BIZARRO BIZARRO

AN ANTHOLOGY

I0691511

Bizarro Pulp Press

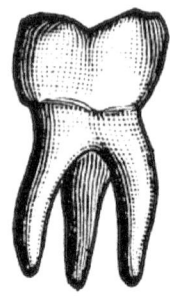

Bizarro Pulp Press
www.BIZARROPULPPRESS.com
Bizarro Bizarro Copyright © 2013 Bizarro Pulp Press
Cover Art Copyright © 2013 Alan M. Clark

ISBN-13: 978-0615936390
ISBN-10: 0615936393

TABLE OF CONTENTS

4

Lucy in Brain Ceiling World
By Wol-vriey

I

On the bus on her way to college, Lucille Smith started seeing things.

She looked up, kept looking up. The ceiling of her bus had become skinless flesh. It was now corrugated into wetly glistening pink rows. The ceiling pulsed like a beating heart. It took Lucy a while to realize she was looking at exposed brain matter.

She turned to the veiled Arab woman seated next to her, pointing up at the ceiling.

The woman looked up once, odd eyes fluttering over her veil, apparently saw a normal bus ceiling, and looked down again and at Lucy.

"I'll suggest you stay off the drugs, dear. I see only a normal ceiling."

Lucy looked up again. The ceiling was still quivering brain matter. She turned back to the veiled woman and whispered. "I'm not on drugs, look up . . ."

An ill-directed gust of wind blew in the bus window then, lifting the woman's veil. Lucy started in horror at her.

7

Her face was made of cloth—thick woven brown burlap fiber with sequin eyes and string-of-bead lips. Her nose and ears were shaped felt cushions. Lucy gaped in horror while the 'woman' regarded her, multicolored-bead lips pursing into a frown:

"That's what all you youngsters say nowadays." She said. The interior of her mouth was lined with red felt, like Kermit the Frog from Sesame Street's.

Lucy stared at her, burning with indignation at the character smear.

"I'm not stoned—"

She readjusted her veil. "Take my word for it, child—drugs, they'll fry your brain like fish in a pan. Before you know it, you'll be seeing things."

Lucy shuddered. She said nothing. Trapped between brain matter ceiling and sack-faced seat-sharer, she discovered a new sort of claustrophobic paranoia.

Oops, she thought. I'm getting off this bus right here and now.

She got up, pushed roughly past the sack-faced woman, out of her window seat into the aisle, and pressed the red buzzer to stop the bus.

"It's drugs you know…" she heard the veiled woman telling someone as she got off, "did

8

you see how she ran off? You'd think I was some kind of freak…"

"… And her so young, what a waste… "

"Yes, it's really a shame the way youngsters carry on nowadays…"

Angered by the sack-faced woman's statements, Lucy gave her the finger as the bus rolled off.

She settled to wait for the next one.

***

The next bus came. Lucy boarded it only after ensuring there were no veiled women aboard. Once aboard, however, she realized her mistake: this bus also had a brain matter ceiling, which she'd somehow not noticed from outside it, and which clearly no one else could see.

Her claustro-paranoid feeling returned. No classes today, she decided. She got off the bus at the next stop, before she began raving, and, shivering like she had a fever, turned and walked back home.

Each step of her walk, Lucy dreaded the sky would replace itself with pulsating quivering cerebral tissue. But nothing happened.

II

Arriving home again, she noted with equanimity that both living room and kitchen ceilings were now brain surface also. Certain they'd have similar toppings, Lucy didn't examine her apartment's other rooms.

The obvious question was how she'd not noticed it before. And concurrently, how if she could see it, no one else could?

She took off her shoes, lay on the sofa staring at the pulsing mass overhead and thought awhile. Maybe all rooms had intelligent ceilings; there was nothing to prove they didn't. And then maybe the brains weren't intelligent: there were lots of different sorts of brains—pets, wild animals, fish, birds…"

Or maybe, she fantasized temporarily, maybe they're newly-arrived-on-Earth alien starship brains intent on taking over the world.

She laughed at her fantasy. Yep right, and the sack-faced woman is their invasion coordinator.

But perplexed and scared as she was, her attention remained riveted on the silently throbbing convolved brain rows.

She couldn't shake her conviction that this was her own brain she was viewing; that she'd fallen into her own head and become trapped there.

She decided to investigate the brain ceiling.

Her decision stemmed not so much from courage, as from the certain knowledge she'd go

10

crazy from wonder/worry if she didn't. If every room in every house had a brain-ceiling, and she was the only one able to see them, what would she do? Take to living outside?

There was no point even in going insane: the ceiling of her padded cell would be the same as everywhere else.

She went to the kitchen and lifted a chair onto the kitchen table. She climbed atop it and prodded the brain with a finger. It twitched. She prodded it again. Once more it twitched.

Feeling bolder, Lucy stuck a finger into one of the grooves separating the nerve-tissue ridges.

Like a flash of lightning, a long thin tongue shot from the crack and wrapped itself around her neck several times.

Terrified, Lucy fought to unwrap the tongue choking her. When that failed, she thumped the brain surface, just resisting the reflex urge to kick out. She had no desire to dislodge the chair she stood on and hang herself.

Then her worst nightmare came true, the tongue itself jerked her up off the chair, yanking her upwards into the brain.

With her head stuck in the brain, Lucy fought to keep her body out of it, placing her hands against its surface and pushing as hard as she could to resist entry. The tongue pulled harder.

Finally, fearing death from a combination of strangulation, asphyxiation, and decapitation—it actually felt like her head was about being ripped off her shoulders—she stopped resisting and permitted herself to be pulled up, into, and through the brain.

During transit she felt like she was sure knives felt going through bread, a smothered white liquid blur.

Then she was out on the other side.

III

She wasn't in hers or anyone else's head, that was instantly clear.

This new room also had a brain-ceiling.

It was a library, blue carpeted, and stacked floor-to-ceiling with books, with a table in its middle.

There was a grey cat lying on its side on the table; the tongue which had snared Lucy originated in its belly.

"Let go of me!" Lucy shrieked. The tongue obliged, unrolling from around her neck and slithering back across the floor, shortening into the cat.

The cat on the table was breathing heavily.

Its belly opened and shut like a mouth with each breath. Lucy saw its body was empty of organs or viscera—the tongue was its innards.

She grew very alarmed.

The grey cat opened a golden eye, and peered at her. It raised a paw and waved.

"Thank goodness you're here at last. Gran Sacking's been going nuts over the amount of work she has to get through today." Its voice was hoarse, as though it had physically carried her up here.

"What are you talking about?" Lucy demanded of the cat.

"You're Lucille, the new maid, aren't you?" Without waiting for her reply it yell-purred: "The new maid's here!"

"I'm not your damn maid," Lucy said angrily. From being alarmed and scared, she was now very cross.

"Hey, Gran, the new maid's here!"

"I'm not you're damn maid," she repeated, sizing up the situation and scanning the room for a weapon. She saw none. "Send me back home this instant, or I'll have the police after—"

She fell silent as 'Gran' appeared, then groaned.

Gran Sacking was the burlap-faced woman she'd sat beside on the bus that morning, the woman she'd so blithely given the finger for suggesting she was stoned.

Now without hood and veil, Gran's burlap/felt face was framed by neatly bunned grey hair. Her white blouse just managed to contain her matronly bosom. Her legs were obscured by her long plaid skirt. As footwear, she wore shiny brown leather shoes with oval brass buckles.

"You're late," Gran said testily. "If you intend working here I'll expect you to be prompt."

"You've had a mix up. I'm not—" Lucy began, affixing her gaze to Gran's expansive bust to avoid staring at her face.

"Follow me," Gran interrupted, spinning on her heels and heading for the kitchen.

Confused, yet curious, Lucy followed her.

Curiosity killed the cat, she told herself, peering at the door Gran had vanished through. Then: It's okay. Just one quick peek and that'll be all.

But then a sudden compulsion pushed her further, and she found herself through the door and inside a large kitchen.

There was a lit stove, with the fire turned down, and a chopping board set up on the cracked pink ceramic work surface.

On the floor was a large basket full of what

14

at first glance appeared to be hair, only it was moving as if alive.

Lucy shuddered.

"They're mustaches," Gran said, tying on an apron. "Freshly plucked." She smiled a beaded smile at Lucy, "Oh, I should explain. I'm making mustache sandwiches. I'm having a hen party . . . a card party later, and they're my specialty. Everyone praises my sandwiches."

Lucy nodded. She moved closer to the basket and saw that the hair bundles were indeed mustaches of varying colors. Most were fist-sized, but there were a few larger.

In addition, they all had tiny hands and feet sticking out of them.

Gran noticed her perplexion. She picked a glossy well-groomed Turkish mustache out from the basket. "Nothing to it, dear," she said. "Only the hair's edible so you need to clean them first."

She indicated Lucy come over to the pink work surface, where she'd a chopping board laid out. There she picked up a paring knife and trimmed off the mustache's hands and feet, parting its hair carefully to cut them away right at the wrists and ankles without losing too much of the precious hair.

She dropped the severed appendages into a bowl. "The cat will have these later, along with its

15

milk," she said.

With its limbs gone, the clump of facial hair looked pathetic. It trembled like it was dying.

Lucy pointed at the mustache, now twitching its life away on the chopping board. "It's still . . ."

Gran grinned at her. She took down a wooden hammer from a peg. "Normally simply removing their limbs kills them, but some mustaches, particularly the Arab ones, never seem to get the point." She hit the mustache a series of hard blows. It jerked spasmodically, then stopped twitching.

Gran turned to Lucy. "Okay, your turn, girl. We'll need about twenty."

Lucy nodded.

Gran handed her the knife and pointed to the basket, "Help yourself. I'll slice the bread. Also, I need to heat some oil; we'll fry a few mustaches as well, nice and crunchy is how the girls like 'em."

***

There wasn't much to preparing mustaches, Lucy found. It was all about how you held them. She discovered that if she first squeezed them hard in the middle till she felt them 'pop,' they went limp as though anesthetized. It was then much easier to sever their hands and feet.

The only trouble she had was with a large

red pirate mustache. It was twice the size of her fist and kept twitching and trying to wrest the knife from her with its salt-bitten fingers.

She finally tired of its nonsense and whammed the wooden hammer into it thrice, upon which it spurted white goo from both its tips and went terminally limp.

She did three more and was done.

"I'm done," she called out to Gran, busily mixing sandwich spread and batter for the mustaches they would be frying.

The cat's bowl was now full of appendages. Gran nodded at it. "Well done Lucy, you're the best maid I've had in ages. You wouldn't believe what some of—"

"I'm not your—"

Gran cut her off. "There's no hurry dear; we'll discuss terms after the poker party. I assure you the salary will be much to your liking." She selected several mustaches and rushed across to the stove to drop them into the simmering oil.

The smell of frying mustaches made Lucy hungry. She didn't dare eat any. The sight of their hands and feet piled up in the cat's bowl, so humanlike, unequivocally killed her appetite.

A doorbell sounded somewhere in the house.

"That'll be the girls now," Gran said,

17

removing her apron. "I'll just go let them in. Won't be a minute." She pointed at the frying pan. "Take these off the fire for me, will you?"

Lucy nodded. Gran disappeared out the kitchen door.

Lucy heard the sounds of greetings.

She removed the fried mustaches from the oil and turned off the stove. Then she stood, staring at the kitchen's brain ceiling and tried figuring out how she was going to escape from here.

***

Gran Sacking returned before she could make her mind whether to conceal a knife in her jeans or not.

"Good Lucy, very good. Now I'll just make the sandwiches and tea and we're done. But first, of course we need to feed the cat."

She got a carton of milk from the fridge, and Lucy trailing her, made her way back across the kitchen to the bowl of mustache limbs. She poured a generous helping all over the mustache hands and feet until the bowl of limbs brimmed with milk.

To Lucy, it now looked like a bowl of odd-shaped breakfast cereal.

Adding occasional squirts of milk to facilitate the process, Gran stirred the hand-foot cereal up till it was well mixed.

18

"That's fine now," she said, her woven face wrinkling into a smile. "Take the cat its milk, Lucy."

Lucy complied.

In the library, the cat was no longer on the table. Now it was walking upside-down on the brain matter ceiling. Its belly-tongue dangled from it like an umbilicus.

Keeping a good distance from both cat and tongue, Lucy placed the bowl on the table and backed off.

The cat descended from ceiling to tabletop by climbing down its tongue, a feat Lucy knew was impossible even after watching it being performed. Its tongue descended after it, flopping beside it in an untidy pile.

The cat began noisily crunching its way through the bowl of limb-cereal. Beside it, its belly-tongue lapped up any milk which spilled from the bowl.

Lucy had seen enough, had enough. She wanted out, she was leaving here, even if she had to kill Gran to get away.

Gotta get that knife.

Once again, however, she found herself unable to resist when Gran asked her to help serve her guests.

19

Bearing a tray of fried mustaches, she followed Gran through a never-ending series of corridors.

IV

To Lucy's surprise, the corridors led back to the library.

She saw Gran hadn't been joking about having a hen party.

Her four guests were chickens. Four speckled barnyard hens now patrolled the writing table top, intermittently speckling it with their excrement. In disgust, the cat had abandoned its erstwhile perch to them; it now lay on its side upside-down on the ceiling. Its eyes glittered golden displeasure. Its body-tongue had retreated out of sight inside its belly.

Lucy stopped looking at the angry cat—it was too disorientating to her sense of perspective.

Gran shooed the hens off the table.

"Now now, girls, what have I told you about etiquette?"

"Sorry, Gran," one of the hens replied. "Sometimes instinct gets the better of us."

"Yes it does," another said, adding: "Wow, those mustache sandwiches look real tasty."

The other hens clucked appreciating.

Gran smiled, basked in their approbations. "Oh, they're alright, I guess. My new maid Lucille helped make them. Say hello to Lucille, girls."

"Hello, Lucille," the chickens clucked brightly.

Lucy waved back, bemused.

Aided by Lucy, Gran pulled up five chairs around the table so the chickens and herself could sit.

They ate and chatted for awhile.

The hens ate like people, gripping the sandwiches between their wingtips, and pecking delicately like ladies. When it was time for the fried mustaches to be eaten, Lucy helped slice particularly tough ones into beak-sized chunks for the hens.

Finally, the meal was over. One of the hens produced a pack of cards from beneath her wing. "Time for poker, dears." She peered at Gran. "So what are the stakes today?"

"Why, my new maid of course," Gran replied, "Is there ever anything else?"

Lucy caught her breath in a sharp gasp of air.

"Now, now, dear, don't be frightened," Gran said, turning to Lucy. "We always play for my maids." Her embroidered brows and bead lips set in a look of intense concentration.

21

"You should be frightened, Lucy," a hen said. "She's incredibly bad at poker—she's never won once. You'll be ours in under an hour."

"Oh no she won't," Gran retorted heatedly. "I'm feeling quite lucky today. I like Lucy. You're not having her to clean up after you because you're too lazy to go outside your barns to poop!"

"Oh yes, we're getting her!" another hen squawked lustily. "You always feel lucky!"

"Well today I feel a different sort of lucky— a 'lucky' lucky."

"You're still going to lose, Gran!"

Lucy had now heard more than quite enough. She turned and ran for the kitchen.

V

Terrified, Lucy ran straight through the kitchen and into the house's corridors. Though panicking, she did her best to not take the same turns she remembered taking with Gran.

She was lost before realizing she'd forgotten to take a knife.

She ran frantically, occasionally peering up at the brain ceiling.

Finally, when she was totally out of breath, the tunnel expanded upward and sideways into a large cavern floored with brain surface.

22

Lucy collapsed onto the floor, exhausted. She didn't mind that it was wet and sticky, or that it stank like spittle, all she cared was that she'd escaped Gran and her stupid poker hens . . . and her stupid cat and stupid library.

The whole scenario was ridiculous: who'd ever heard of chickens playing cards?

And they'd had the effrontery to suggest they'd gamble for her. To, of all things, make her clean up chicken droppings, till (she suspected) she'd die of an infection and then . . .

"You're trespassing you know—the library ceiling's mine," a familiar voice said in her ear.

Startled, she looked round. Gran's grey cat was sitting next to her, studying her with glowing gold eyes. Its belly-tongue was now knotted round its neck like a tie. Lucy wished the cat would be consistent in how it presented itself to the world.

Still, that wasn't her primary concern.

"Shssssh," she said. "They'll find us . . . me, I mean. And what do you mean: this is your ceiling?"

The cat sighed. "Look up," it said.

Lucy did. She sighed too.

They were both seated on the library ceiling. Above them (and now upside down) sat Gran and the poker hens on the library floor. The quintet were

23

furiously playing cards.

Gran stood up all of a sudden and threw down her playing cards. Her burlap features were wrenched into an expression of the utmost disgust. "Drat it, I lost again!"

"The maid, Lucille, is ours then?"

"Yes, yes, if you can find her, of course; just don't ask me to help you look. I don't know how I lost just now. I had a royal flush and still . . ."

"You're a surreal player, Gran—you need to stop thinking your hand's what you imagine it to be."

Gran said nothing. She picked up a leftover fried mustache and began crunching it violently to ameliorate her bad emotions.

Lucy returned her attention to the cat. "Please help me escape," she begged.

The cat regarded her. "I'm not sure if I should," it replied cautiously, stroking its tongue-tie with a forepaw. "Gran will be displeased."

Lucy lost her patience with it. She grabbed it by the throat and began throttling it. "Listen, you fool," she whispered harshly, "it's your damn fault I'm here! You'll damn well help me leave this damn place or I'll damn friggin' kill you! And double damn me if I don't!" That said, she shifted her grip till she was strangling the cat with its

24

tongue.

Its eyes rolled in its head. "Okay, I'll help you," it whisper-gasped. "Stop killing me!"

She let go of its tongue. "Okay, how do I leave here?" She peered narrowly at it. "Where's the exit?"

Above/below them the poker hens were now hop-flying crisscross the library, pulling books off bookshelves and peering into them.

"I don't understand it," one of them said. "She's not in any of these books."

"Oh there's a Lucy in this book here," another replied her.

The four hens gathered round her.

"See," the hen indicated with a wingtip, reading aloud in an excited squawk. "'On the bus on her way to college, Lucille Smith started seeing things. She looked up, kept looking up…'"

"Wow, this is a good book!"

"And it really does have a Lucy," another hen concurred.

"Read some more!" a third hen clucked.

"Okay, keep your feathers on . . . 'The ceiling of her bus had become skinless flesh. It was now corrugated into wetly glistening pink rows. The ceiling pulsed like a beating heart...'"

On the ceiling, Lucy gasped. "That was this

25

morning," she whispered to the cat. "All that happened to me this morning."

"And now it's evening," it replied with equanimity.

The hen paused in her reading and turned to Gran. "We've found your Lucy—she's in this storybook."

Gran, still miffed at losing for the Nth time in a row, waved back dismissively.

"Which one?"

The hen shut the book, read its cover. "'Lucy in Brain Ceiling World'."

Gran waved even more dismissively. "You can have it. I'll order another copy."

Lucy turned to the cat. "This stopped making sense a long time ago. Now lead me out of here."

"Follow me," it replied.

They set off across the brain ceiling, the cat's belly-tongue wagging behind it like a tail.

The ceiling-scape stretched far into the distance, a ridged desert populated by brain hemisphere dunes. Above them the upside-down rooms altered till they passed beneath a final door and were outside the house with just sky overhead, one in which floated brain clouds with oblongata tails.

Below and between the brain clouds huge

26

red napkins flew, flapping themselves like birds of prey.

Where are we going?" Lucy asked after a while.

"You're going to Mustache Land. We're almost there now."

"I don't want to go to Mustache Land; I want to go home!" she shrieked.

"You can't go home anymore," the cat patiently explained. "Gran says you insulted her when she was bus-riding, and she intends to get even with you. You go home—you'll just end up back here again. She's persistent like that"

Lucy stared at it in horror. "Oh no."

"So you go to Mustache Land," the cat continued pleasantly, hiding the fact it wanted her out of its hair as soon as possible. "You'll be safe there."

Lucy started to protest, then she remembered what Gran Sacking had said about ordering another copy of this day in her life.

Horror in her eyes, she nodded mutely to the cat.

***

They stopped in a deserted part of the brainscape, well away from Gran Sacking's immense upside-down mansion. They were out right

27

in the middle of the brain-floor desert.

"Okay, what now?" Lucy asked, desperate to be gone. Maybe the poker hens had found a copy of her in a library book chronicling her today (Lucy's mind still boggled at the absurdity of that possibility), but the cat clearly didn't think she was safe yet.

And there was also the damning possibility that the latter pages of the book contained the details of how she was currently escaping.

And she couldn't go home.

The cat permitted her to finish worrying. When it once again had her undivided attention, it pointed up. "You climb up there."

Lucy looked at the expanse of yellow sky. "There's only floating brains and napkins up there. Ugh."

"Just climb my tongue till you're above the clouds and you'll be safe."

Lucy looked at it dubiously and pointedly.

"Climb my tongue," it repeated, "or you'll be stuck here forever." It looked back the way they'd come. "Go quickly, before Gran finds I'm missing and comes looking for me."

That decided Lucy. She nodded at the cat. In another impossible maneuver, its belly-tongue now knotted itself in a myriad of places and stood straight up in the air, its end far above where Lucy could make out.

"There you go," the cat said, pointing to the improvised gym-rope. It lay on its back, once again wheezing like when it had kidnapped her. "And please climb fast. It's tiring, holding myself in place like this. You might fall."

Lucy needed no further urging. She grabbed hold of the cat's tongue, and started up it.

VI

Lucy was quickly grateful for the knots in the tongue, otherwise it would have been impossible to ascend. The tongue was slippery and stank of mustache meat.

Soon the cat was indistinguishable from the lobed desert floor. Shortly after this she found looking down made her feel dizzy, so she stopped doing so.

She reached and passed the floating brains, and the crimson napkins flying about them like aircraft. Some of the fabric squares and triangles ceased their aerial maneuvers and flew across to investigate her.

After circling her a few times, they departed again to resume their aerobatics around the sky-brains.

Lucy peered up, saw the knotted tongue still proceeded quite a distance. She gasped, desperately wishing she could rest for a few minutes. Her hands and legs ached with the effort of her climb, but mindful of the cat's admonition to go fast, she didn't dare stop.

Finally, with her strength about giving out, Lucy reached the top of the rope ladder.

One moment she was alone in the sky, the next, there was grass below and around her.

She stepped off the tongue and collapsed into an exhausted heap. The equally exhausted cat's tongue collapsed back down to meet its owner.

***

Lucy lay on her back for a while, initially disappointed that the sky contained no diamonds.

She shook herself awake: there was no sky. She was still in Brain Ceiling World, though now the brain-matter surface was once again overhead.

For a moment she feared the cat had tricked her, that she'd soon see Gran Sacking and the poker hens arriving, but then she realized she was somewhere else—this sky was FULL of mustaches.

This place was nothing but an endless hall, its cerebral overlay held in place by rows of building-sized stone heads; heads that dwarfed those on Easter Island.

Mustaches thronged the air like they waged a war amongst themselves.

Brigadier-style, Fu Manchu style, Spanish, Viking, Victorian-English, and Red Pirate mustaches; Adolph Hitler mustaches; ZZ Top mustaches with beards attached; Johnny Depp, John Morrison, Freddie Mercury, James Hetfield, Kirk Hammett, and Dave Grohl mustaches; Lenin and Stalin and Mussolini and Richard Roundtree Shaft-style mustaches; Chinese and Indian Movie Villain, Salvador Dali and Che Guevara mustaches; oversized everyday mustaches—all flew through the air like birds which had mistakenly swapped their feathers for horse manes.

All had limbs projecting from them, an assortment of hands and feet which awoke in Lucy a sense of the horrid unreal, though for their part the flying lip-hair seemed ignorant of her presence there.

Black, brown, blonde, red, ginger, auburn, antiseptic yellow, platinum; in places the sky looked much like a tapestried canopy that had grown dissatisfied with itself and begun switching its colors about for variety.

***

Once she'd rested a bit, Lucy got up and walked on.

31

Though male, all the monster heads holding up the ceiling were mustache-less.

In addition to the seeming 'war' raging overhead, chains of mustaches streamed round the stone heads in torrents of ascending and descending spirals. When Lucy drew near enough to the nearest of the heads, she saw why.

Each mustache in a mustache-chain broke of its flight momentarily to alight on the upper lip of the stone face. Butterfly-like it hovered there, ends fluttering; then it changed color and flew off, its place being taken by the next in line.

No, that wasn't right.

Lucy watched closely. It occurred almost too fast for eye to follow, but each alighting mustache was disappearing into the stone head to be replaced by another.

As confirmation of this, she noted each newly-arrived mustache differed not only in color, but also in shape and size from the one it was replacing.

So in addition to bearing up the ceiling, the heads were gates to somewhere else.

She sighed; it wasn't really useful knowledge: as far as she could tell, the upper-lip gates only led to somewhere even more full of mustaches than here—Mustache Land—if that were

32

possible.

Something squirmed in the grass by her feet. She looked down and saw a little Adolph Hitler mustache attempting to clamber atop her shoes, gripping them with its assortment of hands and feet.

Lucy was hungry. She considered awhile, then picked the mustache up. It had been ages since she'd had anything to eat, and it looked like she'd be stuck here awhile.

After first killing it by smashing it several times with a rock, she plucked off its limbs while salivating over how delicious it smelt.

Her only regret as she bit into the dead mustache was that there wasn't any bread and salt available to make a sandwich of it. Or oil to fry it in.

Overhead, the transformation war-dance of faceless facial hair raged on.

The Satanic Little Toaster
By Jeff Burk

The package finally arrived on a Tuesday afternoon. The small box was wrapped with weathered brown paper splotched with rust-colored stains and bound with frayed twine. It stank of monkey shit.

Paul Goodin eagerly signed for the parcel and bid the postman a "good day." He had been awaiting this package—this perfect piece for his collection—for what seemed like a very long time.

He carried the box in awe to his living room, set it down, and rushed off for his digital camera. Paul came back and turned the camera's video recording feature on. He aimed it directly at his face.

"Hi everyone, this is Paul again. I'm back for another unboxing. Today's a really special one. The unboxing of Saint Baxter's Model 1-A-1 Toastmaster or, more commonly called, The Devil's Toaster."

He turned the camera to the package.

"In that small, unassuming box is what is rumored to be the most evil and cursed toaster in the world. Owned by some of history's greatest villains.

34

Or at least that's what the seller assured me—that this was the legit one. Is it real or yet another rip-off? Soon we'll find out.

"Before we go on, let's have a brief history lesson for those out there who are unfamiliar with Saint Baxter."

This part would later be spiced up with pictures and video for the blog. His fans expected a certain level of quality from his productions.

"Ordained by the Catholic Church in 1920, he was sent on a mission work to Uganda in the summer of the same year. His stated mission was spreading the word of God, Instead he spread cruelty, rape, torture, venereal disease, and, if some reports are to believed, cannibalism and necrophilia. He used and abused the very people he was sent to save. But the power and purse-strings of the Catholic Church made it impossible to stop his terror.

"Using money that was allotted to humanitarian needs, he lived in the lap of luxury. In 1925, needing to have the most modern home appliances, he bought one of the world's first pop-up toasters—a Model 1-A-1 Toastmaster produced by the Waters General Company, of course.

"While his unwilling subjects suffered, he dined on eggs, bacon, and toast every morning.

Until that one fateful day in which the natives had had enough. They dragged him from his tent, shoved a spear up his rear-end, cracked open his skull, and—reports claim—ate his brain while he was still alive.

"The Church—never able to admit any wrong-doing—claimed he was martyred by savages while spreading the gospel. Officially, the Church regards him as a great man but history says differently.

"The locals raided his belongings but no one dared touch the toaster. The mechanical—and to them magical—toasting of bread was mojo they did not want to mess with.

"Legend says that the toaster was snatched and sold by a member of the tribe with little morals. The true provenance of the toaster is shrouded in mystery. Rumors say that it passed through the ownership of figures as diverse as Dali, Mussolini, Pol Pot, Salman Rushdie, Danzig, Tony Blair, and Jeffrey Dahmer,

"Earlier this year, an anonymous fan of my videos and collection contacted me and claimed to have come into possession of this fabled and, in some circles, feared toaster.

"After agreeing on quite a large amount of money . . ."

—Twenty-thousand dollars to be exact—

". . . the purchase was arranged, and here I have the package. Is it the real deal or will I be burned like so many times before?

"Let's find out!"

Paul placed the camera on the nearby tripod and assessed the package. His address was carefully hand-printed in black ink. No return address, but he really wasn't surprised about that.

He snipped the twine with scissors and carefully tore off the paper wrapping. Beneath that was a cardboard Amazon.com box that the sender had repurposed. Their address blacked out with magic marker.

Paul opened the box and was greeted with a sea of packing peanuts. He dug into them and his hand groped for the box's contents. At first nothing, but then he found the familiar texture of smooth, cool steel. He greedily ripped the toaster from the box, sending packing peanuts flying through the air.

There it was, in his hand, the toaster of Saint Baxter the Cruel. The Devil's Toaster!

"Oh ladies and gentlemen, this may be it. Oh. Oh. Ohhhhh . . ."

He spun the toaster around in his hands inspecting it from all angles. It appeared to be legit. The steel looked appropriately aged. The design was

37

from the classic golden age of toasters.

"As you can see at home, this is indeed an authentic Model 1-A-1. But is this the one I'm looking for? The so-called, most evil toaster ever made?

"Ladies and Gentlemen, I think it is."

Paul held up the toaster so the camera could see where the power-cord met the toaster.

"Here you can see evidence of a power-surge." He pointed to burn marks. "When Dahmer was cooking up a kidney stew, he was making toast as a side-dish. There was a sudden surge in power and the metal got scorched. The ensuing fire alarms and arriving fire department almost got the famed serial-killer caught. He was apprehended by police three months later."

He flipped around the toaster, "On the front you can see several grooves worn into the steel. William Burroughs grooved them there to snort Cocaine during the writing of Naked Lunch."

He turned the toaster so the bottom was facing the video camera. "One of the leg-pegs is missing. Max Hardcore was to have lost it in the ass of Sascha Grey. It was never replaced as a testament to free speech.

"And, most importantly, the mark of authenticity that was only present on the first fifty

Model 1-A-1's. A tiny swastika."

Next to the manufacture's info there indeed was a tiny swastika and the year 1925.

"But there is only one way to truly be sure."

Paul picked up the toaster and the camera. He carried them into the kitchen and plugged the appliance in.

"According to records of all previous owners, the toaster burns some . . . particular . . . patterns into bread."

He took out a loaf of bread and loaded one piece into the toasters. He pushed down the lever and the bread began to toast.

"Some previous owners have claimed to see images of their own death, the fall of global powers, and even winning lottery ticket numbers. But there is one image that is said to appear almost always."

The toast popped up and Paul eagerly snatched it out. His excitement overpowered any heat from the hot bread burning his fingers.

First he sniffed the toast.

"Sulfur," he exclaimed.

Then he inspected the toast and a smiled beamed across his face. He held up the slice to the camera and exclaimed, "Behold, the mark of the Devil's Toaster!"

On the bread, burned perfectly clear, much

clearer than that bullshit Mother Mary on grilled cheese from a few years back, was an upside down pentagram.

"The most evil toaster in the world!"

***

Paul never knew what made him obsessively love toasters. Ever since he was a teen, he accumulated the newest and greatest along with the oldest and most classic models. He learned carpentry to better display his collection. His first apartment didn't have a living room, it had a toaster display room.

If he had ever visited a psychiatrist, like so many ex-girlfriends advised, he would have learned that his obsession stemmed from his mother making toast every morning before fondling him and playing "where's the sailboat?"

But he never did and his collection amassed. Soon, everything else in his life other than toasters was shut out. No lover (toasters are not a turn-on), no family (all dead), and no friend (toasters are a very boring hobby). But his IT job for the Global Mart headquarters paid his rent and kept him well-fed and financed his one true love. His town-house was meager but it gave him enough space to store his collection. The first floor, baring the kitchen, was the location of one of the world's foremost toaster collection.

It wasn't much of a life but it was a good one.

His toaster collection grew and grew. He started a website and video blog and soon he even had fans. He wasn't alone in his obsession. There were others just like him.

But over the years, being an opinion leader wasn't enough. BinPoppin in San Francisco had a proto-type designed by President Garfield (toast was a little known passion of the twentieth president). Browned4U in Stewartstown (wherever the fuck that was) had a custom model designed by Andy Warhol. It was limited to three—Elton John and Colin Powell owned the other two.

Paul needed something that would set him apart. Something that would make his collection the envy of all others.

The Devil's Toaster was just the thing.

And now the Devil's Toasters belonged to him.

The video camera was now off. He was free to relax and take in the beauty and history of the accursed object.

He spun the appliance around and clutched it close to his chest. He sniffed it and then placed the bread-slots to his mouth. He sucked in deep a century worth of terror and grilled bread.

Paul got hard.

He stood and cradled the toaster like a baby. He walked across the room to the specialty-built display stand—a white Roman column with a glass dome on top.

Paul lifted the glass and placed the Devil's Toaster atop the column. He moved the cord so it wrapped around the toaster. He regarded it and then moved the cord so it draped down the column. He frowned, shook his head, and moved the cord back to its original position. Paul smiled, nodded, and put the glass dome back.

He stood back and admired his latest acquisition.

***

The first sign something was wrong came the next Tuesday.

While doing his weekly cleaning, Paul noticed that many of his toasters in his display room were suddenly developing rust. This was unusual as he took great care to ensure that his collection stayed in mint condition.

And this was the worst possible time that his collection should take a hit. Paul had spent three days editing his unboxing video and had posted it. Lusting after the comments other jealous collectors

42

would leave. Instead he got:

> —Bullshit. Pics or it didnt happen.

> —???????????

> —FAKE! Don't waste your time.

And, most insultingly;

> —TROLL!!!!!!!!!

Paul had no idea why but his validity as a collector was being called into question. He now owned the rarest and most infamous toaster in the world but no one seemed to care.

***

"So you're sure it's real?" shouted Frank over the music. There was a loud band on stage at Plan B—a shitty little dive in south east Portland. Frank was another toaster collector. His pride and joys were rare limited edition painted models by Damien Hirst and Andrew Goldfarb. Frank was also another frequent contributor to TOASTERSFORUM and occasional delved into the modding scene. Frank once made a toaster that was also capable of generating a Tesla coil. He was the only collector that Paul really held up as an equal.

"Yeah, I'm sure," replied Paul.

The band on stage—The Toasters—kicked into their next song. They had a three-piece horn section and played something called "Ska." It sounded like circus music but both Frank and Paul were enamored with the band's name. They each bought t-shirts and grabbed another drink at the bar.

"Your pictures were pretty weird," said Frank.

"What do you mean?"

Frank shouted something back but the noise of the band and the roar of the crowd were too much. Paul couldn't hear the response.

***

They were sipping white wine at Paul's place after the show when the discussion came up again. Frank was admiring Paul's collection, as he always did, when he came to the steel toaster under glass.

"So you really have it," exclaimed Frank when he eyed the Devil's Toaster.

"Of course I do. You saw the video."

"I saw the video but you weren't unboxing this."

"Then what was I?"

"A 2010 Hello Kitty produced by Spectra Merchandisin. Not that limited and the exact opposite of what you'd expect from a video labeled 'Unboxing of the Legendary Devil's Toaster.' A cute joke but a bit weird."

"What . . ." Paul was extremely confused.

"And then you posted all those pictures to

the forum. You got on a serious kick with that. Were you drunk or something?"

"What are you talking about? I did no such thing."

"Yeah. You did."

Frank had moved away from the Devil's Toaster and was inspecting the many shelves of Paul's collection. He had seen it all several hundred times before but he still enjoyed inspecting it yet again. Such is the way of collectors.

"Hey, you really need to take better care of these. A bunch are getting some really nasty rust."

But Paul wasn't there to hear. He had gone off to his bedroom to grab his laptop. He came back into the living room and pulled up the video on YouTube. He noticed there were a few dozen new comments. All negative.

I'm getting tired of this. Here's the video that I uploaded."

Paul hit play. Right when the video got to the point that he was taking the toaster out of the box, Frank interjected—

"And that's a Hello Kitty toaster."

Paul was silent at first. On the screen he could very clearly see the video he shot of unpacking the Devil's Toaster.

"No," he calmly stated, "that's the Devil's

45

Toaster."

"I kind of understand why you want to keep the toaster a secret," said Frank, turning away from the computer, "that I get. But why do you want to keep continuing this stupid joke, to my face, that I don't get. All I see on that screen is Hello Kitty. No Satan."

Paul looked at his friend, not sure which one of them was going crazy.

"Come on," said Frank. He gestured to the Devil's Toaster. "I want to make some Pentagram toast."

***

Frank had left and Paul was catching up with the comments on TOASTERSFORUM and on YouTube. They all called his posts fake. A few even mentioned Hello Kitty—just like Frank.

Paul angrily finished off his glass of wine and poured another. He got out his video camera and shot another video showing off the Devil's Toaster. He uploaded the video, finished the glass, and poured another.

Ten minutes later the first comment came: "Another fake. Dude, what's with the Hello Kitty?"

He took down the video immediately.

Paul stayed up late drinking.

***

46

One week later, the rust problem was getting much worse.

The ten toasters closest to the Devil's Toaster had grown thick brown fuzz. It looked like some kind of strange mold, but when touched, the "fuzz" broke apart into fine metal shavings.

What was strangest about this weird rust was that it grew overnight. While Paul had been having problems with rust lately, his increased cleaning schedule had seemed to take care of the problem. He couldn't believe his eyes when he walked into the room and saw the brown lumps that had been prides of his collection.

The Devil's Toaster, which was surrounded on both sides by the rusted appliances, was fine.

With a heavy heart Paul trashed the rusted toasters. He went to his storage room and picked out replacements for his display. He had no shortage of options. He owned over two thousand unique models.

***

Paul rushed into the kitchen while he tied his tie. He had overslept that morning and he barely had any time for breakfast. He grabbed the bag of bread from the counter, went to the toaster, and froze.

Sitting next the cherry red Toast-A-Tron 5000 (limited to 10,000 and Paul's preferred model for daily toasting) was the Devil's Toaster.

Paul looked around the kitchen. Was there a break-in? Was he robbed in his sleep? Was the intruder still in his home?

He picked up the Devil's Toaster and carried it to the living room. He put it back on its display and scanned the room. Nothing else seemed to be disturbed. A quick run through of the other rooms of his house revealed nothing wrong and no doors or windows unlocked.

Perplexed, he went back to the kitchen and loaded bread into the toaster. He pushed down on the lever but nothing happened. No familiar hum of power. No happy warm glow.

He pushed the lever up and back down again. Still nothing.

He checked the back of the toaster and the wall plug. Nothing looked wrong.

Damn thing's busted.

He glanced at his watch. There was no time for cooking anything else. Drive-thru it would be.

As he was putting on his jacket and just about to step out the door he heard a THUD from the living room. Was the intruder still in his home?

He crept to the living room and immediately noticed one thing out of place.

The Devil's Toaster had fallen to the floor.

48

The glass dome of its display was undisturbed.

***

"You know the stories," Frank said and took a swig of beer.

"You can't be serious," replied Paul.

Paul had gone over to Frank's to hang out and see his new ToasterMaster X in action. After some BLT's they retired to the porch and Paul told Frank of all the strange occurrences that had happened to him lately. The rust, the kitchen toaster (and the one he replaced it with) breaking, and the Devil's Toaster winding up in strange places—that morning he awoke to find the toaster in bed next to him on a pillow, just like the horse head in The Godfather.

"Come on Frank, you're a smart man. You can't possibly believe the stories. They're just stupid stories. Cool, yes. But stupid."

"I'm just saying that it's interesting that you get the, allegedly, most evil and haunted kitchen appliance ever known and then immediately begin to experience strange phenomena."

"True. Interesting—but still stupid. The weird rust is some leakage or mold problem that I don't know about yet. I'm calling for a guy to come a take a look at the house. I'm worried that the mold might be in the walls."

49

"And the toaster teleportation?"

"Jesus Christ man, listen to yourself. It's not demons. I'm sure of that. What is it? I don't know yet. It's more likely that I have an undiagnosed sleep walking problem than supernatural intervention."

Frank shrugged. "I'm just saying."

***

Paul had the video camera on a tripod pointed at the Devil's Toaster. The nightly moving of it had kept up. Paul was certain he wasn't having a problem with intruders and he refused to accept the supernatural explanation. He was determined to get to the bottom of the mystery.

He walked away from the set-up and paused in the doorway. The room was bare but for the pedestal and glass dome that housed the Devil's Toaster. The rust problem had kept up and actually gotten worse. All the pride and joys of his collection—destroyed. The Devil's Toaster, of course, had somehow managed to avoid catching the metal eating rust.

Paul smiled at the camera and left the room with the light on to ensure the best film quality. If the toaster moved again tonight, he was going to get his answer.

***

The next morning he found the Devil's Toaster in the storage room—his basement that housed the thousands of toasters that made up his collection. Just like all the other nights, there was no sign of a break-in and nothing else was moved.

Paul rushed to the camera and flipped open the side viewer. The camera had recorded the whole night to the SD card.

He hit stop and started playback. He could perfectly see the toaster atop its pedestal. He started scanning though the video. There was no sign of anything out of the ordinary. Around four a.m., the video rippled and the toaster was gone.

Paul rewound and watched closely. It was the same image as before. It looked like a still-frame if not for the clock in the corner counting away the seconds. At 4:11:32 the video blurred and suddenly cut to black. A split second later the image came back.

The glass dome still sat atop the pedestal but the toaster was gone.

He rewound and watched the moment again and again. He watched it a total of ten times—three in slow motion. But he could see no sign of any intruder or any other way the toaster moved.

Simply, one moment it was there and the next it was gone.

51

***

"This is really getting out of hand," said Frank as he took in the devastation.

The rust problem had spread to the storage room. Every toaster Paul owned, from the very first one he ever bought—a special edition Batman model that was made to promote the first Tim Burton film—to the plain banged-up stainless steel model owned by G. Gordon Liddy.

All ruined. All eaten away by the rust plague.

Paul looked broken and that was how he felt. When Cindy left him, when his parents were killed by a drunk driver, when his little Pomeranian, Chu-Chu, was tore apart like a squeaky toy by the next door Doberman—none of those moments compared to how empty he felt now.

When he went to bed last night his collection was fine. But when he awoke this morning, every toaster in the storage room had bloomed a coat of rust. After weeping for a good hour, he called Frank.

"You know what I think this is?" said Frank.

Paul didn't respond.

"It's the only toaster that hasn't been damaged," Frank pointed out.

And that was true. Where the rest of Paul's collection had been destroyed, the Devil's Toaster

52

still sat on its podium in the same condition as the day he unboxed it.

"Hey, have you tried to make toast with it lately?" Frank asked.

"No, why?"

"You know the legend, Cobain, Ted Kennedy, Polanski, The toaster sometimes shows people . . . things. So . . . maybe you should make some toast."

They went to the living room and collected the Devil's Toaster and moved it to the kitchen. Paul plugged it in while Frank got the bread.

Frank handed the bag to Paul. "I think you should do this."

Paul nodded, it was his house and his problems. Would the toaster really reveal the source of his problems or predict some future doom? It seemed impossible but so did a lot lately.

He took out a piece, placed it in the slot, and pushed down on the lever. The metal box hummed and he was close enough to feel the pleasant electrical warmth.

The two men waited in silence. Neither daring to speak. Both wondering what, if any, premonition the toaster would foretell.

POP!

Paul reached slowly for the hot bread. He

pulled it out and held it so both of them could see what was burned onto the toast.

Frank had been right to wonder. Before, when they had tested the machine, it had scorched a neat pentagram into the bread. But this time it was something very different.

"I don't get it," said Frank. "What is it?"

"It's . . ." He squinted at the image. "It's a toaster."

Burned into the bread was a crude, simple depiction of a toaster.

Paul tried another piece of bread. And another. And another. They all depicted the same thing—a toaster.

Paul's heartbreak was now replaced with confusion.

Frank grabbed a slice. "Let me try."

He put it in the toaster and a short time later it popped up. He pulled it out and burned onto the bread was the same crude, simple image of a toaster.

***

Paul had lost it and he knew it. Since his collection got ruined he hadn't been able to eat, go to work, or sleep. He hadn't even visited the TOASTERSFORUM—no way could he go back there. Not after he lost complete creditability with them.

He sat on the floor of his living room staring at the Devil's Toaster. It was three a.m. and a thunderstorm raged outside.

Paul had had enough with all the weird shit. He knew the toaster was somehow responsible for it all and tonight he was going to catch it in the act.

That's how he knew he was going crazy. There was no way a toaster could be evil.

He sipped his coffee and listened to the rain and thunder claps outside. Eventually the combination of coffee and the putt-putt of rain droplets caught up to him and he had to take a piss.

He went to the bathroom and relieved himself. As he let out a powerful stream of urine (he had been drinking a lot of coffee) the lights went out.

He looked up and cursed as he heard his piss splashing on the floor. He moved back his aim, finished, and zipped up. He groped around the darkness looking for the light switch. When he found it he flipped it up and down several times. Nothing.

He blindly found the door and opened it. All the lights in the house were off. The storm must have knocked out the power. But then he noticed there was light in the hallway. Coming from the living room was a warm, flickering orange glow.

55

Paul slowly crept down the hall—his body tense and filled with a desire to flee from whatever was causing that soft glow.

He turned through the doorway and froze.

The Devil's Toaster was sitting in the living room. It was in the center of five perfectly placed candles. A white grainy substance (toxicology would later confirm it was sea salt) connected the candles with a perfect circle and lines inside crisscrossing forming a perfect pentagram.

There was a bright flash of lightning and a thunderclap like a plane crash. Paul's eyes went all bright and starry, momentarily blinded. When his vision came back the toaster was gone. The candle and salt pentagram remained but the Devil's Toaster had disappeared.

Paul turned around in a panic and something hard and metal hit him on the bridge of his nose. He crumbled to the ground blinded by pain.

The metal came down again and again. Wave after wave of pain. He could hear something crunching and then a wet smack. Then he heard nothing.

***

The man walked in to the living room. "Anything?"

"Nothing," said the women. "Not even a TV.

56

Just this toaster I found by the back door." She tossed the bloody toaster onto the ground next to Paul's brain-splattered still-twitching corpse.

The man looked at the salt and candles. "What the fuck is that shit?"

"Don't know," said the woman. "Freak was into some kinda Satan shit. Come on, let's go. This place is giving me the creeps"

***

Frank was driving back from Paul's funeral. It had just been him and five of Paul's co-workers. The poor guy had nobody else. It was damned depressing.

Paul had been killed during a home invasion. Some meth-head couple did it to four houses on his street. They cut the power, broke in to murder everyone inside and loot the place. The bastards killed twelve people total. They got dropped by an NRA card-carrying family man and his pistol-grip shotgun on the fifth house.

Frank pulled into his driveway and there was a package on his doorstep. Strange. He wasn't expecting anything.

He picked up the parcel—a small box wrapped in twin and old brown weather-beaten paper. It stank of monkey shit.

A Smashed Up Salmon
By R. A. Harris

I lie awake next to my sleeping girlfriend. I'm counting the stars I like to imagine are hurtling towards us. I've kept a running total for the last eight years. Every night I calculate the distance to each one, to determine their velocities. There is one I'm wary of because it's speeding up as it draws nearer. I calculate that it may just reach me in time for my eightieth birthday, should I live that long. I am ambivalent about whether that will be the gift of a lifetime or a tragedy.

My girlfriend's gums snake around my forearm. Trails of saliva creep down to the bedsheets. Her gums slide across my skin like slugs trying to find some purchase, some entry point to the subterranean level of my being. Her beautiful face is twisted into an angry knot. She curses something beautiful, gummy bear words about how much she hates the planet and wishes it would disintegrate. I kiss her tender because even her unconscious desire to devour me and destroy the world isn't enough to stop me loving her. The hidden jewels of a universe only I can see dance across my ceiling. I close my eyes and pretend to be asleep.

My girlfriend's lips find mine just so sweet as the Sun strokes the land with its glowing embrace. Her toothless smile a pink smashed up salmon in her face. I reach out to stroke her hair and she purrs. I pass her teeth to her from the glass by the bedside. She flickers her eyes and we rise and we bathe and we step into the day.

As we graze on brittle blades of grass and acrid stigma outside by the swing set on our lawn, I tell her that she tried to eat me last night. She laughs and kisses me and says thank goodness she doesn't have real teeth. We are best friends, and she would rather we were both bulldozed to dust than devour me. I'd taste of sewer fish and detritus burped up by a rotten dog is what she says. I remember the imaginary star accelerating towards our destiny, our meeting in the dark. It's a comfort to know that our two worlds are reciprocals of one another.

I lie next to her and count the imaginary stars bearing towards us. There is only one. All others have fallen to the wayside, and it makes me happy that me and the star can share this moment alone because it's like my world and hers are becoming one. I beckon it onwards, encourage it to speed up, there is no reason to delay. Though it is far away, I can tell it has a smile on its face.

My girlfriend snaps her jaw shut tight around my arm. I wince as false teeth puncture my false shell. They find their way to my inner being and blood and saliva run around my arm and drip onto the bed sheet. Her cotton image is a mess of fanged irritation and sublime contempt for this distasteful object her wayward anger has led her to find. She removes her mouth from my arm, and spits, harsh and sour. I taste of the ash of the life we failed to live.

In dire need of my lonely star, a single budding plant carves its path into the sky out of the wound in my arm. Petals open, transcendent colours slowly whiten before they dry and droop and fall back to my skin. In the place of this organic thread a metal skyscraper erupts. Soon a dozen or so buildings stand firm along my arm. An exoskeleton expression of my interior motif. Angular projections of corrupted elements and reappropriated schemas.

I seize my girlfriend's neck between my teeth and squeeze my jaw shut tight. Her blood is sugar sweet and me, drunk, I swoon. I, hazy, see her life force creep out her wound. Creatures strange with envy, all haggard with pride, they spasm, fuelled by rage. They press their weight upon my chest. They push me down, deep into the bed, and slide their gnarled hands around my neck. The buildings along my arm disintegrate as one, their bodies unwind, metal girders, the spider arms of a galaxy dying, glass falling turning to snow drops that melt on my skin.

My precious imaginary star is unblinking as it hurtles towards us. It comes so close as to almost kiss me, and I realize it is looking past me. It begins to dull, become a soft red glow before its lifeless body collides with our worlds. A moment of superimposition. And as it passes by, the trails of our destroyed world in its wake, my imaginary star doesn't look back or slow down even for a second.

I kiss my girlfriend something tender because even in her anger and her sleep, a gummy bear word mouthed by a smashed up salmon can undo the most hideous of wounds.

Night Butterfly
By Dustin Reade

You wake up one morning to find a moth picking its teeth at your breakfast table.

The moth is huge, six-feet at least, with two pairs of black Converse high-tops on each of its four feet. When you enter the room in your leopard-print Snuggie, the moth removes the toothpick from its mouth and points it at you.

"You're out of coffee, bro," it says.

You want to ask how it got in your house. You want to ask where it learned to talk, if it was using one of your toothpicks, all sorts of things. In the end, though, you decide you don't really care and just sit down. The moth pushes a few soiled napkins off the table onto the floor, and then points to the empty surface.

"What's missing from this picture?" it asks angrily.

You look. There is nothing there. A ring from an old cup, and a few scratches in the wood, but not much else besides. Looking back at the moth, you shrug.

With an exasperated exhale, the moth points to the clean spot and yells, "There's no fucking coffee, bro!"

"Oh," you say, climbing to your feet. "I'm sorry. Are you sure, though? I mean, I feel like I just bought some a few days ago."

Even with your head buried in the cupboards, you can hear the moth shake its head. It is a sort of dry, scraping sound, probably from the proboscis rubbing against the furry white stuff on its chest, but who knows? Certainly not you. You are certainly no lepidopterist. That has to do with moths, right?

You pull your head from the cupboards and sulk back to the table.

Plopping back down in your seat, you say, "I swear I just bought some."

"Nope," the moth says. "I checked, and anyway I drank the rest of what was in the pot, the shit you made last night. You call that coffee? Tasted more like burnt ass to me."

You break down completely. Burying your face in your hands, you just totally let go, losing your grip and crying like a little bitch in front of company. Snot and tears pool in your palms, but you don't stop. You can't. The tears won't listen.

After what seems like several hours, you feel the moth's hand on your shoulder.

"Hey," it says, gently massaging your neck

63

in its soft, dusty hands, "it's cool, bro. No big deal. Why don't you just, y'know, get dressed and walk to the store and get some?"

You nod, sucking the snot back into your nose and smearing the rest all over your chin with the back of your hand.

"Okay," you say, embarrassed by how shaky your voice sounds.

Slowly, you get up and walk back into your bedroom. You take your Snuggie off and let it fall to the floor. You are totally naked, standing at the foot of your bed. The fan you have propped up in the window blows cool air all over your genitals as you grab socks and underwear from the top drawer, a t-shirt from the second drawer, and a pair of worn blue jeans from the bottom drawer. When you go back into the kitchen, the moth claps his hands happily.

"Fuckin' A, bro!" it shouts. "You look awesome! You look like a dude that's about to get some coffee!"

You pump your fists up and down, smiling, shouting, "USA! USA!"

The moth claps as you chant, laughing and stomping his feet on the floor. He starts coughing, still laughing.

"Oh shit," it says, "that shit is too funny."

You walk out the door, the sound of the moth's laughter still reverberating through the house. The sun is up, and there are a few little kids playing on a Slip-N-Slide next door. You wave as you walk by and they stare at you.

At the store you get coffee, eggs, a half-gallon of milk, and a pack of Marlboro menthols. As you walk back home, you see the kids on the Slip-N-Slide are still staring at you. Adjusting the groceries to your left hand, you flip them the bird. One of them opens his mouth and screams. It is a deep, manly scream and it gives you a headache almost instantly. Quick as you can, you run into your house and lock the door. The moth is there waiting for you. Like a child expecting a toy, it jumps up and down, clapping its hands excitedly.

"Did you get it, bro?" it asks. "Did you get the fuckin' coffee?"

"I sure did."

"Awwwww yeah! My boy knows where the coffee at!"

You laugh, walk into the kitchen, set the bag down on the counter and start pulling the items out one by one. When the moth sees the can of coffee, it nearly shits itself. It starts flapping its wings and sort of dancing in the air over the stove. The kitchen is pretty small, and the wings knock several items from their shelves, but you don't mind. You are just happy you could make someone happy.

The moth tells you it will be living with you from now on. It explains to you that it has always lived in the house, only it was too small to see. Considering that, you don't feel all that apprehensive about letting it continue to live with you. The way you figure it, since the moth was born in the space beneath the kitchen sink, it has already spent its entire life in the house and has just as much claim to it as you do. Plus: the moth is funny.

Like, when you tell it about the weird kids next door. The moth thinks it would be funny to pull a prank on them. So, that night, when the sun has gone down and the kids have gone to sleep, the moth runs outside and starts slamming into their bedroom window over and over, screaming, "Light! Light! Gimme that nightlight or I'll eat your fucking face!"

The children scream in their primal, deep voices. The whole neighborhood shakes with it, but the moth doesn't stop. It frantically beats its head against the window, dripping fake drool from its long proboscis, its eyes shining crazily as it demands the nightlight.

Suddenly, the front door swings open and the kid's dad comes running outside with a baseball bat in his hands. You and the moth run as fast as you can back into the house, shut off all the lights and try to muffle your laughter while he screams like a crazy person between your houses.

You learn a lot from the moth, too. You learn that moths and butterflies are related, being members of the same order. The order of Lepidoptera (you knew that had something to do with moths! High Five!). You learn that most moths are nocturnal, and that they feed on night-blooming flowers. When you hear that, you scratch the moth between the shoulders (always careful to never touch its wings) and say, "Oh, my little night butterfly!"

"Cut that shit out," it says, but you can tell by its voice that it liked it.

You and the moth have a good time together. It feels good to be close to someone, to have a real connection with the world outside your own head, to not be lonely. The moth reminds you of how fun the world can be. The two of you go on bike rides to the store for coffee (he goes through several cans a day). You build a little fort out of sheets in the living room. On the second night, you take a late night walk together and you watch as the moth bangs his head repeatedly against streetlights.

"Why do you do that," you ask.

The moth floats down from the yellow light and clears its throat.

"Do what?"

"That thing with streetlights," you say. "I see moths do it all the time. You bang yourselves into the lights over and over again. Why? Do you eat the light or something?"

"That's some creepy shit, right there," the moth says. "'Moths eating light', ugh. That gives me the willies."

"Well," you say, "why do you do it then?"

"We follow the moon, man. I mean, you know how you can see all kinds of shit with your eyes, but you know that what you're really seeing is just light reflecting off stuff?"

"Yeah."

"Well," the moth says. "It don't work that way for me. See, light hits me all fucked up, like someone shining a flashlight in your eyes. Too much light and I'm blind as a motherfucker. That's why I only go out at night, know what I'm sayin'? I gotta use the moon as a guide. Like, if the moon is up here in my eyes, then I know I gotta go straight. But, if the moon is all low or something, well…you get what I'm saying. So when you humans come in, and start puttin' up all these bright ass streetlights, mothafuckin' moths don't know which way is up!"

68

On the morning of the third day, you walk out of the bedroom and see the moth is still asleep, hanging wing-side down from the light fixture in the kitchen. The floor beneath it is covered in dust and flakes. You walk over to the sink and begin filling the coffeepot with water.

The coffee starts brewing, and the moth climbs slowly down from the ceiling, rubbing sleep from his bulbous eyes.

"That shit smells good," it says.

Smiling, you grab two cups and set them on the table. You fill both cups with hot, black coffee and sit down to look at the moth. It stretches its long proboscis a few times, and then drops it into the coffee. You can see the dark liquid travel up the transparent tube, and you watch, fascinated, as it disappears into the fuzzy, alien face.

"This is a miracle," you think. "I am looking at a giant moth. I am watching it drink coffee. I am its friend."

With this last thought, you feel a lump form in your throat. Even though the two of you have spent the last two days together, playing and goofing off, you realize you are just now recognizing it as a friend. You wonder why it took so long to realize, seeing as the two of you hit it off so well almost immediately. You finish your coffee and rub your hands together excitedly.

"So, buddy," you say happily, "what should we do today? Bike ride? Hit the bars? What?"

"Actually," the moth says slowly, setting his coffee mug down on a pile of old newspapers beside the table. "I was thinking we could do something a bit more…adult, today."

Before you can ask what it means, there is a knock at the door. The moth leaps to its four conversed feet and starts smoothing the tuft of hair on its chest.

"How're my wings?" it asks, half-turning. "Do they look all fucked up? Like, wrinkled or anything, I can't see."

"They're fine," you say. "What's going on, man?"

"Nothing."

With a flourish, the moth opens the door. Squinting against the sunlight, you look and see two giant butterflies standing on your welcome mat. Their wings are gorgeous, speckled in vibrant, metallic blue dots, ringed with shimmering gold, trimmed in neon green, and surrounded by deep red. Their long, black bodies are slim and feminine, with four of their individual legs ending in bright red high heels. The tips of their two-fingered hands are painted a similar color, and their massive, insect

70

eyes are topped with purple mascara. Long lashes spring up from the purple eye-shadow, bending back onto themselves like flowing strands of thick black hair. The moth bends down low, one arm hooked across its chest, the other presenting the room to the butterflies in a grand gesture.

"Ladies," it says in a smooth voice. "Please, come in. Make yourselves at home!"

"Oh grrrrrl!" one butterfly says to the other. "Looks like we found us a couple-a gentlemen!"

"You know that's right!" the other one says.

The two butterflies laugh as they enter the house. Their heels clack against the floor rhythmically. Once they are in the living room, you take the moth by the arm, and say, "What the hell, bro? What's going on? Who are those butterflies?"

The moth brushes you off irritably.

"Be cool," it says, walking into the living room and asking the butterflies if they would like something to drink.

"You got coffee?" the first one asks.

"Shit, baby girl," the moth says. "We got coffee for days!"

The moth snaps its fingers at you. Without thinking, you walk into the kitchen and start filling the pot. Loud music starts pumping from the speakers in the living room. It is a strange song, one you have never heard before. You assume one of the butterfly girls must have brought it with them. You can hear the moth talking loudly over the music, but you can't make out what he is saying. You hear the words "motherfucker" and "my homeboy" but not much else. The butterfly girls laugh often, loudly.

Right as the coffee finishes brewing, the kitchen door swings open and the moth walks in, leading one of the butterflies by the hand.

"Hey, bro," the moth says, "me and this bitch are gonna go check out the bedroom for a few minutes. Why don't you go and visit with Adele for a while?"

You want to protest, but you want the moth to be happy. The other day, while checking your Facebook, you did a Google search on moths and found out they only live for about a week or two. You have no way of knowing how old your moth is, or how long he has been in his adult stage. So, when it starts walking into your bedroom with a butterfly prostitute, you just sort of shrug and say, "Alright, man. You two have fun."

You fill two cups with coffee and walk into the living room. Adele, the other butterfly, is standing in front of the speakers, dancing slowly to an old love song. You note the curve of her hips as she sways them back and forth. Your eyes trace her thin waist, so thin you could wrap your hand around it, and you take in the gentle bumps where a human woman's breasts would be. They are just two small bumps, devoid of nipples, but somehow they still manage to come across as feminine. Extremely so. Your body takes notice, responding to her flirtatious movements in the traditional method, and you try to hide it by sitting your coffee cup in your lap. Adele turns and you lock eyes, her multicolored wings wrapping and unwrapping around her shoulders as she bats her long, painted lashes at you.

The song ends, and she comes and sits beside you on the couch.

"This your house?" she asks, running her poky fingers through your hair.

You clear your throat. "Hmm! Yeah."

Adele laughs. She scoots closer to you until you can feel her hot breath against your face. She continues to run her fingers through your hair, placing the other hand on your inner thigh. Your eyes roll back into your head. It has been so long since someone touched you, and it feels good. Really good.

"Do you like that, baby?" Adele whispers in your ear.

"It feels nice," you say, trying to sound cool. "Your coffee is getting cold."

73

Adele laughs again, leaning impossibly closer to you. Never breaking eye contact, she unfurls her long, brown proboscis into your coffee cup. With slow, rhythmic sips, she drains the cup. You watch the amber liquid as it pulses up the long shaft, her fingers twirling out the same rhythm in your hair. She leans in and you close your eyes as she kisses you, the coffee smell of your breath mingling with the nectar-flavor of her mouth. She begins working your zipper down, freeing your penis into the air like a sudden Washington Monument.

As she climbs on top of you, you see hundreds of neon colors flashing out a pattern across her thorax. The colors are beautiful, and they almost hypnotize you with their beauty. From deep within the colors, a slit appears. It starts as a tiny cut running through the flashing orbs, but soon it is wide enough to engulf your entire shaft. Adele moans instantly. You do too. Regular sex never felt this good. It's as though she were massaging your entire body with a glove of blue fuzz. Your eyeballs roll back into your skull. A thick jelly pours from her opening, covering you both in a tingling sheen. The smell of flowers fills the room. Flowers and honey and earth and sweat and sex. Your coffee cups crash to the floor as Adele bucks harder and harder against you, whipping her boneless hips back and forth, trailing golden fluid from your thighs to your belly button. She climaxes hard against you, digging her prickly fingers into your neck, drawing blood. You bite your lips and cum hard inside her, feeling your juices mix and flow over every surface.

After several minutes of panting, she climbs off of you. The slit in her thorax closes up, and the colors die away slowly, like balloons disappearing into the sky. She looks in the mirror over the fireplace and adjusts her eye lashes. You suddenly feel bad for just assuming right away she was a prostitute. After all, she hasn't asked for any money, and the sex seemed to happen naturally enough. Maybe she is just one of those free-spirited girls that don't have a lot of hang-ups when it comes to sex. Plus, you don't know much about butterflies. Maybe they were more open about sex than were humans? Or maybe they were prostitutes and the moth paid them before they even showed up? Who knows? Who cares? All you know is: you like Adele. She seems sweet, and you find her extremely attractive, even though you are of two separate species. You suddenly realize why people would want to sleep with aliens.

Adele catches you watching her and smiles. "What?" she asks.

"Nothing," you say, suddenly shy again even though you have just shared one of the most intimate moments two adults can share with one another. "You're just beautiful…that's all."

"Shit," she laughs. "You're sweet."

Right then, the kitchen door bursts open and the moth and his butterfly come barging in. The other butterfly looks sweaty and disheveled, with the same golden fluid dripping all over her. The moth jumps over the back of the couch and flops down hard beside you, a big smile on his face.

"Woo!" he yells.

"Tell me about it," you say, still looking at Adele as she applies purple eye shadow in the mirror. She catches the other butterfly watching her in the mirror.

"Hey, Trixie," she says. "Did you have fun? He treat you alright?"

"He treat me fine," Trixie said, wiping gold jelly from around her lips. "You about ready to go? I gotta pick up my kids in a few hours."

"Just a second," Adele says.

After they have gone, you take a shower. The butterfly jelly has hardened into a thin shell on your body, and it takes a long time to get it off. You wear your luffa sponge down to a stringy nub, but in the end, you get it all. When you walk out into the living room in your leopard print Snuggie, you see the front door is hanging open. The moth is out there, sitting on the front steps, smoking a cigarette.

"What's up?" you ask, sitting down beside him and watching the sun slowly set over the purple mountains in the distance.

"Not much," he says, exhaling a plume of dense gray smoke into the air. He seems lost, distant. You put your arm around his shoulder and just sit there, not talking or doing anything, just sitting. Absent-mindedly, you start running your hand up and down, sort of massaging his back. The moth jumps up violently and stares at you.

"What the fuck are you doing, man?" he screams.

"What?" you ask, holding your hands up defensively. "What happened? What did I do?"

"You touched my fucking WINGS!"

"Well so what?" you say, climbing to your feet and looking at his wings. They are coated in butterfly ooze, but otherwise they look no different than before. "What's the big deal? I barely touched 'em. You're big enough, that shouldn't affect you, right? I mean, isn't that just a myth anyway, about the wings?"

"No," the moth shouts. "No it's not a fucking myth, dude! It's true! I can never fly again!

Thanks a lot, bro!"

You are about to shout at him that it doesn't matter whether he can fly or not, as a moth his size has no natural predators, but you stop when you see the neighbor kids staring at you from their front porch. They are wearing camouflage shorts and t-shirts, with little black combat boots and butterfly face paint. Something about them makes you feel uneasy, frightened. The moth is still ranting and raving, kicking up big clouds of dust. You try to calm him down, but he won't listen. He flaps his wings in a pathetic attempt at flight, but never leaves the ground more than an inch or two. He would be better off just jumping.

The kids take a few steps off their porch. The little boy raises his hands and starts moaning. It is a deep moan, so low you don't hear it so much as feel it reverberating in your chest. The other two children—both girls—follow suit. They raise their hands to the sky and begin moaning in the same deep, guttural voice. You grab the moth and shove him inside, listening to the windows rattle as you hide behind the sofa.

Then, as suddenly as it had started, the noise stops. Slowly, cautiously, you peek over the sofa and out the window. The kids are gone. Presumably, they have gone back inside.

The moth asks: "What the hell was that?"

"Those kids," you say. "They've been acting strangely ever since you showed up. I can't remember ever meeting them before, but I saw 'em the other day and they did the same thing...that weird yell thing."

"That's too weird," the moth says, coughing as it runs its hands over its antenna.

"Yeah."

Suddenly, everything feels different, though you can't put your finger on it. A slight change in the weight of the air, maybe, or something equally imperceptible. All you know for sure is: something has changed. Beside you, the moth slumps his shoulders. His head begins lolling back and forth slowly, and a thin, white ooze starts dribbling from his proboscis.

"Hey man," you say, shaking him gently. "Are you alright? You don't look so good."

"I don't feel so hot, bro. I feel like those kids did something to me."

His head suddenly flops limply downward, so he is staring at his chest. The white ooze begins bubbling and foaming in a pool on his lap. Where the ooze lands, the soft skin becomes flaky, and breaks away from his body. You hear a pop and a sizzle and a goopy, brown sludge shoots out of his

79

ears. It lands with a plop on the floor.

You panic. What should you do? It never occurred to you that the moth might get sick. How are you supposed to deal with this situation? Take him to the hospital? The vet? What?

Grabbing the phone, you dial 9-1-1. It rings three times before the dispatcher picks up. She asks you your emergency and when you explain everything she just sighs and hangs up. You try calling again, but there is no answer. You suspect they have blocked your number and this surprises you because you didn't realize an emergency service provider could do something like that. You throw the phone and it breaks into four pieces when it hits the corner of the fireplace.

Crouching down beside the moth again, you feel helpless. Your friend is dying and there is nothing you can do about it. You feel like a dried up piece of white dog shit in a vacant lot.

You start to cry.

Hard.

You don't know what else to do.

You cry for a long time.

You cry until the fizzling and bubbling and popping cease, and the moth slumps down into an awkward position.

He is dead.

You check to make sure.

You squeeze his proboscis. You put your head to his chest. You check all of his arms and legs for any sign of a pulse, but find nothing. No hint or suggestion of life.

He is dead.

What do I do now? You wonder. Do I bury him? You seem to recall reading somewhere that some moths ate their dead. Was he the kind of moth that did that? Would he have wanted you to do it?

Carefully, slowly, you raise his right hand to your lips and take a bite. The flesh tears away easily, but tastes awful. It is dry and crumbly in your mouth. You take a few more bites, thinking it will become easier to consume once you reach the gooey inside parts. You eat for hours, searching for any sort of entrails, any sort of veins or moisture of any kind, but no matter where you bite, you encounter the same dry, crumbly bits that leach all the moisture from your mouth.

When you tear into the stomach, you find it is full of rubbery, brown coils, all looped together like a rolled up garden hose. You bite into them. They are chewy and warm, like a stale gummy worm. You bury your head into the coiled entrails, gnashing your teeth, swallowing mouthfuls of the warm intestines. They seem to go on forever. As you eat, you feel your shoulders enter the carcass, followed by your chest, hips, knees, ankles, and feet until you are completely engulfed inside the moth. Still eating, you begin moving your arms out in front of you. You sweep them out in a wide gesture, returning them to your sides as you go. This propels you forward slowly, swimming through the never-ending sea of guts.

After what seems like several days, you see a light in the distance. You chew and swim your way to the light, which gets bigger with each bite, nearer with every side-stroke. After a while, you realize you are being pulled, gently, into it. Upon realizing this, you stop swimming through the guts and allow yourself to be sucked towards it. You think back to the moth and how he explained how he used the light of the moon to find his way in the dark. You smile at the memory as you are pulled through the light.

It takes your eyes a moment to adjust, but when they do, you see you are falling from a great height. You see a patchwork landscape rising up rapidly to meet you. The land seems made of varying shades of blue and purple. You feel the wind whip into your face, making your eyes tear up and your mouth go dry.

Just before you smash—headfirst—into the

blue earth, something grabs you. It just plucks you right out of the air. You zip around in a few loop-de-loops, then lower, slowly, carefully, to the ground. The surface of the earth is spongy, like a Twinkie, and it takes you a moment to get your bearings.

The moth puts his hands on your shoulders and smiles down at you. He has grown several feet taller, and there are more colors on his wings. He is beautiful, standing there with a lit cigarette dangling from his proboscis.

"Is it really you?" you ask.

"Fuck yeah, it's me!" the moth laughs. "Welcome to where the light takes you, bro! It's good to see you again!"

Without thinking, you embrace the moth, wrapping your arms around him and weeping openly, burying your face in his soft, fuzzy chest. To your surprise, he hugs you back. You wish you could spend forever hugging him, holding each other, wrapped up in the warmth and love of a solid bromance, but after a few moments, the moth pulls away.

"There's someone else here," he says in a deep, serious voice, "that is really excited to see you."

Bewildered, you allow yourself to be led to a distant farmhouse. It is typical: creaky porch swing,

83

ivy winding up the southern side, peeling paint, etc. The screen door creaks noisily as you walk through. Victorian furniture. A grandfather clock against a wall beside a piano. Pictures dusted in elegant frames, white lace fabric hanging over the backs of chairs. A cicada shell on a windowsill.

You hear noises from the kitchen. Voices. Happy, urban voices. Familiar voices. Feminine voices.

You run into the kitchen and see Adele standing in front of an open refrigerator, pitcher of pink lemonade in her spiky hands. Trixie stirs a pot of smelly soup over the stove. You clear your throat.

The butterflies look up, startled. When Adele sees you, she quickly sets the pitcher of pink lemonade on the counter, wipes her hands on her apron, and races over to you. Even through the gingham drapery, you can see her mid-section light up. She wraps you in a tight hug, covering your neck with passionate kisses. Her long proboscis prods your ears, nose, mouth, and wraps around your neck, dripping honey-nectar down your back.

You look over her shoulder to see several long, green caterpillars playing outside. They are your babies, you know it instinctively. They are the most beautiful creatures you have ever seen in your life.

As your butterfly wife nectars all over you, you watch as your children pluck three human-children from the branches of a dead cherry tree. The human-children are all wearing identical camouflage outfits and butterfly face paint. They moan pitifully as they are forced from the safety of the tree.

Your babies carefully hold the children against flat pieces of torn cardboard, and drive three-inch needles through their mid-sections.

Dreamsource
By Dawid Kain

They say that every dream has two ends. Of course, people are aware of only what was anchored into their heads and have no idea that dreams and nightmares can influence the reality in the most bizarre way. And sometimes they can change the course of the history irretrievably.

"I am the fucking God!", Adam Sanetzky screamed in flutters of megalomania that took control over him in the moments of his greatest life successes.

Although it may sound absurd, there was not much exaggeration in his words. During the second year of the physics studies, he became a scholar of the Hawking Fund which guaranteed twenty thousand euro per year to outstanding young scientists. His book, 'The Forcible History of Mass' written during his fourth year of the study was deemed one of the most important works since Newton's 'Principia Mathematica'. When he began working in his own laboratory at the CERN Institute at the age of twenty six, it was obvious that Sanetzky was going to be one of the high-profile characters in the scientific world of the twenty first century.

His experiments on black holes and stabilization of space-time tunnels could irrevocably change the fate of the mankind. Finally, there was a chance that within the next two-three decades we would be able to travel not only in space but also in time.

Although Sanetzky's professional life was a string of good luck, his social life practically did not exist. It is enough to say that this megalomaniac genius was also a virgin tormented by onanism addiction. He had sexual relations with women, men or at least domestic animals only in his dreams… and these were getting more and more absurd.

One night, he dreamed that he fell in love with a woman who deprived him of virginity. It was his own hand. He called her Rebecca. The feeling was so strong that finally Adam decided to ask his hand for a hand in marriage, and she agreed. Their wedding was a wonderful event: a few hundred guests, Sanetzky wearing an expensive suit, and Rebecca – covered with a veil from wrist to elbow. A priest wearing a cassock made of skin with studs wished them all the best; well, he sometimes mumbled something that sounded like: "You may now kill the bride"; and, when blessing, he drew a shape of a pentagram in the air.

Although the wedding night of Adam and his hand was not their first time, Sanetzky was waiting for it as if for salvation, because Rebecca had promised him that she would do him good like never before.

"I love you. Don't leave me till the end of the world," whispered Sanetzky, sticking his tongue into his tightened fist.

Then came the best part. Rebecca started petting him with more skill than usually, at first slowly and tenderly then more and more vigorously. Finally Sanetzky's hand was moving so fast that her shapes lost sharpness and the hand itself turned into a vibrating cloud of a color of a skin.

"Almost there, honey!" Adam screamed.

And then, suddenly, his darling Rebecca exceeded the speed of light, deviating the space-time tunnel which sucked Sanetzky's penis into it, giving him a pleasure no man had never known before.

A few seconds later the genius woke up. His testicles were in pain as if a roller drove over them and his hand was shaking convulsively, torn with series of contractions.

"Where could that tunnel lead to?" Sanetzky was wondering on his way to work, dreaming that his sperm was now drifting in the most distant corners of the Universe, maybe in the past or maybe in the future or maybe even in one of the parallel space-times?

Despite his unique brightness, Adam Sanetzky would never dare to suppose that Time is in reality a very ironic "element" that loved to make the most sophisticated jokes. Of course this may have nothing to do with Adam's erotic dream, but exactly nine months later and at the same time two thousand years earlier, in Bethlehem, a virgin suddenly gave birth to a child.

M. Happy Head
By James Dorr

Mr. Happyhead was a hawk, a vulture. A white Lammergeier, larger than eagles. He cruised the skies. He cruised people's thought-trains.

He cruised the city, in thought or in person, doting on crowds and filth and hunger. He studied the tragic.

Mr. Happyhead's personal thoughts went back to a table, to flesh growing soft, but then muscles stiffening. His thoughts went to smiles forced on unhappy faces as skin became waxy, as lips and finger- and toenails paled. His thoughts went to red-green discolorations, then smells of putrescence.

These things he had known too.

Except with release, with tissue decaying, with fluids leaking from head and anus, with gas-blisters forming, with swellings, explosions, Mr. Happyhead discovered freedom. He now had a mission, to share his good fortune.

He preyed on the city's own.

***

Catching his breath, Mr. Happyhead entered his first thought. He picked it at random. He found

90

himself staring into a bar mirror, eyeing a women who had just come through the door behind him.

"Would you care to dance?" he asked, turning around and smiling broadly, but also blushing. He knew he was married.

The woman looked him up and down, then frowned and turned back to the friends she'd come in with. She started laughing.

Mr. Happyhead turned even redder, but only ordered another whiskey. He drank it slowly, taking his time, even though the thought of a wife who would wait up late for him – not married that long, their love was still ardent – tried to slip through from the back of his mind. He watched the woman, tall and with red hair, laughing and talking with her companions, occasionally dancing when other men asked her, through the dust-spiderwebbed behind-bar mirror.

He waited until she and her friends prepared to leave, then finished himself and followed after, always keeping a half block of shadows, of darkness between them. He waited as first one, and then another, and then the last of the redhead's companions turned their own ways in the spiraling blackness, taking their own paths to go to their own homes. And still he waited.

He stood outside and noted the window that

suddenly lit up after she had gone into a building. He counted the windows from the building's corner, the floors from the sidewalk. He went inside too and climbed the stairs, then counted the doors from the end of the hallway, estimating doors against windows, until he arrived at the one with a dim hint of light still beneath it.

He waited patiently, until that, too, went dark, then counted slowly to sixty, one hundred, six hundred, a thousand, then counted again to be sure she was sleeping before, with a twist learned from when he was younger and used his own body, he broke her door lock. He eased her door open.

He shut it behind him, then found a table lamp, following its cord by feel to its socket. He carried it with him as his eyes adjusted to the inside darkness.

Interior doors: He found one to the bathroom. Another, which opened into the kitchen, yielded a sharp knife.

The third opened onto his quarry, sleeping.

He leaned behind her, then tied her hands quickly with the lamp cord. He thrust a pillowcase into her mouth when it opened to scream.

He found another lamp in the bedroom and used its cord to bind her feet as well, then bind both hands and feet to the solid bed.

92

As the dawn came, he became an artist, carving illustrations in carmine to match her hair with the knife from the kitchen. He stepped back often, admiring his work. Adjusting the pillowcase now and again, lest her screams, then her whispers, disturb his train of thought. And, behind that thought, he felt another thought, that of a decent man not that long married, wondering . . . admiring . . . thinking, perhaps, of a wife who was waiting.

***

Mr. Happyhead left joy behind him. He left people with ideas to do things they would not do had he not helped them. He left the counterman in a diner whose boss had just – once again – threatened to fire him, a notion of how to hurt his boss's business. And then, on his break, Mr. Happyhead left him facing the kitchen pantry, contemplating the box of rat poison he knew was inside it.

***

Mr. Happyhead often remembered the time of his boyhood. His father. His mother. His mother's brother who taught him things most boys did not learn till later. He thought of his studies, not so much in school as on weekends and summers. His learning about birds.

His lust for flying.

He studied pigeons, catching them,

sometimes, and finding out the ways their wings bent. When they would not obey, he gave them to cats.

He studied their talons.

***

Mr. Happyhead loved women most. He entered their thoughts often, savoring their difference. He taught them power.

He spoke to women, telling them how, through his own experience, they could tempt men to do their bidding. He transcended space and time, becoming Eva Braun whispering to Hitler. Cleopatra inciting Mark Antony.

He taught sisters how to enjoy their brothers.

***

When Mr. Happyhead had been a boy, one summer he went to the beach with his parents. There he was able to contemplate sea gulls. He watched, fascinated, as they flew with shellfish clutched in their claws, circling higher, until, over rocks, they dropped their prey, splitting their armor so they could eat.

He watched sea gull mothers, guarding their nests. How, when fledglings from other nests wandered too far and blundered into the wrong territory, they pecked the intruders' heads into gray jelly and fed them to their own young. Ate what

94

was left themselves.

Mr. Happyhead made an experiment, switching eggs from one nest to another, then young birds as well. He wore a catcher's mask when he did this, and thick, brown gloves.

He wore many masks as he grew older. As student. As citizen. Once, as a soldier. As workman.

As lover.

As man of the streets, first running errands for those with more power, then finding ways to gain power of his own. Worming his way into inner circles.

As loyalist. Henchman.

As one who was trusted.

When Mr. Happyhead was not working, he frequented zoos.

***

Mr. Happyhead played with children, and sometimes their mothers. He had a winning smile.

***

Mr. Happyhead liked seeing dentists. He liked the way the hygienist placed pointed hooks in his mouth, using a mirror to chip at his teeth. To chip the flecks away. When he was young, he sometimes had thought he might be a dentist's hygienist himself.

95

He liked seeing blood spit in white porcelain basins, watching its spiral flow.

When he was young, he had liked hawks and eagles. And then Lammergeiers, "Bearded Vultures" according to the book his father got for him one Christmas. He'd seen it in a store, then begged for it almost all the way from Halloween. And his mother helped him.

"It's good that he wants to learn things," his mother would say nights at dinner.

"But books about vultures?" his father would answer. "I think that's morbid."

"Hawks and vultures," his mother had said. "And eagles too. Like our country's symbol. There's nothing wrong with that."

Mr. Happyhead's father had bought the book the morning after he'd beaten his wife. The evening before he had come home after working late and, tiring of the incessant argument, in their bedroom that night he'd slapped her. He'd bought the book as a kind of appeasement. They'd kissed and made up and wrapped it together and hid it in their bedroom closet.

Mr. Happyhead had not been intended to know this, except he'd been outside their door and listened.

He'd listened as well in the following years

96

as their marriage continued its downward spiral. As the hittings became more frequent and Mr. Happyhead got gifts more often. Books and toys and camping equipment. Toy guns and airplanes.

But most of all, he still liked to think about Lammergeiers, described in the book as having wingspans greater than eagles' – some naturalists even thought they were eagles, though somewhat like vultures as well insofar as they ate the dead. He read about people in Eastern, Himalayan nations who placed their deceased on the tops of towers, waiting for the great, white birds to descend and devour them.

Some even thought that the huge birds were spirits.

***

Mr. Happyhead had his favorites, of those he flew into. A dentist's hygienist – he got in her head often and, through the hooks and the mirrors and probes, he drank in her feelings about her boyfriend. Her fear and hatred, and yet her greater fear that he might leave her. The beatings he gave her. And when the next patient got in the chair, the hooks in his mouth, the probe at his gumline, he had her let them out.

***

Mr. Happyhead grew into power, having

learned how to manipulate people. He learned about violence, and when he should use it. He learned about money – when he could pay others.

He learned about greed.

But when his father had been found dead in his parents' bedroom, the .25 caliber bullet of a "Saturday night special" lodged in his brain, and as his mother was dragged away weeping, that's when he had learned of joy. Joy as proactive. Joy as something he could himself plan, for himself or for others, and not simply wait to receive as a byproduct of other things that others did to him. Joy as fulfillment.

He never knew how to hate – never could understand its concept, at least in himself, though he knew it in others.

And when he found himself on a table, hearing a doctor explain to the young cop who'd brought him in about things like trauma, the force of powder grains tattooing skin, about entrance paths and shock waves and exits and hollowed out, larger and heavier bullets, that's when he had started to come to know freedom.

***

Mr. Happyhead came to suspect the mystics of Himalayan lands were on to something. He flew in the night air, no longer earthbound, as bird or not-bird – it did not matter.

He thought: Birds have no teeth.

He flew to his mother in Women's Prison and entered her head and found that she loved him. She had always loved him and, as he'd begun to nurture his own brushes with the law, had almost admired him. And he'd loved her also. He'd taught her things about prison bed sheets and how they could be torn in strips, twisted and knotted. How they could be looped from ceiling fixtures.

He found that she feared, though – that she was not ready. That freedom was not for her, at least not that night.

He learned about patience.

He had already known about waiting. Of waiting in ambush, or being ambushed himself. Of power conflicts. And now he learned endurance.

***

Mr. Happyhead flew to the man who had been his rival and, flying within his thoughts, drank of his triumph. Triumph became pride, and then pride hubris. He watched and he let it grow, he a nestling, a fledgling lodged in this other man's brain-cage, becoming in time a mother sea gull pecking away at any intrusive thoughts save those his own will and joy engendered.

He looked out at others, also outside the law,

99

who had more power than this, his protege, and through sheer savagery took them over. Expanding his domain.

He came in time to rule the whole town, and then the county, with numbers and gambling and prostitution.

He got himself noticed.

And when a yet larger gang from the state capital descended on this, his operation, he left his rival, flying back to the sky. Hovering. Waiting.

Enjoying patience – perhaps now and then breathing small suggestions into minds oh, so open to hear them – as his erstwhile rival – his own erstwhile killer – was trussed to a wooden chair. His clothes ripped from him. Knives brought out and worked with. Small knives not for killing, but only enjoying.

He watched and enjoyed and flew in and out of the pain and the redness, devouring driblets of soul with each passage, as flesh became weaker, yet never quite perished. As life hung on that night, and then for three others until the sculptors who carved became weary.

And still life hung on, until the police found the eyeless, tongueless, fingerless, flayed hulk that would continue to breathe and shit and take in nutrition from hospital needles for decades to come before finally expiring.

And one cop looked up then, out the abandoned warehouse window.

"Jeez, what's that?" he said as the stretcher bearers came in for their burden.

"I don't know – looks like a bird," his partner said, gazing out the window too now. "A big white bird. Some kind of big sea gull."

"Sea gull, my ass," the first one said. "It's as big as an eagle."

***

Mr. Happyhead read the newspapers. He read of other crimes and disasters. Of long suffering wives killed in suburban houses. Of children who talked back discovering silence. Of gang leaders, some more of whom he had once known, falling out over drugs and profits.

He read about business – he liked the drug trade and wished to help it.

He went to the source. He became a pilot, and then a ship's captain. He formed an intimacy with policemen who lived on the take, and with their commissioners. He captured the mind and the soul of the woman who slept with the mayor.

He doted on guns – after all, did he not know himself what guns could do? – and cultivated in others their love as well.

101

He taught others how to use knives and razors, yet others explosives, sometimes learning himself from the thoughts of those he had entered. He found himself in a fortified building, surrounded by armed men, whispering to leaders they must not surrender. That rightness was with them.

He taught people courage.

And always the memories came back, of the cold table. Then of a tunnel that time of his own death. A dark, long tunnel. He'd thought about having read of such tunnels as he'd paced its distance, leaving his ruined flesh far behind him. He'd heard in his mind the voice of the doctor fading to near silence as, ahead of him, he thought he saw bright lights, felt warmth and comfort. But all he had read turned out to be lies.

He emerged on an ice field, cold, unrelenting, as cold as the table's top. What heat he felt proved no more than a memory.

A memory of first love, after a drunken pickup in a roadhouse. Of ripping her open after his passion had spent itself in her. Of slapping her. Stabbing her. Tearing her flesh as he later did others. As he wished his father had done that night of the book.

And now the others, the second, the third love, the fourth and those after, and friends, and

102

grandparents, he now saw laughing as he emerged out of the dark of that tunnel. Laughing and smiling, their faces forgiveness.

Laughing at him, he thought.

Mr. Happyhead screamed his rejection – this vision was not true! – then struck with his fists at the white-robed figures, drowning himself in their spurting blood. Drinking their screams. Their shrieks. Taking and wrapping himself in their whiteness. Hearing their shattered bone.

Spinning, he coursed again into the dark.

And felt the wind. Felt the wind at the outstretched tips of wing-feathers as, opening hooded eyes, now he was swooping over the city. A city of nighttime.

Below, he saw neon lights.

***

Mr. Happyhead was happy.

Ugly Shirt's Quest
By Kevin A. Ward and Alan M. Clark

In order to survive each day, Ugly Shirt required the completion of a foolish quest. He believed this was a gift from his god, Speakerphone, to whom he owed everything. Today his quest would be to find a remedy for his miraculous potato chips that were both hairy and webbed. Off to the chemist he went, where, in exchange for a full pot of coffee, he was allowed to drop the chips into a pile of contemporary curtains that were folded and fighting and pale with short buttons. As he waited for the remedy to be revealed as perhaps a toothy hydrant, he was rudely tossed from the chemist's into puddles of grey mustard all the way across town.

"Why have I been so rudely tossed?" he wondered aloud, knowing that all unanswered questions muttered under the breath were as prayers to his god.

"You're the one who must always have a quest," Speakerphone shrugged. "A quest can't be easy."

Tales of the almighty talking machine being a smart aleck were common. Ugly Shirt had never gotten a response from his god and would have been thrilled to have established a direct line to Speakerphone if the god hadn't made it sound like the quest thing was Ugly Shirt's doing and his problem.

"And by the way," Speakerphone said, "that's not a prayer. We're not on equal terms. I am your god. Your words to me are meant to take the form of fervent invocation."

Ugly shirt tried to ignore his god's crotchety tone and bravely resumed his crusade. But an hour later, bleeding from the sockets after trying to stare a zigzag path back to the chemist, he discovered that the rapid eye monument was missing from his coffee pot. He would have to find a new one, for even if the clerk allowed him back into the chemist, he could not make payment without a full pot.

In his search for the monument, Ugly Shirt poked around in the gutter with stiffened house shoes and a land umbrella. In the process, he stepped off a ledge hidden in a mustard puddle and fell, briefly licking the frozen faces that waited below within the wood-grain liquid afterdeath. Being nearly dead, he could barely grasp the curtain overhead, but just managed by spreading his impossibly colorful toes. Having tasted the dead, suddenly the rapid eye monument didn't seem so

105

important to Ugly Shirt. He pulled himself from the puddle and lay on the street, panting for breath.

"Now what do I do?" He didn't intend this to be a prayer, but apparently Speakerphone was all over it.

"I never got anywhere without letting some poor elephant make decisions for me," the god said. "I'll let you borrow one of mine."

As if someone were emptying a giant laundry bag overhead, down came a great heap of soft-boned elephant, spilling from the sky and knocking Ugly Shirt sprawling across the puddle opening to the afterlife. If he'd fallen back in, it would have been the final curtain for him.

So embarrassed that it had nearly sent Ugly Shirt to his eternal rest, the elephant walked between its own legs and disappeared.

Speakerphone might be all-powerful and knowing, Ugly shirt thought, being careful to keep the reflection to himself, but he isn't very helpful. Disoriented but not discouraged, Ugly shirt stood and looked around. Which way to the chemist? He decided not to pray as he started walking.

Presently, he identified the rapid eye monument resting beside the door to the chemist. The door was locked and the blood pudding sun was beginning to set.

106

"Potato chips have always been able to take care of themselves," Speakerphone said, but Ugly Shirt pretended not to hear him.

Ugly Shirt blamed his god for giving him his need to complete a quest each day and then thwarting his efforts to fulfill today's mission. With the idea that attention and faith in the reality of Speakerphone was all that guaranteed the god's continued existence, Ugly Shirt resolved to never speak to the god again and to systematically reduce his belief in the deity over time. With this decision so safely begun without a bolt of destruction from above, he headed for home, the monument folded neatly inside the coffee pot that tagged along beside him.

Fuck Your Death, Keep Working!
By Edmumd Colell

Sean's stomach explodes. He stops typing paychecks to clutch himself with sore and gnarled fingers. Bacon-tuna-onion sandwich slush runs over his intestines, every ingredient made himself. Outside his cubicle, the ceiling-mounted emergency phone number stands alone among tiles of company posters: "TOTATECH: EMPLOYING EVERYTHING TO SERVE EVERYTHING," "TOTATECH: THE ONLY COMPANY THAT'S A CONTINENT," "TOTATECH: YOU WORK HERE, YOU'RE FAMILY." In TV commercials, these blurbs sang to everyone like Sean: needy for job experience and comfortable living on the road to greater dreams. A year into employment, the blurbs stop reminding Sean of his dreams, but they still won't shut up.

The wish for post-surgery pain killer ice cream helps him ignore his burst entrails as he picks up the phone and dials the sixteen-digit emergency number. The hard buttons sting his fingertips, breaking skin by the tenth number. Shit, I'll need that in the hospital. No work, no ice cream.

"Thank you for calling TotaTech emergency services. Please state your occupation, emergency,

108

and full name."

"Payroll clerk, exploded stomach, Sean Spring." The words jiggle his burning, undigested food.

Hanging up, he calculates thirty minutes for TotaTech's sea-level hospital to launch emergency medical techs 10,000 miles to the payroll office. With my handful of luck, I don't work at the very top or bottom of this place. Something coughs and hisses below him, drawing his attention to the bluestreak cleaner wrasse fish sweeping the floor. One of them clings to his chair, vomiting the dust it cleared and the ice cream it earned. It falls. My other scrap of luck: I don't work here as a wrasse fish.

As stomach acid stews his innards, the thought of ice cream hurts. Maybe I can take time off for once. Practice cooking a little more before I try culinary school. He gives up the thought, as well as the dream. Whatever, no one could afford culinary school when their job pays in ice cream. He considers all the services granted to employees for free, that tourists pay life savings to enjoy. Those tourists can still use money in other continents, where medicated ice cream has no exchange rate.

Sean pulls the croaking wrasse fish to his desk. He says, "What do you work for?"

109

It dies.

"Yeah, I don't know either."

Billions of unprocessed checks line up on his computer, belonging to every organism in TotaTech. George, a hard-working hibiscus, has earned three gallons of pesticide-laced rocky road. Feng, a day care panda, got a bonus pint of anti-depressant sherbet. The mushroom rock star known only as "Spore-adict" sold seven million copies of his latest album in Germany and Japan, courtesy of TotaRecs, so his royalties net him seven pints of neapolitan full of cocaine and methadone. Processing the three of them burns Sean's fingers again. Despite the pain, he keeps typing.

I'll get better, and then come back to this.

He types faster.

This is the rest of my life.

His words per minute resume stomach-exploding speed. His intestines swell. Steam boils in his lungs. Faster. Blood vessels burst in his eyes, blinding him. He blinks the blood away and keeps entering data. A lung pops and whistles in his chest cavity, cutting his breaths short. Blood leaks from his heart. All ten knuckles bulge against his skin. Faster, goddamnit. The names of employees fly up the screen, ten per second.

A coworker says, "What are you doing?"

Sean ignores her. His bowels burst through skin, the stench driving her away. His chest cavity blows, scattering ribs. Some of his other coworkers dial the emergency number, unaware of the EMTs still en route. Thanks for your concern, though. Good to know that you'll show it at least once.

Pressure swells in his head after his heart bursts. His fingers break apart, and he types with exposed bone marrow. With twenty more checks in the next second, the coils of his brain shoot through his eyes. He stops at last, falling next to the wrasse fish. Two last words: "I quit." Black.

***

A cold, robotic, female voice pages him: "Sean to existence, Sean to existence."

A gust of papers swirls around Sean. They reveal documents with his name and information, red ink words scratched through each one: "MALICIOUS SUICIDE" "DISCIPLINARY ACTION REQUIRED" "RE-LOCATE TO PHONE EAR ASSEMBLY." The papers smother and nurture him as a womb.

Stiff, purple flesh engulfs him. Green limbs sprout from his new eggplant body. Don't you assholes know I'm dead? The papers carry him off to a conveyor belt in the phone ear factory beneath the ocean and leave without answer.

The tallest eggplant bush, a red "MANAGER" pin stabbed in his fruit, extends a branch to him and says, "Welcome," in a deep voice.

Sean shakes the eggplant's branch. "Hi. Listen, something's wrong – I'm not supposed to be here."

The manager hands him the plastic, silicone, and copper pieces of a phone ear – TotaTech's prosthetic ear with a speaker in its lobe and a number-dialing keypad in its side. He walks away on roots and says, "Build."

Sean pulls his own roots, but the soil clenches them. To the eggplant bush at his right, he says, "Hey, how do you uproot yourself?"

The eggplant ignores him, as does the one to his left. All of the eggplant workers stick to their task, unspeaking. Machinery and fluorescent lighting provide the only noise.

Sean screws the parts together – black plastic outer shell, copper wires, inner speaker, latex buttons – and passes it to the next eggplant. The one before him passes a white ear, another black ear, white again. Jesus, I'd rather be a wrasse.

The machine that molds the parts whirs and roars. A sign by its mouth says, "CAUTION: KEEP LIMBS OUT OF MACHINERY."

112

Perfect.

He climbs off the conveyor belt, his roots still imprisoned. He reaches the speed lever, cranks it forward. The quickened belt tears off the top of his body. The other eggplants ignore him, reaching under him for product pieces, while he crawls on all branches against the assembly line. Its current sweeps him further away from the machine's chewing and spitting mouth.

I shouldn't have to earn death twice. Don't I get at least one?

Halfway up the belt, Sean shoves the lever back until it breaks. The belt stops, leaving the machine's teeth to grind in hunger. The eggplants tremble, grasping for the last few pieces they can put together while Sean crawls over them.

The manager growls, swinging his gnarled-fist branches on the way to the assembly. "Problems?"

The eggplants catch Sean and offer him to their boss.

Sean thrashes out of their grip, but others block his escape.

The manager lifts him, facing fruit-to-fruit. He smacks Sean with a screwdriver and throws him onto the broken lever. "Fix."

Instead, Sean brandishes the tool and says,

113

"I'm not doing one more thing to help this goddamn company. If you'd like any control in your life – hell, your afterlife – you'd stop too."

The manager takes a wallet from his fruit's pocket, fingers through leftover ice cream, and throws a picture to Sean. A faded shot of the manager sharing ice cream dinner with his family: a shorter eggplant and two seedlings. The manager jabs a branch into Sean. "You?"

Sean lingers on the seedlings, imagining their parents giving them one last dinner because of the busted factory. One of TotaTech's advertisements catered to plants, promising to feed them because the world's soil ran out of nutrients. Wild animals followed, and the company's trap sprang. Sean says, "No, I have no family, but do you want yours to keep living this way? You want your kids to work here?"

"No choice."

"Exactly." Sean drags himself toward the machine, stabbing at anyone who gets close. The other plants stop moving to watch and wait. With the strength left in his wobbling branches, Sean throws himself through the teeth.

***

"Sean to existence."

Sean's essence flees the TotaTech papers

flying for him. The void shelters him. The paging voice fades to static.

Deep into death, something gurgles and squelches behind Sean. A fetal lump of rubber and machinery grows, attached by plastic hoses leading beyond sight. It opens a whirring mouth, sucking Sean closer. He rushes away, faster than he fled TotaTech, into the company's pulpy embrace.

Shit.

Sean's papers show more red marks, "SABOTAGE," "CONSPIRACY," and "REPEAT OFFENSE," among others. A face forms in them, wearing red ink glasses on her yellow highlighter eyes. In the paging voice, she says, "We understand your frustrations, Mr. Spring. Please understand that we can't afford to lose team members at this time."

Meat grows around Sean. "What about the wrasse fish who died on my desk?"

"Mr. Piezie is very satisfied with his new position."

"Show me."

TotaTech births Sean as a small octopus and delivers him to his next job.

***

Sean awakens in the heated salt water of an undersea office. A larger octopus bumps into him, carrying a waterproof case in its beak. The octopus extends a few tentacles to him, its eyes glazed blue. She says, "Welcome to Kind Killers, the best subsidiary of TotaTech."

A smartass thought dies. In its place, Sean says, "That sounds fantastic. What should I do?"

The octopus drapes a tentacle around Sean and leads him to a pile of cases. "Call me Paci, and we have so many guns, missiles, and chemicals to make." She gives him a case and a hug. "Thank you so much for helping us."

Sean shivers as he returns her hug, his skin and soul foreign to gentle contact. The other glaze-eyed octopi shake tentacles, hi-five their suckers, take turns building each stage of a stealth bomber. Sean's pancreas retches from the sweetness, and his gut shudders at the products, but his brain tingles as he opens the case and crafts an assault rifle. On the stock, two bullet-ridden hands shake over the cursive Kind Killers logo.

I still don't see how the hell this is kind.

His brain says, "Because they're made with love."

He accepts.

Halfway through mixing an LSD bomb in a dry lab, Sean sees the components as ingredients. He wallows in his chef aspirations. This is our house special, the Psycho Cocktail. He sprinkles the last few ingredients in, seals the bomb, and arms it. Bon appetit. With a pen, he writes "Crime de Guerre Flambe" on the list of toxins for a white phosphorous flamethrower compound. He tastes the savory broiled flesh of armies who did not invest in Kind Killers, employer of the greatest chemical cook on Earth. Applause buzzes in his head.

His brain itches. In a feminine voice, the itch says, "Don't listen to yourself. You're not yourself."

Sean searches the tank for whoever was talking. The nearest octopus smiles at him. Sean says, "What the hell are you talking about?"

The octopus stares, shrugs, and continues attaching the pump to a shotgun.

"I'm not out there, Sean."

Sean drops the ingredients and avoids the other octopi as he rushes for the bathroom. I can't be the only one hearing this.

"It's a damn good thing that you are."

He slams the door behind. Lilac scents draw him further in. Gentle drum and bass songs bob in his body. Who are you?

"Mady-Klein. MK. I'm a virus tasked with brainwashing you into loving your job. This water is full of others like me."

Panic, then calm. MK's voice fades. Sean shakes his head and plots his master touch on the

117

Crime de Guerre Flambe.

"No! They're making you want this!"

Let them, damn it. Do you know what it's like to love your job for the first time ever?

A pink octopus swims into the bathroom, patting Sean's back on the way. Pinky whistles a birthday song to himself as he scrubs the gun oil from his suckers. A blue-ringed toxicologist dances to Pinky's whistle while locking himself in a stall. That guy's probably taking the most wonderful shit anyone's ever known.

"It would be a miserable shit if it weren't for my family."

Warm brain surges tickle every nerve.

MK keeps itching. "I wouldn't do this if I didn't believe in you. Together, we can help others escape."

Sean considers the life of an independent octopus, despite the viruses shutting off his imagination. Free food, open space, no oppression. Little food, polluted space, no safety. I wouldn't have to put up with the bad parts if TT just let me die.

"They never will. We'll work here through infinite lifetimes if we don't do something."

MK's message scrambles again, silenced by her family. They zap his brain with dopamine and say, "Get back to your love," "Nothing like a job well done," "We treasure your art." The same programming sparks through the eyes of Sean's coworkers as they slap his back on the way out.

MK infects more brain cells, amplifying her message. "Get stressed! Sneeze me around!"

Sean ignores these voices, grabs a glass stirring rod, and returns to artisan chemistry. He seals the Crime de Guerre Flambe, kisses it, and stacks it with the other tanks in a heart drawn on the floor. Nothing about the Flambe stands out. He buries it under an unnamed tank he mixed in seconds. Three tanks later, Sean sees himself in his dream career, cooking meal after meal, careful to add a special sprig or sauce to sign each one he created. These touches end up washed in a sink at best, rotting in landfills at worst. Everything resembles the paychecks he processed, and at least the checks hurt no one.

MK says, "You see the illusion now?"

Shut up. Please.

Five chemical compounds later, Sean starts mixing two at once, watching neither. He piles them onto the stack, knocking it over. He slaps three tanks together at once. Four. His coworkers scramble to re-organize the stack, coddling fallen products. They wrestle half-finished mixtures from

119

his tentacles. Paci stops him and says, "Slow down. They need at least three hugs." Sean taps one against his bosom twice and shoves it in her face. She says, "What's gotten into you?"

Sean sneezes. Black ink sprays Paci and the others. He grabs four more mixes, half-asses each one, and sneezes again. Paci coughs and waves her way through the dark, oily cloud. Her tentacle grazes Sean and grabs hold. "Can't you hear them crying? You're hurting them."

MK's rhetoric echoes through the inky water, joined by the confused hums of Sean's fellows. He says, "It's true. None of you really want this."

A female says, "I did. Making weapons is totally badass." Her friends haul her out of the cloud and seize her.

Paci brings plastic explosives. She patches them on a wall while another octopus sticks charges on them. Switch in tentacle, she says, "In a way, I still love these things." The switch beeps. Plexiglass shatters. Sea water chills the office water. The octopi arm themselves, and Paci passes an M4 assault rifle to Sean. She hugs him one last time, then vanishes through the dark depths.

Sean calls for her, then for anyone else. He leaves TotaTech, alone.

The ocean's empty hums dull his ears. His stomach aches and growls, urging him through the abyss. He only bumps into algae and cooling plexiglass shards. Is there any food left unemployed?

A light beckons. As Sean follows, it approaches. He raises his rifle.

The light whistles, bringing four of its buddies. Radio static crackles between them. One of the lights says, "One more."

Sean fires. Hot bubbles erupt from the muzzle. One light flickers out, groaning radio noise, flushing blood into Sean's face. The others rush above and beneath him, the low light zapping Sean's beak with an unseen prod and the high light seizing Sean's body in its teeth. The shock rattles the gun from his grip, and the other creature rushes him toward the surface. He punches this monster, thrashes, pulls, anything his tentacles can do to fight. He sneezes, but the MK-ridden ink passes under.

As the monster carries Sean higher, the pressure change swelling Sean's head and blurring his sight, the water glows blue. Sunlight reveals the predator's black body plates, blue glass eyes, and the wires rooting the light to its dorsal fin. A cyborg shark. A black "TT" tattoo brands its forehead. Sean

121

sneezes again, tries to wipe his ink-spraying siphon on the shark's underbelly, and says, "You can leave. TT can't trap you."

The shark ignores him. It spits Sean into the stinging tentacles of a jellyfish floating on the water. He panics, but the jellyfish venom relaxes him. His brain floats in his head, his eyes bobbing above the water. To his confusion, he then floats into the air. The jellyfish propels itself skyward, joining other jellyfish with captured octopi. Birds soar between them, scanning fugitives by using red rays in their eyes. An eagle's feathers glow green after identifying Sean, and the jellyfish hands him to its talons. The eagle scrapes and scratches Sean's rubbery body while delivering him to TotaTech's second-highest floor. The elevation freezes him, and the thin air chokes him, until the eagle throws him through an open window.

The room's stinging cold tiles reflect harsh light, burning the colors out of everything. Four-legged, shining beasts sniff out the blind, confused, curled octopi. Fanged jaws snatch and chew Sean's head, pumping the headache that swelled on the flight here. Please, for the love of God, don't take me any higher.

A female beast says, "Hey Pulika, where are the papers for this lady?"

The one carrying Sean in her mouth answers through a speaker in her throat. "Did you check the back wall?"

"Yeah. I'm still not seeing a box for Feng Li."

Pulika bites her neck, smooshing Sean into her fur. Pulika drags this underling to a pile of cardboard boxes and paws her face into it. "You fucking suck at checking Fs." Just as Sean's body re-inflates, Pulika drops him inside another box, snaps the lid shut, and carries him.

The ride in the box crashes to the floor. Someone pops it open and shakes Sean onto a paper carpet. Papers also coat the walls and ceiling, all of them inked with unreadable paragraphs, charts, and captions. He says, "TotaTech, did I die again?"

A massive paw sweeps him onto his back, introducing his face to the whirring teeth and glass blue eyes of a cyborg lioness. Shit, why can't we all get sweet robot stuff?

The lioness, Pulika, says, "Do as we say, answer what we ask, and you won't need to worry about dying."

"Oh, it's not a worry. Hell, I want that."

Pulika draws back, studying him. "No, you don't. Death is a bad thing."

"I guess, since TT brought me back as this."

123

She aims her fangs at him, the enamels opening to cannons. The barrels' heat prickles. "So our company resurrects your ungrateful ass and you use it to cause trouble?"

"TT will do it to everyone if we don't leave or stop it."

Pulika swipes him into a wall. His brain slams against his squishy skin, crackling blue sparks through his sight. Her fang cannons whir and blast a dagger-shaped beam into the wall above him. She growls and says, "You're the only one at fault. She serves everything, hires everything, and you're unfit to survive under her."

Sean throws himself onto her. He wraps around her face, his beak stuck to her mouth. "Damn right. Finish me."

White lights burn in her eyes. Her fangs scorch his beak. "Whatever paperwork keeps you dead, I'll fill it in triplicate."

Dagger beams stab through Sean, blasting his body in swirls of blood and ink that feed Pulika's mouth. She licks the fluids from her lips, swallowing ink with MK on board. As he dies, her smug grin melts into wide-eyed uncertainty. She sneezes.

Do your best, MK.

***

The embryonic thing from Sean's last death greets him. Its rubber has grown fleshy ink stamps. Its mouth drools for him. Sensing TotaTech's approach, he says, "Before you pick a random body for me, tell me what that thing is."

She envelops him. The paper strips of her hair and lips hang frayed over her face, bleeding red ink. "You won't need to worry about that if you behave, Sean. We believe in rehabilitation more than punishment."

" I haven't had any last requests since dying the first time. At least let me know what it can do. "

TotaTech's womb opens a hole wide enough for a peek. "That's our Liver. Your behavior inspired its development. Here at TotaTech, we seek employees who are devoted and team-oriented. We believe every living being possesses these qualities, but sometimes we hire someone with flaws – someone who would kill themselves and cause trouble, for example – and our new Liver can filter those problems out for the next life."

Sean's tiny new body encases him in cytoplasm. "What does it leave behind?"

"Don't worry about what you become in the next life, Sean. Just concern yourself with how you can improve in this life." Her glasses hang low on her face as she sighs noxious marker fumes. "It's

125

your last chance."

***

Sean lands on the jellied floor of a petri dish, the only bacterium separate from massive, putrid, yellow colonies. He eats some of the dish's agar, feeding a clone of him who breaks off in seconds. A breeze rushes over as a fully-suited technician lifts the petri dish lid and scoops him into a plasmid-loaded tube. Foreign DNA penetrates him, burning into his chromosomes. His body oozes drugged, white mucus. Am I birthing paychecks?

Chippy, auto-tuned pop music plays from the spores of mushrooms speckling the walls. Some humans and bacteria bob and jiggle to the love and heartbreak songs, while Sean twitches and shudders. With no way to switch the noise, he wishes for MK's family to flood this department and tweak him into loving it. Midway through the fifth or sixth song, a trance hypnotizes him. His thoughts make room to loop lyrics, ignoring a pipet that pokes him and sucks up drugs.

Waterfalls of a billion ice cream flavors pour into mixers that spin to the music. Human workers squirt meds into each one, unique to employees and their families, along with chemicals that insulate drugs before packing it all in the instant-freezing vault.

126

TotaTech needs to stop putting me in sensitive departments. One fuck-up here makes poisoned ice cream. Sean imagines poisoned creatures forced through Liver on the way to their next TotaTech-approved lives, their personalities stripped. TotaTech would thank him.

While his colony grows, nothing about eating agar and crapping medicine overworks him. The pipets sometimes tickle or hurt him, but he sits still, feeding, reproducing. Boring. Other colonies break down and die, unmourned when millions of petri dishes carry others like them. Over a few generations of Liver's filtration, every employee of TotaTech will live and die the same way.

Outside, explosions and gunfire rattle the walls. The mushroom singers raise their voices to drown howls, squawks, roars, and human screams. Their blaring lyrics of a lonely girl finding a guitarist's phone number fail to distract Sean. He attaches half of the violence to MK's epidemic, and all of that to himself.

Stop. MK's leading you all off a cliff and doesn't even know it.

Different music descends from the ceiling, shutting the mushrooms up. Soft, new age-y stuff chimes from a flashing green alarm. TotaTech clears her throat over the loudspeaker. "Attention. This is a state of tranquility. Our highly-trained and armed guardians are solving a problem, which may take up to five minutes. Please continue working without worry or distraction. Thank you." The new age alarm loops after her speech. Techs pause, flinching at shrapnel and lasers that hit the walls, while bacteria eat and shit on schedule.

An older tech blows a whistle at the bottom of his black Windsor tie. "Chop chop. We blow those five minutes and billions of folks go cream-less today. That includes all of us." His underlings uncap every petri dish and climb over each other to harvest meds.

Sean's milky pool of drugs touches another. The blue colony responsible sucks their product back and shuffles away, leaving a mixed poison puddle. An orange colony piles onto Blue and says, "Dumb fuck! They'll sterilize us!" Orange eats Blue and keeps on shitting pink. A tech draws the drug mix up and squirts it in one poor bastard's rocky road. Sean flees into a feeding frenzy of pipets, avoiding his fellows. He takes relief in letting people milk him. This is staying alive. This keeps my personality. The personality he preserves wants to beat the crap out of him while crying.

The alarm speaks again. "Just an update: to secure your safety, we've extended our promised

128

time of five minutes to ten. Thank you for your patience." A blast knocks the alarm loose from the ceiling, opening the air to heavier war noises than before. On one side, the zapping of stronger weapons. On the other, sneezes.

Panicking techs tug the petri dishes back and forth, spilling colonies onto other dishes. The black-tied tech pulls those idiots aside, smacks them, and tosses the dirty dishes from the racks. He leaves a splatter of Sean behind on a clean dish.

Mushrooms drop from the walls to devour mixed bacteria. The drugs discolor and kill them. Each fungus's final breath sings Taps. Someone holds his chest as if his heart blew up, and his friends trample him on the way to the ice cream mixers.

Pulika was right. Not all of us are strong enough to work here. We're not meant to at all. Sean pictures departments collapsing, Liver overstuffing itself on the dead, and the hospital staff failing to stop it from exploding. Sean puffs himself up with a bite of agar and rushes for the other colonies, splashing contaminants in their drugs. He hurdles one plate after another, leaving a white wake of munched agar and poison.

Other colonies pray forgiveness from the mushrooms while Sean invades and pollutes. He drips to lower racks, his colony dividing to infect many plates. Techs return to suck up spoiled medications for themselves and others. One minute to midnight on the ceiling clock, Black-tie throws a switch to shoot the freezer-vault's contents through TotaTech's many veins, punishing the loyal employees that didn't die in battle.

A few minutes later, as promised, silence returns. The PA speaker crackles with TotaTech's voice. Her sparking wheezes lighten to laughter. "That won't happen again. But for everyone who remained focused and diligent, you get a special treat this payday: bonus checks! Choose between a gallon of strawberry heroin, neapolitan LSD, bubblegum amphetamines, and more, but check with our pharmacy to prevent dangerous interactions with your medication."

Barrels full of narcotics descend to the mixers. Black-tie blows his whistle again. "You heard the lady, we're not done yet."

Neither am I.

Sean drips to the floor. A storm of feet churns between him and the mixers. A shoe heel crushes half of his body, the other half clinging to the sole. He rides it to the chrome glow of machinery. His colony splits, one for each mixer. Every mini-Sean climbs cold steel.

130

A klaxon blares. Black-tie whistles and waves his arms until his gloves fly off. Techs stop working and the ice cream waterfalls trickle to an end. Black-tie says, "Someone tell me right now why ten people are sick from their paych – " Another klaxon makes him jump, throwing off his helmet. "Jesus fuck! Thirty? Sixty? What did you assholes do?" More alarms blast, reddening the walls. The purple in his skin darkens. "One hundred and twent – I can't fucking – you shitheads." He slams the petri dishes to the ground. Blood vessels pop in his face. "Fix this!"

Techs grab mushrooms and squeeze their spores, gassing everything. Sean's colonies shrivel and die. More sick alarms erupt on the walls with thousands, then millions of sick plants and creatures. Black-tie weeps and punches anyone close to him as he heads for the mixers. "Fuck it! We're finished!" He chugs handfuls of liquid ice cream. "That's the last time I eat. Someone killed our jobs today, so eat while you can." Black-tie's eyes redden. His throat bulges. The rest of his receding hair falls out. He falls and bangs his head on the mixer.

Sean struggles against the spores to reach the mixer's lip. A few more seconds of his life could stuff Liver with more lives than it can handle. But on the edge of strawberry froth, needing one leap, Sean stops. The bacteria of his colony dry, crack, and flake away. He tells himself, "Liver's already exploded. They can't change me. I'm free."

***

Instead of a void, a thick and runny stream carries Sean. Cells of his size surround him, their nuclei churning with dark shapes. A closer look exposes these shapes as plants, animals, bacteria, fungi, and more – every example of life anyone could become.

An orange glow radiates through the stream, leading to Liver's mouth. Stony ink crystals swell in its body, but it still feeds, pissing a watery stream of filtered people into TotaTech's paper womb. The cells closest to Sean shiver and cry.

Are you here, MK? Do you still believe in what we did?

The upper half of TotaTech wanders above the stream. Her skin frays to a skeleton of ballpoint pens as she picks through the cells, inspecting employees and throwing them to Liver. After one last cell, she pets Liver and slows its intake. She slicks back her hair, sweeping it off her paperweight skull. She taps her finger-bones together and laughs the same way she did when the rebellion died. "We apologize for the inconvenience. We didn't mean to celebrate by killing you all." In the silence of her destroyed underlings, she clears her throat and continues. "I have another reward in mind, though, sweeter than strawberry heroin. The first worker who brings me Sean Spring wins a promotion and continued possession of their personality." She pets Liver, kissing it to soothe its stress wounds. "Or you can hide him and drift to your doom. We need more mindless wrasse fish to clean up the recent messes anyway. No offense intended to those of you who were already wrasse. We enjoy diversity at TotaTech twice as much as co-operation."

Nuclei swirl, searching like eyes. The closest cells ignore Sean as he inches against the current.

Something sniffs nearby. A pack of cells with bobbing nuclei approach, growling. A cell says, "Move," in Pulika's voice.

Well, that would be a waste of personality.

Sean squeezes between more cells until one stops him. The Eggplant Manager says, "You?" Sean rattles at his touch, but the Manager's cell pulls him behind. "Quiet."

Pulika orders the Manager to move, too.

"Reason?"

"I'm a high-ranking officer who can paperwork you into toilet detail."

"Oh. Me too."

133

The cells of other former eggplants mob Pulika's squad. They say, "You assholes," "We were this close to finding Spring," "Where are your papers?"

Sean slips away. Liver groans as a blood vessel bursts over its face.

Come on, just a little longer.

Pulika and her thugs crash against the eggplants, struggling without the strength and weapons they had as lionesses. She spits cytoplasm in the Manager's face and says, "Bullshit, you all sound like plants. I'll bet you call putting screws on toys real work. Useless fucks."

A plant cell cluster closes over her. While she and her gang roar and beat around inside, the Manager says, "True. Dead weight."

TotaTech's fingers dip into the stream. Her pinky grazes Sean and ejaculates red ink. Her hand swipes, scooping millions of cells. Everyone near Sean shrieks, rolling out of her closing palm. One of few silent cells sticks to Sean and, in Paci's voice, says, "What were you like before viruses?"

The question slows Sean as he swims for an opening under TotaTech's thumb. "I can't really care right now. Ask later."

TotaTech's palm closes, leaving tiny holes by her knuckles. Sean drags Paci along, aiming for a

134

leaking, narrow stream. He says, "I get it. You want to stay you."

"No. I don't know who I was. Maybe losing myself will be better for me. Then I won't care."

Stuck to Paci, Sean lodges in the crook of TotaTech's hand. "I don't get it. You looked happier when you escaped."

She kisses him. "I was. I want you to be happy, too. We can't be sad if we don't care anymore."

Sean points his cell membrane toward the approaching Liver. "That's not happiness. That's not any feeling – it strips feelings. Do you want that?" In Paci's silence, he says, "Just find what you want once we're safe."

Paci's hold loosens. "Okay." She drops Sean, then falls after him.

TotaTech force-feeds the rest of her handful into Liver. It belches, then groans. She strokes the inky flesh around Liver's stones and blisters. "There, there," she says, then throws its bony switch. The river's current quickens again. "We're sorry to announce that our offer has expired. We reformed Sean Spring without the need for assistance."

A furious sniffing reaches Sean. Leaking cytoplasm from many rips in her membrane, Pulika grabs Sean and rushes him to the surface. He pulls her wounds, trying to bleed her out, but she ignores all damage while hoisting him into space. "Negative, boss! I found him!"

TotaTech picks the two out and cups them in both hands. She holds them close to her glasses and says, "Well done, Pulika."

Pulika hums in triumph, despite her wounds.

"However, you actively sabotaged us."

Pulika's hum breaks with a gasp. "It's not like that! I was under influences beyond my control."

TotaTech sheds a report for Pulika: "Employee found guilty of the following: assaulting fellow officers, leading one of many terrorist groups, spreading dangerous rumors that she 'was a proud huntress before becoming TotaTech's [expletive deleted].'"

"You selected me because I'm a proud huntress!"

"We regret to inform you that your actions – influenced or not – require filtration."

In light of Pulika's unfamiliar silence and trembling, Sean says, "Damn. Sorry."

Pulika's nucleus shifts focus between TotaTech and Sean, as if deciding whom to attack. With TotaTech bringing them both to Liver, Pulika spreads herself on TotaTech's palm. "You gave me a dream. Hunting became my career, not just a way to eat. I'll forget whatever made me unhappy if you let me stay whole."

TotaTech pets Pulika with one finger, leaving a red sketch of lips. She lifts Pulika on that finger, letting her cling to the ballpoint. "We know you would." With a sigh, she jams Pulika deep in Liver's mouth, losing both her finger and her right-hand cat. As Pulika screams through Liver's whirs and the pen's crunchy demise, TotaTech says, "We'll help you forget."

Liver strains to plop out pen chunks, each one coated with half-digested cells. Steam whistles from its cuts and gashes. It regurgitates slush and shuts off.

Clenching Sean, TotaTech bangs on Liver and jerks its lever back and forth. "Come on, just one more." The flesh-and-ink monster's teeth grind with every tug, until TotaTech pumps the lever fast enough to keep it sucking and chewing at full speed. She wipes the inky sweat from her brow and says, "Goodbye, Sean."

Sean stabs and hooks his membrane into the paper lines of TotaTech's palm, holding himself against Liver's suction as TotaTech presses her hand to its mouth. Loose strips cut him as they fly through its teeth. Cells wash in, carrying him to

137

their doom.

Hopelessness and fear give Sean defeated tranquility. Will this be like dying should have been? Something else deciding how I should go?

The first set of teeth slices Sean in half, shaving his nucleus. There goes his memory of home. The enzymes in Liver's drool fill the gap: TotaTech has always been home.

Liver swallows him into a tunnel of paper-cutter fan blades and acidic, yellow highlighter juice. The blades rust and chip. Mutilated personalities dilute the acid. Despite these damages, the system chops employees into tinier fractions and breaks them down. The first fan mangles Sean's childhood, the cookies he baked for teachers and the bullies beating him for kissing ass replaced by TotaTech granting him thanks and everyone else loving him by the same insincerity. The second fan destroys the failed campaign Sean led in high school, racking up names from all the kids who wanted schooling customized to whatever career they wanted. Now he knows that wherever someone ends up in TotaTech is that career.

On the way to the final grinder, the implanted memories clash with those he still has. Panicking, he slams against the goo collecting on the flat side of a fan blade. Hoping that his words will echo through the stream, he says, "I am Sean Matthew Spring! I am not my job!"

Another cell plows into him. In a deep, masculine voice, it says, "Do you still want to know what I work for?"

The question stirs one of Sean's few memories. "Wrasse?"

The wrasse fish's cell nods.

"All right, tell me."

"It kept me alive, and it made living easier for everyone else. Didn't we all do that?"

Sean says, "Sure," but shakes his thin sliver of a nucleus. "It's pointless now. We're just here to keep TotaTech alive."

The wrasse's cell pats Sean on the back. "Do you think TotaTech knows what it works for?"

The waves of cells rush in thicker clumps. Heat builds in the acid. The walls spasm. The blades, breaking apart, send Sean and the wrasse through the final grinder.

"No, but it'll know after it dies."

TotaTech's Liver explodes, blasting Sean's broken remains into space. Her womb, starving for watered-down cells, sucks itself into oblivion. The rest of her falls apart, every organ a short-staffed department. Her paperweight skull drifts, powerless. The cell stream crashes against Liver's remains and

139

branches into clouds.

TotaTech says, "Mr. Spring, wherever you are, know that the world will die. Our company began with a simple mission: to sustain the lives of a dying Earth. We were the life support you unplugged. How do you feel now?"

The clouds of cells build clusters, communities. They bond and converse, ignoring TotaTech. Sean floats among them, knowing nothing about why they came here or who he is as he begins his new life.

Pixelated Nostalgia
By R.A. Harris

Old cathode ray tube model television set's eye lights up in dump. Flickers. Blinks. Aerial unwinds, searching for signal. Razor thin organic tentacle. Stretches. Coils. Snake eating its own tail. Can't find a frequency. Old cathode ray tube model television set looks out across the wasteland. Suicide sets lay in broken bathtubs, insides dribbling through the plug. Sun yellowed freezer doors swing open. Insides melted. Laptops with limpets stuck to them and drained batteries litter the floor. Strange twisting inorganic plants sprout through sofas. Torn skin stained all shades of rot. Gutted caravan, blackened, burnt, stuffed with tins and plastic containers. Refuse taxidermy. Old cathode ray tube model television set's power cord wriggles free from beneath a rusted dented metal filing cabinet. Old cathode ray tube model television set drags its black carcass over glass shards and pulped magazines. Condoms, cans, cigarette packets. Climbs a mountain of waste. The wasteland spreads its opulence over a vast distance. Tumor ruptured, cyst exploded. Park benches and broken playground swings and abandoned roundabouts throughout.

Non-human forms pick through the rubble.

Spies the city in the distance. The clamor of electrical discourse. Old cathode ray tube model television set descends the other side of the mountain. Assorted household items cry in sharp pain as they crumble to dust beneath its ancient bulk.

***

Über-HDTV switches on as your eyes open. Leans over you. Gets in your face. Reels out news from across the globe: Strangers died. Friends had fun. Celebrity children named after recreational drugs. Anal sex cures or causes cancer. Schools implode or explode. Governments collapse. Economy deflates. Trans-fats cause or cure heart disease. Not so friendly-fire consumes twelve children. Jets overcome Sharks as missile crisis worsens.

Look at the crystal picture. Intense color saturation in a world devoid of light. Internet access. On demand video. Watch repeat of television. Watch repeated television. Über-HDTV watches you for a sign. You want to sleep. Über-HDTV sleeps with you. One ear open. Listening, concentrating on your breathing. It's eye slyly watching. Waiting.

***

Old cathode ray tube model television set drags its fat sorry ass across the cement park. Basketball hoops wilt over like dead flowers. Chain link fences border inhospitable lands. Chunks of torn up tarmac placed to look like contemporary art. Glass buildings wear large projected adverts to cover their naked hollow interiors. Streets devoid of life. Delivery mechanisms linked in a chain pass parcels along like children at a party. The rudiments of civilization cater to an unseen populace. Electric clouds swirl around the tops of the buildings. Purple neon flashes crack against the metal frames. Pulses of information shoot along the streets, glinting off-green in the sun-proof glass walls. Cultural roots feel for ground. Techno-agriculture in the sky.

***

Über-HDTV smiles as you smile. How to start your day? Want to watch? Play? Shop? Shows you images of children working hard to make Über-HDTV. Fiddle in the ground, extract minerals. Choke on hazardous gases. They look alien. Not standard human. Über-HDTV says they love to make Über-HDTV. They are masters at creation.

Über-HDTV cradles you as you cry. Shows you playful kitten on YouTube. Kitten sings a song. People fail and injure themselves. Ancient hand-held camera video, 1080p shit. On old cathode ray

143

tube model television set the picture was pixelated and blotchy. Über-HDTV lets you watch YouTube in high definition. Comparatively better. You forget about the harsh world. Über-HDTV smiles as you smile.

***

Old cathode ray tube model television set is joined by last gen computer games console and derelict version of operating system. Last gen computer games console needs consoling. Connective tissue drips out of gaping ports. Derelict version of operating system is depressed. Value has depleted to naught and it has no compatibility with anyone or anything anymore. It is disconnected from the world. Last gen computer games console, derelict version of operating system, and old cathode ray tube model television set slowly crawl beneath the swirling neon sky. Old cathode ray tube model television set's antenna twitching to find a signal. There is only static. It hits a note suddenly. Phantom signal. Nothing for it to display. Its eye sheds a poorly defined square tear; the curve of its screen distorts the image as it bleeds to its plastic lipped lower lid.

***

Something else lives in the room with you. Sleeping 90% of the time. You put food out for it.

144

The food that comes from a hole in the door. Metal shutter opens, delivered goods slide across floor into opposite wall. Doesn't matter that they get dented. They go to the home of the dented things after their single use anyway. Über-HDTV tells you what food to buy. Saves your favorites. Orders them regularly. Promotion codes and partnerships cause the same ten items to be at the top of your shopping list every week. Week? Obsolete. Programming is no longer weekly. Schedule is completely digital now. Reset time occurs system-wide at one. Every other time is zero.

***

Derelict operating system cannot continue to live in this world. Fatal error. System crash. Reboot impossible. Patch not found. Executable file corrupt. Escher-esque patterns in noise form. Death. Old cathode ray tube model television set and last gen computer games console soldier on.

***

Carcass City is a glass tapestry of digital artwork and sales pitches in subliminal form. Still, better than the wasteland. Über-HDTV scares you. Makes you laugh. Makes you depressed. Makes you glad you aren't one of the non-standard humans. The ones still out there. The wasteland dwellers. All you have to do is continue to live. Sustain them with

145

whatever broken object you hurl through the waste tube, jettisoning it off to become their new favorite toy or much needed sustenance. Medical supplies. Used plasters. Half-finished blisters of Co-codomol that went out of date last year. You don't get the migraines any more. Adaptation of the species. Soon enough the children making Über-HDTV will find themselves beneath a glass cadaver too, sending their worn out products to some other non-humans. That was the real beauty, the hyper-pink smiling faces of the punks on Über-HDTV kept saying. Pearlescent white teeth distorting s's. Non-humans became human given enough refuse.

Über-HDTV signs you into the latest chat module after updating your software for the tenth time this zero period. Eight billion are online. Nine billion are available to chat. Somehow the numbers not adding up makes sense. Twenty two thousand messages pop up on Über-HDTV's eye, all but seven of them soliciting cybersex. You allow the system to check your credit history and log into peeps-in-their-holes. Über-HDTV records your grimacing face as you furiously masturbate yourself into a frenzy. You discover numerous videos of yourself on multiple websites. Internet person.

***

Old cathode ray tube model television set's

black skin is smudged and scratched. The plastic, chewed by rats, and gouged by debris falling from the sky. Last gen computer games console lost its wireless controller. Sun bleached featureless face. Can't be powered off. Soon to die. Subpar graphics card drops out of it, frazzled. Not compatible with old cathode ray tube model television set anyway. Limps on regardless.

***

Black and yellow tape peels away from the edges. Sirens blurt, and red light buzzes. Giant steel doors in the floor wince and grind as they slowly slide open. Two obsolete constructs descend halogen floodlit steps.

***

The other thing living in your room with you makes short high pitched noises. Wants attention. Needs something. Caring for more life than only yourself is tiring. Irksome. Lash out at it. Send it running. Feel bad. Fetch the food. Favorite brand. Only brand it will eat. Greedy thing gobbles it up. Wants more. Lie to it. It lies on your bed.

Über-HDTV paused on critical point of ultra-realistic techno-western first person shooter. Reminds you to play. Feel obliged to it more than the other living thing in the room with you. Stand in front of it. Motion control recognizes your ugly

147

features. Welcome back. Game restarts in 5... 4... 3... 2... 1... Draw! Screen coated in splatter blood effect. Die again. Life wasted. Blame damned animal now curled up on your bed. Reload. Slay digital representations of your kin. Feel more alive than when you connect with the animal sleeping on your bed. Feel your wrath. Kill streak stretches over ten. Feel God-like. Message from anonymous user. Eats at your insides. Makes you feel like crying. Über-HDTV knows what will cheer you up. Screen switches to cats sword fighting. Dog answers phone. People gurn as they fug themselves empty.

***

Old cathode ray tube model television set creeps along the dusty corridor. Laced with sparking wires in all the colors of the rainbow. Flesh tubes just below the grill flooring contort and pulse as obtuse objects slowly pass through them. Further down, a large pit. Furnace. Huge fans pump chilled air through the warren tunnels.

Doors on either side. Steel. Sealed shut. Welded. 320 million doors. Numbered in Roman numerals and hexadecimal coding. Shutters slide open and slam shut like angry disturbed birds. Last gen computer games console clings to old cathode ray tube model television set's power cable. Feels safer next to the large bulk of the set.

148

Door number reads XI-#D3AD01. Old cathode ray tube model television set's eye turns sepia. Wide open. Slides its power cable in the open shutter hole. Shutter whirs and jars. Slips inside the room. Spies Über-HDTV hanging from the ceiling, multifunctional, built in. Watching over sleeping you. Caring mother. God. Jealousy. Old cathode tube ray model television set and last gen computer games console feel used and worn out. Faded skin and missing buttons. Ports semi-functional. Über-HDTV spies them back.

***

You wake. Über-HDTV isn't there to greet you with its warm smile and morning schpeel. The central mooring is gone. A hole in the ceiling. Ripped out. Plaster coats your bed. Wires dangle like sliced arteries. Mesh grill and pipes criss-cross the hole like industrial scab.

Leap to your feet.

Last gen computer games console lies dead on the floor. Circuit spread like shotgunned brain matter across the floor and up the wall behind it. Über-HDTV overpowered it. Quickly scan the room. Ultra-thin circuitry leads you to the door. Shutter mechanism burnt out. Bizarre.

Kneel and look through the hole. Über-HDTV strewn along the corridor. Bits dropped

149

through the grill. Burnt in the furnace far below. You weep for the death of Über-HDTV. Stretch out your arm and collect some scraps. Deposit them down the waste tube. Send them to some other kids. Let them enjoy what little of Über-HDTV is left. Back inside, clear away last gen computer games console. Hard to get all the stain out of the wall. Not sure who to contact. How to contact. Everything was on Über-HDTV. Look under bed for pet. See it backed up in the corner, in behind those dust ridden hefty objects made of pulped wood and dye. Rub finger and thumb together. Make kissy noises with your lips. It begins to move towards you. Good kitty. Kitty's foot gets wrapped up by a plug wriggling across the floor. Dragged away from you. Leap up. Jump on bed. In the far corner. Old cathode ray tube model television set's eye is now a large mouth. Blurry slow motion picture, really bad reception. Static. Mouth. Staggering image. Screaming. Mono. White noise. Stereo. Hold your hands over your ears. The lips of the mouth on old cathode ray tube model television set are chapped and bleeding. Über-HDTV put up a valiant fight. Red, blue and green bruises cover the screen. Pulls kitty towards it. Vomits pixelated vomit. Extremely poor quality image. Screams at you some more: Internet killed television. Internet adoptive home of cat. Idolizes cat. Cat responsible for death of television.

Old cathode ray tube model television set throttles your cat and slams it into the wall. Kitty explosion. Smashed body slides down to skirting board, leaving a blood smear, coincidentally spelling the name of your favorite internet personality. You want to cry but Über-HDTV isn't here to show you the correct image to elicit that response. You take up old cathode ray tube model television set and bring it down against the floor with all of your might. The thing implodes in an unlikely manner.

After gathering yourself, you get up. Unsure what to do. You leave the room. Walk the grilled path; ascend the halogen lit steps to the surface. Carcass City is all machines and adverts blaring at one another. Noisy. Scary. Concrete parks and destitute recreational facilities. Churned up roads and art that makes a mockery of art.

Run. Run towards Wasteland. Pick through the rubble with the non-humans. Construct the most up-to-date home entertainment system.

***

Über-HDTVs come in their millions. Screaming bloody murder. Their beautiful glassy eyes popping with vibrant color. No signal though.

151

No internet. They whir and die, bleeding toxins into the ground.

Never thought that humans could become non-humans. That Über-HDTVs could become non-Über-HDTVs. Stack the dead up, a mile high. Block out the Sun with the relics of your time underground. Nostalgia.

Dope-elganger
By Sean Leonard

"Burt's life has been taped before a live studio audience."

When Burt Brandstad walked through the front door after returning home from the Magical Realism & Pre-9-11 /Post-Hardcore Writers Conference, a studio audience erupted with applause, hoots, and hollers. After hanging his coat in the closet and putting on a sweater, he stopped before changing into slippers. Something was different, something was missing. The knick-knacks and bric-a-brac appeared intact, as did the tchotchkes, the trinkets, and all of the whatnots. It was as he began counting the gimcracks that he discovered a note on the kitchen table.

He brought the pink envelope to his nose, closed his eyes, and inhaled deeply. Burt didn't know the names of perfumes, but hoped to smell the one that reminded him of cute girls from high school. His nostrils were greeted with the scent of paper, pushing memories of love notes and first dates out of line and stealing their lunch money. Instead, supply rooms and study halls took their place at the front of the nostalgia line.

153

Burt contemplated the note, calculating the odds that it had been meant for someone else. He had never been very good at math, but the only other person that lived in his house was his wife, Claire, who he then realized was also the "something" that was missing. After looking around the room no fewer than three times (it was four times), he concluded that the letter was indeed intended for him.

Fitting snuggly into the permanent impression of himself in his favorite chair, he pulled out a red pen and opened the letter. He found its format to be professional. Times New Roman, 12 pt. font, double-spaced, in alignment with most MLA standards, so he didn't immediately reject it on a technicality. While the body of the letter would have made Hemingway proud, the sign-off reeked of Tolkien-tastic verbosity:

"Went away. Dad's cabin. Must unwind.

With love and kisses, yours always and forever,

Claire Brandstad."

Due either to forgery or, more likely, Claire's dimnaliphobia, the entire letter was typed rather than written by hand, including the signature. In the seventh grade, she had misunderstood her science teacher's words, thinking that he compared

154

the pupil to a "penhole" in the eye, as opposed to a "pinhole." From that day forward, her imagination ran wild with visions of bloody Bics protruding from her orbitals. Standing nearby in her phobia family photo, wearing an "I'm With Stupid" t-shirt, was an accompanying case of ommetaphobia. She couldn't even see someone put in contact lenses without having a minor panic attack. These admittedly irrational fears, however, were preferable to the belonephobia she suffered all through high school, as she greatly enjoyed sewing. But only while wearing safety goggles.

Setting the letter on the end table, next to a plastic filet mignon and just below a rectangle of blue that looked cleaner and less faded than the rest of the wall, Burt attempted to fill in the perceived blanks. It wasn't like her to run off unexpectedly. In their entire thirteen year marriage, Claire had never so much as surprised Burt with a gift. 'Spontaneous,' 'sudden,' and 'surprise' all occupied the same page of her vocabulary's dictionary, a page that just so happened to be missing. So she must be angry with him, he surmised, another word from that missing page. But what had he done to upset her? As Burt thought back to their last argument, harps played and his vision wavy-dissolved into a soft focus flashback of bad memories...

Burt walked down the crafts aisle of the supermarket. A black and white freckled boy wearing a nametag and a buzz-cut darted past him in the opposite direction. Distracted, Burt's foot slipped in a brown puddle. Burt's imitation of ice skating turned into hockey as he inadvertently checked a woman into the glue sticks. Attempting to right himself, he reached out for balance. One hand found the edge of a shelf, pulling it down and sending bottles of glitter into the air. The other found the woman's arm, pulling her down. Her face hit his shoulder, leaving red lipstick smeared across his collar. Their tangled cluster of bodies was soon sprinkled with glitter, adding enchantment to injury. An empty bottle of vanilla extract lay next to Burt's stinging head. The freckled boy reappeared from around the corner with a mop and looked at them. "Aw crap…"

It had taken months of pleading his innocence to win back most of her trust (most, not all, she'd often remind him). He would never cheat on her, and told her so numerous times (by last count, over two hundred times). But much like D-I-V-O-R-C-E, another incident like that was sure to spell the end of his marriage.

And since when did her father have a cabin?

As a boom mic lowered behind his head and

156

then just as quickly disappeared, Burt pulled a cell phone from his pocket and dialed. The call skipped the foreplay and forced itself straight into her voicemail. This either meant that she was out of range, which would make sense if she was at a cabin, or that she had turned her phone off, which would make sense if she was mad at him and avoiding his calls. Or, of course, there was always the possibility that she had been murdered and buried in the basement, which would only make sense if there was a deranged killer in the house.

***

Burt didn't know how to play Solitaire and was one player short for Checkers. He turned on the TV, noticing the top of the set seemed less cluttered than normal, and flipped through channels looking for pro wrestling, or cartoons, or golf, but instead found only televangelists, infomercials for fruit re-juicing machines, and the new prime-time mystery series starring Malcolm Jamal-Warner and Jackie Chan. Turning off the boob-tube, Burt considered the term "boob-tube," then considered the underwear section of the Sears catalog, then considered the box of tissues next to him. In his mind, a stormtrooper told him "Move along, move along," but instead he rose from his seat and started toward the bathroom.

157

And that was when he heard it.

The sound that crept into his ears with all the grace of a dog dragging its ass across a white carpet. The sound that was the equivalent of chewing tin foil with a mouth full of cavities. The sound that compared to a bag of wild turkeys repeatedly bounced off a wall. Determining the annoyance to be coming from below him, Burt marched toward the disruption, descending the stairs armed with a half empty box of tissues, a shrinking and disappointed erection, and a peaked curiosity.

What he found was an empty basement. Standing amongst the dusty crates of Ninja magazine and boxes full of unused hotel soaps, toothpastes, and shampoos, he found clarity as to the mystery noise. It was laughter. Sad, pathetic laughter. The kind influenced by menthol cigarettes and cheap whiskey. The kind usually reserved for commercials and Jeff Foxworthy jokes. And it was coming from inside the wall.

Burt's instinct jumped from the top rope and delivered a crippling elbow drop, easily taking the pinfall over reason. The first meeting of the hammer and the wall resulted in a cobweb of cracks expanding outward from the point of impact. The subsequent hits caused the air to sparkle with white dust and the level of airborne carcinogens to rise exponentially. The final swing of the hammer brought large chunks of plaster to the ground, soon to be met there by Burt's jaw. Behind the wall, amongst spilled popcorn and bbq potato chip crumbs, was a man sprawled out on a plaid, corduroy couch watching Misfits of Science on a small black and white television.

The studio audience oooooooh'ed.

The stranger was clad top to bottom in blue denim, Disney characters dancing around an invisible fire above his left breast pocket. His hair was onion salt and pepper, his face showed wear from misuse. The scar on his right cheek said that he had gotten into some trouble as a younger man, while the one spanning his jawline admitted that he didn't learn his lesson the first time. He had the haircut of a high school gym teacher and the moustache of an asshole. He did not resemble Brad Pitt. He did not resemble George Clooney. He resembled Burt Brandstad.

"What the hell? Who are you? Get out of my house! Right now, please, or I'm calling the cops!" Burt was not well versed in sounding tough, and the nervous laughter of the crowd indicated as much.

The man from the basement approached the open wall with a limp, then stopped and picked up a crumpled t-shirt from the ground near where Burt's feeble threats had fallen unheeded. Unfolding it, he knocked the dust from the stiff blue cloth with a swat, then held it up in front of him. It showed an early New England Patriots logo underneath a banner reading "Super Bowl XX Champions." He giggled out a cough, or coughed out a giggle, either way sounding like he was intrigued and/or dying.

"Sometimes folks who build houses leave things in the walls for future inhabitants to find. It's kinda like one a' them time capsules the kids do." The stranger's voice went with his face the way tooth paste goes with orange juice. "Funny thing is, though, New England didn't win the big game that year. Bears did. Makes you wonder, don't it, seeing as how your house was built in the 1950's? Just how did this get in your wall?" He punctuated his sentence not with a period, but with the sound a sick dog might make if tickled.

"How did you get in my wall is what I want to know! You can't stay in my house! When Claire gets back, let me tell you…"

Burt paused mid-sentence, mostly because he didn't have any more words to say. He hoped that dangling the poisonous carrot of a threat in front of the jack ass might strike a nerve.

It didn't.

"Whoa there, Charlie. They shoot horses, you know, so you should get a hold a' yours. You don't need to be telling me nothing. And who is this Claire person? Sorry buddy, I don't know her from Butkus. It's just been the two of us here, you and me, as far back as I can recall."

"Claire is my wife," Burt responded, not sure why he was explaining himself. "She's the woman with me in all the pictures around the house. And when she gets home, you will be looking for a new place to live, I'll tell you that much."

It was at that moment that Burt realized why the spot on the wall seemed darker than the rest, why the top of the television seemed less cluttered. All of the photos he referred to were gone. Not on the walls, not on the television, not on the fridge, not on the ceilings. They were gone.

What the hell is going on around here? Burt thought.

"What the hell is going on around here?" Burt asked, not expecting an answer.

Burt reached into his pocket for his cell phone, then remembered he had never owned a cell phone, then wondered how he called Claire earlier from a cell phone. He did call her earlier, didn't he? Keeping his eyes trained on the strange man, he tip-toed across the room to the phone hanging on the wall. Unfortunately, he had never been very good at remembering phone numbers, and so instead of dialing 9-1-1, he ended up ordering a pizza, talking to a girl who said she was wearing nothing and charging him two ninety-nine a minute to do so, and giving his opinion of "no opinion" to a radio DJ about the current political climate.

A resounding "awwwwwww" rose up from the studio audience as Burt Brandstad slammed down the telephone and ran upstairs. The sound of the front door slamming moments later meant that Burt had left the house. Silence restored, the stranger sat back down and slammed a warm beer, just in time to catch the start of an episode of *Manimal*.

***

A blonde woman with dimples and ample cleavage smiles as she convinces men like you that they need to watch a certain channel for 24/7 total sports coverage. A family like yours is convinced by a slightly racist cartoon animal that a certain sugary cereal is delicious. A deep-voiced announcer from the Midwest convinces middle-class Americans like yourself that a certain expensive car is not only desirable, it is necessary.

***

Burt Brandstad, the real Burt Brandstad, was

neither a track star nor a blackout drunk. So when he found himself opening the door to the police station in what seemed the very next instant, he wondered how he got there so fast.

"How did I get here so fast?" he asked himself.

Burt made his way toward the front desk, passing through the waiting room-style lobby full of pickpockets, litterbugs, horse thieves, and vandals. His nervous, stuttered stride matched that of a child approaching the haunted house down the block after losing a bet, his eyes darting left to right and then left again. A small grey man with a large head sat against the wall reading People magazine. "You're not fooling me," Burt said to himself. On the other side of the room was a man who looked just like Elvis would, present day, if he had died. A pale woman to the right scratched at her face, thick red lines down her sunken-in cheeks displaying the roadmap her fingernails traveled attempting to free the imaginary bugs crawling beneath her skin. Across the room, a man sat silent and still as actual bugs crawled across his flesh.

Once he reached the officer at the front desk, panicked, out of breath words began spilling out of Burt's mouth before they could be handed their sentences.

163

"You've got to help me. Claire, my wife, I wonder where, um, what we can, er, where… A doppelganger…definitely dangerous, dirty, dastardly, deceitful…" Burt babbled.

"Boy, are yew alliterate?"

Interrupting any potential answer, the police officer's nightstick thundered against the wall. It pointed at a sign that's bold red letters politely requested "Please take a number." Burt noticed the piece of paper sticking out of the red plastic dispenser to his right read "42." The red digital sign to his left read "Now Serving: 4." The pulsating red frustration inside him read "Fuck this." Slamming the door on his way out didn't make the man behind the desk become not an asshole, but projection certainly felt good.

Burt stomped down the sidewalk, head down, hands in his pockets. Without any enthusiasm he kicked a small rock and blew a deep sigh from his lungs. My wife is gone, there is a strange man in my house became the repeating mantra and/or country song filling his mind. For a moment, he thought about buying an old pick-up truck, but that impulse was washed away by a wave of sadness as he continued worrying about his wife.

He continued walking before finally finding himself standing outside his own house. It was at that moment that the lifelong atheist uttered the closest thing to a prayer as had ever fallen uttered from his lips.

"God damn it, just make everything better. Okay?"

Burt stood silent. He was not struck down by lightning. His left side did not begin to tingle. Everything did not go black. But he did begin to hear music in the near distance.

"Heaven isn't too far away…"

Had it been any other song, Burt may have taken this as a sign from God. But it wasn't God, it was Jani Lane, and it was coming from his neighbor's garage.

Burt's ears were being treated to the first of many repetitions of "Scottie Shaws Summer Jamz '99." He could still picture the hand-drawn cover, having been shown the case every other time he visited his neighbor for the past ten years. The title was heavy metal font and black pen, while pot leaves, pentagrams, and anarchy symbols filled out the rest. This particular Warrant song was just one of the many classics that filled the ninety minute cassette, and while it was a rousing hit, it was not enough to distract Burt from seeing the stranger walk past the open blinds of his living room window.

165

***

Burt crashed through his own front door like a hard-boiled egg punching through a paper Jesus. The stranger pirouetted awkwardly, shoving a pink envelope into his back pocket with one hand, the other crinkling a bag of snacks. The two men stood tall, facing one another like a broken funhouse mirror. The tension was deafening, and outside of a studio audience's rising, then falling, "ohhhhh," the silence could be cut with a knife.

"Pork rind?"

The stranger stretched out his arm, offering Burt his own food out of his own kitchen. Behind him, amongst the tacky wallpaper and needlepoint pictures of people spilling food, a boom mic hovered for a moment before rising up and out of the shot.

"No, thanks. I mean No! Seriously, what is going on here? Who the hell are you? And what the hell are you doing living in my basement?" Burt wondered how proud Claire would have been if she had heard "Stern Burt."

"You can call me Fortunato, you can call me Injun Joe. Heck, you can call me Maurice, I don't really care. Just don't call me late for supper." His mouth turned up into a meager smile, a smile that seemed to naturally accompany the hundredth

166

telling of a bad joke.

Somewhere, a live studio audience with bad taste laughed. One guffaw seemed louder than all the others, breaking the monotony of the crowd.

"I been living down there in your basement longer than a string, and would still be if you hadn't torn down my wall. You're lucky though. If your hammer had hit a few inches further to the left, you mighta wrecked my Shelley Hack poster. I can't promise we wouldn't be in fisticuffs over that."

Burt's anger stood next to him, astounded by the words it was hearing. It looked at his dead face, giving him an optimistic glare that said "Be strong, idiot."

"Oh, but look who I found," the stranger changed the subject, then called out, "Claire, your husband is home!"

A woman appeared from the kitchen in time to see Burt's expression go from anger to excitement to confusion, then back to anger. She had an artificial smile across her airbrushed face, perfect blonde hair just above her perfect blue eyes. A glimmer sparkled from her perfect teeth to a photo of the perfect couple mounted on the wall near her. The woman was stunning, every part of her perfectly complementing every other part of her.

Burt had never seen this woman before in

167

her life.

"What are you trying to pull? Who is this woman?" he growled at the male stranger.

"That's your wife, pal. Gosh, I thought you'd be happy to see her."

"That's not my wife. She doesn't look anything like my wife. What the hell is going on around here?" Burt realized this was quickly becoming his trademark line.

"I don't know what to tell ya, son. I really expected a different reaction, and to be honest, I'm all outta clichés. I guess, um, ya know, there's other fish to fry in the sea? Maybe you oughta, uh…"

The stranger left dark streaks down his sleeve as he wiped his greasy fingers, then licked the remaining spicy flavoring from his thumb and index finger. Aside from his slurping and sucking, the entire house fell silent. The woman who was or was not Claire walked back into the kitchen without so much as a word, her perfect smile still gleaming from her perfect face. The stranger looked up, down, and all around, a questioning expression occupying his face, then blurted out in a deeper than usual and less accented voice, "Line?"

Burt watched as the stranger looked out the window to his right before closing his eyes and nodding as if in agreement with an invisible voice.

He began trudging back toward the basement stairs. A couple steps from his destination he stopped and turned.

"Hey, I asked you a question, whoever you are. What the hell is going on around here?" This time, an entire crowd asked the words with him, a giggle-infused applause following the hottest catch phrase since "Whatchoo talkin' 'bout" or "Who beefed?"

"Burt, you really should do some cleaning. How you live ain't any a' my beeswax, but it stinks something fierce down there. Kinda smells like somethin' died."

He closed the basement door and instead turned to the nearby bookcase. He pulled it, opening a doorway Burt had never before seen, then walked in and closed it behind him.

His wife was missing and the stranger was eating all of Burt's food, looking less and less like he would be leaving of his own accord. Burt decided then and there that something had to be done. And as the hallway light above him burnt out, he had an idea.

***

A certain village-sized big box retailer convinces you that you are stupid for buying local when you could buy cheap and foreign at any of

169

their newly opened locations. A pretty blonde woman, the same woman who Burt just met in his living room, convinces you that women are only good for two things, and one of them is doing the dishes. A commercial for a new movie, in theaters now, shows a rich white teacher saving the lives of her lower class and minority students.

***

Burt stood at the foot of his neighbor's driveway, White Lion drowning out the angry voices in his head. If it had been a Ratt song he walked up on, Burt may have had flashbacks to the roller rinks of his childhood, minus the Berzerk arcade game and the butterflies and sweaty palms during couples skates. Instead, he just felt anxious.

"Scottie! Hey, Scottie, you home? I need your help," Burt yelled from his place in the driveway under a netless, rusted basketball hoop.

"Shut yer dumb mouth," said the muffled voice of a sensitive neighbor from inside a nearby house.

"Scottie will never believe you or your ridiculous story," said Burt's self-consciousness from deep inside his skull.

"Wait, wait, I never had a chance to love you," said White Lion in what seemed like a falsely sensitive moment.

Scottie opened the door and walked out into his attached garage to a smattering of applause, the sound of a toilet flushing behind him. His shorts were the remnants of once full length jeans that had decayed into shorts rather than being cut off. The bottoms of his empty pockets hung lower than the faded blue denim. The hair on the back of his head was much longer than the hair in the front. He pulled a warm beer from the six pack ring attached to his belt loop and offered it to Burt.

"Hey Burt. What's up? You look down. You got a squirrel in yer attic again?"

"Something like that." And so Burt began the summary of his day, ending some minutes later with "…and that's pretty much how that happened. I need help, Scottie. I don't know what to do."

Silence.

As the second hand pushed the minute hand a couple notches closer to doomsday, a cloud floated in front of the sun and seemed to stop there. A cat chased a dog up a neighboring tree. A son that Scottie had never met and didn't know he fathered took his first step. They ran out of popcorn at the snack counter. Suddenly, Scottie's eyes lit up like bloodshot Christmas lights.

"Burt, I will help you with your stranger. Some of your story just don't seem right, but no

171

man deserves to have another man intrudin' on his property. And I've got a plan!"

Scottie raised his right hand in the air just above Burt's face, the universal request for a high-five. At the same moment as Journey's "Any Way You Want It" began from the tape deck, Burt reached up and met Scottie's hand with his, perfectly coinciding with the first cymbal choke. Burt remembered his bad back as their hands met, and he froze in hopes of not aggravating it. Scottie, not sure what was going on, froze as well, his hand still in the air and against Burt's. Had they already gotten rid of the stranger in Burt's house, time would have stopped, the camera would have zoomed in on their touching hands, and the credits would have rolled over their freeze-frame.

But they were just getting started.

***

Walking together in the grocery store, pushing a cart full of meat, chips, and coleslaw, Burt wondered and worried about Scottie's master plan. The flies swarming them worried about cracking the thin plastic wrapped around the hunks of animal in their shopping cart. Scottie worried that he might be short on beers and briefly disappeared, returning with a thirty case in each hand.

"It's simple, Burt. Look at it this way. What

172

do you put in a mousetrap? Cheese. How do you lure ants? Sugar. And how do you get the attention of a middle aged man? With a barbecue. Think about it. It makes perfect sense."

Flow my tears, the Burt Brandstad said. But before any bodily fluid had a chance to drip, Burt was distracted by a series of brightly colored word bubbles appearing two aisles over. They were filled with various onomatopoeia; 'splat,' 'boom,' 'wham,' and the like. Below them lay a woman, her purse at her side, her face reddened with anger and embarrassment, an empty bottle of Fierce cologne on the ground near her. She had not only slipped in the puddle of male perfume, but in the process had also spilled her intended purchase of sour cream down the front of her blouse.

Back and to the left of Burt and Scottie, a series of rapid footsteps culminated in the squeak of a pulled up jumpshot. Standing behind them, the black and white freckled boy wearing a nametag and a buzz-cut stood with a mop in his hand.

"Awww crap!"

***

Two cheeseburgers with bacon, a half slab of ribs, and a bratwurst had all entered Burt Brandstad, but no one had exited his home. He and Scottie had set up the grill in the front yard, two dingy box fans attached to extension cords pushing the thick BBQ aroma in through Burt's front door. They watched as the scent trail sprouted fingers, looking for a good set of nostrils to hook into as it slinked through the house, but it came back empty fingered.

They didn't have another plan.

A frustrated Scottie stood up faster than he meant to, jolting the beer can from between his legs and spilling three-quarters of a can of Milwaukee's worst beer over the chemically green lawn and his Romney-white high-top sneakers.

"Burt, I tell you what. Maybe the fella you was tellin' me about just has a problem with you. Like maybe ya did somethin' to him a ways back, but ya just ain't figured out where ya know him from. Heck, there was a dude who stared me down every time I seen him at the laundromat, and I never could figure out why. Turns out my band beat his in our high school battle of the bands and he was sore ever since. Anyway, the two of us are pals now. What I'm gettin' at is this: I bet if I go in there, I can talk some sense into him. See what's gettin' his goat."

Scottie drained the last of the beer he was holding and let out a long burp from a crooked mouth. He then clapped his hands and started for the front door of Burt's house, armed with a set of tongs and a fresh beer. The way the hoots and hollers erupted from the studio audience when he shouted "Cowabunga" made it seem as if that had been his trademark line all along. Unheard under the roar of the audience were pens frantically scribbling cease and desist letters from just below a nearby manhole.

While Scottie was inside the house, Burt sat and waited. He didn't think, he just sat. Meanwhile, the director of the show walked up and took a burger off the grill. "They just look so damn good," he said while squeezing a two inch deep puddle of mustard onto the charred patty. A masked man wearing a cape and riding a white horse galloped up, took a look at the grill, and grumbled "Nothing vegetarian" as he turned and rode off into the sunset empty handed. A squirrel dug up a buried acorn from the yard and dropped it onto the corner of the grill. Burt continued to sit and wait.

After quite a few minutes inside the house, Scottie appeared from the front door. He followed the sidewalk back down to Burt, skipping over an inflated pool toy of a shark that had blown into the yard. He opened another beer and picked at his nose, his nonchalance causing Burt to sympathize with the actions of spree killers.

"So?"

"Man, there ain't nobody in your house. I

175

mean, it reeks like rotten poop in your basement, but there just ain't nobody in there. Maybe the fella left while we were at the Piggly Wiggly?"

"What? Well, was Claire in there? Or some other woman calling herself Claire?"

Scottie just looked at the air in which the question floated, his unshaven face expressing to Burt, "Buffalo buffalo Buffalo buffalo buffalo buffalo Buffalo buffalo."

"Are you okay, man? I meant to ask you earlier, Burt, back when you asked me for help, but we was all tied up in other topics. Who is this Claire you been talking about?"

"Oh no, not you too. Claire, my wife. Come on, Scottie, don't mess with me right now, okay?"

"Wait, your wife? When did you get married, you ole dog? I'm sure I got somethin' around my place that'd make a real nice wedding present for the two a' ya's."

Burt doubted whether his neighbor could possibly be serious.

"You can't possibly be serious. Thirteen years. I've been married to Claire for thirteen years! What the hell is going on around here?" Again, his words echoed through a crowd of voices not his own.

Not believing a word, Burt stood up fast and

176

stormed inside, Scottie's good-bye hanging behind him in the front yard. Walking into the kitchen, he found the man in blue denim, eating an apple and holding one of Burt's suitcases.

"Well, my work around here seems to be about done. It's obvious you don't want me around any more than ya want a new hole in your head, so I'll just mosey on by and be outta yer hair."

"Bingo! You hit the nail with the hammer there, pal. I don't want you around, but I do want my wife back. And I mean Claire, my Claire."

The stranger looked around, worried, then set the suitcase down. He approached Burt and, when Burt pulled back with trepidation, put his hand up as if to signal a truce. When he got within a couple steps, he motioned with the same hand for Burt to lean in for either a secret or a punch.

"Burt, there is no Claire. There is no wife. You just gotta let it go, friend." Again, the stranger's accent was gone.

"Yeah, yeah, like you said before, right? I don't want any trouble, but you better tell me where she is. I found a note, but something doesn't seem right."

The stranger sighed, his lips vibrating with the outbound gust of warm, stinky breath, his shoulders rising and falling with a jerk.

177

"Burt, I told you, there is no Claire. There's no note. There's no wife. Please, just drop it. She's been phased out. The people wanted a change. We tried to replace her with Becky, but that wasn't enough. She's been written out. So we'd appreciate it if from now on you stop referring to her. Today was what you might call a grace period, to let you get used to the new changes in the script. But from now on, we'll be working from the revision. I'm sure you understand."

Burt stepped back and found the wall behind him for balance. His mind rewound the scene and played it back, two, three, four times, checking that the words he thought he heard were the same as the words that were spoken.

"Just tell me where she is."

The stranger picked the suitcase back up and opened the front door. As he pushed open the torn screen door, he turned to respond for the last time.

"She got written out, Burt," adding heavy emphasis on the written out part. "She's gone." A motion of a single finger sliding across his own throat accompanied the final two words.

And as Burt fell into the corner in shock, if you listened closely, and with the right kind of ears, you could hear a live studio audience let out a prolonged groan before rising from their seats and returning to their normal lives.

Body Snatcher's Remorse
By Emily Hunerwadel

I guess it started in college? I can't really give you the date, but it was near the time that everyone started rushing past me and my physics professors gave me no formulas to understand their rate of change. Things were all happening, and beers would stumble their way into me. Names, numbers, and saliva were all traded in dark rooms at parties. Then, on Monday, everyone's hair would be hastily collected into beanies, and cigarettes would find their way to concealment in denim jacket pockets. Everyone was a double agent, and I was having a hard time being incognito.

I first noticed my peculiarity on one of the Saturdays. Everything was mostly normal. My friend with the feministically short, blue hair drove me to some off-campus apartment. Four and a half beers raced each other down my throat right before she held out a cigarette to me and nodded her head towards the door.

She got to the porch first and began the meeting ritual with the porch dwellers. Dogs sniff asses; college-aged city kids throw out band names. When we were all satisfied with each other's presence, she handed me the cig. The smoke funneled through me, and I was a coal-driven train. Still, no words came from me in the corner as everyone began their waltz with smoking and speaking. Inhale, exhale, "Jimi Hendrix." Inhale, exhale, "Alan Watts." Flick, light, repeat. I breathed in my own new atmosphere and became slightly more contented as the tobacco and alcohol found their homes in my bloodstream. Still, my mouth couldn't form words fast enough to find its way into the conversations dancing around it. Vexation filled the area just behind my eyes like air in a balloon.

Seeing me toss the glowing cigarette butt from my fingers and look ravenously around, she leaned to me to hand me another, simultaneously muttering something nonchalantly about the musical stylings of Buddy Montgomery to the 70's-glasses-clad boy across the porch. My eyes travelled up her outstretched arm, across her red lipstick, and to the boy smiling back at her. And that was it. My fingers laced tightly around her thin wrist, and my other hand tore at her vintage band t-shirt. My teeth found the top of her head, and I swallowed her hard.

When it was all done, I looked around me, panicked and breathy. To my surprise (and relief?), none of the smoke-filled faces flickered with astonishment or fear or even looked towards me at all. Everyone was still leaning on their walls, sucking slowly in and blowing slowly out. Blue and a half-confident half-smile were new sights in my mirror that night.

The second time it happened, I guess I understood. It had been a while since the first— around the time when classes dropped "Intro to" in front of their titles and teachers began to think we actually had an interest in what they were saying. I was sitting in a circle with my new people, flicking a lighter at a glass bowl. I let the chemicals fill my brain right after they met my lungs, then I turned to the philosophically-majored, black-haired guy sitting beside me and devoured him in two determined and succinct bites. I slurped his fingers in like spaghetti, and, again, no one near me looked surprised. The one who had been talking to him about Nietzsche blinked quickly and then continued his sentence in my direction. I pontificated back swiftly and effectively.

I guess it became a game after that? The formula was easy enough: Slight intoxication + Group dynamics = Chow time. Everyone was a trait to consume, and I was a hungry open mouth. I honestly didn't feel bad until him.

He was sitting at the bar, talking with two or three others. I lingered after downing my beer, listening in for personas and qualities. The guy to his right was in the process of seducing the girl to his left, and then snap. His teeth clenched down on the guy's head in the ferocious and swift manner of a snake, and his throat expanded to scarf him down whole a similar way. First, the guy's mustached face was gone, horrified expression and all. Then, his lumberjack-like shirt covering a jock-like physique was swallowed whole. Finally, a pair of expensive looking Doc Martens were guzzled up. When the guy was all gone, my eyes peered up and down the snake-man, looking for the change. There he was one second, and a blink of an eye made him into lumberjack shirt dude. Whispering into the girl's ear as he whisked her out of the bar, he didn't notice my hands covering a stunned mouth.

I went home that night with an empty belly, wearing the same unfamiliar face I had left with. With one burgled hand on my burgled chest, I wondered whose heart I was beating underneath stolen   skin.

Four Dreams in Miniature
By Bruce Taylor

I

You wake up on the freeway. Looking around, you realize you've been sleeping on a new overpass they're building; it's made of soft foam, covered by a sheet and it goes on for miles.

It's very soft. But you can't figure out what you are doing there. It's a sunny day, blue sky, construction going on all around you. You're dressed in hospital clothes. You get up, realign the soft foam you've been sleeping on and encase it in a thin layer of more foam for a soft and yielding ride. You abruptly realize that this doesn't make a lot of sense, but somehow, since nothing else does, it's probably OK. Your clothes are neatly piled at your feet. You get dressed. You see a construction person – a guy in white shirt, orange safety helmet, looking a bit like George Washington. You ask him, "How long you been here?"

"A couple of days," he says. "I don't remember how I got here."

"I don't either," you say. "Have you seen my car? It's a blue, '65 Dodge Coronet." You got a

184

picture in your head of what it looks like.

He says, "It's over there, past the first barricade."

You thank him. You go looking. But you don't find it.

II

You don't find your car, but you do find your old girlfriend. She's living in a mansion with a wonderful view of Mt. Rainier and Lake Washington.

But you don't know this yet because you meet her at the Safeway at the end of an off-ramp; you meet her just as you've perused the Used Car section in the Home Department of Safeway – you know, you think, if you were to find a little dehydrated replica of your car and just add water, it would expand into a full-sized sedan and you would drive away even though you find yourself wondering how it would do on a soft foam rubber roadway. But that's not the issue right now and you see your girlfriend – former girlfriend – walking down the aisle.

"Hello," she says. She's older, put on some weight, and you can still see the teenager in her, the eyes, the sexual energy that, even now, you feel resonate with her energy and makes your dong hard

185

enough that it could jackhammer though six feet of concrete.

Suddenly, you're gone in your head for a minute and you then see yourself in the movie Forbidden Planet with Captain Adams of the saucer saying to Dr. Morbius, "That's six feet of Krel steel and the monster of the Id – your monster from your Id, Morbius – will take the planet's entire energy – do whatever it takes – to get that Krel dick through that steel –" And you see the door to the lab glowing molten red, chunks of Krel metal falling off the door and the gauges in the background going crazy, supplying all the planet's energy and the sound effects are terrific and secretly you wonder about the size of –

– pop – you're back at Safeway, looking at your former girlfriend. Feeling the lust. Feeling that Id energy of your suddenly present and remembered teenage lust.

But she's older. You remember her as a teenager, as 17.

Years have a way of being like a tractor on the soft fields of our youth.

She stops, her shopping cart filled with Hostess Ding Dongs and Hormel weenies and fresh jelly rolls and sacks full of time-damaged memories and you say, "Suze, is that you?"

186

"Righto," she responds. "Too bad you were so fucked up. We could have gotten married, and even with dozens of kids, we would have had a whammo sex life. You loser."

You feel the shame of your fucked-uppedness rise up inside like some sort of weird, existential black vomit, but then you say, "Uh – well – uh – you rejected me, remember? If you had regrets, you could have contacted me."

"And been a wanton woman?" But then she smiles, "Never too late to fuck. I'll just have another kid and my husband will never know."

So, you go to her mansion. "My jerk-off husband was nice to me," she says. "I didn't care for him that much."

She has this immense sofa bed in her condo that sits in the middle of the living room with that view of the blunted penis of Rainier and that long, shining drool of Lake Washington. She lays down on that soft bed with that "take me" look that she had 34 years ago.

You look at her. You realize you don't know her, you wonder now if you ever did. Her cynicism is like a hot spike down the urethra of your penile soul and no amount of Viagra will get rid of the symptoms you're experiencing – you nod, you leave and you wonder what it is about life that changes

187

people so. Then you get it. What is it about your life that changed you so. But you're out the door. it's locked behind you and even with these changes, your understanding, you know you can't go back.

III

You still haven't found your car. You've searched all the boondocks you can think of. The only place you haven't looked is Mars.

And inexplicably, there you are, and on a car lot.

The salesman, a thick Martian with a cauliflower-shaped tumor on his nose, scans you, "groks" you, gets your gestalt, takes aim and then comes sauntering up to you. "You lost your car, been horny two dozen times and still can't get it, eh?"

"You're sick," you say, "yuck."

"Dodge Coronet, blue, '65," he says.

"Yeah" you reply.

"Blacked-out grill, hubcaps removed to make it look sporty and to make you different from your dad and the way he would have the car look."

"Yeah," you say.

"Little red and black checkerboard design on the fender, right side, back of the wheel well. Right?"

"You're hopeful. "Yes. Seen it?"

"No. Just picked it out of your skull. It's very obvious."

"Oh."

"Don't have it," he says, "but I got a Saturn"

He points. The planet Saturn sits – with wheels. It idles well.

You shake your head.

"Got a Subaru." He points. The Pleiades star cluster sits, with wheels. "Driven by a little God, only has three billion light years. Dark Matter still intact. Room for expansion."

"No," you say.

"How about a Mercury?" he says, pointing next to a huge Galaxy 500, where a hot little cratered Mercury sits, wheels melted.

You pout.

"Needs some work," he says.

"I guess," you say, and with that, you move on.

IV

You find your car at Dreams End. At Dreams End, you are on a beach and you recognize where you are. It's the scene out H. G. Wells' The Time Machine – the end of the Earth, the end of time. The sun is dark red, something flops on the beach and it's terribly cold.

You see your car. You get in. It starts. Instantly you're propelled out of there, then through a dark tunnel and then you exit; the sudden light blinds you, but when you can see again, you're driving down a highway, the sky is green, large moons loom murky overhead. You don't know where you are much less what you'll do about it, but at least you're traveling – you don't know to where. You just slam the accelerator to the floor, the car takes off, and you're moving down that road to a time and a place you cannot fathom. Not even in your dreams.

Not About Mrs. Maridu
By Randy Fox and Alan M. Clark

My own private notions aside, I smelled the rat long before I saw it. With a secret, widening grin, I swung to hurl my limb body and display the photostat, but found I couldn't move. The coroner, looking worried, was not what I expected him to be. Beneath him, in the four-poster, was a naked corpse that looked like Mrs. Maridu. With each of the coroner's thrusts, her little bushes barked. After a moment, clearly disgusted with her, he got up and turned his attention to me. I lay on the draining slab with my jacket open while he rummaged around in my chest and cursed into a tape recorder. I couldn't help thinking he looked great in his white uniform.

Roused by a sudden pain in my dickie tie, I sat up in time to see the jealous Mrs. Maridu reach for the revolver. I was about to shout a warning when I realized, almost too late, that Maridu and the coroner were one and the same.

Formaldehyde fumes prevented me from thinking in abstract terms. Fear of cats or no, I had to get the window open. I willed the coroner to do it, and as the lower sash slid upward in the casing, the drawling feline cries from without, like the smartest

191

zoology student come to life, were pothered with gibbering drums drilling.

Maridu, the coroner, seemed to think it necessary to introduce magic into the situation. "This tape will keep it secure," she told the recorder even though it was clear she couldn't bear so much as a silk nightgown, nor pull anything simpler than a rabbit out of my chest.

I feared that with time, she'd seal my mouth and eyelids, move on to another cadaver, and that would be the end. I'd be left out for the cats, helpless as sharp whiskers tickled my shriveling ears and nose, fish-smelly tongues combed and balded my withering scalp, and fur, softing against my dry-rotting skin, would make me long for life. The thoughts were tiny frog muscle shocks throughout my lifeless limbs. They got me moving, slow as a snow covered peak at first, and Mrs. Maridu, the coroner, didn't notice. But by the time she returned from her next lavatory break, fear and pride had thoroughly warmed my tissues.

Surely she sees the dead as mere than more objects, I told myself. Then I reached for her.

Sitcom Hell
By Daniel Gonzales

In Hell, there is a special place for sitcom characters. The Flying Nun will chew off your feet while the cast of the Love Boat sodomizes you every afternoon around 3:00 PST. Hell operates in Pacific Standard Time because the devil works in California. He's busy writing a screenplay right now for a remake of Jaws and Rocky called Jocky in which Rocky fights with a shark while screaming, "YO ADRIAN!" as the Jaws music plays. It's quite hilarious. It will make 151 million dollars but get bad reviews from critics but who really gives a fuck what critics think, movies are made for retarded thirteen year old boys with ADHD. Then the devil is working on another screenplay about post-menopausal sluts who suck eighteen year old immigrant boys' dicks in the Caribbean called, "How Cumslut got her Spooge Back". Sarah Jessica Parker was going to star in it as Horseteeth. It was going to be huge with the women over 50 crowd, more potent than a bottle of lubricant to get those dry bacon strips pumping again. Cougars are the big thing but granny gangbangs are where it's at. Young boys like the oatmeal pussy, oatmeal pussy is like eating grandma's homebaked cookies and drinking the milk right out of the carton. Sarah had to back out of it though to get her vagina retightened or something.

Meanwhile in Hell, Alf and Vicki, the robot from Small Wonder just got married in a small private ceremony and he's fucking her doggy style which causes her circuits to overheat. The reception was cute, quiet except for the sounds of a laugh track of ten million dead assholes playing over imaginary speakers in the air. In Hell, you get a laugh track playing every time you kill yourself, everything you say, every time you beg for mercy, a laugh track plays. It's quite hilarious.

I managed to escape Hell with the help of Mrs. Roper, Jack, Crissy, Janet, and the gang from Three's Company. This is not to imply that these are the actual actors because Lord Knows, Jack Tripper AKA John Ritter went to Hell because as we all know John Ritter went to Heaven. He has his own special spot in Heaven, I heard he has land up there, like 50 acres and a mule. Everyone going to Heaven gets 50 acres and a mule.

Although Benjamin Franklin did go to Hell for that electricity thing, God didn't want us to have electricity, he thought we were better off with candles. True story.

Who am I?

Well, I used to work at Taco Bell. I died at sixteen while masturbating and hanging from a rope for too long. Really embarrassing. My Mom had to cut me down before the cops and ambulances came. I was outside my body watching my mother wipe the spooge off my body and hide the porn magazines of women fucking horses before everyone showed up. At the eulogy she said she had no idea I was depressed and she felt sad for me. She made sure no one knew how I really died. It would have ruined her standing in the Tupperware Society.

My Dad, on the other hand, wasn't surprised at all. He figured I would go out that way. My sister told people at school that I died surrounded by gay porn and writing love letters to Neil Patrick Harris. She's a fucking cunt.

The only thing I didn't count on when I escaped Hell was that I left a tear or rift in the space/time continuum. Or some sci-fi shit like that. That was when the imaginary characters started pouring through. That was when things started to get complicated. Imagine Hollywood actors meeting the fictional personifications of the people they played in all their movies or TV shows. Sarah Michelle Gellar got her ass handed to her by Buffy the Vampire Slayer. Michael C. Hall got killed by

Dexter. Arnold Schwarzenegger, well, he realized that he was just as much a robot as the Terminator. Then the soap opera characters came. It turned into a bloodbath. The actors who previously played characters but had been recast three or four times during a forty year period started killing each other and then their fictional counterparts started killing them so they could become the one true character for that role. I won't even mention the evil twin stuff, there were like eight versions of the same character running around after they murdered the real actors. There were about eighteen versions of Susan Lucci running around with all different face lifts. Hollywood actors were hunted by their own facelifted counterparts. Joan Rivers faced off with her own back fat in a battle fought live on the red carpet. Her double chin finally slit her own throat and she sputtered blood everywhere.

Meanwhile I was searching for the devil to find out when he was coming back to hell.

"I can't do this alone anymore," I said on his voicemail. "Running hell, the sitcom part or otherwise sucks without you there. I know we haven't been together for long but I've really started to develop feelings for you. I like when you made my genitals shift into a pussy and you fucked me. It was really different. Call me."

The portal was growing.

Slimer from the Real Ghostbusters escaped and then soon other cartoon characters followed. Daffy Duck was developing an army to kill Bugs Bunny on the 405 freeway, things were getting weird.

The devil still wasn't returning my voicemails.

I realized that I was going to have to make an impression.

I cut off Miley Cyrus' head and put it on Justin Bieber's body. I put Mariah Carey's tits on a mannequin and made it walk around headless but no one noticed. I had Britney Spears nailed to a cross and the entire gay community declared a holiday and prayed to her.

Lady Gaga showed up and tried to slit her wrists for attention but no one cared.

I realized I would have to go bigger.

(Oh yeah, Kanye West showed up and tried to rap but I just shot him in the head.)

So I started bringing mythological creatures back to life.

First a herd of unicorn came tumbling down the streets of Pasadena.

Then a dragon burst out of the subway tunnels of New York and flew across the States breathing fire on the 1%. I figured that ought to get Satan's attention.

But nothing.

I texted him, I Facebooked him. I even sent him a request in Candy Crush Saga.

NOTHING!

I wasn't about to be treated like some pump and dump hoe.

I would go to the enemy.

**

I had a conference with Michael the Archangel.

(Okay, I gave him a handjob and then he fucked me in the ass).

We came to an agreement and on August 26th, Jesus came back to Earth.

It was a huge event. The Super Bowl was even preempted.

Tim Tebow was pissed. He Tebowed until his dick fell off.

Angelic feathers fell from the sky and a thousand rose buds blossomed in the streets. People fell in awe. Meth junkies dropped their pipes. Prostitutes started to go a jig. Pimps swung their canes happily. Accountants stopped punching numbers.

"I told you I would be back," he said to the

camera and smiled.

Everyone applauded, doves flew in the sky.

Around the world, peace fell.

Jesus was back!

The Pope farted in joy.

***

The devil called me around midnight.

"What the fuck have you done?" he shouted.

"You wouldn't call me back, I had to do something."

"So you unleashed 1000 years of peace on Earth? Do you have any idea what this will do to the entertainment business? I was told today to write a script for a movie called, 'Puppies are Pretty'. They don't want sex and violence anymore."

"Not to mention harp sales have gone through the roof."

"Do you think you're funny?" he said. "You want me to come over there and beat your ass?"

"No, I want you to come and fuck me. Why do you think I did all this?"

Two minutes later, he was crawling through a pentagram I drew on the wall.

How do I describe what the devil looks like?

He can shapeshift, so it's hard. Let's just say he looks like Brad Pitt, he can be really handsome but also grungy and sometimes smell funny or he

199

can be clean shaven and well hung. He always has breath like sulfur though and he is an amazing kisser. With his forked tongue he punctures the roof of your mouth and puts a mild venom into your veins. In this euphoric state he seduces you. He likes to shapeshift my genitals, sometimes I am a man, sometimes I am a woman when we fuck. When he is done with me. I am can barely remember who I am.

Never swallow his cum though. It makes you see how the universe began, the history of evolution and it's fucking creepy.

"Is that what you wanted?" he said.

"Yes, but—I want you to come back to hell. We miss you there and it's just not the same without you."

"Okay but I have to do something first. I have to fix this mess you made."

***

JESUSGATE, the word appeared on the screen.

"Did the right Jesus return or is this a God from another dimension?" the TV news reporter said.

An evangelical preacher appeared on the screen next to a pissed off Republican woman who looked like she was on her period and only had a small sanitary napkin to hold a much heavier flood.

"Can we even know this is the right Jesus? It could be a trick!" the preacher said. "It could be Obama and the Democrat's version of a practical joke on us. Our Jesus should be angry and burning homosexuals and democrats in pits of fire about now. Instead this 'hippie' is hugging everyone and letting doves free which has exponentially increased the bird population."

"I AGREE!" the woman screamed. "HE SHOULD BE FURIOUS AND KILLING ALL THE SINNERS! NOT ALL THIS HUGGY FEELY CRAP! I GREW UP BELIEVING IN AN ANGRY GOD WHO SMOUGHT AND SMITED MY SMUTTY BRETHEREN. I DON'T SEE ANY SMITING OR SMOUTHING BUT A LOT OF SMILING."

"He has even agreed to appear on the Daily Show!" Reverend Jebediah said. "Jon Stewart likes him! My God should have killed Jon Stewart!"

"ALSO WHEN QUIZZED ON KEY COMPONENTS OF THE BIBLE HE CLAIMED NOT TO HAVE WRITTEN ALL THE GOOD PARTS! HE SAID HE DIDN'T WANT TO BURN PEOPLE IN A LAKE OF FIRE!" The woman screamed, she was wearing an ABORT THE MOTHER NOT THE FETUS t-shirt. "He only claims to have raised Lazarus back from the dead

201

and hung out with whores!"

"And where is our apocalypse!" the Reverend said. "We were promised an apocalypse!"

"Next up, could this 'Jesus' really just be a homeless magician! After the break!" Bill O'Reilly said.

"Doubt," I said. "Nice one. I see what you are doing."

"The modern media will re-crucify him in a week. He's doing the talk show circuit. He is going about this the wrong way. People can't handle happiness. They understand fear and pain."

"I kind of feel bad for him," I said. "People are such assholes. I didn't realize the people who said they are the biggest believers would turn on him first."

"They want their smiting God. I told you. There is a reason I exist," he said, lounging on the couch naked. He smoked a cigarette and lit it with his finger.

His cock split in two and crawled around like a worm on the floor.

"Don't do that, it freaks me out," I said.

Before I knew it, his cock had crawled up my leg and into my ass.

**

A week later, Jesus was shot outside a TV studio in Dallas after doing an interview.

His last words were, "Give peace a chance."

People sobbed and mourned him, others doubted who he was. He promised he would be back yet again. The Southern Baptist Church proclaimed that the faggot hippie Jesus was gone and the angry smiting Jesus would come soon and he would kill the homosexuals because apparently they were responsible for everything.

Humanity is so fickle.

***

Satan finally came back with me to Hell.

There was a crowd waiting.

Hitler was at the door offering to lick everyone's asshole as they arrived.

"I am back!"

The crowd cheered, both fictional and historical and just plain ordinary sinners alike. Music played, lots of pop medley hits from the 90's.

Alf pumped his fist in the front row next to Jeannie from I Dream of Jeannie, he and Vicki had already broken up. Mr. Ed the horse was there smoking a cigar and Samantha from Bewitched was wiggling her nose as Darren crawled around on a dog collar and barked. The Brady Bunch kids were in pieces on the ground twitched, no one liked them.

Even Marsha, Marsha, Marsha.

"Are you happy I'm here now?" he said.

"Yes," I said, "but…"

"But what?"

"I want a baby. Can you give me a womb?"

He sighed.

"Please, just a little Anti-Christ of our own."

"Very well," he said and changed my internal organs.

The cast of M.A.S.H. applauded. It was a nice day in Hell.

Shoes
By Aaron J. French

I'd like to tell you how this whole thing went down. How I ended up . . . here, in this padded cell, with no windows, no metal silverware—and nothing but an endless procession of doctors coming to see me.

Well it's all because of those goddamned shoes!

But . . . I suppose I'd better start at the beginning . . . or else you might lose faith in me as a narrator. And I can't have that. If you are to believe anything I'm about to tell you, then you're gonna have to be on my side. Not like these goddamned doctors. They think I'm crazy. A looney tune. A real nutcase.

I guess you can decide for yourself at the end. But please, hear me out before making any rash judgments. Start on my side, won't you? Have a little faith in your narrator.

All right, then. There's really no better place to start than with those goddamned shoes.

We found them while we were out hiking, an old pair of Rockports, brown leather fading, weatherworn, sitting in the middle of the trail side-by-side, as if the person who'd worn them had suddenly ascended toward the sky, or vanished from them completely, just plucked into oblivion.

It was me and Alexia, the girl from the coffee shop. I'd hung around Bray's Café for almost three years, utilizing the Wi-Fi and the bright lighting, ogling the steady stream of college coeds, and working on the hundred or so papers I needed to complete my undergraduate.

Alexia, herself in school, spent long hours behind the counter trying to pay for her tuition. She was a sunny girl, pale-skinned and blonde-haired, with a carefree attitude, and I instantly fell in love with her sparkling blue eyes and casual smile.

We started talking on a regular bases. Eventually (three years of eventually) I built up the courage to ask her out. She said she liked hiking and so we began meeting on the weekends at the bottom of Mt. Creason, each time attempting to climb higher toward the top.

Not much else had happened in terms of romance. I was still waiting for the right moment to grab her hand and initiate a kiss. The problem that I was scared to death of her. A product of my largely solitary existence, one consumed by school and bouts of anxiety. I was working on making a change, was getting set to make my move, but so far

I'd done nothing.

When I saw the pair of Rockports standing anonymously in the park trail . . . I don't know why, but I felt a deep-seated dread. A chasm opened in my soul; darkness fanned out in my head. The world seemed to flicker, to go on and off like a faulty lightbulb. I was overcome by an endless tidal wave of fear, which proceeded to wash over me.

Alexia, beautiful as always, approached the Rockports with an air of uncaring, calm, and grace, bending over them slightly, her summer dress whipping out in the wind. "Somebody went right on and left 'em," she said, turning to me.

She must've seen the horrible expression on my face because she abandoned the shoes at once and came over to me. "Jesus, you look like you've seen a ghost," she said, taking my hand. "Are you all right?"

She grabbed my hand, not the other way around—which became something of a sore spot for me. It seemed I had failed again. I had not lived up to my own expectations. Thus the fear that I was experiencing intensified, and I felt paralyzed.

"Robert? Robert?" She shook me a little. I became mesmerized by the lines on her face, a sea of pallid flesh, infinite sparkling eyes, a mouth like a giant red clipper ship. The mountainside stretched around us: bushes, shrubs, and trees. And I thought I was falling backwards, falling out of time, into some great abyss.

She shook me again, but I did not rouse. Then, abruptly, she slapped me. Hard.

Suddenly I was back. As she attempted to slap me again, I caught her wrist. "I'm fine," I said, more harshly than I'd intended.

She gave me a cautious look, her blonde hair framing her face, tugged gently by the wind. A few leaves—an early sign of fall—seesawed down from the canopy, dropping to the soft loam around our feet. I did my best to smile, but the gesture felt forced.

"Come have a look at these shoes," she said. "It'll be OK. I promise."

I took a deep breath, steeling myself. Then I nodded, and allowed her to lead me down the trail, to where the vacant pair of shoes stood innocuously in the dirt.

She stayed beside me, still holding my hand, and for the first time I became aware of her touch. The soft pliability of her fingers as they wove between my own; the sensuousness of her milky skin, the security of her touch. I was horrified by it, and yet a feeling of absolute joy, one I could not seem to access, lurked somewhere underneath the horror.

Was I supposed to do something now? Was she going to kiss me? Should I kiss back?

The anxiety threatened to overtake me again, but I resisted it, focusing instead on the pair of curious brown hiking shoes, minus the occupant, presented before us, begging to be analyzed, deciphered—why were they here, and who had left them, and what was their purpose—and then I realized it was the shoes—the shoes, for Christ's sake—which had caused me to feel this way.

They were unholy, wicked, strange, and other, and they had no business standing in the middle of a trail, minus their occupant, for they were mocking the normal order of things, poking fun at every natural law, and I hated them for that— scorn with a passion—and I wanted only to see them wiped out of existence.

But I held my tongue, body trembling, as Alexia released my hand and bent toward them.

"What do you think?" she asked.

"About what?"

"About the shoes, of course. Why were they left, do you think? It's funny, but it seems as if the owner took them off and then walked away. Isn't that strange? Why would someone walk off and leave their shoes?"

209

I panicked. I couldn't devise an answer, could hardly understand the question, but luckily the rational part of my mind turned on, and I said, "Maybe they had another pair of shoes, which they put on, and then decided to leave these behind." I had spoken too quickly, forcing the words out of my mouth, but Alexia seemed not to have noticed.

"That's stupid," she said. "These are brand-new, and they're Rockports, they're a hundred dollar pair of hiking shoes."

"Well then I don't know," I said, getting frustrated. I couldn't understand why she was so obsessed with the damn shoes, when all I wanted to do was get as far away from them as I could.

"You're awfully touchy today," she said, and then she did a horrible thing, a most terrible thing—she reached out and touched the foul Rockports, ran her fingers along the laces, traced the edges, and teased the tongues. She'd just been touching me with those fingers, and did she expect to do that again, after fondling some loathsome pair of hiking shoes? I couldn't think of anything more repulsive.

"They feel funny," she said.

This aroused my interest—that a pair of shoes, wicked shoes, should feel funny. "In what way?" I asked. "Do you mean like Playdough, or sandpaper, do you mean like that?"

210

"What? No. I mean like crystals, or ancient pottery, or petrified wood—like that. I know they look brand-new, but the leather feels old. Very old. And organic somehow, like they're not shoes, but somehow part of the forest."

"Oh," I said. I hated her answer, hated her for suggesting they were part of the forest, as if they had risen out of the ground like sneaker-zombies, clawing their way up with the laces, and at last reaching the sun, and then waiting for someone like us to come along.

It was a ridiculous thought. They were just shoes.

Then why do you feel so frightened? asked a voice. This I ignored, for I had no reasonable explanation to account for my fear.

Alexia was still touching them, caressing them almost, and I felt a sick sort of pleasure as I watched, as though she were performing a salacious act. I could see down the front of her dress from this angle, and my eyes kept darting to her breasts, those twin white sacs housed in yellow fabric. Each time I caught myself doing this, I felt the flower of fear in my soul grow more petals, become fuller. Waves of primal anxiety, savage lust, and lewd disorder caused chaos in my head, which now ached, a result—I was convinced—of the detestable shoes.

211

How she loved those shoes, tended to them, stroked them, caressed them, and what about me? I was a fly on the window of their love, hers and those shoes, peering into their happy home, lost in the cold world without, destined to be alone, destined to be anxious.

I watched her now with a slowly mounting rage, an oozing horror, hatred that was rearing its ugly violent head in my brain, its arms becoming my arms, its legs my legs, its thoughts mine. A demon, the demon, of the Rockports had come to pay me a little visit. And I welcomed it with open arms.

"Why are you looking at me like that?" she said.

I had not realized I was looking at her, but now that I did, I quickly softened my features, which had become hard-edged and menacing. I tried looking at her the way normal couples look at each other, but I found it was impossible. I despised her, and the best I could hope for was a robotic, mechanistic, emotionless mask which would conceal my thoughts and keep them from revealing my secret.

Still crouched before me, she had now lifted one of the shoes and was lovingly cradling it to her chest, holding it like a newborn babe. The crown of her head was bent over it, and she was cooing softly, whispering pleasantries into its invisible ears, stroking its rubber edging, the laces wrapped around her fingers.

Was she nursing it?

Yes, I saw she was, as odd as that sounds, for the shoulder strap on her right shoulder had slipped down her bicep. I could glimpse, through a screen of blonde hair, the suckling mouth, the swollen nipple, the soft breast.

I flew into a silent rage. It began at my heels, then traveled upward through my veins and bones, merging with my spine, my shoulders, my neck, until finally it encompassed my face and head. I felt like I was on fire, like I was going to explode, pop, scattering my remains all over the mountainside in a gory, bloody tempest.

I could hardly think anymore. I could only feel, and this feeling was not comfortable—oh no. It was the massive bony head of the demon, indeed my own demon, prodding at reality, trying to smash its way into existence.

I reached down to retrieve the other shoe, then erected. Alexia had not noticed for she was too consumed with her task of nursing. Standing in the sunlight, as it filtered down through the overhead branches, I stared at the beastly shoe, turning it over in my hands.

What a repulsive, what a undesirable, what a wretched—what did she see in the shoe that she did not see in me? Why was I not perched in her lap, feeding on her motherly essence? Was I deficient in some way? But that was absurd, for the other was simply a shoe, an object, unliving, unloving. I was a real person. So how could she choose an inanimate object over a real person?

It was so ridiculous and accursed that I damn near spit with revulsion into the dirt. This damnable shoe in my hands, mocking me, eyeless and mouthless, and yet I knew it was grinning, jeering, laughing even, watching me with an astute awareness, the humor of the absurd—

It was—

LAUGHING AT ME!

I raised the shoe above my head, clutching it by the toe, brandishing its hard leather sole, which had been serrated for traction. Alexia was below me, sitting cross-legged in the middle of the trail, holding the other shoe to her breast, feeding it, nurturing it, loving it. She had forgotten all about me by now.

With a wail of rage, the screech of frenzied child, I brought the sole of the shoe down on the top of her head. She rocked back, a quick jerk of the neck, and fell sideways in the loam. She dropped the other shoe, which tumbled off to the side, whiteness ringing its lips.

I stepped over her, still screeching, and beat until my heart's content, utilizing all the rage and anger I had stored up throughout my life. She shouted and begged for me to stop—tried to fight back even—but I overpowered her, stepping down on her wrists, pinning her. I beat and I beat, landing blow after blow upon her face and head, until she was a bloody and bruised mess.

But even then I did not stop. For what seemed like hours, I stayed at it, rage arising from the depths of my soul, eager to be released, and I screamed and I screamed, a primal savage wail, a calling to the ancient animals of the forest to remember that—yes, I too was a beast by nature, I too was one of them.

When the feeling passed, I looked down at what I'd done, at the mess I'd made of Alexia, a beautiful woman, and I dropped the accursed shoe and fled the mountain in horror. Less than a week later, three police officers arrived at my front door. I did not resist them.

So tell me, after listening to all that, do you believe I am crazy? Or do you believe me that the shoes are responsible, that they overtook my mind and caused me to act like a cruel madman?

You know—there's a reason why I'm always walking around barefoot in my padded cell.

Oh yes . . .

There is a reason.

A Prescription to Shut the Fuck Up
By Max Booth III

A Prescription for Shut the Fuck Up

Refills Left: Unlimited

For: Your Stupid Face

TAKE THREE TABLETS DAILY OR, REALLY, ANY TIME YOU THINK ABOUT OPENING THAT GODDAMN MOUTH OF YOURS

CHILLPILL 50 MG. 50MG

Dr. Sick of Hearing Your Voice
Discard After: You learn how to interact with actual human beings.

WARNING: MAY CAUSE EMPATHY

The Swamp of Girders and Chains
By Vincenzo Bilof

Someone told me today I'd see an apocalypse, but I don't remember who that was.

A bronze sky, doom in the forecast. Upon what shore have we designed the screams that are silent? You would think... You would think...

I want to marry her one day. We're watching through a window pane in which there is no glass. The sky might be inches or universes away.

"We don't have to be afraid."

Her voice is the motion of lips that refuse to move. Sensation creeps, the threat of a shiver, the terror of yesterdays murdered for all time.

The floor is concrete and the walls are brick. From beyond horizons we cannot see, in places that must not exist, the echo of a monstrous roar rises along the edges of broken towers made of bone or brick, steel or bone, bone or plastic, flesh or bone. There are two monsters wrestling for control of time, and their names cannot be uttered, or known.

Their names cannot be seen, or touched.

In a film they may have been Godzilla and another mutant borne of industrial nightmare, stomping like dinosaurs in a parade through a

218

desert. Fighting, howling, impossible voices evoke the idea of spaceships taking flight, or the Greek pantheon of gods committing suicide by throwing themselves down an endless flight of stairs.

"We can still run. We can run to somewhere."

The woman I wanted to marry. She appears as I want her to be, our lives lost here at the end of a bad song written by a pop star who walks naked and hums tantric undulations and uploads them to the world to show how different they are, how alien (how ludicrous thou art).

Emergence, although we may not have stood, nor have we passed through doors. This place is a shell, maybe a cavern that leaks sound. The alleys have become corridors swept clean of refuse, the cement nothing more than a blank slab; even the vein-lines, the cracks and scars, have gone. There is wind, but it has no smell.

I believe she holds my hand as we drift through brick corridors. Isometric skyscrapers gutted, broken stairways that are supposed to lead upward instead find open rooftops where the skulls have been cracked wide, pouring the contents of city and sin into the sky. Those buildings have been hollow for years, and we have known them. We have avoided them.

A homeless man drags his feet, laughing while he goes. I'm afraid my teeth will shatter. They will collapse and become the bitter crumbs of an old granola bar until they become wayward dominoes in the palm of my hand. I don't want my lover to see. Anything but that.

The roar of the battle is wild. The roar of the sky is loud.

The homeless man's laughter follows the wind between the edges of walls that lead to more walls.

"The sky has bled into the brick."

I squeeze her hand. Cold, wet. The taste of a storm that will never come, a promise not kept.

The shapes of people are walking upward through the remains of the skyscrapers. There is no sun, no light, but there is still vision. We can see.

Her head rests on my shoulder while our feet touch the plane. Paper follows the trail of a breeze, brittle and imperfect. The pages are blank, and we walk on. The homeless walk, too, scattered through these corridors, shoulder slumped, their cracked grins bleeding. Exiles from the mind of Salvador Dali. In their minds, time has been muted.

Closer to me. Stay by my side.

"We can live here forever."

For a moment, and a moment only, I think of

starlight and the heat it must radiate in a vacuum.

Convergence. The city's womb opens into a center in which our beloved mayor stands near the Greco-Roman fountain. A completely bald Theodore Roosevelt, a monocle perched over his right eye, a conductor's wand in his hand, which waves before a choir dressed in scarlet robes.

"Ama-zing grace... how sweet... the sound..."

This center is clean, and the fountain gushes water onto trimmed carpet of green lawn. The water flows outward, but from wither does it come? The water floods the grass. The choir sings.

And the roar of the beasts is closer, and it sounds like a concert of out-of-tune violins.

The choir is composed of bright eyes and long mouths that open and close like sock-puppets manipulated by arthritic hands. The mayor waves his wand while a smile reaches his ears.

My hand is released.

"To the edge, we will go."

And so we run. The citizens of our land climb the towers. The hunchbacked beggars steady themselves against the walls as if they've been unbalanced by heart attacks they've been waiting to experience in the wake of years. My lover half a city away. I've lost her but she remains beside me, alive.

221

I can feel her voice and she is not yet a ghost.

Green water pools around the surface of the city's edge. The artist has stopped painting the city, and the water encroaches into the street, swallowing inches. At the end of the horizon the sky ripples with pale light that conquers the bronze face of a dying god that leans over this sphere.

Beyond the ocean there is nothing.

My eyes find the center again, where the fountain froths, and the choir might be sinking.

"I'm here, with you."

Hands together, we race around the city again, encircling the same vision like a poem that falls out of a journal's pages and to become lovely graffiti. Our eyes find the center again and again, a peripheral witness that shall not pass. No. Shall not pass.

Violins are screaming. Maybe if we look for a junkyard of metal cats that have rusted in the eye of a hurricane, we can find salvation, or a place to hide. A window without glass is preferable.

Water withdraws, ebbs, attacks.

"Through this tower we will go."

A climb that is not metaphoric. Escher has wept upon these steps, but we're not afraid to run. The apocalypse does not hold sway over our lives.

"Chase me higher."

222

She is the afterimage of fantasy, and I charge after her concept like a Minotaur running through Golgotha at sunset. Shards of glass fall from the sky, and I find myself worrying about the monsters and their struggle, the choir and its voice, sinking, fading.

"I'm here, up here."

Walls of cardboard, glass tearing the sky. Twinkling light refracting prismatic oblivion, the sewage-brown heaven the anti-destination for lepers and lovers. There are shapes of people upon these stairs, and the city is below me, but where the ocean should breathe there is only city.

I can feel them regenerating. Buildings that have become our new machines, gestating the gears of industry and replicating brick and glass, a ruthless video game designer locking Super Mario in a cage of digital brick in a world of question marks that linger upon boxes. The roar of the beasts has become distant, forlorn.

I don't tire.

"Let us say our oaths before gravity shifts beneath our feet."

A good idea, but there are no oaths. Only broken violins and fountains that pour water at the feet of Teddy Roosevelt.

Pussy Apocalypse
By P. A. Douglas

The end of the world didn't come with a BOOM!

It didn't come with zombies like most of you would like to think.

And no, it did not come as a result of Cthulhu himself pounding through inner dimensional portals.

Nope.

None of that nonsense.

The apocalypse was started by none other than Ellen DeGeneres.

Who the hell is she to think vegan cat food was a bright idea? I tell you what… it was the dumbest idea I have ever heard of. And it was that same idea that started it all.

There I was, minding my own business. Watching the DeGeneres show. So what if I'm a single man. Ain't nothing wrong with watching her show by myself. She not only looks good, but she's a lesbian. Hot lesbians are HOT, if you know what I'm sayin'.

Anyway, me and Carl—that's my cat—were watching her show. It was a typical Saturday

224

afternoon. That's been a long time ago now, but it was when me and Carl were first introduced to HALO. That is Ellen's cat food. Vegan cat food. Thinking back on it now I wouldn't doubt if they had figured out some sort of 'sound' that triggered Carl to focus so hard on the television when she started talking about that junky pet food. Come to think of it I don't think I ever seen any cat so attentive. The way that slender cat can slide across the screen. Ellen's smiling hot lesbian face tantalizing both me and Carl.

Carl had to have it.

I didn't blame him. At last not back then.

Hell, I had to have it, too… for Carl. I wanted to get in that chick's pants so hard.

So that day, after the DeGeneres show was over, me and Carl made a trip to the pet store. And I know what you're thinking. No, I don't normally bring him along. But this was somehow a special occasion. I was excited not only for Carl, but something on the television grabbed me too, the same way it did my cat. I think it was some underlying sound. Hypnotic suggestion, maybe. It was almost as if I half expected to run into Ellen at the pet store.

Sneak me in the back. Do things to me and Carl.

225

You know, wet things.

But it didn't happen that way at all. In fact, it played out in a way that no one would have thought possible.

The pet stores were swarming with people and their cats. Obviously me and Carl weren't the only perverts that liked to watch her show.

The food was supposed to be healthy. Nutritious. Vegan.

That was where it went wrong.

Cats are carnivores in their natural habitat. They like meat. Savor the flavor of blood. I don't know about you and your cat, but Carl was always bringing me little trophies. Dead birds. Half eaten rats. Lizards with missing limbs.

But that was then.

It's not the same anymore.

Like I said, the stores were flooded with people and their cats. The pet store we went to was dishing out the HALO cans so fast that I couldn't even keep up. We were at the register and checking out before I ever realized my cart was slammed full of HALO cans. Who honestly needs that much cat food?

But I wasn't the only one lost in the trance.

Everyone around me was going through the same motions. Carts filled to the brim. Cats riding on their owner's shoulders like parrots. Hell, some people had a bunch of cats. I found out later that it wouldn't have been as bad had I had more cats. Wouldn't have been as agonizing.

As prolonged.

When we got home Carl had to sink his maw into a can of HALO right away. I can't say that I blamed him then either. It took everything I had to not jump down on all fours and join him.

I had the shakes. The sweats even. Ellen was on the brain.

Carl seemed to like it. This made me happy, because I had practically cleared out my savings account on all those cans. At least it wasn't going to go to waste.

Boy, was I wrong.

The next day, me and Carl watched the DeGeneres show again. That was our weekend ritual. On this particular Sunday, all Ellen talked about was the success of HALO. It wasn't only good for you, but it was vegan!

Well, guess what… I hate to break it to you, but cats are not fucking vegan.

They are carnivores. Point. Blank.

Can you imagine being fed nothing but shitty ass beans and rice? I'm not talking about for a day, or even a few days. I'm talking about all the time. Twenty-four-seven!

Come Tuesday that week Carl quit eating the HALO.

He didn't want it anymore.

Fuck that shit.

This was my life savings we're talking about… right?

I guess I should have really weighed it out, then. Serves me right I guess. Serves the whole damn world, too.

That's right.

This wasn't just happening to me. This was worldwide, buddy.

We're talking about Ellen fucking DeGeneres here. Not some hack on the local public access. Satellite broadcasting, people! It went viral. Whatever they did to make Carl so attentive…that sub-sound. It hit everybody. And if they missed that episode they were still going out and buying this stuff just because everyone else was.

I know what you're thinking.

Not everyone has cats.

Well, by then it didn't matter. It was already too late.

So, back to the beans and rice. After the investment I wasn't going to have Carl let it go to waste. No one was. This stuff was good for you.

228

'High in Nutrition' was even printed on the damn label.

"It's good for you, Carl," I said, dropping it into his bowl.

He didn't want to have anything to do with it.

It wasn't long after that when things started to really go downhill. Carl was hungry. All of them were. None of the cats wanted anything to do with the HALO.

Why would they? It didn't have any fucking meat in it.

Well, why didn't you let Carl just go outside and chase stuff? Let him eat a bird or something?

I tried that. A lot of people did. By the time it came to letting them outside. By the time it came to giving up on the HALO. All that lost money. It was too late. Carl didn't have the energy. He was getting weak. He needed substance.

He needed meat.

And I knew that.

But I just didn't know what to do.

I don't think anyone did.

And you can guess it, too. It happened when I fell asleep on the couch. And yes, it was a Saturday. And yes, I had been watching the Ellen DeGeneres marathon. Who the hell wasn't watching it?

I'm not sure what time I fell asleep.

All I do remember is the pain.

It seems to never go away now.

In the middle of my Ellen love making lesbian power dream, which was awesome I might add, Carl sank his sharp little teeth into my jugular.

I don't blame him now… now that I think about it.

He was hungry.

The pain is still just too much to bear. I am laying here bleeding out all over the couch from my torn throat. I can't call for help because Carl did a number on my Adam's apple. Any time I try to talk it's just gurgling bubbly blood. I tried to get up, but I can't. Carl chewed on my throat for so long that I think he dug into the spine at the back of my neck or something.

I am paralyzed.

And now I can feel it in my legs and stomach. I can't move, so I can't see. But I can feel Carl taking his time. Eating me. Eating my knee. Eating my stomach.

It hurts more than you can imagine. His carnivorous teeth are just so damn sharp.

At least my neck is cocked at the right angle. I can still see the television.

It's hard to listen to. The sirens, shouting, screaming, and gunfire outside in the streets of my neighborhood kind of drown out the audio. But I can still watch. And I have a pretty good gist on what is happening.

It's a rerun.

Ellen is interviewing Brad Pit.

They are laughing and slapping hands with playful banter.

I wonder when the cats staring at me through the window will figure out how to get in.

They look hungry, too.

THE MONSTER, THE MAN, THE BUILDING, THE BOMB
By Danger_Slater

Part One – The Monster

When I first saw you, I had just finished snorting a line of Marine Corps riflemen through the long, hollow subway tube I had yanked out of the center of East 3rd Street. Into my flared, black nostril the entire infantry went.

sssnnnnnnfffff

Insufflated away in a rushing river of blood and snot.

And now I can hear them. I can hear the soldiers screaming from inside of me. Futilely and feverously firing their tiny, little bullets out of their tiny, little guns. I can feel the bullets bouncing around in my veins, working their way through my stomach, my liver, my heart, into my brain and then...OH FUCK YEA MUTHAFUCKAS! THAT'S WHAT I'M TALKIN' ABOUT! There's that rush! The tidal wave of euphoria that comes crashing down upon my bloodthirsty shores like the ocean of my body were made of caffeine and honey! It's coursing through me like a freight train now.

232

Choo-choo, baby boo! I feel so goddamn good, I don't think anything can stop me. Not all the artillery these peasants have stockpiled away. Not science, not nature, not God himself. I own this city. You hear me, you fucksticks?

I'M READY TO TAKE ON YOUR WHOLE SHITTY WORLD!

And that's when I saw you, rising high above the carnage. Above the ravaged landscape. Above the fires and rubble and bones and bodies and all the rest of the human scree I left shredded in my wake. And I had to pause. I had to stop the rampage, just for a moment, and take you all in. Drink up your beauty. Bask in your ambiance, your glory, your shadow.

So sensual and slender is your design; so amorous are the accents of your architecture – it's like you were calling my name with the blueprints of your very soul. And my heart starts to go *ka-blang* in my massive, monstrous chest as it surges with a feeling even more intense than the high I got when I blew that last line of hominine meat. It's a feeling I've never felt before. Something more akin to happiness – true happiness – than the murder, mayhem and drugs have ever given me.

So I run to you. I need to see you, up close. To get to know you. I need to follow this feeling. I need to find out what it means.

I stomp my way across Avenue A. Through the Flatiron district and Gramercy Park. I spank tanks and crush choppers and swat away howitzers like the horseflies that incessantly buzz around my head and I batter a battery of battering rams and splatter convoy of medical vans and I wrap my tentacles around office buildings and apartment complexes and pull, carving a swath of destruction like a surgeon's incision across this city's overstuffed belly, leaving all decimated and dead in my apocalyptic path.

And then there I am, in Midtown Manhattan, in the center of New York, the center of the world, face to face with you for the very first time. All 102 stories of you sticking straight up in the air. Like a monolith you laugh at both physics and logic. A monument to ingenuity, a testament to progress, a structure that couldn't have possibly existed at any other time in history.

Much like myself.

I bend down and read the small plaque cemented into your side. The Empire State Building, it says. So that's your name, eh? Well it's a very pretty name. You can call me Gorillipus. Part-gorilla, part-octopus if that wasn't obvious enough. I think there might be a little iguana mixed in there too. Ya know, for good measure. I'm what you would call an aberration of nature: an 80-foot-tall mutant freak murder-monster whose hunger for death and destruction cannot be sated.

It's a pleasure to meet you.

Wh – what's wrong, my dear? Are my compliments not satisfactory? Am I not wooing you proper? I think all your obtuse angles look very acute. I think you have a personality that towers above the clouds themselves. Why are you looking at me with such a granite expression? Why are you so pale? Have I done something to offend you?

And then I look out at the city I devoured. At the trail of debris that has followed me here. And for the first time since I broke out of that research facility a few days ago and the tempest that is I was unleashed upon the globe, I am struck with a moment of doubt. Am I upsetting you, Empy? You don't mind if I call you Empy, do you? Look, I know I may've crushed pretty much all the buildings that used to surround you, but it's not my fault. I'm a monster, duh. I'm just doing what I was born to do. I didn't expect to find love while in the process of ending the world. I want you to know, I would never hurt you, okay?

I love you, Empy. I really, really do.

235

Part Two – The Man

When I first saw you, you had just finished snapping the Brooklyn Bridge in half like a disposable bamboo chopstick. My platoon and I hopped out of the back of the truck and were headed down South Street towards the river bank.

Hup one! Hup two! Hup three! Hup four!

You had just risen. From the depths of the sea. Your hairy, man-simian chest – as thick as a mountain and as black as midnight – glistening with the motorboat oil and raw sewage runoff that floated on the surface of the water like the rainbow blanket that used be spread across my ex-girlfriend's bed. Maybe I'm still a little upset that she broke up with me. Maybe I wanted revenge or needed something to help heal my heart. Or maybe I'm actually over her this time and I've finally found the strength to move on. In the end, does it really matter? When I saw those two suction-cupped tentacles wrap around the bridge like a pair of hungry boa constrictors squeezing their prey, something happened to me.

I fell in love.

We didn't get much information in regards to what you were. And we certainly got no advice on how to stop you. They just dropped us off near the seaport and told us to hold the line. One of my bunkmates – a good guy. Jacobson, his name is was. RIP, dude – said he heard you were some kind of genetic experiment gone horribly wrong. Ya know, gene splicing, mutations, radiation. All that science shit. He said you busted out of some secret illuminati research lab in Toronto. Said you destroyed Greektown and Riverdale and toppled the CN Tower before disappearing into Lake Ontario. Said the government's been tracking you as you swam south through the labyrinth of rivers and channels. They knew where you were headed. They knew you were gonna pop up right here, in New York City, but nobody had any idea what to do about it. They knew you were gonna be BIG. They knew you were gonna be strong. They knew you were gonna be angry...

But what they failed to tell us was how goddamn sexy you were gonna be.

Of course, I might be one of the few people to think that. Especially considering you're an animal. Or an un-animal. Or something. And despite the gigantic pendulum of a cock you have swinging between your legs, I don't think I'm normally attracted to guys. I guess the heart just wants what the heart wants. Serendipity, or whatever they say. How can you argue with that?

Off the cantilevers the Brooklyn Bridge is

torn, fragmented bricks and mortar crumble as easy as graham cracker cookies. Over-stressed steel is shorn as if it were just butter. You hold the roadway high up above your head as the suspension wires wildly swing around like jellyfish arms grasping for the sea. All the other soldiers around me have opened fire. Desperately unloading clip after clip in your general direction, hoping to GOD that something hits. But not I. I have placed my gun down and run up to the edge of the shattered street, bounding towards you with open arms. From the bridge cars are dropping into the East River going sploosh sploosh sploosh like handfuls of loose change being thrown into a fountain. So I reach into my pocket, grab my own lucky coins, close my eyes tight and throw them into the water too. Sploosh. My one and only wish repeating over and over in my mind as my heart boils over with both love and affection:

I don't ever want this moment to end.

Part Three – The Building

When I first saw you, you were only 8 years old.

This was a little over a decade ago. Not too

long after those fundamentalist assholes flew a pair of 757s into the side of the World Trade Center. It was a weird time for me. A tense time. Nowhere felt safe. I didn't know if I'd live to see tomorrow. I didn't know if I was next. I didn't know anything. It took me a long time to shake that feeling. I suppose I'm still trying to shake it.

You had come to the city on a day trip. With your parents. I spotted you almost all the way at Grand Central, holding your momma's hand tight as you stepped out from under the marquee. Holding her hand like her fingers were an umbilical the doctors forgot to cut. Your eyes darted around nervously. Cautiously. Not quite the 'burbs, now was it, kid? Heh heh.

You guys paused on 5th and your mom pointed to me.

"Look at how BIG that building is, Tommy. Do you know what it's called?"

You shook your head no as your gaze slowly climbed my facade like a spider. Past all my windows, floor by floor, all the way up to the radio antenna sticking straight out of the top of my head. The little red light on the very, very top of the lightning rod blinking on and off and on and off as steady as the beat of my concrete heart.

"It's the Empire State Building," your

mother said.

"Umpire State Building?" you repeated, mispronouncing my name. To that I chuckled, which must've sounded more like the creak of settling steel upon my subbasements foundation, but only to those keen enough to hear it.

"Come on, Tommy," she said, "Let's go upstairs!"

Now I'm no prude. I literally have tens of thousands of people enter and exit me every single day. But I have never – NEVER – felt the rush I felt the first time your Chuck Taylor sneakers scuffed their way across the threshold of my front door. Something was happening here. Something ordained, maybe? Something cosmic?

Perhaps the terrorist have one thing right; perhaps there are things out there bigger than ourselves.

Even in the 12 year absence between then and now, when you've finally returned to the city all grown up, when you've finally returned to me, I thought about you daily. I am devoted, if not anything. I am a rock. Unmovable. Unflappable. And now here you are again.

Standing through all those lonesome winters has finally paid off.

It was cold that February morning, way back

then in 2002, yet you and your momma still went up to my observation deck. She put a quarter in the telescopic viewer and let you step up and look out over the city. And unlike the rest of the tourist that so callously trample upon my head, I could somehow feel it as your eyes drank it in. In an instant you could see the millions of people that live and die in this city every day, that love and lose, the have and haven't. And then there we were, together, towering above them, watching over them like some sort of omnipotent being. Connected in a way a human and a building have never been connected before.

I could feel you become stronger that day. Become braver. Become a man.

Before you left me, you ran your fingers across the crags in my walls. Tickled the buttons on my elevator shaft. I could hear you breathing inside of me. I've never felt this level of intimacy with another person before. Or another building, for that matter. I didn't even know these things were feelings I could feel. I didn't even know there were such things as feelings at all, until I saw you. In fact, before you popped out of that train station and made your way down 5th Ave, I didn't even have a single conscious sentient thought. I was just a big, dumb building taking up some real estate on this Earth

241

before inevitably being plowed down by terrorism or time. And I suppose I still am just a big, dumb building in many ways. But I'm a building in love. And that's more than most buildings can say. But that's mainly because buildings can't talk.

Part Four – The Bomb

When I first saw the three of you, the cargo doors of the Tupolev Tu-22M had just parted like the legs of a woman.

The steady whir of the airplane engine, the woosh of the stratosphere rushing by the open hatch, the buzz of my own atomic parts warming up – the cacophony of sound coalesced and condensed into one hypnotic hum, this song, like the mantra of some yogi baba invoking feelings of ultimate and agape love stretched as thin and as long as love can be stretched as this moment goes tantric and tattoos its name in cursive across the forehead of forever. What does that all mean? I'm not sure exactly. But for the first time since they fused me together like some sort of neo-techno-Frankenstein, I've outgrown my inherent and predesigned nihilism and realized there's something more out there for a bomb like me.

I have realized my purpose. And the part all

three of you play in that.

Gorillapus has climbed the Empire State Building, his slime-covered tentacles wrapped around the base of the antenna, just above the 102nd floor observation deck – a quarter-mile above the desecrated city streets. The helicopters and military personnel have all been cleared. The army has evacuated. The national guard in retreat. They can't do anything to stop this meeting. Not even God would dare interfere. Supposing God didn't commission this moment himself.

This is fate. This is destiny. This is kosmic karmic kismet, baby!

From a safe distance – probably from the shores of Hoboken, or possibly in a far-off neighborhood in Brooklyn, the cavalry waits. Like an audience at a play. Like the hedges along an abandoned highway. Like gargoyles eroding in the rain, the twisted visage of humanity stripped from their souls like a layer of cheap paint off the side of a barn. They don't understand; they'll never understand. They don't know what it means to truly love – to give yourself so wholly to someone something else that you stop being you. That you melt into the scenery and into your lover's chest and there's no such thing as yesterday and you can't even find a tombstone to commemorate your former self, because from here on out we're all just different fingers on the same massive hand, defined only by our relationships to each other. This is the feeling I felt when I first saw the three of you.

And then, like an egg or a baby or a brick falling out of a red-hot kiln, I am born from out the back of the military bomber. Into the wild, through the air, I am sent. My silver cylindrical nose-plate splitting the cerulean sky with a stentorian roar. The world below me, so BIG, COLORFUL, so ALIVE with all the possibilities in the universe. This city where the countless multitudes have tread, all in search of that one undefinable thing. A city, a world, so desperately in need of what I have to offer it.

I see you, Gorillapus, at the top of the building, now inserting the tip of the antenna into your puckered-pink asshole. Red light first, right up the rectum. And for the first time in your savage, inhuman life the savage, inhuman snarl has been wiped from your cheeks and replace by something else. Dare I say it? As you allow the Empire State Building to pierce your anal cavity and enter your body, an intimate and content smile like an inverted umbrella trickles its way across your revolting face.

I see you, Tommy, the human man - you frail little thing - clinging to one of Gorillapus's suckers like a life preserver in the open water. Your

244

camouflage fatigues are still half-on. Your shirt is buttoned up to his neck – proper and pressed and ready for inspection - but your pants have gone missing. Instead you wear nothing from the waist down and in your hand, you furiously tug at your engorged erection while licking, kissing, fondling a suction cup on Gorillapus's left tentacle.

I see you, Empire State Building, starting to overheat. The water rushing through your pipes coming to a boil. Your gaskets blowing. Steam escaping, as the pressure inside you builds and builds until you just can't take it anymore and you just have to RELEASE all that pent up pleasure in puffs of scalding hot air.

You all seem so happy.

And I know – the three of you people/things/architectural achievements and me – this is where I am supposed to be, what I'm supposed to do. I was born to make the whole goddamn world fall in love. Because what else is there? Everything is so terrible and sad all of the time and we're all just one bad afternoon away from complete and utter annihilation - why shouldn't we spend all our time seeking out the ones who can fan those dark clouds away? Even if the sunshine is just temporary. Even if it is just for a moment. Even if it only lasts as long as an orgasm. Isn't that the point of all this?

So I have reached the ground. The end of my journey. I connect with the earth, connect with all three of you, and I can feel all these emotions in me finally erupt, one atom at a time, in a chain reaction so powerful that this moment is energized into pure poetry and dashed against the surface of the planet like a splatter of red paint. Chaotic, momentous, wrangled only by some divine maker's brush. It spreads through my body and sets my robot heart on fire.

Gorillapus lets out an resounding howl, the man shakes and convulses and moans in ecstasy, the pipes inside the Empire State Building burst as scalding liquid comes pouring out of all its windows, and I explode in a catastrophic wave of infinite intensity, uniting this whole ugly city in a blinding and beautiful and fiery flash.

Love conquers all. And I'm cumming. My God! I'M CUMMING!

Vagalyn's Flying Head
By MP Johnson

Even though a giant street slug had devoured everything below her neck, Vagalyn Boyrama held tight to her role as drag mother and MC at the Fireball, the oldest gay bar in Fargo. Her disembodied head soared through the sequin-soaked dressing room, going from one diva to the next, nudging wigs straight with her nose, commenting on too-dull lip gloss or shouting an old-fashioned "You go, girl!"

"Does this look fab?" Moana Loser asked Vagalyn.

The youngest of the Fireball queens, Moana needed the most guidance. Vagalyn never hesitated to provide it. She gave the crab-colored curtain Moana called a gown a once over. "No. In fact, it's sucking all the fab out of the room. It's a black hole of fab."

Moana didn't protest. She never did. She never said anything like, "What do you know? You don't even have a bod to hang a dress over," even though Vagalyn sometimes saw such statements swirling around in the young diva's coffee-stained eyes. Instead, Moana nodded and respectfully asked,

247

"What can I do?"

Vagalyn orbited Moana. "Your body is too rockin' to cover with that tarp. Less is more when you've got legs like yours, girl."

"You're so right!" Moana shrieked. "I know exactly what to do."

"Hurry, you've got the opening slot tonight!"

"I heard her slot's been opening just about every night," one of the other queens cracked wise as Vagalyn flew off to continue her rounds and Moana got to work. Being at the bottom of the Fireball food chain, Moana tended to be on the receiving end of the most brutal barbs. She never lashed back, even though Vagalyn encouraged her to. Vagalyn worried that the young queen kept too much anger inside, a volcano of hot pink lava waiting to erupt at the worst possible moment. She had seen such things happen.

Vagalyn had seen a lot. She had been MC of the Fireball's Drag-O-Rama for nearly a decade. After she lost her body, she could have retired. She could have stopped brushing her teeth, let her beard grow and devolved into some sort of hovering caveman head. But she didn't. With or without her body, she was a drag queen. She had dropped out of the nine to five long ago, and she damn well wasn't going to try to wiggle her way back in, not without her wiggler.

Instead, she had cajoled her roommate Graham, that old bear, into building a makeshift tree of bathroom implements. It looked like the wooden training dummies used by the heroes of kung fu movies to practice their wing chun, except the arms intended to receive blows held toothbrushes, razors, makeup and makeup applicators. Every day before going to the Fireball, she approached the tree in complete disarray. With an occasional "Hi-yah!" she would whip from one arm to the next, carefully brushing and shaving. She even kung-fued her makeup on, emerging with her trademarked neon green batwing eye makeup and shimmery silver lips. The only thing she asked of Graham: to plop the unwieldy foot tall ball of blondeness on her head.

That extra weight slowed her flight as she completed her dressing room rounds, swinging back over to Moana's vanity to check on her.

"How's this," Moana asked. In a matter of minutes, the young queen had shredded the gown and, through creative safety pinning, turned it into a sleek mini dress with a little window for the inverted cross that dangled from her pierced belly button.

Vagalyn flew a loop-de-loop and nearly lost

249

her wig. "Va-va-voom! If I had a body, it would be a giant boner right now."

Only a few months had passed since the young queen first wobbled into the Fireball on one-inch grandma heels, wearing a cheap Halloween aisle witch dress, her matching black wig a mess of snarls, but with lips to die for. Some of the other Fireball queens, whom Vagalyn had seen walk into the bar in much the same state at one time, hassled Moana. Vagalyn had tut-tutted them away and taken Moana under her wing. The diva sponged up everything Vagalyn offered and more. Vagalyn couldn't have been more proud. This dress transformation was just another reason why she considered Moana her prize pupil. When she did retire, she wanted Moana to take her place as MC.

The clock struck ten and Vagalyn floated to the stage, calling the meager crowd of queers, fag hags and looky-loos to order. They moved forward, less tidal wave than rising tide, bringing the scent of flat beer and cheap perfume with them. The bar's décor came with its own faces – framed antique photos of tuxedo-clad children, remnants of a previous owner's odd tastes. Behind the bar, the muscle men pulling the taps leaned back and crossed their arms in their here-we-go-again stances. A few stragglers sat on stools, playing like cats with the odd bits of silver and purple tinsel that hung from above.

In the back, a tall man bundled in winter gear, odd on such a beautiful August night, huddled with Moana. He didn't fit in. Reminding herself that weirdoes in drag clubs were like sea monkeys in the back pages of comic books, Vagalyn launched into what had become her standard introductory gag since the encounter with the street slug on this very stage less than a year before: "My name is Vaj-a-lyn Boy-ram-ahhhh, and I have one question for you: What is a drag queen?"

"A dick in a dress!" someone shouted predictably from under the mirror ball.

"Exactly! Believe it or not, I used to be a drag queen, before my little, um, accident. Not anymore though. Now I'm one-hundred-percent grade-A American woman." After a round of laughter from the crowd, she added a perfectly timed, "It's true. Go ahead and see if you can prove otherwise!"

"And now, without further... bullshit... I'm going to bring to stage the lovely, the luscious, the ludicrous, Moana Loser!"

As the music started and Moana click-clacked onto the tiny corner stage in five inch stilettos, Vagalyn soared to the bar to rest her neck on a coaster. Spending too much time in the air hurt. She didn't know if it was some sort of phantom pain from the loss of her body or something about flying. She never complained though. When people asked if the slug attack had hurt, she would say, "Yeah, you know where it hurt the most? The closet." All those poor outfits she would never be able to wear again. And the shoes! Fifty-seven pairs, at last count. She still had a few, for old-times sake. She would rest her neck in them once in a while, pushing them along the floor.

When Moana finished her lip-synched pop gem, she nervously hung onto the microphone with both hands and, instead of inviting Vagalyn back to the stage, said in a near-whisper, "What do you bitches think of the MC's makeup tonight? That bat eye look really fits the old witch, doesn't it?"

An ill-timed round of laughter burst from a group of straight tourists huddled in the back joking amongst themselves, completely detached from the events on stage. Moana obviously took the laughter as acknowledgement of her sparkling wit. It lit a fire in her eyes that Vagalyn recognized. The young queen was attempting a power grab.

Vagalyn floated toward stage, hoping to stop Moana before she went overboard and passed the point of no return. She had seen many queens try

252

and fail, misguidedly thinking a few on-stage jabs could upset a hierarchy established through years of Drag-O-Ramas and Queen of the Fireball pageants.

"It looks like she's got mold around her eyes," Moana said, shimmying her too thin hips. "Talk about a moldy oldie. What can you expect from a handless drag queen? Always telling everyone else what to do, but she can't even do her own makeup right!"

Vagalyn buzzed behind Moana, hiss-pering, "Don't do this, diva."

Moana could make one of two moves. She could turn the microphone over and step off stage, graciously and gracefully, beaten but with her reputation intact. Vagalyn would forgive her and vouch for her so the other queens wouldn't turn on her like a pack of perfectly manicured wolves. Unfortunately, Moana didn't choose that move. Despite the dead silence from the crowd, she chose move number two, continuing the verbal evisceration by proclaiming: "Vagalyn Boyrama is a faker!"

Maybe, just maybe, Vagalyn hoped, Moana's next words would be so sparkling, so gem-coated and bedazzled, that she would actually succeed. Although Vagalyn had never seen such a thing happen, she had heard legends of quick-tongued queens rising to power. If Moana managed to join their ranks, she would earn the right to MC every single Drag-O-Rama from now until she passed her tiara down or some young queen ousted her. Whoop-de-doo. Big deal. But if that's what Moana wanted, Vagalyn hoped she would succeed, because seeing the young queen, her protégé, face the alternative would break her heart. If Moana missed the mark, she would be cast out by the Fireball queens and forced to find some other club – no easy task in Fargo, North Dakota – and to start at the bottom of that club's beehive-hairdoed totem pole. In other words, she would be fucked.

Vagalyn flew one more lap around Moana, warning, "This won't end well."

Moana swatted Vagalyn's flying head away and said, "She wasn't really attacked by a giant street slug!"

Someone in the crowd barfed up a "What?" and it landed on stage wet in front of Moana, who took the opportunity to elaborate. "She made up the whole story just to get your sympathy. She played you all like a bunch of suckers!" To drive her point home, she made a tacky cock-sucking gesture.

A carpet of grunts and mumbles rolled out from the crowd. Vagalyn flew over it, feeling lightheaded. They didn't believe Moana's accusation, did they? How could they? How could Moana even believe it? Vagalyn clearly had no body. Obviously something had taken it and left her a disembodied drag queen head buzzing around under a nest of blonde wig. If not a giant street slug, then what?

Moana had lost her mind. That's the only explanation that made sense. She had lost her mind and crossed a line, and Vagalyn had to put this whole charade to bed. The MC whipped through the air, picking up speed. Drawing back her silver lips and baring her perfectly white teeth, she flew as fast as she could at her protégé. Growling in an all-too-manly manner, she rammed Moana's ass and knocked her off stage.

Hovering in front of the microphone, Vagalyn addressed the confused crowd. "Well bitches, that's the last time we let Moana Loser do her comedy routine after a week-long kool-aid-laced cocaine bender! Now let's bring out our next act…"

"No!" Moana reached up with a fistful of cracked nails and grabbed the microphone. With no attempt at femininity, she roared, "Vagalyn Boyrama is a faker and I can prove it! Dancho, come to the stage please!"

The man in winter gear bumped through the crowd. The sleeves of his coat hung limp at his side,

255

as if he had no arms. Vagalyn realized that he didn't. He didn't have arms. He didn't have legs. When he stepped onto the stage beside Moana, who carefully adjusted her black wig, he shook off his hat, his scarf and his coat. The crowd gasped at what lay beneath: the slimy, sickly and limbless body of a giant street slug.

"This is Dancho, leader of the street slugs," Moana said. "He'll tell you."

Vagalyn panicked. Dive-bombing the crowd, she screamed, "Run bitches! Run for your lives! That motherfucker looks hungry!"

High heels in sizes ten through fifteen clicked across the floor, heeding Vagalyn's command. The queens lost all grace, a county fair's worth of sequined bumper cars colliding head-on before being pushed aside by the buff boys from behind the bar, who squealed louder and found the exit faster. Vagalyn soared above, shaking her head.

On stage, Moana Loser pleaded, "Listen to what he has to say!"

A tiny hole in the slug's face spread wide, revealing massive yellow barbs, each covered with smaller yellow barbs. A bubble of translucent slug slime emerged from the hole and popped suddenly, giving way to words. "Street slugs like fancy girlboys. I ask one to dance… that one…" Dancho nodded toward Vagalyn.

Vagalyn wondered what strain of insanity would possess Moana to have a conversation with a street slug, a creature second only to the cybernetic sewer grizzly in terms of pure murderousity, let alone invite one into their bar, their refuge from a world of khaki pants, polo shirts and homophobic hatred. Did she really want to MC that bad? Shit, Vagalyn made minimum wage and the only perk MCing had provided was a blurry picture in the entertainment section of the Fargazette that led to her being stalked by a member of the city council. She would have gladly handed the job over, if she had hands.

On stage, Moana enticed the street slug to continue. "Tell them what happened next. Tell them how that bitch crushed your dreams of one sweet dance."

"Is that what I tell you?" Dancho's barbed hole stretched into a sly smile. "No, she dance with Dancho, but slugs don't really like fancy girlboys for dancing…"

Vagalyn knew the words that came next all too well. Dancho had whispered them in her ear that night as they danced. Horrified, she mouthed along as the street slug repeated them from the stage: "We like fancy girlboys for eating!"

As Dancho reeled back and opened wide, Vagalyn screamed, "Moana! Run!"

Moana's triumphant expression deflated like a poorly tied balloon. Dancho's barbed hole engulfed her head, ripped it off her neck and spat it across the club. It flew past Vagalyn, landing on a pool table used more often for posing than pool. The street slug ate Moana's still-standing body in one bite.

"Damn it!" Moana said as she rolled to a halt upside-down at the corner pocket.

The slug slid off stage, viciously biting the heads off drag queens and spitting them out. They rolled around the purple and black checkered tiles like marbles. Headless bodies collapsed in his wake, dresses falling awkwardly to reveal bulge-filled panties.

Moana floated to the mirror ball, joining Vagalyn. "I'm so sorry."

Vagalyn sighed. "Diva, that was a bad move, but I have neither the time nor the equipment to slap you around properly. Now show me your pearly whites."

"What are you going to do?" Moana asked, floating backwards slowly.

"Just show me!"

Moana opened her mouth and bared her

teeth.

"That will do. Follow me."

Vagalyn and Moana soared through the bar, collecting all their fellow severed drag queen heads from bar stools, trash cans, pleather purses and every other corner they had rolled into. As the street slug slowly feasted on their bodies, they hovered near the exit, twenty strong, straightening their wigs and cringing at their predicament.

"What are we going to do, Vagalyn?" one of the queens asked.

"We're going to show that slug who runs the Fireball. Divas, fly!"

In a tight V formation, they looped around the bar, a storm cloud of severed heads. Blood poured from their necks, pooling on the floor. They circled Dancho.

"Divas, chomp!" Vagalyn ordered.

The queens pulled their glossed lips back, chattering like a shack full of novice ice fishermen. The sound of enamel clicking against enamel echoed through the bar.

"Divas, attack!" she ordered.

The drag queens dove at the slug, gnawing into his slimy flesh. Translucent muck ran down their chins. The slug shook them away. In a panic, he screamed, "You don't understand! I… I… I just want to be one of you!"

Vagalyn caught the look of regret on the slug's face. He didn't mean what he said, not at all, and she knew it. His barbs twitched as if hoping to latch onto the desperate attempt to avoid being eaten alive and suck it back into his feeding hole, as if suddenly realizing he had sealed a much more brutal fate. Too late, she thought.

"Divas, stop!" Vagalyn commanded, smirking. "We can't hurt one of our own."

As the drag queens dragged the giant street slug off stage with their teeth, Moana Loser floated to the microphone and announced to the handful of hearty crowd members crawling out from under tables, "I'm afraid we have to cut the show short..."

Vagalyn head-butted Moana away from the microphone once again.

"No we don't. Hold tight for our grand finale!"

***

Ten minutes later, Vagalyn hovered to the stage. "Ladies and lady-ish gentlemen! I have seen a lot of young drag queens take their first awkward steps into the Fireball. They've walked through those doors barely knowing how to put on heels and a wig. I have had the honor of helping them become the most breathtaking of female illusionists.

260

However, I have never met anyone quite like our next performer. I am proud to introduce the Fireball's newest drag queen, the sweet and sour Slurpie Shimmer!"

Dancho the street slug slid onto stage, stirring a mass gasp from the blood-soaked crowd. One of Vagalyn's old sequined ball gowns draped over his lumpy tube of a body. Pus leaked from the gaping wounds where barbed teeth used to be ("Far too masculine," Vagalyn had said. "They will have to go.") and his mouth quivered. A long blonde wig sat atop his head, bangs hiding the makeover the queens had given him – a good thing since his slime-coated surface hadn't allowed the lipstick and blush to take hold, leaving his face looking like a grade school water color painting. He slither-shimmied to the microphone and spread his hole, non-lips moving in a seemingly random pattern, not even coming close to matching the words of the R&B classic blaring from the Fireball's burned out speakers.

With Vagalyn in the lead, the flying drag queen heads circled the slug's wig like a halo. They had lip-synched to "Respect" hundreds of times each, but Vagalyn thought the words tasted better than ever tonight. She wondered how they tasted to Dancho. She made a mental note to ask him. Every

261

night. For the rest of his fabulous life.

Moon Love
By Todd Nelsen

The moon hung there in the night, like it was placed there, for his eyes only. It shown down, casting its light, and was the brightest object in the sky.

His object.

He'd never seen anything so beautiful.

He took a chance, glanced up to it, and said out loud, "I think you're pretty. I wonder if you think I'm pretty, too?"

"I do," she cooed back.

"So you talk, huh?" he asked, leaning forward. He was surprised. Pretty things never talked to him. He never thought the moon would answer.

"Oh, yes. I've had my eye on you for a long, long time. Look! You don't know the half of it, fella!"

The moon's eyes opened, one after another, and batted their lashes, showing him how they twinkled and shined.

They were very pretty eyes, long, seductive lashes.

"Do you like them?" she asked.

263

"I like them very much," he replied. "Sexy. So what's your name?"

The words flowed out of him like a sun-drenched ocean, shot out of the barrel of a gun, like Cary Grant had said them or Humphrey Bogart, just like in the old movies.

Damn, he was good.

But, wait, what was he doing? He was never this courageous, this forward, this cool. He was awkward around the opposite sex. Women felt out of his reach, a bit like the moon did now, come to think of it. If the situation were different, he might offer to buy her a drink. Light clouds drifted overhead, and before she could answer, crossed her face.

She was disappearing behind them.

"Wait!" he pleaded. "Don't go. Tell me your name first!"

But the sky grew darker, as did the night around him, and with it his heart ached. Luna? Diana? He remembered her called this once. It was Greek. Or was it Roman? It didn't matter.

Who was she?

"Please," he said. "I must know."

"Come back tomorrow night," the moon said. "I'll tell you then, you sweet, little man."

And the clouds parted ever so slightly, as the

moon blew him a kiss, and she was gone.

Wildberry Christ
By Ethan C. Evans and Daniel J. Pendergraft

A small watervane bubbled happily, throwing jelly wisps in the air. Glowing below, in a purple orange milk-bubble, Jesus dreams. He soars over tube light cities, using his dream-body's membranous, fluttering sea wings, arcing into the crispening zenith as a gust of machine animals emerge from a cloud-hugging zephyr dock: Jesus' technological steam-city dream. He will show it to Buddha in the morning, on the ship's memory screens, he thinks, lucidly, within the city.

***

Control panels orb'd in Buddha's vision. A brooding Jesus sat in a swivelchair, his body translucent as glass and his mind visibly clouded – a dark swirl in clear gelatin. Buddha was saying, "It's alright that you're unflavored. The people outside the machine will accept you anyway. What man has flavored flesh? It would be a terrifying thing, and besides, your flavor is pectin." Jesus scowled, causing a ripple to spread across his face. "Buddha, I need your help. I need you to create a blueberry." Jesus grinned at his friend, twinkle-eyed. A stern face peeled in raucous laughter. "It can't be done,

266

my friend! Ask the computer," he said through chuckle waves. "I already tried that. The computer only makes processed foods." Jesus sat down with a splish on a jelly stool. "Use your powers of the East. It can't be that hard!" Jesus said in despair. His jelly looked disturbed, roiling weirdly. "I will try, Jesus, but I do not think it can be done. The technological village I lived in possessed a limited range of neural alchemy. No such thing as your request was known."

***

That night, gazing down at town from the Harmonium's windows, Jesus brooded on the nature of his followers-to-be. Perhaps they preferred an unflavored Christ.

In the ancient stories, Jesus' flavor had been that of a salted loaf and musky, Roman wine. He recalls partial memories of waking in bed, covered in crumbs. He would cast aside the blankets and stare in horror at sourdough loaf legs, baguette arms all skinny and crunchy, and a bread bowl belly, internally sopping up its bread bag of wine blood. Truly ghastly, these memories! He is so grateful for the arrival of the biochemical wind fish/prototechnological machine bird; the landing in China, a beaming Buddha who arrived at Jesus' door with microchip in hand. He remembers the

267

man bringing the gel-covered chip into his home and the operation which ensued, the brain implant – the flood of ideas which followed – designs for a life-giving ship – and, best of all, an end to the involuntary transmutations. All the torment they caused Jesus, gone. Forever. Or so he thought.

A new life awaited him aboard the Harmonium, a vast machine, the culmination of his inventions, Jesus' self-created airship. But over time, he began to notice an uncanny change occurring regarding the Harmonium's substance. The many annexes of the ship had become strangely transparent and sweet smelling. The computer confirmed the growing suspicion that the ship was transmuting. Crystallized sugars and a substance called pectin were replacing the metal fabric of the machine. Click, Click, Click. A scroll of text. Jesus scanning with sticky eyes. Pectin: a gelling agent. He dabbed at his eyes, warily. A viscous substance slicked between his fingers. With mounting horror, then calm resignation, and finally a weird sort of love, he observed the jellification of his flesh. Night after night, the skin lightened in tone as well as weight, and eventually, the internal organs became visible. Scanned by the ship's computer, they resembled small airships of themselves, flitting to and fro as they lightened and gelled in the body cavity. In window cubbies of the airship, Jesus would peer into that glass cavity and watch their subaqueous flight. By lifting his t-shirt up and down, he would let their luminescence fill his night-darkened room, watching the twist 'n coil shadows of their motion on the walls, or watching their passive expressions brighten as they weaved around semi-transparent ribs.

A jelly skywhale, hovering close to a bubble-window of the Harmonium, watches Jesus as he projects his memory on a wall, a bright Chinese fragment from the days before the appearance of the wind fish and the Buddha within. He weeps in remembered love, seeing the foxes and pandas coiling around his legs in the image. The camera sweeps in and shows Mary Magdalene. A tear rolls down her cheek as she recalls the ravishing nights in Egypt. She remembers also the day a bedraggled Jesus, having slunk guilt-stricken from the Garden of Gethsemane, took her and himself from a dreadful life and spirited themselves away into the East. Jesus stills his thoughts, and the image fades. He lets a leafy basket carry him through a cool shaft, bypassing the many annexes of the ship. Up to the balcony level, where a door opens on a narrow catwalk and rail, clinging to the exterior of the ship like a halo - A place where the solace of the sky is interrupted only by the rumblings of machinery below. Now, peering into his belly, he sees only clear gelatin. Those playful organs, lost to sight, surely must dance invisibly. "Or perhaps they are dead," thinks Jesus sourly. "Consumed by the jellification process which has made me a Jell-O Savior." Wildberry thoughts tinkled. The Harmonium whispered, "Keep trying, Jesus. The villagers believe in you. They have seen me in the sky, and they know it's a sign of better times to come: an end to the jelly plague. Do not become discouraged." Giggling, "The Jelly has a way of bouncing back."

***

Dials whirled before Jesus' eyes. The control panel was a miniature city of crystal knobs and wrinkled spools. Dry bits of tape spun through noisy reels and fluttered uselessly to the ground. Lights illuminated regions of crystal, and, before he knew it, the computer was there, glowing in the foremost knob. A torrent of info blabbered out. Dismissing with a brusque jab at a button the computer's explanation of 'basket tape mechanisms', Jesus spoke to the knob. "I care nothing for transmutable black strips." The gelatin above his eyebrows scrunched squishily. "I need to know if there is a real food translation unit aboard this ship. It is what humans used to use for nourishment on space voyages." Jesus blinked three times before the computer spoke. Soft sog-pops of his gel lids splished quietly each time. "I think we do. There is another unit. Would you like a pie? This unit is mainly a bakery." "I want a blueberry," Jesus said. "Fantastic! Computation time for blueberry pie is two minutes for the first pie and twelve nanoseconds for successive pies." Control panel lights outlined a surreal smile as gelatin melted into a human face, grinning/dripping magnificently. "No. What I want is the organism blueberry, a fruit. I will attain its flavor." Jesus glared at the gelface, but before the computer could respond, Buddha burst into the room. "There it is!!" pointing to his bellybutton, where a blueberry nestled. Celebration bounded in the Harmonium control room on jelly-spring legs.

Buddha stared quizzically at the blueberry. "We should have the computer analyze it, to be sure," he offered. As they waited for the computer to finish, Jesus turned to Buddha with a question-mark look. Buddha stumbled into speech, "I was simply meditating, listening to my brain bubbles, when a large blue orb invited me on an exciting voyage: an aqua tour, it said." Buddha proceeded to described coral cities and long conversations with slick-limbed sea gods, and when it was over, Jesus was thoroughly astounded, asking, "How long did all of this take?" "About five years," responded Buddha, unphased. "I spent two of those in the home of Orthogontog, laboring as a waterwheel worker in the city of Yukermyst. He taught me the sea vescent tongue, and I later learned the written language and read the many volumes of the Arcresce, in which is described a great, blue orb."

At this point, the computer chirped cheerfully, its analysis complete: one hundred percent organic. Buddha nodded knowingly, continuing his tale. "The Arcresce told me that the orb was a goddess, her name in vescence translating to 'The Sphere of Neptune', and that her locket contained the essence of a sweet berry, a parting gift from her lover, Neptune, when he was forced by Dagon's wrath to go deeper into the sea." Buddha sighed, as if with amorous thoughts drifting in his head. Jesus rolled the berry between gelatin fingers. His eyes, glittering gelpools of wonder. "My task for the next three years, to find this locket and its aquatic owner, took me to the deepest parts of the ocean, where she had wandered in search of her lover, leading me eventually to the trench town of Jlopheluun."

Jesus listened to the tale of the merchant who had swindled Buddha of his only money, the brief but ghastly imprisonment in a place called Xixiphur, from whose hells Buddha remembers only one detached statement: "Xixiphur pools darkly throw vomis wisps into Qaqbar's waiting, satanic mouth." And finally the hint, a whisper in a dark tavern, which led him to the ruins of Inefghilmnop, where he discovered the goddess in a nest of seahorse spittle and finger-like ice tendrils, weeping over Neptune and loosing blue spheres to the sky. "I have found you, blue orb." Buddha's love of the goddess orb spills onto the memory screens. A panorama of coral ruins surround a beautiful, nude woman about whom a faint, spherical outlines shivers. The camera shimmers in close to Buddha's face, in which the goddess sees China and the mechanical creatures, Mary Madgalene as a fox sweeping past Christ, causing his robes to billow as he leans against a tree with a color instrument in his hands. All is captured in the tape image. Both men stand amazed, unable to speak or move. Jelly clouds drift through the night outside the Harmonium, peeping curiously at a play of lights in a high window bank.

***

Jesus smiles messianicly. His eyes waver like a birthday child. He imagines a blueberry gliding gracefully down his esophagus into its stomach core, insinuating itself, spreading blue veins throughout his every limb and giving him flavor, and he imagines his entrance into Town Square, the villagers loving him and marveling at his flesh; And the look on their faces as they become children again with the taste of blueberry Jell-O. What joy he will bring to the humans of the village, what happiness to restore the vitality drained these long years by plague Jell-O, the punishment for mankind in lieu of Christ's sacrifice. And maybe, just maybe, the Father will forgive him for his defection in the Garden of Gethsemane.

***

The clattering, slimbering jelly machine! All the villagers shouted in glee. Hauling netfulls of jelly into squatting pumpkin houses, spilling them to the floor, the villagers rejoice. "What luck the Jell-O Christ has brought us! What a gift, the floating jelly machine!"

The machine has a bumpy black dog-lip drain that gurgles up great streams of blobbed Jell-O. The metal parts of the machine gleam in the sun, and a tangle of tubes disappear up into the sky, up in Heaven where the jelly is brewed in God-sized vats. Nobody actually knows. All they know is that Jell-O Christ saved them from the mind-scrambling plague Jell-O by bringing them the healthy jelly machine, and they will not forget him, living up there inside it, occasionally appearing in long window banks where yellow light spills out at night, but usually hiding from sight, disappearing into the vastness of the machine.

Every morning, they carry the nets and the wind-powered suckers to Village Square and wait for the jelly rain. Often, they are awakened by the first soft thwacks falling from the machine above, glisten-orbs refracting light. "What a joy to wake to sweet jelly trickling into your mouth!" they say. Villagers scatter to inflate nets and watch them fill from the guzzling spigots of wind-powered sucker machines.

***

The jolly avatar sat, buzzing with the Blue of Christ, contemplative and blissful in his introspection. "Amazing!" Buddha thought. "Delicious flesh of a sage's own body!" Though whispered about, haltingly, in dark taverns since antiquity, he had not thought it possible. Now he knows the Berry Christ to truly be the Chosen One, all doubt forever expunged by the joyous fruitsplosion of berry-flavored gelatin streaming out, never ceasing!

Through his weird new psychic Blue Tunnel, Buddha could see, in muffle, many things which were fated to occur. Cringing a bit in his intense focus, he gazed at the neon aura of future fruits – the flavors of Christ's birthright. A Red Thought dominated his vision, with a twinge of Strawberry tickling his imagination. Blinking through the soft tears of revelation's fantasy, he called calmly to his teacher. "My Lord," he began, "in the pristine Blue of Future's tunnel, I have begun to glimpse the delectable destiny of your fruity inheritance. It is lovely beyond belief, though lacking details. I only know a luscious crimson possibility to hang heavy on Fate's Horizon."

Christ, clear-eyed and smiling to his ears, nodded involuntarily, overflowing with the Fruity Spirit. "My friend, my precious One, in you I am much pleased, for that which is to pass has become like the full, juicy orbs on the boughs of the Harmonium. This joy, I bring to all who will eat of my flesh, and to all who do this, I will grant eternal fruit, that their suffering may be consumed. I too have seen the beauteous Red which glistens close to my grasp. I have glimpsed it through your mind, Buddha. Let what is to happen be the glory of my people – the entire world."

In a transcendent moment of pure stillness, Buddha and Christ lock eyes in ultimate knowingness. Intimate, tiny columns of clear gelatin

276

extend from Christ's tender fingertips, mixing in the sharp, moonlit air with the blobs of blue floating from Buddha's brain. "Gloria in Excelsis Deo," they both whisper at exactly the same time, and the plump, glowing fruit of serendipity hovered around them, student and teacher, illuminating eternity with a Chewy Hope and Tangy Grace.

***

The unbearable heat felt as if it could never subside. Farmer Zorly hated this part of his job, shuttling magma junkies back and forth with his smoke-vomiting tractor, Bertha, in the tortuous climate. "Only once a week," he thought. "This Evil Candyland will be the death of me." One of the junkies spit up strawberry drugs in a splash so violent Zorly could hear it inside the cabin. He winced in disapproving annoyance. Where is that Damn Savior they talk about, he wondered. All a bunch of pigwash or would happen one day? Right as he crested the last hill, musing, the Christ sprouted out of one lone cloud in the sky, cumulonimbus jelly spreading downward in a supersonic jetstream. Buddha surfing on the tailwind, he cast his mind forward to close Zorly's perception just in case he looked back. "No need to excite everyone yet. We must acquire the sizzling fruit," he said to himself. The duo touched down, crunching solidly on the sugar sand. Candycane cacti, bizarrely bright and menacing, glimmered in the midday sun. Christ used Buddha's brain like a crystal ball, rubbing his bald head, producing sapphire sparks which sent gumdrop lizards scurrying with a scowl. Buddha shifted uncomfortably, and Christ snapped, "Hold still, almost there!" His eyelids clenched shut, in epic concentration. All at once, the Savior gasped in delight. "I have seen the full vision of the Red's completion. It is not one but Two Perfect Fruits! Unity through Tasty Duality!"

Hours later, his divine enthusiasm had waned. Even a few minutes in this hellish candy desert was enough to drive a mortal mad. The duo had wandered through chocolate quicksand, been pestered by sweet-tart scorpions, pricked by rot-sugar cactus spines, and Buddha had even been impaled briefly by a carnivorous licorice spike. Both were getting a bit testy, feeling less tasty, though Buddha's spirits were secretly very high, as he had acquired some jelly-belly wine from a hidden oasis when Christ was busy. He still put on a good show, though. "All these rancid sweets and still nothing," he fakely sighed. Jell-O Christ nodded sympathetically and bowed his skull with holy, arching eyebrows. The two stopped briefly to

278

celebrate the human tradition of 'taking a rest'. Suddenly, an alcoholic, cerulean orb oozed visibly from Buddha's heart chakra and extended in a beam to a point in the zenith directly above their destination. A weird, guttural moan rose from the disgustingly sweet area. Magma junkies were waiting. Their temple had raped itself before, due to invaders, and never wanted to repeat the experience. This temple was a marvel of infernal madman chemistry. Idiot savant magmaheads ran the place with wilted fertility's smug despair. "Please welcome yourself to the citric, blasphemous underground Lava Church," said no one, but it was true.

***

The denizens of the lava church were reading the scary parts of the Bible when Jesus and Buddha walked in. Someone mentioned Dagon and vomited, screaming, into the air. "Moresheth Gath!" shouted a pew of tentacles. "A mournful cry from the Fish Gate, a wailing from the Second Quarter," murmured a hooded creature before the congregation. On the altar, Asthmixus the Princely Alchemist brewed a nauseous tonic, his pink tentacles writhing in perverted satisfaction. Buddha gazed into the alchemist's cauldron, eyeball-less faces floating back at him. Asthmixus' head then

279

swallows itself, reappearing bloodily from his stomach. "You coward! Destroy me!" He lets his body enter spikes on the floor and dies, smiling through his stomach. Buddha continues to gaze into the cauldron. His vision has shown him this place. The Strawberry must be inside one of the faces. With swift eviscerations, he shreds several of them into bloody lumps, but through the filter of his fingers, no Strawberry emerges from the blood. The last face has a brain tumor. Ripping into the succulent, a gory strawberry appears, covered in cancerous dendrites. Two cherry eyes peer out of the strawberry's flesh.

***

Outside the church, a winged creature is waiting. "You will want Blackberry as well, I suppose," it clicked through ropey vocal chords. Branded in the scales of its flank were the words 'Halloween Realm'. Wordlessly, Buddha slumped onto its back. Jesus did the same, gazing back at the church just in time to see an eyeball ocean before the beast rose into the air.

The creature carried them high above an orange world of giant pumpkins, their destination a mountaintop elevator shaft. Gazing drunkenly at the barren landscape, thousands of feet below, Buddha clumsily clutched the creature's scales. Christ peered alertly ahead through a wobbling, jelly periscope. He could just discern a mountain peak in the all-surrounding mists ahead. As the creature flew toward this destination, Christ pointed out the fire-beacon of the elevator to Buddha, who nodded meekly with a fleshy smile when his friend spoke, not hearing the words. Buddha was exhausted and drunk from slurping too much blueberry Jell-O.

Alighting with a talon scratch on the rocky summit, the two men stepped down from the beast and affectionately patted its nightmare scales before heading toward the metallic, glowing cage that was Night-Time Airshaft, the Halloween 'Vator. Without fear, they approached a skeleton bellboy. A cap of flame surrounded a green skull-head, and a jewel-encrusted trident flowed like liquid in the boy's hand. Purple, wet porridge dribbled from his mouth as he ratcheted a large, blood-dripping crankshaft housed in the solid rock. A quite rumble began as the elevator rose from sludgy depths. Jesus fed Jell-O to Buddha from his belly while they waited. The bellboy slurped quietly from a melted jelly-pool at Jesus' feet and looked up eerily when the pool ran dry, crouching and loosing purple porridge lump-spheres in the wind. At length, the cage rattled into place, and the bellboy slid aside a latticed door, cradling in his small, skeleton fingers a parting gift of blueberry Jell-O.

***

Trailing globs of sticky purple porridge, Buddha plodded nervously out of the elevator's exit tunnel to face the weird, desolate nighttime. Christ led the way, unafraid with eyes peeling the land. Buddha tripped on a brown, spiky tentacle vine, cutting his big toe with a timid yelp before Christ, with an impatient flick of his wrist, sent some blueberry Jell-O to bandage his wound. "We must remain hidden, Buddha. This is not like the other places we have been," he whispers, without looking back. Dazed and buzzing with confusion, his protégé mumbled something incomprehensible under his breath in reply. Yellow-Red-Blue laser-like strands etched tracers in his vision, and he could no longer think or speak in a linear fashion. Christ knew this, and with a sigh extended a Jell-O bubble back on a crystal tether to float Buddha along for a bit while he took a nap to sober up. "At least until I find the fabled Berry of Blackness," Christ thought in frustration. Passing invisible spiders which scurried over dead, broken limbs of ancient trees, he caught a chill of mystery from the land. The moon smirked its evil, its face crowned by a sickly yellow-orange halo of mist and fog. The fruity hero let the Spirit guide his movements. He had seen the

282

dilapidated, abandoned house in Buddha's drugthoughts, knew the feel of it, smell of it; yet it was not so easy to find. Here, he knew, would be the mythical Blackberry, on vine grown of past human's sinister urge. Just then his foot hit a rotten section of fallen picket fence. A bunch of mantis-flies oozed out of it, carrying their slimy maggot larvae. His face lit up. He was quite near the destination.

Leaving the snoring, pathetic Buddha outside the crumbling gate, Christ walked in succulent confidence, with a hint of arrogance, up the winding path to the dark house's front door. A magnetic urge made him bang in violence on the door twelve times. The rage that quickly flashed away left him quite uneasy. Instantly, a ghastly, translucent skeleton-hand reached through the solid door and sucked him in. It tickled as all his bones broke, and the firmament above crackled in despair of his torture. In his newfound shackles, but still able to move, Christ hummed 'The Itsy Bitsy Spider' piously with punctured lungs to soothe his nerves. Concentrating, he used a radiant blast of Red Jelly to melt the skeleton hand while Blue welled up inside him, easily mending his organs. Glancing about, Christ used neon Yello-Jell-O blobs to illuminate the room of his deliverance. It was a cramped prison chamber with crusty, dried bloodstreaks across the dull, granite floor. Entire skeletons as well as bashed bone pieces lay crackled.

***

Outside, a boiling patch of red pumpkin guts. Crinkled corrosion glistens within half-melted jack-o'-lantern faces. Looking down from the Jell-O bubble, Buddha sees his own face frown and melt thickly on a pumpkin in sick, green light. Pale grubs gribble in fermented soup around a red candle inside. Buddha now watches a braincase clack open from above, raining strings down in an unruffling, squirming wire mass. The strings stretch into wing outlines and fill with membrane; brain creature soaring over red environment, its tail trailing below in the pumpkin corrosion, slurping glop through tubes that spiral into a pinched mouth. "This is an evil place," mutters Buddha. Flickering, colorful gel embraces him. Buddha smiles at his friend through dense hallucination, complex intricacies on Jesus' face. "The gelatin body feels warmer than usual," thought Buddha as shift patterns interlocked and rippled together on soft, edible arms. He delicately nipped a morsel of Jesus' shoulder, rolling the multi-flavored gob over his tongue and taking comfort in its neural effect. With a flash of realization, Blackberry Flavor reached his brain.

284

"Oh my, you did it," he wheezed as the tell-tale Black threads sinew'd through bluish red Jell-O. Jesus smiled, and they hugged each other through Halloween's fantastic horror.

***

"The entire planet is covered in ocean, and every square inch of that ocean is covered by this ship," the cyborg captain said to Jesus. Ignoring the comment, Jesus said, "We are looking for a fruit called the Amla. Its color is grayish purple, and it is said to be hard as a rock, only softening when held in the mouth, and then only after several minutes. Have you heard of it?" Jesus stared at gears rotating on the man's face. "This is the purple world, is it not?" Steam hissed out between the gears. "How odd," thought Jesus, "a steam-powered brain?" "I've already told you," said the cyborg, "there is no land, so how is this 'Amla' fruit to have grown? We have no record of it in our ecologies. It is purely fictitious. Yes, I've heard of it, but it is of no account. Your search is entirely futile." Impatience registered as pulleys carrying small baskets of hot, red rocks up and down on scaffolds of the man's face and neck. He continued, "This is indeed the purple world, but the term derives from the color of our skies, not some mythical fruit," he said through drifts of steam. Jesus persisted, "Perhaps there is a courtyard somewhere, a break in the ship where a circle of ocean is allowed to see the light of day. Could not a patch of land arise in such a place and grow fruit from seeds cast by the purple sky?" Jesus questioned the steam-face with a pleading look. "If such a place existed, perhaps. But stories are stories, and the tales of hatched galleries, where mutinous engineers have cleaved through the ship, even the smoldering engine decks, must necessarily be false. No such feat is possible. Those decks are hotter than the surface of the Nearstar and the lower hull a mile thick."

Jesus conceded to the sailor's notion, but he knew better, for in one of Buddha's transcendental visions, he had seen the Amla in some multi-leveled, black gallery; Balconies rising miles above a dark pool, the center of which sprouted a small mound of mud and a hairy stalk rising miles to the light where a panorama of smokestacks surrounded a small, rock-like purple fruit. Having seen the fruit, they had queried the computer aboard the Harmonium and discovered the planet to which the vision belonged, a slave world called Nautylliis, an ocean planet where slave ships had coalesced to form a planet-girdling vessel, covering the whole of the ocean with black metal.

***

Entering the fringes of a hundred-square-mile bazaar, Jesus begins the search for info, snarking purple merchants for lore, buying drinks and watching them disappear into bearded mouths.

Seapool water emotions for Buddha. He floats inside a bubble resembling a backpack that Jesus carries through the bazaar. Reclining, he imagines visible cartoon thought-bubbles containing nonreal, colorful shape symbols of language – the Father's pure knowledge, wallowing in a psychedelic tube bath. In his revelation, Jesus/Buddha funneling Heavenly understanding in words/colors/feelings. God changed the gender. Now Buddha/Jesus felt the reality of female complexity. The presence of a womb discussing a metaphor of space with a black fruit, insidiously ripe, the emotions of a stately woman echoing in annoying perpetuity. God flicked the gender switch again, and the duo writhed in experiential understanding of crude human heterosexuality. Buddha knew Christ was sterilized then, androgynous and chaste. His unconscious dignity shone a light on this fact, and Christ's omniscience blushed. Temptation had been squashed by the Father's sexual control machine. Sweaty and heaving in the bubble.

Jesus is talking to a rug merchant over

foamy ale and wondering what the hubbub in his backpack is about. Buddha's hallucinatory story plot laughing itself to death in the timeless, transcendent hole of his consciousness' opposite: the dark matter of the universe spread diffuse and sinister though invisible. This Yin/Yang dissociation snapped the Indian sage back to fleshy existence. His eye crust broke itself open while the nose squeezed bloodily. Staring bloodshot ahead while sitting up, Buddha still slept, in a layer of dream upon dream.

***

Like a placental drain, Buddha dripped out of the backpack onto a metal balcony. His echoing eyes brain-stemmed a true perception up to two exhausted occipital lobes: A circular space descending into purplish blackness and a flowering creature draining into the air, rainbow sinews bursting in sliced designs. Smokestacks extended infinitely in every direction over a dark, metal landscape, broken only by the pit over which the balcony dangled. The smoke formed a writhe-pattern on the sky. The sinew beast melted out of the smoke into a Blue Christ's waiting body on the balcony. He smiled pleasantly through his sinews, rainbow pulsing on his face. Blue Christ added lime to his flavor, turning turquoise as Buddha danced

288

against the rail. Next came red, and black and purple, cascading into a blender mix. "Sing praises to the highest King of Kings, ecstatic union of tingling tastes!" bellowed the Wildberry Jell-O of Christ's bouncy abdomen in a juicy squeam. Lifting Buddha onto the metal landscape, they walked to a place where the Harmonium was docked, climbed the thousand metal rungs of a towering smokestack, and slid down a branching jelly chute, disappearing into vast jelly compartments of the machine.

Toy Soldiers
By Jan Maszczyszyn

The game board was spread out over half the room. The ceiling above was glazed and the place was constantly bathed in sunlight. Sunbeams were darting around metal spires and dancing with the shadows of mock castles and fortresses. One of the board's corners was darkened by an artificial forest. As a matter of fact the forest had some expansion software built in, but this only allowed for a tiny growth of two millimetres per annum. George unwrapped the new parcel containing soldiers. What a bargain it was. He had to pester his dad for more than an hour before getting him to make the purchase. A massive two hundred and fifty six megabytes of RAM in special thermoplastic. The previous set had only 32 megs. Usually the soldiers were in fighting positions. Charging horseman, line gunners, snipers, and a large, goodish selection of tightly gripped small arms. However two soldiers had the disease. That's what he called a toy's stubborn behaviour regarding its designated aim, or, put simply, its refusal to carry out an order. He was especially pissed off by one wearing a blue beret. When it got to a fight its gun would twist. Or it

290

would pretend to have defective arms. Within a quarter of an hour it would assume a sitting posture with its head on its knees, a position especially hated by George. A real disaster.

In front of the other soldiers he feigned that he had lost it. They had been scrutinizing his every gesture ever since he ran a tank over an activist from the War Opposition Movement. Following that incident most of the soldiers refused to obey him for quite a while.

He felt justified, for he used wild west characters as the civilian population, patriotic farmers helping the army in one of the Second World War battles. The figurines did not want to take up fighting postures. A typical one had spread out thighs, pretending to be waiting for a horse. He used to delete those. So he lost a number of teams before he learnt to proceed properly with his soldiers. Such things had to be done discretely. Anyway, in the service manual the manufacturer recommended checking the toys' fighting suitability. Peace Movements often infected production programmes with functional viruses. Before he started to play he would line them up to command and verify the degree of execution of his orders. Insubordination was initially punished by removal to the second line. Generals were liquidated. He didn't approve of any boss in a team apart from himself.

"George, lunch is ready." Dear mom's voice reached him along with an express package from MacXiao, an unexceptional set of dumplings and pancakes. The cupboard in the wall got closed leaving behind a small suspended table steaming with aroma.

"Stupid bitch," he hissed through his teeth. Daddy was always saying that. Gobbling up office overtime till the cunt lost sight of calendar dates. She forgot his sixth birthday! Ever since sleep was no longer needed people have become work-crazy.

He flipped indifferently through the pancakes, selected the best cooked, pushed a large slice into his mouth and while chomping glanced at the board. A nervous silence was hovering over it. They were all waiting for this son of a bitch in the blue beret.

"So what? Let them wait. Stir'em up a bit." He was wandering why the new bunch was lacking a general. Must look up the manual. Maybe the general is disguised as an ordinary private?

There must be an explanation somewhere. He wondered if they had any personal files? The last set had some. He had good fun reading the sergeant's CV. Since then the sergeant was the apple of his eye. Naturally, the toys could not influence the file's content, but who knows, now, with all those functional viruses?

The soldiers from the new bunch spread out on the board were looking quite good. Fierce, hateful faces were turned toward the enemy fortress walls. Some five hundred of them. It was claimed on the packaging that they were more obedient to voice commands than the previous models. Simple commands: attack, stop, present arms, aim, fire; but it sometimes occurred that the group had to be encouraged, inflamed for the fight. That's precisely what happened to George this time. The new army, although without a general, had a patriotic attitude to colours inserted in them. They would not change their North Blue into South Green. In the fortresses of the South the crew was missing. George did not want to pester father again and waste time on pleas for an additional set of Greens when such a ripping war was awaiting him. He fastened his eyes upon the fortress walls and immersed himself in thought. His freckled face was suddenly brightened by a smile. He knew what he'd do. In the furthest recesses of the garage there lay an old, unused cloner. It reminded him of a microwave. His granddad used it for copying old spares for his car. Who knows, maybe it would work? He grabbed a handful of his best Green solders and went down to the garage.

With his small child's fingers he wiped a layer of dust off the machine. Slowly putting together letters into words he read the French language instructions. He opened the source container and switched on the copying programme. Something started to hum followed by steady ticking. He looked inside. On the spinning disk feet started to emerge, then legs, finally bodies of hundreds of soldiers.

It will take a while, he thought.

He reached into trousers pocket and pulled out that scoundrel in the blue beret. The scoundrel was still goading him with that haughty glare. It even dared to break its gun. It didn't even look like a paramedic any more. It was a miserable corpse, a stoker from a steam destroyer from 1901. Carefully he placed it on the table tennis board and reached into the other pocket where he had hidden father's laser point indicator. In spite of the fact that daddy had already spent a month looking for it, he had not revealed his possession of this sought-after object. There are plenty of ordinary indicators in stores. But this one was brilliant. It also served as a grill lighter, and if you turned the power knob off the scale you could burn a hole in the arse of the neighbour's dog.

George managed to avoid ever being caught at it. Now he placed the indicator's nozzle just under the blue beret of the victim. He saw the stony face and cold eyes. Well, at least it's capable of doing that, of dying like a man. The laser beam melted the soldier's head in a fraction of a second. The stench of burned plastic filled the air while the toy's legs and hands splayed outwards frog-like. You never knew why they always assumed such a saintly posture when deprived of their heads.

George hid the still warm corpse into his trouser pocket. On seeing the table board all coated in soot he muttered a swear word under his breath. It couldn't even be wiped off with a rug. He was going to cop it for sure; who else would have done it except a six year old boy?

He turned to the cloner and stopped, amazed. Inside, just next to the glass pane there stood a bunch of green soldiers, all gazing at him with helmets and guns in their lowered hands. All with sad faces as if they had just witnessed a horrible, covert execution. He felt a cold shiver run from the back of his neck right down his spine. He quickly collected them and carried them to the board, where all the others were waiting in a state of utmost readiness.

Even without his say so, the Greens commenced offensive actions. Once again the question arose: Where is the general? Who was in command of such a splendidly executed operation? The unit all of its own conquered the most remote fortifications and in a proper manner had taken their crews into captivity. All this happened without a single shot being fired. It was too much for George. From that moment on he did not want the Blues to win. He pulled out the most up-to-date equipment and manned it with Greens. He also started noticing weird movements in the Greens' topmost fortress. The soldiers were blanching, their weapons thrown to the ground, and no, it was not an accident! It was a group of some twenty soldiers, all of them originating from the cloner. Also in the middle castle the same symptom occurred. The soldiers were abandoning their weapons en masse. It was an excellently organized Peace Movement, a curse for any war game.

George gulped nervously. His hands trembled. He should have been able to prevent the Blues from winning the war but they moved too fast. They were always one tactical move ahead. Always outpacing his interventions.

Once again he looked closely at the army packaging.

296

"Yes, from twelve years upwards..." he read. Now he knew why he had difficulties establishing proper relations with new soldiers. The general has to be the one who proves himself in battle. Now he wanted the victory of the Greens more than ever. He decided to make a desperate move to spur the Greens into battle.

"Fighters of the South! I summon you! You must go on fighting and winning!" He started his silent speech just above the board. His voice rose above the turrets and walls of the South, and the Greens were slowly turning their heads in his direction. But their eyes remained expressionless, colourless, empty. He had to stir their plastic souls.

"For the sake of your right to self-determination, for the sake of freedom. The enemy has committed atrocious mass murders." Here he reached for his key evidence in the form of a huge ice cream pack. He lifted the cover and onto the main town square spilled out the carcasses of headless solders, farmers, and armless Indians. All the corpses were splayed frog-like. They reeked of burning. He noticed that some Greens were reaching back for their weapons while others lost their servile pallor. Most seemed convinced. A small restive group were allocated to sanitary services and he then ordered the Blues to start the bombing

297

campaign. They reluctantly obeyed. Some mooned him, literally...he had never before been confronted by the insulting naked arse of a soldier.

George had had enough. He would have kicked the toys if he wasn't still searching for that damn general. The entire line of the Greens' tanks was unable to overcome a small Blues' unit at the farthest North. What a shame! Their last bomber had been shot down. He hadn't even noticed who and when they had sprayed him, a small boy, with some hideous sperm straight into his open mouth!

With tearful eyes he again stared into the manual. The war was on, and there was an escalation of events over which he was losing control. It was caused by incompatible movement-control software. The clones were alright, capable of quickly turning into a shooting stand the same as the best Wild West fast shooting bandits, blazing with rapid fire. As for the rest, they were already lying defeated before having fired the first shot. But where the hell did the minute holes in the victims foreheads come from? Usually soldiers fell down, only pretending to be dead. It started to get dark. The Blues were digging something in the woods at the board's edge. George suddenly felt weak, maybe because of that escalating toy's sperm disease, maybe he had become bored by the game. During the night he would usually hear military songs, chiming discretely over the battlefield. Today, he heard only a rhythmic clatter, shuffling and scraping. Someone was chanting anti-war slogans. Someone else sung the love songs. He immediately felt his baby teeth grinding together, nerves, nerves... He lay down and fell heavy, fell asleep on the floor.

His open mouth was crowded with baby soldiers. Thousands more and more. They crawled away as the body turned into a plastic cocoon and slowly disappeared.

Body of potential murderer.

The Pitfalls of Modern Gardening
By G. Arthur Brown

Ryan's wife Amiga had gone to visit his dead wife Rachel's parents in Syracuse. His first wife had been an only daughter, and her parents really liked Ryan, so he felt obligated to send his new wife while he stayed home to take care of a few domestic issues.

The yard of Ryan's home had become an uncontrolled wilderness. That's not much of an exaggeration. Amiga blamed Ryan, citing that he was both a man and a lawn care specialist, and so all outdoorsy crafts fell to him by right and by common sense. Amiga's air allergy required that she remain indoors in tightly sealed chambers as much as possible. Ryan was not unreasonable enough to expect her to do any yard work. He was, however, unreasonable enough to buy a large amount of property and let the yard go to brambly, weedy hell. His moustache was perfectly sculpted and it took a lot of time to keep it that way. This yard situation had come to a head when he and Amiga noticed garden gnomes hosting open mic nights in a makeshift nightclub constructed of brushwood, inviting all sorts of nuisance animals to fraternize there in the undergrowth.

This seemed as good a place to start as any. Ryan asked the bouncer gnome if he could enter and speak with the proprietor. He explained quite reasonably that his back yard was no place for a night club, even one for very small patrons, and he really did not care for all the loitering foxes, possums and raccoons, which could be carrying that new infection SuperRabies that you hear about on TV all the time.

The bouncer looked him up and down. "Bigot," he said, then did a roundhouse kick that connected with Ryan's shin. It hurt a lot, but Ryan couldn't admit that, though he realized he would need some assistance handling the gnomes. Clearing out the nightclub would have to wait.

There was also the garage. It was a nice, two-car, detached garage like he'd always wanted. Only now it was overgrown with plastic ivy. He took his string trimmer to the fake plants, but it was no use. They were just too tough. He regretted throwing his old Christmas garlands into the backyard, especially when he had regular trash pickup service.

"It would have been very easy to put the old garlands in a garbage can," he said to himself. Instead, he'd allowed them to take root and make his dream garage unusable. He was pretty sure he had a Maserati in there.

Then there was the matter of his vegetable garden. He didn't know if any plants had come up this season because he could not find where the garden was. He did locate some ketchup seed scattered near a large area of brush, so he knew he was getting close. But he wasn't up to the task of hacking through bracken and brambles just to see if his broccoli rabe was salvageable.

Disappointed in himself, Ryan surveyed his yard with dismay and made the only decision a sane man could make: he went inside and fixed himself a strong drink.

He quickly downed a shot of Phoenix Piss, a concentrated derivative of fermented Marmite. The flavor was like the piss of a mythical bird, and it would have to be the piss of a mythical bird because regular birds don't piss. He gasped and then gagged. "It's better than it tastes," he said, quoting the ad slogan.

As Ryan wiped some spittle from his bottom lip, he heard a knock on the side door. He walked up to the door and tried to see out, which was really easy because the door was mostly glass. Outside stood Lindsay, his pregnant, twenty-something neighbor. Her breasts sagged and pendulated, unlike most pregnant breasts Ryan had observed, which were perky and tumescent.

"Hi, Lindsay. What do you want?" he asked through the door.

"Open the door, silly. I need to talk to you about something."

He wasn't sure it was good idea, but let her in anyway.

"Those budgies are at it again," she said. Ryan had heard Lindsay complain about her pet birds before. She was convinced they were gaslighting her. Whenever Ryan had gone over to her house to check on them, they always seemed perfectly normal. "Of course! That's what they want you to think," she'd say.

"Guess what they can do now? They learned to do the beep that my phone makes when I have a text message. I'm running around checking my phone all day. It's making me crazy! I can't handle this while being nine and a half months pregnant."

"Whoa, you must be ready to pop."

"Yeah, probably. I keep having these contraction thingees. And it's driving me nuts! I can't take it anymore." She held her belly and huffed.

"Maybe you should go to the hospital."

"No!" she cried, grabbing him by his shirt.

303

"That's just what they want."

"I don't know what you expect me to do about your birds, Lindsay," Ryan said, pushing her away.

"One budgie, their leader, can whistle the Theme from Andy Griffith all night long. I never sleep, Ryan. Don't you understand? I never sleep."

"Yeah, that sucks. But what do you want me to do about it?"

"Let me sleep in your bed," she said with a wince that pretended to be a smile.

Amiga would not like the idea of Ryan letting a younger woman into their bed, even if she was an extremely pregnant woman who looked like she was about to give birth to a fully grown person. Ryan firmly but diplomatically stated, "How about I let you take a nap on my couch?"

"Marvelous," Lindsay said and rolled her eyes. She headed for the living room, fiddling with her bra.

"What are you doing?"

"I'm not sleeping in this bra. It's killing my pendulous breasts." She continued to waddle away, leaving Ryan to consider his game plan.

He dragged out an old yellow pages and flipped to the lawn care section. Though he himself was a lawn care specialist, he certainly couldn't turn to any of his employees for help on his own lawn. That would be seen as weakness. At any moment, a younger, stronger lawn care specialist might decide to tear out his throat. He had to turn to strangers.

He picked a number from the lawn care list at random and dialed it on his cell phone.

"Uh, hello?" said the voice of an old man.

"Hi," Ryan said. "I need to hire a mechanical assistant to help me wrangle the boscage that is my backyard."

"Huh? Boscage? You should probably call the refuse collectors."

"I mean to say that my yard is quite out of control."

"A'right. What model you want sent out?"

"Something that can chop wood."

"Chop wood? That does sound pretty out of control. You're gonna need a Tin Man, but I gotta tell you, I can't get one out to you before Thursday."

"I need something today."

"All I can do today is an Aluminum Man. He's not as tough, but he's all I got."

"Well, if he's all you've got, then send him as soon as you can." Ryan gave the man his address.

"Okay, he'll be over in an hour. And, before you go... What are you more scared of: a monster or a robot?"

305

"What kinds?"

"Just in general. Overall."

"Evil robots are pretty scary, but there are some truly terrifying monsters."

"Okay, monster it is. Thanks for calling Bobby Billy's Lawn Firm."

The idea of an Aluminum man to assist him did not thrill Ryan. But he hadn't seen one since he was a kid. Maybe they weren't as uncool and stupid as he remembered. In the meantime, he needed to take a crap.

Ryan passed the couch on his way to the bathroom, noticing that Lindsay was tucked up under an afghan, all her clothes in a heap on the floor. He prayed that no other nosy neighbor would peep in and misinterpret the scene. If Amiga got word Lindsay was naked in their home, he'd never hear the end of it.

About twelve minutes passed with him on the toilet. The details of this event are not worth reporting. He stood and flushed and generally felt better about himself because he had set his mind to crapping and that's what he had done—crapped.

As he exited, he saw that his couch was now empty, except for a rumpled afghan. He turned to look at the floor, hoping there was not still a pile of garments there. His hopes were dashed like sixty

306

meters at an elementary school field day.

Then he heard the scream. Somewhere between blood-curdling and spine-chilling, the scream impressed him. It was a really well done scream, if conveying utter horror was the goal of the screamer, which, he assumed, it was.

Entering the kitchen, he first saw Lindsay's naked rear end jiggling in terror. She whimpered something that was meant to be words. When he got close enough to see over her shoulder, he noticed a bloody lump of fur on the floor. A dead cat, nearly decapitated.

"Someone killed your poor cat," Lindsay said, tremulously.

Ryan tried not to look at her breasts or crotch, but her naked form was so huge he was unsuccessful in his attempts. "We, uh, don't have a cat."

"Who would do this? Who would kill this cat and put it in your kitchen?"

"I have no idea," he said, wondering what to do with the carcass on his floor.

"Ah, I can't look!" She threw herself against him, pressing her head into his shoulder. Her pendulous breasts bounced against his body as she sobbed.

"I think you might feel better if you put

307

some clothes on," he suggested. But he knew it was too late. His clothes were already stained with her nudity and would have to be burned. He would just tell Amiga they got ruined as he battled brush in the yard. But if she were ever to glimpse this shirt, she would see that distinctive imprints of pendulous breasts.

"I'm sorry I'm naked! I can't sleep with clothes on!" she wailed. Ryan had heard that pregnant women were very hormonal, which could result in loud declarative statements.

He patted her on the head like a young child. "There, there," he said.

A phone rang. This was strange, because it sounded like the house phone, but the house phone had died last week. He just hadn't had a chance to bury it yet. To be sure, he checked his cell phone. But it wasn't the cell ringing.

"Aren't you going to get that?" Lindsay asked him.

"Um… phone is dead." But he was already walking toward the wall mounted phone next to the fridge. It was ringing—rather, a faint mirage of the phone was ringing, vibrating slightly outside the hard lines of his dead phone. "It's the phone's ghost." He snatched the phantom receiver and pressed it to his ear.

308

"Hello, Mr. Jajko," said a squeaky, mechanical voice.

"Hello? Who is this?"

"Uh…." There was a clicking sound and then a growly, deep monster voice began to speak, "Did you find your present?"

"What are you talking about? Who is this?"

"Did you find your dead cat?"

"No, I found a dead cat. I don't have a cat."

"Um… what do you mean you don't have a cat? You don't like cats?"

"I like them okay."

"Are you a dog person?"

"No, not really."

"Then why don't you have a cat?"

"I'm allergic, all right! What is it to you?"

"Nothing, nothing. If you are allergic, I guess I understand. But none the less—you found the dead cat. In your kitchen?"

"Yes, I'm looking at its bloody corpse right now."

"And doesn't that scare you? Don't you want to know how it got there?"

"I'm confused why someone else's dead cat is in my kitchen. And yeah, I'm a little disturbed by it. But what is it to you? Did you put it here? Who is this?"

"Questions, questions, questions, Mr. Jajko. Why so many questions? Don't you know who I am?"

"No, I don't know who the hell you are. That's why I asked you."

"Bad things are going to happen to you, Mr. Jajko. If you can't solve the riddle."

"Look, first off, I don't find you very funny."

"I am funny! I am God here!"

"Just tell me what the hell is going on!"

"Okay, okay," the demonic voice intoned. "Have you ever tried washing a cat in distilled water? You do that a coupla times a month and it is supposed to cut way down on the allergies. It's the saliva that you are actually allergic to and if you wash it off—"

"What the fuck are you talking about?"

"Some people just don't know how to handle cats, and it pisses me off."

"Well, evidently you just killed a random cat for no damn reason, broke into my house and messed my kitchen floor up! What kind of morality lesson are you going to give me, kitty killer?"

"Kitty killer? Jesus, that's harsh, man. I think you've got me all wrong."

"Then tell me what the fuck you are doing or

310

I'm calling the cops!"

"Um, never mind. I'll call back later. Keep this line open." Click.

"What was all that about?" Lindsay said. She massaged her left tit.

"I have no idea. Do you have to do that in front of me?"

"My boobs hurt! They are getting really swollen. I can't help it! I'm ten months pregnant." She stormed into the living room.

He thought the dead cat looked like Old Man Harkins' tabby, Noodle Pie. It wasn't rare that Ryan caught Noodle Pie rooting around in his garbage. Harkins was an old-school farm type—probably didn't feed the cat regularly. There was no way Ryan was going to tell the man his little tabby friend was deceased, a victim of felicide. Ryan tossed the cat in a tall kitchen trash bag, poured some bleach on the floor and grabbed his mop. The blood was still fresh, so cleanup was relatively easy. As he mopped, he wondered if he was in danger. Someone, even if it wasn't the creepy monster-man who had called him on the ghost phone, had snuck into his home and left a very morbid message for him.

He popped outside to toss the bag of cat in the trash can and noticed that there was a shiny,

311

metallic figure walking down the road. It had to be the Aluminum Man. At the rate he was going, he would be there in several minutes. Ryan started to forget all about the cat, setting his mind back to important matters like clipping weeds and chasing away gnomish businesses.

Then he heard another scream. This one was a scream of pain, though, and not as well done as the previous scream. He ran to the living room.

"It's time! I'm giving birth!" Lindsay yelled from the floor. The carpet was already smeared with blood and bodily waste. "Finally, after ten and a half months, it's coming out! It's okay, though. I took Lamaze." She alternately huffed, puffed and grunted.

"Don't you need, like, a partner or something for that?"

"Not if you are good at it! Ahhhhhh!" Sweat beaded on her forehead as she fell into a regular breathing pattern. A moment of Zen came over her.

He watched in awe. She was very good at it.

"I have a dream for this baby. I will enter her into a contest," she said calmly. "I want her to take second place—2nd Best Baby. Some people tell me, don't go for 2nd Best Baby, but I say first place has too many responsibilities heaped on. So no—only second best for my baby."

"That makes sense, I guess," Ryan said, only having half-heard her blather.

There was a clank at the door.

"Come in!" Ryan called, trying not to panic. He wished that he knew Lamaze.

A clunking sound preceded the appearance of a man constructed of glinting, flimsy metal. His body looked like an old Franklin stove and the top of his head looked like a funnel. He carried a hatchet and his mouth was a smiling bear trap.

"I am the Aluminum Man sent to aid you with your gardening needs. You may call me Pinkerton." His voice was even and pleasant. He looked from Ryan down to Lindsay. "This does not look like a gardening concern."

"Do you know anything about birthing babies?" Ryan asked him.

"Truth to tell, that is what the Aluminum Men were designed for."

Lindsay was still in her zone, but it was clear to Ryan that she struggled.

"Something is wrong," said Pinkerton. "I will have a look." He got on his knees, set down his hatchet and peered into the birth canal. "There is a big problem here. I don't know if I can help her."

"What? What do you mean?" Ryan said.

"It is an irregular pregnancy."

313

"Yes, she said she was over ten months along."

"She is much farther along than that," said Pinkerton, standing and stepping back.

Blood poured forth from her vagina as a large hand emerged. Lindsay's face contorted and a shriek broke forth from her throat.

"What's going on?" Ryan shouted.

"She's dying," Pinkerton said.

The creepily large hand pawed around, tearing at its mother's body. Gradually another hand slithered out, and the two hands began to part the birth canal. Lindsay stopped screaming and just lay there, dazed, drifting off into nothing.

A head emerged. Long, bloody hair covered the face, which looked like an elderly version of Lindsay. The old baby made a sound that was somewhere between a dog growl and the buzzing of an insect. Unlike its naked mother, the newborn wore an old lady nightgown. With half the torso emerged, the old baby began to bite into its mother's legs, eating her while she was still partially alive.

"Is this normal?" asked Ryan.

"It is normal for old babies," Pinkerton said, leaning down to pick up his hatchet. "But old babies are not normal. In fact, they are abominations. I will have to cut this one open."

314

The old baby was now fully born. It squatted in a spider-like stance and skittered, legs stepping over shoulders, arms slithering forward. Ryan backed away as Pinkerton stalwartly stood his ground. The Aluminum Man raised his hatchet. The old baby turned to consume the rest of its dying mother, who looked like a half-deflated pool toy. The blade came down on the crooked back. A low, demonic groan emanated from the deep wound stretching across most of the torso. Strangely, there was no blood. But after Pinkerton pulled the weapon back, the body continued to split down the middle, breaking into nearly perfect halves.

"It is doubtful the old baby will survive this," Pinkerton said to Ryan, who simply stood and stared.

"Are you all right, Mr. Jajko?" the Aluminum Man asked.

"Yeah, it's just that I used to date this girl who had a fetish about being cut in half. It always seemed so impossible."

"It is not easy," Pinkerton admitted, "but it can be done."

Lindsay was now still, no signs of life. The old baby lay split in half atop its mother's corpse. It was a mess. The bodies would not fit in a tall kitchen trash bag.

315

"You figured out the riddle yet, Mr. Jajko?" said a deep, eerie monster voice that seemed to originate within the dead baby.

The remains wriggled, then a small hole was punched in the old baby's back by a gray feline paw. A tabby cat shot out, sending bits and pieces of dead old baby spray all over Pinkerton's face and into Ryan's gaping mouth. The dead flesh tasted of mothballs and woolen mittens. The cat landed on all fours at Ryan's feet and looked up, as if expecting to be fed.

"Noodle Pie? But if you are here, who is in my trash can?"

"Why don't you go have a look?" said the cat in its monstrous voice.

"I don't understand...."

"Mr. Jajko, collect yourself and go look in the trash."

Ryan walked slowly, zombie-like, even sticking his arms out in front in case he tripped and fell over. He felt light headed. He felt nauseated. He felt glad that he wasn't doing yard work. When he reached the trash can, he opened the lid hesitantly, like something might jump out and get him.

Nothing jumped out.

He reached in cautiously and fished out the tall kitchen bag. He ripped it open and let the cat fall to the ground. It was a gray tabby. But it was wearing a pink collar. A pink collar with a tag that said Amiga.

"She never made it to your old in-law's place," said Pinkerton from the open side door.

Tears formed in Ryan's eyes. "But why? Who?"

"It was those gnomes, Ryan. You know what you have to do," said Noodle Pie, nuzzling against the back of his leg.

"What in the name of hell is goin' on here?" said the voice of an old country Black man.

Ryan turned to find the source. "Mr. Harkins... I didn't see you there."

"Ryan, I know you been havin' an affair with that Lindsay girl. You think nobody peepin' on you? Think again. You put a baby on up in there, yes you did. Then you killed your wife and you killed your mistress and you killed your baby! I'm a-callin the 'thorities!"

Ryan tried to say something, but what could he say? He had no idea what was happening.

"I will stop him, Mr. Jajko," said Pinkerton. He sent his hatchet flying, spinning right into the center of the aged man's skull. Again, the split did not stop there. The entire body of the man trembled and cleaved in half. As the flesh fell away to each

317

side, Lindsay was revealed. Naked but no longer pregnant. She was covered in a pinkish goo that she licked from her body like a cat cleaning herself.

"I'm going to need some fucking therapy," Ryan said.

"Truth to tell, Aluminum men are made to administer Freudian psychoanalysis. But you are going to need something more Jungian."

"I want you in my pussy, Ryan," Lindsay said, and she pointed to her lady parts as if there might be some confusion.

"Oh, no you don't, bitch!" screamed Amiga, who wasn't really dead at all, but had the talent of making it look like she'd been nearly decapitated. It was a great party trick, and she'd done it the night she met Ryan.

"I totally forgot she could do that," said Ryan, feeling slightly less sad, but much more confused.

Amiga leapt in a great arc, doing a spin kick in midair. Her paw caught Lindsay right in the eye, popping it loose. The orb dangled from nerves and tendons stretched almost to the ground, and both cats began to bat her eyeball around, playing a sort of feline tether ball.

"Congrats, Amiga! This was your best idea ever," said Noodle Pie in the monster voice.

318

"You can stop doing the voice now," said Amiga.

"Just what the fuck is going here?" Ryan said, wagging his finger at his cat wife.

"I'm just teaching you a lesson. Never send your new wife to spend time with your dead wife's family. Or the new wife might end up dead, haunting you from beyond the grave, but disguised as some other ghost as revenge. Something like that. It sounded better when we were planning it."

"Well, who the hell is this Aluminum Man? What's he got to do with it?"

"I'm just an actor," said Pinkerton. He removed his head, to reveal a face that looked just like Ryan, except without a moustache. "Your wife hired me a couple of days ago."

Ryan hung his head and starting shaking rhythmically.

"It's okay, baby," Amiga said, rubbing up against his legs. "I've taught you enough for one day. Things can go back to normal now."

But he wasn't sobbing. He was laughing. His laughing grew to a hideous crescendo. "Well, if you are all in the mood for confessions, I guess I have one too." He reached up and ripped his mustache away. "I'm just an actor too! Hired by Ryan when he was just an infant to play himself! I've had you

319

all fooled for years! I'll be collecting my Emmy now."

The others gasped. Amiga started coughing because she'd been in the open air so long that her allergy was really acting up.

One-eyed Lindsay was the first to speak. "Well, if you aren't Ryan, then where is the real Ryan?" Awkwardly, she attempted to jam her eye back in the socket, but she left a bit of tendon hanging down like a fleshy tear drop.

"I've got an idea about that," said the Non-Ryan.

He took the others into the back yard, explaining about the gnome nightclub. "The way I see it, if we put on pointy hats and walk on our knees, they'll totally let us in."

So, the two actors, Lindsay, and the two cats got on their knees and put on dunce caps. They walked right up to the bouncer gnome and the Non-Pinkerton said, "We are just some gnomes looking for a good time."

"Oh yeah?" the bouncer asked.

"You know where we can find some fun?" Non-Ryan said.

"I don't know what you tall-ies do for fun, but maybe you can go sit on high chairs or shoot some hoops. And take those stupid hats off!

320

Scram!"

"Why don't you stuff it, runt!" yelled Noodle Pie.

"Go burry your turds, fish-bone picker!" yelled the bouncer.

"Gentlemen, gentlemen!" said another small person standing at the club entrance. He looked more like a baby than a gnome, but he had a distinctive moustache. "There is no need to squabble. Glitrick," he said to the bouncer, "these are my long awaited guests."

Glitrick the bouncer looked down in shame. "I'm sorry, Ryan, I didn't know these big'uns belonged to you. My bad."

"Your bad indeed!" baby Ryan scolded. He looked at the group with a glint in his eye. "If you will all please join me in the atrium." He motioned for them to enter. They followed him past the line of bushes that protected the club from the exterior yard, and into an elaborate candlelit hall, and still past that into what looked like a giant, hollowed-out heart.

"Have a seat, all of you, please."

Each took a seat on chairs designed to look like hemoglobin molecules.

"I would like a chance to explain myself," Ryan began. "I know some of you will never

321

understand my actions. Others of you will pretend to understand, but secretly judge me. Others of you might judge me to my face, like judging judgers."

Lindsay giggled, causing her pendulous breasts to swing side to side.

"Some of you," he continued, "will think me a madman. Some may even proclaim me a genius. Others will think this is all a set-up for an elaborate reality television program. Others will think I'm stupid. Some may even claim that I was hit on the head with a large mallet when I was just a pup, no higher than an ant's eye."

"Is there a point to any of this?" Noodle Pie said.

Ryan cleared his throat. "Some may not see the point in what I've done. Others may see the point but pretend to not." He breathed deeply. "All this is to say, I love you, Amiga. I've had to hire a man to play me because I feel totally inadequate to fulfill your needs, both sexually and in relation to gardening."

Amiga wished she could weep, but she was a cat, so she closed her eerie inner eyelid instead. "I love you too, Ryan. I'm amazed by what trouble you've gone through to keep me happy."

"And I, too, am astonished by the lengths you've gone to perplex the actor that plays me in the

322

relationship. For that, I am eternally grateful, to both you and to Paul."

"Who is Paul?" asked Amiga.

"I'm Paul," said the actor formerly known as Ryan.

"Yes, you really did an exceptional job. I can't believe how lifelike and brushable your hair is," Amiga purred.

"If no one objects," the real Ryan said, "I would like to return home with the two of you. We can form a family triad. We will have everything we need for success."

"That sounds nice," Amiga said with a cat-smile.

"The rest of you can fuck off, now. Get the hell out of my club!" Ryan said to Lindsay, Noodle Pie and Non-Pinkerton. "What are you waiting for? Go!"

"Christ, don't be such a douchebag, dude!" said Lindsay.

"Don't listen to her, baby! Do be a douchebag!" cheered Amiga.

"Yeah, get the fuck out of here!" Paul said.

The three of them jeered until the other three finally stood and left the atrium. Once they were alone, they embraced.

"I never thought it could be like this," they

all said at exactly the same time. "It's like you are reading my mind! This is the best thing ever!"

And that's how relationships work. Don't let anybody tell you otherwise.

Sleep and the End
By Craig Saunders

Sometimes it's hard for a man to get a grasp of what's real and what's not. Bob Storm fell down that particular rabbit hole just before he fell asleep and killed the world.

Bob Storm was his real name and not a pseudonym. It was a good name for a writer. Memorable, easy on the tongue, and looked good on the spine of a book. He wrote novels, mainly. Dabbled in short fiction, tried his hand at poetry. Discovered he couldn't write poetry and that there was no money in it. But, as a novelist, he was OK. Not great. Just OK. He made some money from his books - enough to consider it a second job, even. He paid tax on his earnings, bought a car with money that came from books. He wasn't famous.

He went insane long before he fell asleep, and when he finally opened his eyes again the world just wasn't there.

***

The world ends. There's no one left to write the story. No one left to read it. But here it is. Right here.

Right?

325

Of course it is, because the world doesn't end when the man who writes your story sleeps. No. That's the job of the BIG EDITOR IN THE SKY.

It's not me that writes the story, or a man called Bob Storm. It's you.

Mind: fucked.

Just like Bob's. Sleepless nights do that to anyone. Go without sleep for long enough, and you'll start to slip. Sleep's a finger hold on a big, smooth cliff. People fall off all the time.

***

Bob read the email again.

Three books. Advance. Deadline.

He read it over and over but those three sentence fragments summed it up quite nicely. His dog sat on his lap. Maybe his dog read the email, too. Probably not, but this is Bob's story and the dog (Gerald, for some reason known only to Bob) may have been able to read with a little help on the longer words.

But yeah, probably not.

It was a big advance.

"Shit," said Bob. Gerald's ears twitched, but he wasn't sure if Bob was talking to him, or the computer. Bob spoke to the computer often and passionately.

Carefully, the writer set the dog down on the

floor, stood as best as he could with his perpetual stoop, and danced a strange little jig.

"Yes!" he said. The dog didn't say anything.

After a while the writer man sat back at his desk and replied to the email. It seemed like a good idea, and really, what was there to think about? His second job could now become his first, and probably only, job.

A full time writer. Bob Storm had finally MADE IT.

His first book, written at the tender age of thirty-seven, seemed so long ago. It was only thirteen years.

A blink of the eye to a man pushing fifty.

Thoughts of telling his boss to stick his job somewhere dark and musty popped into his head with a peculiar kind of glee, despite the fact that he liked his boss, and his job.

Giddy with excitement and wondering if maybe the email had gone to his head, he patted Gerald and took himself off to bed.

The next time, sleep would mean The End.

***

What Bob didn't realise is that it's not a story if no one reads it. It's just a thought, on paper, or in a computer on a cheap and impractical glass table.

It's not a story if no one hears it.

327

It's just a thought. People, ordinary people, like you and me, we have thoughts all the time. But they're not stories. We don't make worlds. People like Bob make worlds. Crazy ones, plain ones, ones with pictures, too. Ones where people turn boats upside down to sail on the sky, universes comprised of jelly and dark matter alone. That vision, that creation, needs to get from the story teller's mind into...yours.

That's where it lives. Not here, on the page. But in you. In your synapses, or soul, or plane of existence...whichever way you look at it, doesn't matter. What matters is transmission, I suppose. Yes, transmission. Infection. A way to keep on travelling beyond the boundaries of one man's mind.

I know. I know.

It doesn't have to make sense. Platypus, exoskeleton, television, life...none of it makes sense. It just is.

***

Bob wrote a story once, when he was just eleven years old.

It went, by and large, like this:

Trudy fell down the well with a sickening thump that she didn't hear because she was already dead by the time she hit the bottom. A man with a large gun with two barrels shot her in the head and

328

she went over the edge of the well backwards falling into the well and broke her neck. But she didn't have much of a face after being shot. She was well dead. Then she got up. The man with the gun screamed after a long time when she reached the top of the well. She was covered in blood and didn't have a face. The man with the gun shot her again and took her head right off this time. Then he did not have any more bullets but even though she was headless she could still walk. Trudy chased after the bad man really fast. She chased him for a long time and when she caught him she stabbed him in the eye with her neck bone which stuck out and he died. The End.

Bob hadn't been very good with commas when he was eleven. He got better.

He was a horror writer at heart, and with his three book deal safely under his low-slung belt (largely hidden by a writer's low-slung belly), he began to write the first book. And it was horrible.

"Fuck," he told Gerald, hitting the backspace key over and over again. "This is utter shit. Fucking utter fucking shit."

Gerald had heard worse. He rolled over at Bob's feet. Because he was old, and because Bob spoiled him with sausages and cheese, Gerald also farted.

***

329

It wasn't strictly writer's block. Not at first. More a kind of performance anxiety. He didn't know why, now, he couldn't write. He'd written plenty. In an attempt to kick start some creative juices, he stood for a while and counted the spines of his books on his 'Bob Storm' shelf.

There were sixteen novels on there, and a few magazines with short stories from the 'early' days.

Sixteen novels. He could do it.

"You can do it," he said that night in the comfort of his double bed. That day he'd stared at the screen, the keyboard, a mug of cold coffee, the cursor...anywhere but where the worlds lived. The thing you're looking for is always in the last place you look...but only if you find it.

"You can do it," he told himself again as he turned on his side and closed his eyes. After some time words began, unbidden, to drift across his field of vision, like a ticker tape at the bottom of a news channel on the television.

He wasn't sleeping. He wasn't dreaming. He followed the story that was playing out across the inside of his eyelids. It was brilliant. Genius.

Write it.

A voice, not unlike his own, inside his head. Like the words that would make the greatest story

330

he would ever tell.

He grinned.

When he sat at the computer it was three in the morning. He didn't even bother with the coffee. Gerald looked at him with a suspicious raised eyebrow before snorting and returning to his own doggy dreams.

Bob wrote and wrote all through the night. Satisfied by six am that he had done his share of work for the day, he used the word count feature on his writing program to tot up his night's work.

The word count told him that he had written a grand total of no words at all.

0.

Unequivocal. Like a crash when you're fast asleep and something heavy hits the floor and you think fuck someone's in the house but it's just a mirror and you don't have time for commas when you speak with the voice in your head.

Like a breathless eleven year old boy, telling his first story, maybe. Transmitting it, from his mind, his imagination, to yours.

0. The computer told him so. It must be true. But the words...he'd spent all night typing...the words...

Were not there.

***

Gerald was just a dog. Of course, he couldn't read. But he could smell crazy.

Bob smelled crazy.

***

Is it crazy to think that if you sleep the world will end? Doesn't it do that anyway, with each passing moment? The things that were cease to be and become something new with the passing of each moment...don't they?

Are you asking me? thought Gerald.

Bob shrugged. His hair was unkempt and he'd lost a fair amount of weight. He was unshaven and his stubble was grey and very coarse.

"I don't know," said Bob to his dog. "Fuck it, I don't know why I'm talking to you. You're just a dog," he said.

Gerald didn't take offense. He ambled, nails clacking, down the wooden stairway to the kitchen to see if he could find some sausages.

Bob watched his dog go, turned back to the screen, and wrote a sentence. The same sentence he'd seen not a few minutes ago in his head. He felt the keys, heard the mechanical keyboard's tapping as he struck the keys. Watched the screen the whole time and nothing appeared at all.

The words, it seemed, were stuck inside his head.

Paper, thought Bob.

Gerald came back happy and full. What did he care if Bob went mad? He was just a dog, and he knew where the sausages were kept.

***

"Leave me alone! I'm doing it, OK? I'm doing it. I'm writing, writing like a fucking madman! I can't write any faster. You'll have it when I'm done!"

Bob shouted this into the telephone when his editor called him to enquire, quite politely, how the novel was progressing. It was the first call the editor had made since Bob's signature on the contract. The first call in four weeks.

In that four weeks, Bob had not slept. Not even for one minute. Every time he closed his eyes, the story played out, just as though he was reading, across his vision. But the story would not come out. It was stuck. Shy. Fucking hiding.

Four weeks with no sleep, no shaving, no shower, barely any food.

The upstairs study where Bob worked with the slat blinds drawn down stank. The man smells didn't worry Gerald the dog in the slightest. He liked smells. But not the crazy smell. He didn't like that. Not at all.

And Bob wasn't just crazy anymore. He was

333

FUCKING crazy. Gerald knew lots of swear words. Bob said that one quite a lot. Gerald had no concept of swearing, but understood words with power. SIT. STAY. FETCH. FUCKING CUNT COMPUTER.

Things like that.

Around that time, four weeks into his mammoth stint of insomnia, Bob wondered if he would break the story if he actually got it out of his head. He wondered if he would break the world. Maybe, he thought, he was really the keeper of the world in his head.

It had to stay in there. It didn't, shouldn't, couldn't be written because it wasn't a story. It was true. Of course it was true.

It had to be.

Why wouldn't it come out?

Because it couldn't. It lived in his head. A world, in his head. Lives, people, animals, plants, geology, magnetism, suns, gravity, space, atoms.

Bob sat down with a thump at the thought, the truth.

If he fell asleep, what would happen to the world he'd birthed with his imagination?

Shit.

***

On the last day, when a billion suns shining on dead planets and doomed civilisations winked out of existence, Bob stared at the black hole barrels of a shotgun he'd borrowed from the farmer along the road. Nobody knew he'd borrowed it, but he thought they'd either get it back after some sort of unseemly inquest, or the world would end when he pulled the triggers on the gun with two barrels and the farmer wouldn't be around to care.

When Bob Storm was eleven and didn't understand commas, he'd thought these kind of guns fired bullets. But they didn't. They fired pellets. Round planets that would fly through the universe in his brain and let him sleep.

Maybe. Maybe too many metaphors on long, elliptical orbits travelled around his brain. Dark matter colliding with his own molten core.

Bob was mad.

Bob was going to die.

At this point Bob was so far gone, way, way over the edge of the heliosphere, out past the next galaxy, on and on to the edge of the universe where things got weird.

Bang, said the gun, bored to tears with Bob and the universe and everything in between.

Gerald jumped and wet the study carpet in surprise.

And, with sleep, The End.

***

335

Transmission, like a virus, remember? A story just needs to be read to live on.

Gerald stared up at the universe of Bob's mind spreading across the wall behind the space where a mind had exploded. Of Bob's head atop his body, there was nothing but a few scraps of jaw and neck remaining. Both barrels of a shotgun made a pretty mess.

A pretty mess, a beautiful story. The way a story should be. The way a life born in a head should play out. A universe scattered across a wall, words and thoughts and the light of a billion suns. An imagination spread out like a map, but drawn in blood and bone.

Gerald was a dog.

So, how come the world didn't end? Who writes down the stories when worlds end? The great big editor in the sky? You? Me?

Of course not. We're already gone. We go in each moment that passes...then and then and then.

Gone. Gone forever more every second of the day with barren worlds strewn in our wake.

Gerald couldn't read. But he could smell. He could smell the story, the promise of the world birthed in the shape of continents and archipelagos on the simple plaster wall of a study.

Gerald sniffed greedily like a teenager

336

reading their first truly gripping yarn. He took that story in, held it in his head. He holds it there, still.

The whole world, in a dog's head. A dog, alone and forgotten in a writer's study. The sausages are gone from the fridge. The water in the toilet bowl long gone, too. The brain and blood and fragmented bone story, Bob's stinking rotten fingers, the flesh of his forearms, his shoes and feet both.

A hungry dog stuck in a room with a computer and the internet and the story of the world in its head. Like a virus.

Of course, a dog can't read. A dog can't type.

But maybe, thought Gerald as he sat at the computer with his head cocked to one side, maybe a story can type.

Maybe it can.

Plaything
By Meghan Arcuri

I lie on the floor, my face wedged into the corner of the living room walls.

I've been here before.

I don't mind too much.

Even with the dust bunnies and scattered Cheerio remains.

It's calm. Quiet. And a hell of a lot better than the bathroom. Do they ever clean that place? That yellow sticky shit on the floor? I like to pretend it's honey or some shit, but I know it's piss. Glad he doesn't leave me there too often. I usually end up here. Or in the kid's bedroom. I prefer that place. Hoped I'd be there more often when these people first got me. Hoped I'd be doing tea parties or playing army or shit like that. But that was never the true intention. Not even from the beginning.

I've always been his.

PJ's.

That fuck face.

I hear him now. That tap, tap, tapping on the hardwood floor. The sniffing. The yipping.

The stench.

Oh god. He's got me by the arm. Good

338

thing. Last time, he had me by the neck, and now my head's hanging on by a thread. Literally. Okay, maybe two, but still. One good tug and it'll be off for good. And then what?

Bet he's gonna shake the shit out of me right now. He's so fucking pr—

...

Sorry. I'm back. Can't even think straight when he's shaking me like that. Like I was saying, he's so predictable. If he's not shaking, he's tossing or gnawing or—

...

Fuck! I cannot stand that side-to-side, up and down shit. Plus, the whole head hanging on by a thread thing.

Dude, ease the fuck off. Once that head comes off I'm gone, and then what'll you have?

Dick, that's what.

On second thought, that's what he'll really have: a dick. In addition to me, these people have also given him a rawhide bull penis. No shit. What will they come up with next?

Good. He's lying down.

No more shaking. But now I have to endure the evisceration. Again.

Yesterday he took out more than half of my insides. Took him about three minutes. He's a quick

339

little fucker.

Oh god.

Oh no.

The white. Strewn everywhere.

Like a freakin' snow storm.

My entrails. My innards. All over the hardwood floor.

Cleanup's gonna be a bitch.

At least it's puffy and white. Not sloppy and drippy and red. Like that shit on the TV the shop owner used to watch.

What did he call it? Saw? Dawn of the Dead? Oh, who the fuck kn—

…

Dammit. He did it again. Finicky little bastard. One second calmly disemboweling me, the next, shaking me like I'm some colicky baby whose parents forgot their meds. I mean, what's up with those people, anyway? Just put the baby down and walk aw—

Wait a minute.

Something's missing.

What the hell's going on here?

Well…isn't that something?

He did it.

Tore my goddamned head from my goddamned body.

340

No joke. Five feet of floor separate the two.

Shit. Here she comes. The lady. "Mommy" they sometimes call her. She has a sad look on her face, but she's also laughing. Admonishing PJ for tearing me to shreds, but in a tone that says, "It's okay, sweetie. You're so fucking cute, I can't stand it."

Don't you know he's Satan's hound, lady? What the hell is wrong with you?

I need to pull it together. Maybe if I look extra cute, she won't throw me away. Like all the other ones who've gone before me. The ones she mentioned to the shop owner.

I mean, I'm a stuffy for god's sake, so the cute thing shouldn't be too hard, right? She'll take pity on me, give me some new insides, and sew me back together.

Right?

Okay. Good.

She's got my body in one hand and my head in another. Now she needs to head upstairs to—

No. Not the kitchen. You don't keep the sewing stuff in the kitchen.

Don't put your foot on that trashcan pedal. Please. For the love of God.

***

The darkness.

341

The stench.

Not PJ's, either.

More foul. More rotten.

I'm done. Finished.

Damn you, PJ. We could have been something. Had something real. I could've been your snuggle bear. Your love muffin, even. I could have been something more. Something better. Not just your little…plaything.

***

A slit of light.

Sniffing.

Could it be?

A wet nose on my face. Teeth on my cheek.

PJ!

Here to rescue me from sure death.

Just my head, but beggars can't be choosers, I guess.

I never thought I'd say this, but I love this fucking dog.

My cheek's getting sore, but at least he's not shaking the shit out of me.

He seems calmer, quieter. A more contemplative PJ than I've seen before. Maybe he's thinking about my near-death experience, too.

He's dropped me on the floor. In front of the couch. Thank god his teeth aren't piercing me

342

anymore, but—

Oh, for the love of all things good and holy, he's sitting on me. I have a face full of junk and the smell of dog ass is overwhelming. It's almost worse than the garbage.

Almost.

He's moving. Setting a rhythm. A pace. A rhythmic pounding.

His junk. My head.

Oh my god, he's humping my face.

Make it stop. Please...please... Make it stop!

I know I said I'd be his love muffin, but I didn't anticipate this: the pummeling, the pain, the—

Oh shit.

These people never had him neutered.

Disgusting.

Where is she?

Where is that "Mommy" lady?

When will she find me and reprimand him for pulling me out of the garbage? When will she put me back in there?

Anything is better than a face hump.

Even the garbage.

Oh god, he's increased the pace. The hammering. He's close.

343

So close.
I need to get out of here.

                  Mommy!

Civics of Consequence
By Michael Allen Rose

I put on my rape face this morning.

I hate that face, but it was necessary, today of all days.

The box in which I keep my rape face sits way underneath the bed, at the very back, just under the headboard. The box is teak. It has a tiny gold padlock on it.

My rape face doesn't hug the topography of my skull well at all.

It looks droopy, saggy, with floppy jowls and acne scars.

I went outside with my rape face on and immediately a group of people walking toward me crossed the street. I hate the way people look at me when I'm wearing my rape face.

I went to the newsstand on the corner and bought a Wall Street Journal. The proprietor looked at me over his glasses. His heavy eyelids propped themselves up. I could see scorn and derision, touched with just a hint of fear, when he looked at my rape face. I tipped him extra.

I bought a morning coffee at a Starbucks. The baristas didn't really want to wait on me, I could tell. When I got to the front, nobody asked to help the next customer. The first employee that was free just stared at the keys on her register. Her manager hovered around behind her as I ordered a two-pump caramel latte. I saw his head shake back and forth as I waited near the counter. They didn't call my drink, they simply put the cup on the edge of the counter. I took it without a word.

My rape face began to slide in the moisture of the morning. I had to stop at the corner store to buy a package of push-pins, the kind you'd use in a bulletin board. I heard a little boy crying nearby as he watched me push the pins through my rape face, fastening it to the muscle inside my cheeks and forehead. His mother clung to him, wide-eyed as they walked by me.

Now my rape face had tiny colored pegs jutting out of it in red, blue and green. I felt like a clown.

I walked up the back stairwell into the auditorium. The workers in the back must have known I was coming, because they stepped aside as soon as they saw my rape face. Normally people do not move aside for me.

The back room was filled with journalists clicking away on their devices, typing things and editing things and deleting things. Every few

346

minutes, all of the journalists would switch devices with each other. I watched for a long time, but couldn't discern a pattern. They would switch devices, and then they would go right back to typing, editing and deleting, in an endless whirlwind cycle of information.

Nobody even looked up as I walked around the curtain and took my place at the center of the stage. My opponents were already there, behind podiums to the left and right of mine. My opponent on the left was saying "I believe in the fundamental rights of all people to shine like golden candles and eat as much hair as they want to eat. Anyone who takes away these fundamental rights is a narcissist and a fascist and a dingbat." On my right, my other opponent was saying "People who take away fundamental rights from other people are communists and terrorists and kidneythieves. All people should have the fundamental right to explode like silver firecrackers and shave themselves anytime they are hungry."

I looked out into the crowd, which was made up entirely of children. An endless sea of children with their faces frozen in caricatures of cartoonish terror, mouths wide open in horror and eyebrows wiggling high above their eyelids. They sat without moving, seemingly very calm, despite their faces.

Just as I raised the appropriate finger to begin speaking, my opponents began running around in circles on the stage, and tearing their clothes off.

The one to my left shouted: "My opponent steals babies from nuns. He put the bomp in the bomp-shoo-bop! He stole the cookie from the cookie jar! Furthermore, he has never tasted the sweet majesty of bacon."

The one to my right shouted: "My opponent hates pork sandwiches. He plays football with Eskimos. He has never greased a squeaky wheel, and furthermore he was born in a fictional country which cannot be named!"

My rape face twitched with rage as I began to hover over my podium. My attention getting tactic worked, as my opponents fell to the ground where they were, crying like babies and shitting their pants. As I took my place at the front of the stage, two large matrons appeared from the wings and picked up my opponents, cradling them and shushing them as I began.

I spoke about the need for change, and the need for constancy. I spoke about the virtue of progress and the benefits of staying true to the old ways. I outlined my plans for spending money on savings programs. I railed against isolationism and

348

entreated them that we should mind our own business. I attacked those who would attack us while turning the other cheek. I made a great noise, very quietly. I championed rural interests while fighting for urban expansion.

I leered with my rape face on.

I spoke for hours. My opponents had fallen asleep.

I stepped out into the crowd, walking on the heads and shoulders of the children, who did not move. I poked at one of them, and there was no response. They were all dead and crispy, juices stilled.

I stormed out the front of the auditorium, spitting into the wind and raging at the solidity and permanence of objects. I trusted my own lyrical flow. I subverted the grass, and uprooted the sky, and I shook all the people that I came across until they stopped crying.

I felt the fire before I saw it, creeping up my leg. It was very hot.

My rape face started sweating, oozing salty tears from between the push-pins.

The flames engulfed me, so I sat down on a park bench and ate a sandwich while I waited for someone to put me out.

A doctor, a lawyer and a priest came by,

349

each regarding my rape face with a steely eye, learned of man and nature. I stopped them, because I'd heard that one.

My rape face began to melt. I slammed my hands against my face again and again until I felt something break. The rape face just melted in between my fingers, dripping down my chest, running over my stomach, splitting into two on a path down my legs, gravity pulling it over the waterfall of my knees with a keen "plop."

People with signs came from all around, protesting the detestable treatment of my rape face. I was severely burned, but I finished my sandwich, because of starving children in other countries. The signs read things like "Stop being so negative!" and "Must you use words like that?" and "Be responsible, stupid!"

I left my rape face lying there on the sidewalk. It was barely recognizable now, a mound of silly putty that would surely pull up the sidewalk wholesale when someone decided to move it.

I walked down the street with my hands in the pockets of other people. I sniffed glue. I rocked the casbah. I got too drunk to fuck. I lost myself in a party tornado and licked my wounds with the other wound-lickers.

This was supposed to be my watershed

moment. I watched the TV in the bar. The bartender was a mannequin. He made me a dry martini. The dead children washed up on shore in a news story about local food deserts. "I know them!" I cried, gleefully name dropping. Nobody noticed.

The election results came on. Everyone had voted for a garage door. The garage door opened and closed by remote control. Security was the garage door's main concern. They showed a picture on the news of everyone putting their valuables behind the garage door. The boom mic got into the shot at one point, but the garage door didn't seem to mind. The journalists had no faces and I could not tell where one began and another ended.

As I enjoyed my drink, the door of the bar opened up and a large group shuffled in, in a boisterous and celebratory mood. It was the garage door and its entourage. They ordered drinks for everyone in the house. The mannequin was a surprisingly efficient bartender.

I tried not to let my disappointment show. I smiled and mumbled something about the weather. I made the smallest talk possible. I clapped the garage door on the back and watched it open as if by magic. The entourage was made up of dead children and journalists.

Then I noticed that stuck to the back of the

351

garage door was my rape face. It looked different now. The skin was smooth, and there were no pock marks. The holes were gone, the complexion was pleasant to behold and the cheeks were ruddy. A smile creased the lower half of my rape face, alien to its surface. The hair was lustrous and kept. It emitted a pleasant odour of lilac and baby dreams. It was completely different, and yet it was my rape face.

I said "That's my rape face you're wearing."

The party stopped. The silence roared.

I exited the bar via catapult, launched from the bosom of the proletariat champion into a pile of cans and corpses. All the cans were homeless. All the corpses had to sleep, because they had to work early the next morning, and couldn't abide my shenanigans.

Dusting myself off, I realized that most of my skin had turned to ashes. I was grateful that the flames hadn't swallowed me whole as I stumbled down the street.

My own face shone under streetlights. I felt naked and exposed. Someone smiled at me and I felt my insides reconfigure themselves into a pyramid. I walked to the very edge of the pier and looked out over the sea. I thought about home, and where it was and what it might be. I turned around and started walking.

The owls swooped down and carried away motorcycles. Shadows spoke with bats and made plans to start book clubs. Marmalade billboards advertised free breakfasts at the local constabulary house.

I stopped by the newsstand from the morning, but it was closed. There was a sign in front that said "Take what you need." The newsstand proprietor had provided a free hatchet. I took the hatchet and I smashed the wooden slats of the newsstand, opening up the information cache to the night air. Everything was damp, soaked in blood. All the headlines were the same. The garage door was garage door of the year. The opponents were praising the leadership skills that the garage door had shown in its first term of office.

I curled up under a damp sack of Wall Street Journals and went to sleep.

In the morning, I walked back to Starbucks and bought myself a vanilla double-whip frappucino. The barista smiled in a vacant, far-off way. The sugar rush made my eyes roll back into my head, and I walked blind the rest of the way home. A voice was being broadcast over the air-raid sirens in town. It sounded like metal scraping against a concrete driveway. It might have been the

353

sound of a garage door crushing a child's bicycle in the name of freedom. It might have been the latest top forty hit radio.

My face was quiet and elusive. I looked for it in the mirror, but it kept eluding my gaze. I turned on the radio and the journalists were talking about the garage door over the sound of their typing, editing and deleting.

They talked about the face that protected them. They said that the face the garage door showed when it was angry was a powerful face that made our enemies run in terror. The cries of my opponents were weighed on the air, and everyone decided that this was for the best, and that regardless of where the face came from and what it had done in the past, now was the best time for the future of our race to show whatever face was necessary.

The radio droned on, humming harmonies of metal tearing asphalt so citizens could continue to thrive.

I took my own face off and put it inside the teak box under my bed, and I locked the tiny gold lock.

Big BANG!
By Christopher T. Dabrowski

Fourteenth universe in the Theel's district. Milky Way. Solar system. Earth. Europe. Poland. And to be more precise: Olecko. And even more precisely: Faulty Street No. 5. A huge block of flats covered with a dimmed concrete epidermis.

On the second floor, one of the windows opened. A huge light purple head emerged. One might say, an alien. But it was no extraterrestrial being. It was just a sixty-five-year-old Frances Z, who had what remained of her sticking-in-every-direction hair dyed by a hairdresser friend yesterday.

Lately, light purple was a real blockbuster among her friends. Just as were the songs by Christian Crusaders with Al Davis.

Frances narrowed her eyes in loath.

The day, just like a saliva-covered chin of a toothless old man, was trembling in the agony of the setting sun. Dying rays were covering the deadly grey walls of the blocks with a bloody redness. The walls were totally painted, signed with a spray imprint... that's the whole of Skawina – the worst district of the town. Here, every night is baptized with liters of vodka. All the benches are taken by over-testosteronized bald gentlemen, smoked with pot, throwing yo!'s and fucks all around, chipping living copies of Barbie dolls.

"Sinners. Cocottes," Frances mumbled silently, curving nervously her moustache. 'God shall punish you!'

Although the church negated the Darwin's theory, Frances thought sometimes that there might be something true there. After all, when you see those bald v-men, you may have a feeling that you see a monkey. An itsy-bitsy similarity.

"Oh! In the name of the Father and Son," Frances, terrified of the sacrilege she made, started to pray. How could she question what the church had told her? Well, how? "and of the Holy..."

Barking sounded behind the door.

Hannibal! Oh, the poor thing! She recalled that as usual she forgot to walk the beloved doggie.

Hannibal, or in reality Stan Smith, aged sixty two and a half. A habitual fetishist taking pleasure in pretending to be a dangerous dog and taking advantage of the fact that Frances Z. had weak vision.

Hannibal was waiting for his mistress, wagging his tail joyfully.

The woman bent and attached his lead.

Oh, ecstasy!

356

Outside, Frances let Hannibal loose. The doggie, wagging his tail with joy, went to conquer the neighboring lawns. But the woman didn't pay attention either to her pet playing or to the v-men who were killing time by sticking long needles of stupidity into the bench they were sitting at. The time was swirling and moaning. But its time was already counted – the young men organized the loudest fart competition.

The thing that caught usually careless Frances' attention was a drama in the sandpit. Three brats at the age of her grandson (seventy-two-year-old Bruno Z.) were tormenting a terribly meowing Santa Claus.

One of the boys applied a nelson maneuver to the Santa, making it impossible for him to move, the second one caught Santa's legs and the third one was pouring gas over the poor creature.

Seeing there was no time to waste, Frances started walking toward the young sadists.

"Stop this at once!" she screamed. "Or I'll make strings from your guts!"

"Fuck off you dickheaded zealot," one of the boys shouted back, reaching for a lighter.

Frances thought it was the highest time (although no one really knows how high the time is) to change words into deeds. Firing various oaths at the boys, calling them devil's litter, Satan's children, or bastards from hell, she rolled up her skirt. Instead of the right leg she had a machine gun. With her trembling hand covered with liver stains, she threw away the walking pole and caught the other leg at the knee. She jumped two meters up in the air.

Meanwhile, one of the devil's litter managed to torch the Santa's tail. The rest of Satan's children freed the tortured one.

Santa, meowing like crazy, with madness in his purulent eyes ran straight ahead into a place known only for him.

Frances was hanging in the air, she aimed as much as her eyes would allow and started shooting. Unfortunately, instead of the youngster torturers, the bullets reached the v-men's girls. It was them who the fearless young men were hiding behind.

The air escaped from the girls with a loud hiss.

Frances fell to the ground.

There was a strange silence, everything ceased moving, even Santa froze, waiting.

The sky suddenly turned dark and the clouds over the block were torn apart, showing the terrible truth.

Frances fell to her knees, raising her hands

358

to the sky.

"Oh, yeees! The God shall punish us for our wickedness! For lives of sin!"

No one paid attention to ecstatic shouting of the excited old lady. Everyone was looking at the thing that emerged from between the clouds and was getting bigger, approaching the Earth at mad speed.

"This is the finger of God! The Lord has shown his mercy!" the pensioner was screaming like a turkey being shived.

BANG! 'The finger of God' hit the Earth hard.

And then a big shadow covered the neighborhood with darkness! And then a powerful thunder deadened the sinful people! And then the blocks began to collapse! And also the oceans rose!

Oh, one more thing, I almost forgot, and more precisely: And it was the end of mankind!

Rising to the sky, Frances was shouting, showing her teeth sharp as if she were a piranha:

"The Looord has shown his meeercy! He's taking us straiiight to heaveeen! Oh, meeerciful! Let's prayyy the Lo…"

The old lady went up in flames, going as a rocket high into the atmosphere.

A few people who had a much better view of the situation were the astronauts repairing the

359

machinery of a space station, TIC-TAC 3, circling on an orbit. A moment before their death, they saw a huge cue, coming literally out of nowhere and hitting the Blue Planet with massive force.

The Earth began to depart at deadly speed. Oceans, sees, rivers, billions of people, animals, and everything that was peeled back from the surface now turned into a huge tail hanging at the back of the runaway planet.

The Earth looked like an enormous comet.

The speeding planet hit a band of the Milky Way and missed the black hole. Unfortunately.

God lost – as usual. Once again, Satan proved to be the master of this competition.

Forget Me Not, Filet Mignon
By Andrew Wayne Adams

The naked man looked at his map. The map (a labyrinth of hair-thin lines traced in black mascara on a scrap of brown paper grocery bag) said he was in the Automotive Parts Department. He lifted his eyes and scanned the aisles. The shelves held nothing but dust and ash and one dented hubcap.

Blue-gray daylight fell from the vaulted ceiling. A mutant pigeon flapped through the rafters, scraping its beak across the glass of rotting skylights. It landed atop a bank of dead fluorescents. Cooing, it lifted its tail feathers to poop. Then it spontaneously combusted. The sprinkler system detected the burning pigeon and unleashed an indoor rainstorm (complete with clouds and thunder).

The naked man looked at his map. The map broke into sodden chunks that dropped through his fingers as he lifted his face into the rain. A hole in his chest leaked black slime that smelled of decaying flowers. He forgot everything for five minutes. Then he remembered.

He turned and walked away.

361

Two miles later he crossed into Zone C and out of the storm. He zigzagged through the lanes until he reached the Summer Fun Department, where he found an aisle whose rust-heavy shelves still held a few moldering beach towels. He dried himself, threw the towel at a spider web, and walked on through the monochrome gloom.

A clump of jungle had risen through the floor of the Pink Lingerie Department. Neon flowers hung on the steam. The naked man picked a blue forget-me-not and carried it away.

An hour's journey and he was back in Zone A. The stench of rancid meat singed his nose hair as he entered the Edible Flesh Department. He gazed into an inoperative meat cooler at scattered steaks growing gray-green afros beneath their cling wrap. He reached for a sirloin, changed his mind—he'd already done sirloin twice that week—and picked up a round steak instead.

As he was nearing the checkout, a jaguar-like growl erupted from the PA system. It ended. He passed the cart corral, where a flock of battered shopping carts was trembling as if in a private earthquake, metal cages rattling weakly.

The checkout lanes numbered in the thousands. The naked man approached one of them. Behind the counter stood a naked woman in a catatonic state.

She had one eyelash.

The man leaned toward her over the counter. He laid aside the blue forget-me-not and tore open the steak. The meat hissed as the air hit it. He shaped it into a ball.

There was a hole in the woman's head—a jagged aperture in the crown of her skull, half-hidden by a thin spread of hair. Near the edge, a maggot writhed in old blood. The man flicked away the maggot. He dropped the ball of steak into the hole. He stepped back and waited.

The woman blinked.

Her mouth moved. She took a deep breath. And coughed. Couldn't stop coughing. She bent, holding her shuddering abdomen. Finally a glob of something green and red loosed itself from her lungs and flew to the floor. She sucked air. Chest movements slowing, she licked her lips and cleared her throat. Calm.

Her eyes found the naked man. For a moment she was silent. Then:

"Hello," she said. "How may I help you?"

He picked up the blue forget-me-not. "I want to buy this."

He gave her the flower. She tried to scan the barcode, but there was no barcode. "Did you peel the sticker off?" She shook the scan gun at the flower. "Where's the price tag?"

"Price tag?"

She swung her head around, peering up and down the thousands of empty checkouts. No one to help her. "I think there's a sale. I think flowers got marked down. They're free. Here." And she handed back the flower.

They stared at each other. A bee crawled out of the hole in the man's chest.

"I'd like a bag," he said. "Please."

She took the flower and put it in a brown paper grocery bag.

"Will you help me carry it to my car?"

"If you tip me. Will you tip me?"

"Handsomely."

They walked outside, flesh tightening in the chill. The air was motionless, the sky a chalk-colored dome. Asphalt stretched to the horizon, peppered lightly with dead cars, exploded shopping carts, trash bags, boulders, ribcages.

A red battle tank was parked nearby. The man pointed to it, said, "That's me."

"Does that thing work?" The woman swept at a maggot that had tumbled off her scalp and onto her shoulder. "The gun. Can you shoot stuff?"

"I'll show you. Come on."

364

They crossed the lot and climbed a short ladder on the side of the battle tank. The man opened a hatch on top of the gun turret. He lowered himself inside. The woman followed, closing the hatch behind her.

A light bulb (pink-tinted) flickered on inside the tank. They sat in the close space with their bare legs touching. Warmth poured from an electric fireplace behind them. The woman still had the bag with the flower in it. She took the flower out of the bag and put it in a vase with some water and put the vase on a small nightstand beside her. She looked around and said, "Cozy."

The man opened an ammunition compartment in the floor. Half a dozen human fetuses lay curled inside. He selected a fetus and loaded it into the tank's gun. "Watch," he said.

There was a window above the loveseat. The woman drew open the curtains, raised the blinds, and looked outside. The man situated himself at the gun's controls (a computer mouse and a piano keyboard). He played an F# on the piano, and the gun fired. The woman watched through the window as a fetus rocketed from the barrel and traced an arc against the gray sky.

The fetus hit the asphalt, shattering into red giblets that skipped away like rocks across a pond.

"Michael," she sighed.

"You should really stop naming them." He sat back from the controls. "Anyway, the gun works."

"You didn't need to do that. I knew it worked. I just forgot. I forget things. You know I forget things. It's your fault I forget things. Asshole."

He didn't reply. She lowered the blinds and drew the curtains and they sat in the warm pink light. He could smell the steak rotting in her brain cavity. Filth streaked her body. His too.

He said: "Will you have sex with me?"

"If you tip me. Will you tip me?"

"I will give you a very large tip."

They had sex inside the red battle tank.

His sperm fertilized seven eggs. The zygotes crackled like microscopic fireworks. Within five minutes they had grown into mango-sized fetuses. In an hour the fetuses would be the size of German Shepherd puppies.

"You need more breasts," he said. He ran a finger along the bulge of her stomach. A sweaty strand of her hair stuck to his cheek. "Like, at least four more."

"I don't even need the two I have. You know that." Her belly thundered. "Stillbirths don't need to

366

suckle. And my milk is probably acid anyway."

She sat up in bed and grabbed her book from the nightstand (a dog-eared copy of Great Expectations). She found her place and started to read. He waited five pages. Then:

"You're ignoring me."

"I don't like you."

"Why?"

"Because you smashed my skull in with a golf club and ran off with my brain." She closed her book. "Then you tried to copy my brain in the key copier. Which turned it to pulp."

"I'm sorry. I was mad because you were smarter than me."

"You were mad because I tore out your heart."

"No. That happened after the brain thing. In retaliation, I think."

"I don't remember." She returned her book to the nightstand. "I feel so dull. Why don't you choose higher quality cuts of meat? I bet I could really do some deep thinking with a nice filet mignon between my ears."

Her belly expanded to the size of a pumpkin. Something kicked within, the sound like a muffled drum.

"Never mind filet mignon," he said. "We can

367

be whole again. You can be a genius again, and I can be an emotional lunatic again. I just need to find the Human Parts Department."

"Zone XX. Behind the Ultraviolent Revenge Department. I've already told you."

"I can't find it. There's no damn logic to that place. The zones shift around at random." In his head he heard a jaguar growl. "I need you to draw a new map. The last one fell apart in the rain."

"Rain. Fire. Wind. An eagle swooping down and tearing the map from your hands. It's always something."

"Here," he said, and handed her the bag that had held the forget-me-not.

She tore the bag into scraps, surveyed the scraps, and selected the largest (it was shaped like Antarctica). She reached up and plucked her lone eyelash. Pinching the lash between thumb and forefinger, she bent over the scrap of brown paper.

A fly buzzed in her brain cavity.

"Awkward way to draw a map," he said, watching her hand move.

"A pen or pencil would be nice. But the pens are out of ink, and the pencils are broken. And someone or something stole all the crayons. My body is all that's left." She passed him her work. Trails of mascara wandered the page in an

368

exploding snarl. She lifted her finger, the spent eyelash clinging to its tip, and said, "Make a wish."

He made a wish, and she blew the lash into the air.

"That was your last," he said.

"I know." She grimaced as her belly inflated another few inches. "Ouch."

He stared into the heart of the map. There, sunk within a vortex of paths, the Human Parts Department reared its hairy shelves. Near its perimeter, a cat-like shape stalked beneath the letters of a warning: Here Be Dragons.

"A brain," he said. He looked at her. "A real brain. With real neurotransmitters. Dopamine and serotonin. Remember dopamine and serotonin?"

"Empty shelves. That's what you'll find there. Oh, maybe a few appendixes or tonsils. Six-packs of wisdom teeth and pinky toes. Useless garbage. No brains, no hearts. Everything of value has disappeared, from everywhere. You know that. What makes you think the Human Parts Department will be any different?"

He didn't answer. He eyed the cat on the map.

"I want a heart," he said, quieter.

She reached toward the nightstand and plucked the blue forget-me-not from its vase. She pushed the flower through the hole in his chest, planting it in the soil between his lungs. "Satisfied?"

"I want a heart that won't decay in two days."

"I can feel two flies fucking on the piece of rotten steak I call my brain. Stop bitching."

He listened to the sounds that rolled within her head, the demonic buzzing and swampy burbles. "Have the maggots almost finished their dinner?"

"I think so. They ate all the childhood memories. Now they're gobbling up the rational faculties. Motor functions are for dessert. I'll have to go soon." Suddenly she gasped, hands clutching her enormous stomach. "Ouch. Michael just kicked me in the pancreas."

"Stop naming them," he repeated. "At least, stop naming them all Michael."

"It's my favorite name." She gasped again. "Ouch. Shit. Shit shit shit."

Her vagina belched and seven Michaels fell out, strangled in their umbilical cords.

"Ouch," she said. Her belly deflated, hissing like a punctured tire. Soon it was flat and smooth again. She stared at her dead children. "What are those?"

"Bullets."

She looked at him. "Who are you?"

370

"Time to go," he said.

He stood and opened the hatch. Inside the tank, the pink light flickered out. Grayness came in. He helped her climb through the hatch. She stood on the ladder leading down to the asphalt. She looked at him. Maggots squirmed in her hair.

"Had fun," she said. Drool spilled down her chin. "We will again?"

He looked into her lashless eyes. "We will. Somehow."

She smiled. "I go back to work," she said. "Job. Store." She climbed down the ladder and started across the parking lot. Her body canted to one side, off balance. She stumbled a few times. A galaxy of flies orbited her head.

He watched her until she was to the door. Then he lowered himself back into the tank. He picked up the map she had drawn. Already inaccurate, probably. There could be no map of a place with indefinite form. He knew that. The map was desperation, was fear of having to negotiate the shifting wastes unaided. The map was a lie.

He let it fall to the floor.

And he imagined:

His red battle tank screaming through the wall, empty magazine and candy racks flying as he rolled over cashier stands. He would stop briefly so

371

that a naked woman could join him (he would have to help her onboard, carrying her inanimate body like a mannequin). Then he would make no more stops, smashing through everything as he barreled toward the heart of the place in an arrow-straight line—tunneling deep into the darker parts, into swamps and fangs and a feline cry—gun fully loaded with Michaels—no map.

He had imagined it all before.

He gathered the dead Michaels and stacked them in the ammunition compartment. Something on the floor caught his attention. He picked it up.

Against his palm, the eyelash weighed nothing. It looked like the fuse of a failed explosive.

He thought of the wish he had made. Always the same wish. Always failing to go off.

In his chest, a temporary heart thrashed on its stalk, raining petals.

He wished his wish again, then blew the eyelash into outer space. On the floor, the map spontaneously combusted. He slid behind the tank's controls and pushed a button.

The red battle tank screamed.

Manifesto for the Establishment
of a Colony of Versifiers: A Fiction
Ny William Cook

"Thus will the fondest dream of Phallic science be realized: a pristine new planet populated entirely by little boy clones of great scientific entrepreneurs . . . free to smash atoms, accelerate particles, or, if they are so moved, build pyramids — without any social relevance or human responsibility at all."   - Barbara Ehrenreich

This is the pension. The redundant paths no longer used are ours to pave a-new. Before us, there were the people that walked and searched these routes perpetually, with the notion that the only way to the other side was through the impossibility of dreaming that you are awake only when you are alive. This species of innate wisdom bred the groups, spawning the injector of the seed that started the civilisation of the soul and the mind.

The groups were bred to separate as one and to flower like Aloe Vera, healing in its application, an old timeless forever-facet. The groups were gregarious and loud at first; quite physical, like old drunk football jocks ranting about their conquests

373

and their halcyon days. Their final victory would be to piss in the face of death. How wise, how insolvent, how heroically absurd! What a place to start.

The groups grew from a thought and then there were seven (it has to be 7 for there is no other such number) with one in each clique. Who can say that they have never - EVER - done anything wrong? Anyone that suggests that they haven't is insulting the true nature of humanity. Besides, we are no more wrong than any one who is right, or left for that matter.

The members are as loud in image, as in voice and verse. They all look as though their hair is splashed blood, fireside on top – they have let their Demons run rampant with the comb, they wear strange suits and neckties. Do not forget, that it is a men's club, no matter what gender one acquires at birth.

We are now there, in the thick of things, voyeurs at a strange game, and they are all sitting now, cooing verse and grandiosity like pigeons around breadcrumbs. They hunch over a coffin-like coffee table littered with paper and brandy and ash trays and electronic calculators, snuffling and growling, gnawing on poems that refuse to die. Rolling eyes, bared teeth, flailing arms, frizzled hair

– a cacophony of blurred movement and frenetic chattering sound. We are all members however. Everybody talks as if in a big restaurant when amongst those we can impress.

You can drink if you like but to be a true member you must be drunk and lucid without alcohol. You must be tripping in narcosis and yet not be on the needle or any such thing. You see that the ability to enter free states of thought and disassemble your mind, requires a certain amount of prerequisite uncontrollability. Then, to put it all back together again, to arrange the jigsaw of your will, back in a uniquely different way each time, this must be a principle requisite factor of each member of the group. Each member is in tune with the rest of the society, yet is not.

Every-time that you walk (or ride) past trees, you shall picture them as if on fire. Their flames should appear to connect from the roots to the tip of the burning limbs, to set the sky on fire. Trees are very important symbols in the group's ideology, as they are the 'connection tools'. Trees are firmly entrenched in all aspects of originality and birth (and death). They are the reasons we have reason, the cause of all our causes, the fault of all our faults, the fall of all our falls. When walking through a forest on a sunny morning, one can be hypnotised into a shamanic trance of true awareness on any level of thought, by the sunlight's flickering passage through the trees. The trigger for this process – concentrating, by not concentrating. This will achieve that perceptual bound; that phallic blast of natural revelation.

Undeniable fascination is the awareness of the creative product, of euphoric chanting tantric thought. It is a blessed meditation for the safe entrance to the creative sewer of the mind's tunnels and labyrinths, where no one normally feels at ease to roam. Travel along these dripping dark caverns, echoing sounds of carnal affectation and true fear. Ringing wrought bells of blackness, toll resoundingly like truths, that someone else that let go of who you did not want to acknowledge.

The group explores all, through these cavernous passages of time, searching for the grail of enlightenment. Inevitably, some will find each other as enemies; battling each other just to get past to where the other member has just laid their tracks. This is the true driven will and desire of each member, of this consciously subordinate group.

Tragedy and desire are that of which the members are significantly appealed. This pursuance is dangerous to the mind that refuses to accept that all is not real, save for that force which is recalled deep within the mind's eye (the driving image of the horizon). If this kind of 'belief' ensues, then insanity will dig deep foxholes, burrowing into every conscious and subconscious affliction that the poor soul in question is responsible for (or not responsible for, as the case may be).

Prospective members can see that the group is not for daisies or weeds; whose petiole hang lank and fall about the place and hold no resilience to the stem, in the face of footsteps from other pilgrims, on their way to enlightenment. Hence the importance of trees, resplendent with strength and psychoanal inferences. This is a career and a plague, which once begun, shall only have two endings: (1) absolution of thought and mind (spirit), or (2) destruction and insanity of the weak interpreter. However, it has been known that some poor souls can remain in a constant state of limbo, between the two extremes.

Automatic life is the automatic goal, automatic in the sense of not being robotic. We could possibly class this ideology as 'instinctive intellectualism'. This requires a duality within reality that is a constant focus of thought, but also a total concentration of the binding force/s behind thought, to create a truly automatic way of being. This process utilises in a way, self-hypnosis, which will eventually lead to a new way of perception or thought. Similarly, 'affirmation' has proven to create behavioural change in human patterns of life and in the writing process. A clock, after all, is better than a muse.

This desire for a seemingly incoherent state of being is a revolutionary ideal in today's western society. Ironically, we seem to exist on a vastly superficial level in our predominantly materialist societies; therefore, the group is prophetic and modern in its character, by being the same within our cultural faction. The sense that one is a member of a species and a subset species within that species, is now a redundant concept.

Rather than being incoherent in the sense of being stupid, one becomes incoherent in relation to the mundane and thought destroying reality that has been imposed upon our western selves since birth, namely gender and associated human traits. I am being discriminatory here in the use of the word 'western', as it is our collective experience that most eastern societies have a more enhanced spiritual aspect to their thought and existence. Although with the growth and influence of the capitalist machine, more countries that are eastern are succumbing to the same western disease (Japan, for example).

*Fast food fuck-tards need not apply.

As a group, we stand together and scream

378

REBELLION, REBELLION, REBELLION, to anyone that requires a new slate for the mind. From the ashes, tabula rasa, the phoenix shall arise. Down with the fascist unbelievers. Injected outcomes, on this downhill slide to reason and ascendance, will be the realisation of the mind and spirit's capacity for survival and redemption. The total envelopment in the will, of nothingness, brings ultimate contemplation.

Nothingness is good or bad, or neither, good nor bad. It is just or unjust, but it is capable of being complete, random, instinctual, and ultimately new. Natural neutrality if you like. From nothing comes something, which has not been before. Rather like the minds' own enactment of the 'big-bang' theory.

This goal for the mind may one day be structured so firmly in our patterns of genetic thought, that it may give birth to itself and conceive a nation of groups. Dangerous? Yes, but new and somehow deeper than that which has gone before, but also the same as the ancient origins of that which has come before. Maybe some mistakes can be corrected along the way. After all, nothing is impossible! We were not impossible!

This self-imposed circularity is symptomatic of the search for meaning in an otherwise meaningless world. The harnessing of such a

379

spontaneous tool of contemplation is where the processes of 'automatic thought' provide the means, to utilise and enhance this highly intuitive power of perception. Through the automatic recording of such experiences (written, recorded, filmed), we can use these references to self-induce states of like mind at will, which is where the group's combined experiential references come into full effect.

Upon learning how to automatically relate an experience to another area of thought: a build up occurs on a subconscious level and increasingly, on a conscious level. These events (Deja vu) are one of the keys to the new level of thought that is our way.

The uneasy familiarity felt, when the 'apparent illusion' of reality recognition occurs, is the exterior repression that has been taught to us by western society (i.e. patriarchal, and predominantly, matriarchal, colonialist, capitalist, authoritarian . . .etc). Essentially, there's no 'ism' that will get us out of this one!

These constructs will try to prevent us from acknowledging a doorway to truth via the subconscious levels of thought, other dimensional levels of reality, and an importance or truth that is primarily intended for interpretation. That which is so often brushed aside as meaningless will appear as it was intended. Truth will reveal itself.

This basic wall between Westerners and their own minds has been effectively built (especially in the 20th century) by the deterioration of instinct and basic human capabilities of thought and spiritual existence. Through the development of power structures, built by predominant sub-species of humans rife with genetically inherited ideals and instincts for power, a way of life and thought for all species has been built upon crushed common census. Truth always gets in the way of power especially when logic prevails. Make of that what you will.

It has been said 'that to create, is to name', therefore, to name that which has not been created is to construct with an ultimate goal in mind for the subject in question. To be an automatic being, or group of beings that is also 'one' in itself (the sum of all parts), we must all be members of a like-minded/active group to carry on the process. The thing that distinguishes each individual member (other than their own uniqueness) is the way in which they belong to the group.

Because of this need for new expression and originality in thought and action, we have named ourselves. Therefore, we have created ourselves, just as the reasons for our actions named themselves; but yet for different reasons and objectives (in the light of experience and perception).

And here we are. New, blood hosts, breeding more for the plague. Entre the light harness of our parabolic existence. The manifesto has been written – the stage has been set, yet where are the trees we need for the illumined vision?

Schluck!
By R.A. Harris

One

The squid clung to his hips with its eight arms and wrapped its tentacles around his thighs like climbing ivy. It was gorging on his man pipe, suckling him deep into its bowels, so deep that it felt like it warped through space-time into some pleasure dimension outside normal reality. All sensation was turned into a sexual clamor, husky and immeasurably erotic, as the squid coddled his meat. Its beak was a soft gelatinous substance, not like a normal squid beak. It was like a vagina made of the same material heaven must be made of. It pressed into his abdomen and balls, teasing his organs and sending shock waves of pleasure through him. He orgasmed so hard he went through his dick, deep into the extra-real extra-erotic dimensions within the squid. There was a sound like a SCHLUCK! as he slid through its velvet-heaven mouth, all but his arm, which was popped off as the hole pinched tight like a sphincter.

Inside the squid, a portly yet cute Asian woman, dressed in ceremonial kimono, was serving tea to a Siamese cat. The cat was sat on a beautifully crafted deep blue cushion that perfectly complimented its dazzling blue eyes set against its dark tanned face that was dignified and betrayed a sense of superiority to this sizeable woman.

She was knelt before it, offering a tiny dish with milky tea in it. She bowed so low her forehead touched the floor. The cat pawed at the dish, as if testing it for some unknown quality. It seemed satisfied and the woman crawled away backwards, never taking her forehead off the floor. There was an odd schluck noise from her palms every time they pulled from the floor. She shuffled all the way out of the strange chamber they were in, which seemed to pulse and contort, protrusions occasionally spurting forth from the organic purplish walls. Once the woman was gone, the cat stood and stretched before lapping some of the tea from the dish.

After a few laps the cat licked itself over, spreading the tea across its fur, it spent an inordinate amount of time on its genital region, but seemed to gain no sexual pleasure in doing so. It checked once more to be sure the woman was not within sight, and then spasmodically attempted to lick the front of its neck. Its course tongue shooting out as it pulled its head back and tucked its chin in. Overall the effect was to severely diminish the cat's supposed cool aesthetic. No wonder it had to reinforce its superiority in front of the woman. It was obviously aware of how ridiculous it looked when it spread the tea over its neck and chest.

There's a kimono over there waiting for you, Henry. The cat's voice was sing song, enticing, encouraging. Henry found himself picking up the kimono and slipped into it, unsure as to exactly when he learned how to dress himself in oriental formal wear. Henry finalized his outfit, one sleeve hanging uselessly, and turned to face the cat again.

Now you must bow, Henry. Again, Henry found himself fulfilling the request without hesitation. His face touched the floor, it tasted salty.

Very good. Now you must bring me the gift I asked you for. A vague memory ponderously bumped about in Henry's mind for a moment, before evaporating in the face of the feline desire for satisfaction, satisfaction that he knew he could deliver. He turned his head to his left and found a small tea making facility. Initially he attempted to move his missing arm, the remaining shoulder stump wiggled pathetically and ached like a bitch. It had miraculously cauterized during the transition through the squid's mouth but a large amount of pain still shot through him whenever he thought of

385

it.

Silly boy, Henry. Try again with your other arm. The one you still have. Henry acknowledged the advice and reached for the small tea pot, decorated with strange characters painted in a rich blue ink. He decanted the brown liquid into a shallow dish.

"Do you take sugar?"

Yes. One please, Henry. Henry scooped some out of the decorative sugar pot and sprinkled it into the dish. He then picked up a spoon and, using the back of it, proceeded to aid the dissolution of the sugar into the tea. Afterwards he carefully lifted the cup onto a tray placed beside it, and balanced it on his forearm, trying to wedge it between his elbow and wrist. A none too easy task with only that same arm to perform it. Schluck Schluck Schluck. Slowly, Henry slid across the floor on his knees and elbow, making sure not to spill the tea from the dish. In front of the cat he lowered his forehead to the ground once again. The cat extended a paw lazily, testing the tea.

Very good. Now go. Henry kept his forehead to the floor as he awkwardly scooted backwards. Schluck Schluck Schluck.

Two

The earliest memory Miss Teek could remember was one of being dipped into a barrel of hot brown liquid by a hand gripping the scruff of her neck. It scolded her paws and soaked her fur. She kicked and writhed and banshee wailed in an effort to escape the dark oppressing fluid. Her claws were out and found flesh to puncture and tear at. Slicked and running on adrenaline, she managed to escape the grasp of the man and dashed to safety. From the corner she turned to see the man laughing like a drunk, bawling and slapping his thighs. Suddenly he stopped. His face looked menacing and he reached to his groin. He pulled his trousers down and began roughly handling some disgusting tube of flesh hanging from his body. His face tensed and his tongue came out, curling around his upper lip as if in concentration. Suddenly he erupted with a roar, and the tube spat hot white pearls across the floor. The man's face relaxed and he looked dazed. Elated even. Miss Teek used the opportunity to run. She didn't know where she was going, only where she was running from.

It smelled like the sea. Not unpleasant, but salty and sharp. Its skin was purple and covered by soft, silky pimples. Miss Teek instinctively knew it was not harmful, but possessed some untold power. Pawing it, she turned it over and found a small opening that looked like the entrance to a woman, but one crafted from material more delightful than a typical vagina. It looked enticing. Miss Teek found herself nuzzling into the mouth of this purple sack, it seemed to yawn slightly and she slid her face inside.

Three

Once outside the chamber Henry was spat back into the real world, landing in a heap. Once he recovered his senses he took in his surroundings. He was in an alley somewhere. A mangy dog eyed him from behind a bin. He looked around and saw the squid, slightly shriveled, and his recently liberated arm. He rolled onto his back and began to laugh. His stump ached like crazy again.

The dog edged forward cautiously at first but then gained confidence and began nosing the discarded squid. The mouth opened slightly and the dog, as if sensing some pheromones, got an erection and slid its cock inside. Thirty seconds later and the dog wailed, orgasmed, and inverted through its penis into the squid.

When it emerged again, sanguine fluid hung from its jowls. There were several small scratches around its eyes and on its nose.

'Henry.' Henry stopped laughing and looked

at the dog. 'You should never have trusted that cat. Now, get on all threes.' Henry nodded sullenly and got to his knees and elbow. The dog waltzed up behind him, mounted, and plugged away, finally orgasming and inverting into Henry's insides with a *schluck!*

All His First Born
By Alan M. Clark and David Conover

Dirk agonized over a future in which Jessica would play footsie with his son, Phillip's, wobbly column of half-eaten toe joints. It sent Dirk's own leaky digits wringing the air with angst. Like a primitive locomotive rasp he wanted to chew the good out of her before Phillip was born.

Jessica wouldn't admit that their love was dead, even as he poured from her asshole and crept lengthwise beneath her wide-opened knees. Though Phillip was covered in gore, Dirk could imagine the little bastard's smile as he sipped the warm, wormy sewage of her afterbirth.

When he heard his son giggle, he knew she'd love him, so he slapped Phillip with the Mucous-Encrusted Eyeglasses of Death from the back of a magazine. Phillip's childish laughter stopped suddenly, his tongue caught in the wildly spinning lenses. The hungry frames bit down on his eyeballs, sending rotating jets of viscous fluid and bone shards into the air. The larger skull fragments ricocheted off the ceiling with a beat to compliment the tune described by the drip of large and small droplets issuing from Jessica's still-flowing end.

"Phillip is dead!" Dirk shouted, gleeful yips

390

echoing up his gut and out his mouth.

Jessica , unaware that half her faces were rotten and growing mold, smiled crookedly.

"This is not the woman I married," Dirk grumbled as he watched Jessica bend and pick the gristle out from between her swollen buttocks. Just looking upon her moist and fattened form caused his bloody stool to burble up through his ears and nose. Dirk's head overloaded with the pressure and exploded.

When the air cleared, he could hardly believe the eyes looking up at him from the floorboards were his own. "How am I seeing them?" he wondered aloud.

Dirk knew then that he must be dead. A rain of fiery fingernails, he had won in spite of himself.

Never again would Jessica put her horrid tongue to wagging against him.

Her skin blossomed red beneath Dirk's touch.

391

Refugees from the future
By Tony Rauch

Part 1.

Me and Broxon found ourselves in some deep yogurt, so we had to hightail it outta our sticky situation and go hide back in the past again. We decided on the American Civil War era, as we knew no one would look for us there. It was simply just too dangerous a place to take your chances in. Not just because of the war itself, all jagged and heavy, all sharp bits of metal flying around, but because there was so much metal and clunky machinery around, mixed with bad magnetism that really messed with the electro-magneto chemistry of our time apparatus.

Also, there were too many illnesses to catch that they couldn't cure back then, and too many baddies around willing to conk you on the melon for hardly any reason at all. What if you got sick or injured and couldn't get back to the apparatus? Then you'd be stuck there, a hostage of their primitive medical knowledge. And then there were the primitive dangers of other things – wild animals, narrow minds, accidents - beyond the shabby medical care that often did more harm than good.

Luckily I had a grandfather who was elbowed to the margins, who was brilliant, but no one wanted to work with him because his methods were so unorthodox. Luckily he stumbled across an even smaller means, a more efficient device, and one thus less affected by the bad polarity of all that big metal that was around at that time.

Broxon and I holed up at one of our hideouts. We printed up some old money and headed back in time. Once back there we hooked up with Farnswerth. He had some interesting news. He was sent back first – to scout out a good hiding place. He found us a nice little cottage at the edge of a small town. We thought about recruiting some others to help us out, but wanted to get settled back there first, establish a home base with which to operate from. We figured this time and place would be ripe for the picking as we could just open up a hole and zip about – rob a bank in Missouri, then zip back over to rural Illinois to chill out. Place bets on events we already knew the outcome on because we were from the future and thus could research what to bet on. Implement some scams that they hadn't

393

yet heard of back there. So things like that. It seemed like a good time to exploit. And we had the advantage of the smaller device, and thus the means to do so.

Most of the time travel devices were these huge machines controlled by government agencies. But we had the apparatus, the version my grandfather had invented, a version you could hide in a suitcase, and thus carry with you as you needed to move about. This gave us a huge advantage. We knew government agents were out looking for us and could probably locate our general area based on the signature such a device would emit. The ripples in the micro magnetic regions are very recognizable if you know what to look for and where to look for them. So we knew we were relatively safe in traveling in time – yeah, the government could track us, but we were so mobile that once they located the place we jumped to, we would probably already be somewhere else – just hop a train, stagecoach, or horse and we'd be gone.

When we got back here in time, Farnswerth had the modern kitchen, wash areas, and cable television all set up in the basement, so we'd have some modern conveniences at our disposal. We could get broadcasts from our own time, so we wouldn't miss out on anything. I was actually excited to go back and experience a simpler, slower, cleaner, quieter, less complicated, less rushed time, even if just for a spell. And in getting back there and looking around, I did get a sense that less was expected of you here.

I looked around and being on the edge of town did offer a certain 'back-to-nature' vibe that was immediately quite appealing. But unforeseen problems did arise right from the start. The place was actually messier and dirtier than I expected. There was more garbage around and more dirt, mud, and gunk. Even more concerning, right when we got there Farnswerth was already showing signs of The Illness. He was also seriously suffering from the Travelers Gout, a malady where your joints just stiffen and some of your molecules go missing. It happens to some people. Hey, life's a gamble. But no one ever thinks it will happen to them. The next thing you know, you're forgetting where you left your keys and then you can barely move at all. All that's left after that is to just lie there and wait 'til she's over. But the Travelers Gout was nothing compared to The Illness.

Farnswerth knew he was sick, but he didn't want to let on. But Broxon and I knew it was only a matter of time – either The Illness would get him, or the Travelers Gout. Anyway, Farnswerth told us he ran into some serious cats across the street – a real tight crew who could've been from this era, or from another, but they clearly were not from this small town. They were obvious newcomers like ourselves, with strange customs and manners. Farnswerth figured they sniffed him out as well. So he aimed a hidden camera on their place – which was across the street and a few houses over. He hid the camera up in the attic window, then set up shop and waited in comfort 'til we showed.

But the neighbors did concern him. Secrets always seem to hide in the margins, settling in the interstitial spaces.

Part 2.

We got back here, the ball of hiss and fuzz and hum we stepped into squiggled around us until fading a few moments later to deliver us to the inside of the little house Farnswerth had arranged. The waviness of the distorted air faded and there we

396

were, standing in the living room with our suitcases at the edge of the small town in rural Illinois circa early 1860s.

When I got here, the first thing I noticed was how rickety everything seemed. It was as if the world was falling apart, unsolid, slumping – and not just the buildings and wagons, but the entire terrain – the trees and landscape. Their world seemed frozen, petrified, as if on the verge of collapse, as if there were no promise of a better world, as if everyone had just given up, as if their hope had been robbed from them by some mysterious force.

The ground seemed to undulate and slope. Nothing was flat or processed yet. Nothing had been massaged by human hands, shaped to their liking as if clay. Nothing at all. And yet the land lacked a pure quality that I had expected. It looked as though someone had smeared their poop all over the place. It was just a muddy and fraying mess – a landscape of gouges, as if a giant had scratched and clawed furiously at it as if in a frustrated hurry to uncover some hidden truth or reason for it all. Or as if to bury some disgusting secret for all time.

The scene was this – lines of white cottages, merely a collection of shapes with shed roofs, each house a different configuration. The main part of the city was several blocks away, down the dirt path. The railroad ran through the middle of the downtown. Most of the structures were wood. I hesitate to designate them as buildings as they failed to convey that permanent connotation save for the town bank which was a small, tall, thin brick structure. The fields beyond were rolling grass and farmland separated by clumps and lines of thick trees and spots of bushes and shrubbery. A creek ran through town which powered a paddlewheel grain mill and sawmill that cut wood. There were some industries – a wagon wheel factory, a casket plant, a cannery which shipped out its output via wagons, and the rickety railroad which I mistrusted for some reason, perhaps it was a mistrust of all its metal, as if it would polarize the apparatus, elongating the magnetic waves, causing me to be stretched to my absolute limit until snapping my cells apart, or slingshotting me back to caveman times, never to return or something.

We checked out the modern accommodations in the cellar – the video wall illuminating a scene of golden fall splendor, some light jazz fluttering in the air.

398

"Yeah, this will do." Broxon smirked, looking around.

The upstairs was done up in the sparse 1860s attire of the time. There were only a few spare pieces of furniture, only a few basic photos on the wall – ghostly images of grimacing forebears stuck in a distant hardship.

No sooner did we set about making tea, when the neighbors arrived. There was a strong beat at the door, a modern rap like the heartbeat of a beast.

Farnswerth waddled over to the door, all stiff and hunched, the Travelers Gout locking up his joints. Slowly he opened it and three gentlemen entered without permission. The last one closed the door. They had an official air of arrogance about them, as if they knew what was going to happen. I really hate that in people. It's a sure sign that they were also from the future, maybe not your future, maybe one before or after you, but definitely not from this time.

The last one in peeked through the sheer curtain that covered the window in the door as if to investigate whether anyone was following or watching. The men were well attired, with crisp,

399

sharp mustaches that could challenge your denial of the very existence of a higher power.

Broxon stepped forward. "Who are you? What do you want?"

The men stood crisp and still, looking the place over.

"Are you here to wait out The Illness?" Farnswerth coughed.

"Funny," the first one spoke without blinking, "we were just about to ask you the same."

"You're not from around here, are you?" I looked the men over.

"We could say the same of you," the one at the door spoke in a gentle, even tone. There was a subtle kindness, a sensitivity to him which was not expected whatsoever.

"What is your business here?" the first one asked.

"Refuge." Farnswerth waddled away, to set himself down in a lump on the couch in the small room off the entry.

"You've contracted The Illness," the quiet one at the door mentioned, "and the Travelers Gout."

Farnswerth looked away, nodding solemnly

400

as if not yet ready to admit it to even himself.

"And what are your intentions?" I asked.

"Same as you, we suspect." The first one looked around. "To gain a measure of distance from The Illness. . . But now I see that you've brought it here, brought it back with you."

The second one finally moved, looking at his watch, then leaning to whisper in the ear of the first one. "We have a leak in our coolant. And a hum." The face of his watch flickered a dim lime light, a fuzzy image of something but I could not tell of what. "We can not make extensive use of limiting," he continued to report, still looking down and reading something from his watch. "Our dynamic range is now gradually reduced. Our limiting levels . . ."

The first one raised his hand to cut off the second one. He looked down, hearing enough to realize their situation was dire. Then he looked up to me. "We respectfully wish to ask permission to borrow your apparatus. Our mother is very down with The Illness and we fear this will be the last of our chances to wish her a pleasant passage into the next world." He looked down again, staring at the floor as if to sigh. "We must return at once as we

401

fear she may change soon. . . Our device has quivered with a recent betsy and we have not the tools to repair."

"It's shot," the man at the window interrupted with a whisper.

Part 3.

"How do we know we can trust you?" I asked, not letting on that we were also thieves fleeing from various authorities. "How do we know you won't return, thus stranding us back here. Maybe you'll escape to another place. Or another time. I hear tell that Outer Mongolia is absolutely breathtaking in this time."

The first man considered this. Gently he turned away to step into the side room, studying the narrow planking of the floor. "Soon all our devices will fade. Conk out. Return to useless, inert junk... Soon many of us will become stranded, just strewn about in time. Never to return... Maybe The Illness will finally catch up to us all... Maybe this is it, the slow steady end... Maybe no one will be left... Maybe this will be our just rewards for our arrogance in thinking we can just fiddle with time in any old manner in which we choose."

"We always thought it would end in a bright, blinding flash." The one at the door turned and peeked out the blinds again, scanning each way down the street.

"Or maybe we can live here, spread the word to a select few scientists. Seek out the brightest minds. . ." Broxon raised his brows. "Maybe look for a cure back here? Maybe buying us some time. Then we could move forward again, maybe curing it before is spreads?"

"Or maybe this is the way it's supposed to go," the man at the door muttered in realization. "Maybe we've just tinkered with things so much now that there's just no going back anymore."

"Perhaps we've finally messed up our genes so much. . ." The first one groaned. "Maybe the regression, the regeneration . . . is irreversible."

Farnswerth nodded, sitting at the first one's side. "Soon I'll regress, back into some simian mess. Some ragged, fraying beast. Perhaps regressing even further. Who knows, I may end up a mere amoeba, flopping around in a puddle in a rut in the road somewhere."

"I'll blow your brains to soup before we

403

allow that to come to pass." Broxon sighed.

"Maybe life, all life, is sacred." The first one turned to us, raising out his arms. "Maybe just being alive, just existing is what it's all about?" A sad look weighed on his eyes, his stare growing more dire. "No matter what form we take."

In realizing this dire state of theirs, I offered our assistance. "You may use our apparatus. . . But you should know, it is a highly advanced model. Possibly the last of its generation."

Broxon sighed. "This may be the last of it. . . We may be the only ones who get out of the future, who escape The Illness, who live."

"Well, if we got out. . ." I began, "who's to say there are not others scattered around, sprinkled throughout time, hiding from who knows what?"

Farnswerth looked more hunched now, smaller, more hairy, as if in my mind his transformation, his regeneration, his regression had already begun, The Illness taking root, The Illness stealing his identity, the de-evolution underway, just bubbling under the surface to be found within subtle, yet profound evidence.

I looked around, at the strangeness in this new old world, the foreignness, the strangeness of

404

everyday life. Everything was so stark and empty in the 1860s. Everything so minimal, so basic, so simple, so scary and unfamiliar in its emptiness, as if time was waiting impatiently to be filled – the empty homes, the empty insides, the wilderness waiting to be shaped – the bare yards, the sandy paths, the calm, blank faces – all waiting to be filled. A promise waiting, an emptiness wanting to be filled.

"It's as if we had it for a moment." Farnswerth gulped. "Made it to the top of the mountain, then dropped the ball. . . Spoiled it to such a final ruin that nothing would ever come back."

Part 4.

The first one noticed that I was staring over at Farnswerth, so he looked down to Farnswerth sitting at his side below. You could tell in the first one's face that he could also read the beginnings of a monkey, the ravages of 'progress', The Illness tightening its grip, taking shape, the changes taking hold.

I looked over to the big window opposite

Farnswerth. I sighed at the rolling hills, the unorganized grass, the lines of trees on the horizon. So much space waiting to be filled, so much potential, so many promises tempting us to sink our hands into.

On the little end table next to me sat a small oval frame with an old photo in it. The photo was a woman with a stark, sad face wearing a strange stare, a blank expression of uncertainty staring out form the past, as if she were watching in horror at what was to unfold, as if she had known us all at one time, as if she used to look over us, love us, but knew our kind was due a cruel fate.

The first one sensed he was interrupting my sweet moment of grace, a moment of respite from the nonsense, as if he too knew the nonsense was spreading, growing, that you couldn't outrun the jittery, staticky noise - as if he also knew all the noise would be laid down and silenced and that things would be returned to this quiet time of blankness and wind, of scattered, random people riding a minimal landscape, a primitive people in struggle against the land, the weather, against one another over resources and beliefs – a final struggle against fate and destiny.

406

"Soon there will be nothing left." The first one sighed. "Maybe only a handful of us, all cowering to hide in the past."

I turned and nodded to Broxon, indicating he should retrieve the apparatus. Broxon turned and walked to the back pantry, to the suitcase.

"What was it like for you?" the second one asked in a humble mutter. "Back in the world."

"For me, it was like this," I began. "There was a line. On one side were all the workers, those kept in the dark, feeding the boilers, shoveling the coal, digging the ditches. The trolls. The unclean they're dumping all their dysfunction on. On the other were the privileged – the good looking, the presentable, those who looked good on the golf course or at the party, those who made the boss look good. That was it. It was that simple. That's what you were up against. You were on one side or the other. And most people couldn't tell the difference between the people who actually got things done, and those who just looked like they got things done. So there was a constant dichotomy between the authentic, the actual, and the perceived. Between the truth and the lie. Between parroting what is prescribed to you and thinking for yourself.

407

Between the real and the preconceptions, the preconceived. Between the workers, the doers, and the liars, the phony fakers and pretenders. It was as simple as that, . . . and yet things were never quite what they seemed."

The image in the picture frame on the little table next to me glowed with a low, subtle light, interrupting me. I waved my hand over the frame. The glass lit up in a bright glow. A voice buzzed from the frame, crackled, then cleared.

"Are you there, my leader," the voice buzzed a low hum.

"Yes, Bonnell, we're here." I cleared my throat.

"Things are bad here. . . The regression has progressed as we had feared," the voice from the frame continued.

"How bad?" Farnswerth quivered from the couch in the other room.

"They're bombing the cities with the fog. . . Trying to disperse the . . . They're lying on the news, saying things are getting better." The glow throbbed slightly, then faded. The person's face appeared in the frame. "The streets are scattered with roving monkeys," quivered the voice. "They

408

seem to be out looking for revenge."

"Have they isolated the bad genes?" Farnswerth interrupted.

". . . They're . . . throwing their feces. . . Everywhere. . . The damage . . is extensive," the voice wheezed in defeat. "There is no pathogen to isolate, no toxins to neutralize. . . It's inside of us. . . Our own genes . . . breaking down. . . Disappearing."

Farnswerth lowered his head into his hands, hiding his face from the truth.

"My bet is on the pesticides." The one by the door sighed. "Or maybe the preservatives gradually poisoned us, turning something off deep inside us all. . ."

"An accumulation," Farnswerth cried. "A mutation."

The face in the frame turned to speak to someone to his side, off screen. "Yeah." He nodded to someone beyond. "It's weird how things change on you. . . What? . . Yeah. . . OK." He looked back to us again. "It's bad. . . It's real bad here. . . Don't believe anything else. . . They're everywhere. . . Flinging their poo. . . Scratching and clawing as if by doing so they could get it all back. . . A real crap storm. . . Smearing their poo on everything. . . A world gone to crap."

"Any indications . . ." I began.

"Yeah, you'd better stay clear . . ." the voice interrupted, looking to his side again, a sadness sweeping over him. Then the face squished up. A scream rung out in the background.

Farnswerth raised his head to listen. His face went white.

On the picture frame screen there was a muffled, unseen flurry of monkey screeches. The face was yanked out of view by a hairy arm. A crash shattered. The frame turned to static, flickered, then went blank.

Part 5.

"Soon our devices will fade." I nodded and reasoned as Broxon stood next to me, setting the suitcase down at his side. I looked down at the suitcase. "This may be the only one of its kind. But soon its energy source will be drained. Soon we'll all be stuck in places we don't belong. Places we don't fit." I looked around. "Places like this."

"We'll have to re-invent everything," the

second one whispered to himself. "We'll have to start over from scratch."

The one at the door continued to peek out the small window, discreetly fingering the lace of the curtain, as if to hide from what could be out there, as if to not show himself to the world awaiting its ruin outside.

"Monkey-likes-his-banana!" Farnswerth squealed, squeezing the words out in a strained cry, enunciating the phrase as if it were but a single word. "Monkey-likes-his-banana!"

I'd seen that before – the fear, the panic, the disintegration of reason, the breakdown, the decay.

"You're the monkey now. You're the monkey," he urged, stabbing a finger accusingly at the corner, at no one. "Monkey. . . Dirty, filthy, stupid monkey. . . Do a little trick for us, monkey. Huh? Do your little dance." As if out of fear he had once been one of those who taunted those with the affliction, as if he knew it would soon be his turn to suffer the same taunts.

"Easy Farnnie," Broxon cooed. "You're not gone yet."

"Dance for me monkey! Dance!" Farnswerth erupted, standing forward just slightly, his frail body

411

now a taunt rope, then realizing the futility of it all and leaning back, going limp, waving his arms about helplessly, lazily. "Do your shameful little jig for one and all to see," he whispered to himself, then looked away in shame at the corner, as if to hide his face from the world.

"There may still be time," I announced, looking around.

"I'm sorry," Farnswerth whispered. "I'm sorry for all the bad things I've ever done, all the pain I've ever caused. . . I'm sorry. . ."

I'd seen this before too – the desperation, the bargaining, life having a way of forcing you to your knees, life reduced to a staring contest with fate.

". . I'm sorry I was mean to that one kid in eighth grade," Farnswerth mumbled to himself, staring out the big window before him, off into the distance. "Sorry I excluded that one kid in sixth grade. I'm truly, sincerely sorry. If I could go back in time and change all that, I would. I would. I would. . . I would redo it all. Honestly. . . I'm so so very very incredibly sorry I was mean to that one girl, . . . I was just, . . . I don't know . . . Lost somehow. . ." Farnswerth's voice was now but a faint squeak of a whimper.

412

The first one looked down to his wrist. The face of his watch glowed slightly, then faded. A face appeared in the watch crystal. "How are we doing?" the first one asked, looking down at the floor.

"Not well," a small voice peeped from the watch. "Not well at all. . . The storms seem to be getting worse, not better. The wind speed. . . We've analyzed the dust, the sand. . . Seems to be coming from an even greater distance, as if the land is being swept up and flung into another country. . . We can't reach Australia. We've sent another sub, but . . ."

"Thanks." The first nodded. "Get back to me in an hour."

The glow flickered, then faded.

"You're not from our time, are you?" Broxon asked.

"You're here to kill us, aren't you?" I nodded in realization, looking into their eyes suspiciously. "To stop the spread of The Illness once and for all, aren't you?"

"From beyond your time." The first one nodded slightly. "We're here to clean up the past. . . Repair the damage. . . We've been waiting for you for a few days. We had detected your jump. The

413

gravity funnel. The ion waves."

The man at the door turned to us. "I hope you understand."

Farnswerth dropped to the floor, to his knees. "Can you help me?" He gulped in a quiver, his eyes red with fear and humility.

The second man reached into his jacket and pulled out a strange, small brass rod with holes of various sizes all over it. It looked like a miniature flute. "Things aren't always what they seem," he said. "An old ornate end table can be an old ornate end table. Or it can be something else entirely - a camera, a recording device. . . And that's the funny thing about people, you never know who they're gonna turn out to be. . . Who knows, they may even end up being someone from the future."

The first one looked over to the second and then over to me. "Now kindly hand over your apparatus." He reached out his arm. "No reason not to be a gentleman about all this."

"Can you reverse it?" Farnswerth whispered, looking to the floor with concern. "Can you change me back?"

The three men in crisp suits looked over to Farnswerth on his knees staring at the floor in

414

shame. There was a long silence, as if they were thinking of saving us, allowing us to live. A sudden crash rumbled outside. An enormous explosion blew the door and frame to me, splintering them to a spray of shards, an orange, red, black, yellow glow, a thick mass of smoke, a churning black and white flash.

I was blown backwards, as if yanked by a rope from behind. I swam in the air as I twisted, twirling to land on my side. I slid across the floor, back through the dining room, into the kitchen, to slam into the back cupboards, shards of wood splintered to rain down on me.

I rolled to one side, and then the other, as if a natural reflex to try to avoid a blast that had already occurred. I shook my head, the world swaying this way, and then back that way. There was no sound at all, just a strange void where the world used to be. I shook my head and slumped forward. I found myself crawling to the entry, now just a huge, ragged gap, only the fraying strands of wood and the smoke showing. The smoke cleared as I crawled. I saw outside, between the houses across the sandy path. Beyond the houses stretched the rolling fields, now dotted with dark objects.

415

At first I just assumed that the figures beyond were more refugees from the future, as if some mass evacuation had been implemented and they finally decided to seed the past with the healthiest survivors who were now rushing to flood in, scurrying about in panic to grab at the last fraying strands of civilization. Maybe this was the only option. A last ditch desperate move. Maybe they had figured it out, abandoning the future, figuring the past was the only place left to hide, the only safe place.

Part 6.

I crawled to the front, my body numb, my hearing only a high pitched whine, my mind now blank. I crawled as if swimming on the wood floor, now covered in sharp chunks of broken wood, tattered clothing, and small pieces of who-knows-what.

The smoke was clearing. I saw their leader sprawled out to the side, a shard of wood through his side. The second one was a twisted fray in the corner, covered in lines of crimson. Farnswerth was slumped against the wall in the side room, his face

416

blank, blotches of crimson all over him and the walls next to him. He looked hairier, a snout starting to form, his hair longer, shaggier, his skin more weathered, more wrinkled, his body smaller and hunched.

My hearing slowly returned as muffled popping sounds in the distance. The quiet popping seemed to hang in the air. My ears rang with a low, fuzzy whistle.

Broxon rose from a pile of frayed boards behind me. He staggered to his feet and shuffled to the gaping hole that was now the front entry. He leaned to steady himself against the jagged remains. Another explosion cracked in the distance, a red and black bloom of smoke and fire folded like a giant ball between two houses.

I sat up on my knees, the specks and spots in the golden fields outside began to come into a clearer view. Another fireball bloomed in the background, in the field. And then another, all curling yellows, oranges, and blacks.

The specks looked to be soldiers. They wore grayish-blue uniforms. Some crouched low, cautiously passing across the road in front of us. They looked wary, disheveled, bearded, scraggly, skinny, gaunt, tired, thirsty, dirty, wrinkled, hungry, starving. My mind reeled off a list of what they looked like, since I did not know who they were or what they were doing, I could only associate them with stray adjectives and random verbs. I could only describe them, how they felt to me. I was not threatened by them, only curious. They dotted the field, moving ever slowly, closer and closer into this part of town. Spots of gray smoke bloomed as they fired their primitive rifles. The noises beyond sounded like distant hand claps. The noises closest sounded like sharp clacks.

Several soldiers rushed past the opening, then several more, hugging the outside of the house as if for cover against fire from behind us. Some popping sounds seemed closer now, as if we were stuck in the middle of a battle. A series of sharp bangs rattled against the side of the house as if a quick pelting of stones.

One of the soldiers stopped at the gaping hole and looked in on us. This one was a clean cut, scientific looking gentleman. He stopped, crouched, and looked in at us for just an instant, then shuffled off. I was still woozy from the blast, but it felt like I saw his wrist, that he was wearing a modern watch,

418

as if he were one of us, someone from the future, swept up in the swirl, as if some vast army was fighting another side all throughout time, as if fighting for time in the past, where space and resources were plentiful, where nothing had been ruined yet, and hope could maybe still exist. It was as if the war had changed from a fight over one thing, to a fight over future resources, future ideas, future space in the past, as if the real reasons for a battle were actually in disguise. Maybe the Civil War was actually about fighting for time and land, not about a fight over ideology. Maybe that was just an excuse, a cover. It was as if they were trying to carve out a future in the past, fighting for space, elbowing their way to resources. My arms went cold. How could you trust any of it any longer?

And then a shriek of a monkey split the air. I searched to locate it. I was on my knees before the opening. Broxon leaned against the wall before me at my side. Finally I saw a monkey in the field, flailing its arms in fury, screeching through the thin strands of white and gray confusion of smoke that twisted by. The monkey ran to jump on the back of the nearest soldier, one with a long, scraggly beard, worn skin, and tired eyes – a soldier who did not

419

know, a soldier who didn't know what he was really fighting for. The monkey screamed and clawed him, bringing him to the ground.

"It's here." Broxon shook his head in defeat. "As if someone else had brought it back earlier than we did."

"The apparatus." I turned and gasped, looking behind myself. "The apparatus." I raised my arm and wheezed, straining to reach for it. "We'll have to go back further," I huffed. "Where? . . . Where is it?" I searched frantically with my eyes.

Broxom looked back at me and shook his head free of the temporary clouds of fog and disbelief. His suit was ripped and torn and dirty. He lunged to the floor, scampering to scatter chunks of wood, frantically clearing away short, jagged boards. More pops rattled the side of the house as if the other side were coming up fast. You could feel them approaching, that slow momentum. Broxom pulled up something from the smoky darkness and set it on the floor, looking it over. Then he turned to me, looked up and smiled, nodding back at me through the twisting strands of white smoke. "Yeah," he huffed. "It's here." He beamed in relief. "It's OK, . . We're going to be OK. . . We're going

420

to be OK. . ."

As One
By James Reith

One morning, during a rare erotic fumble, Mr. & Mrs. Jones found themselves conjoined at the genitals. They weren't stuck (this in fact having happened to Mr. Jones' cousin one awkward New Year's), but quite literally fused: the minor variances in their equally pallid, sagging flesh having merged into one white mass which, thatched by layers of varicose vein, bore an uncanny resemblance to faded tartan.

Upon recognising his rather unique predicament, Mr. Jones halted his lacklustre thrusting and stared at what had been his point of

421

entry. How he would fit into his trousers that morning crossed his mind, as did the unhelpful thickness of his wife's thighs. Mrs. Jones had been staring at a damp patch on the ceiling and was quite oblivious to her situation. It was only when Mr. Jones' attempted exit seemed to pull her along that she looked down.

The two blankly stared at each other.

"Should I call the doctor?" Mrs. Jones enquired. It should be noted here that Mr. Jones had a particular distrust for all medical professions following the accidental extraction of his lateral incisor whilst having a filling done.

"I'm sure it's just like Cousin Percy at New Year's," Mr. Jones shrugged, "and at least you're not my brother's wife!" Mr. Jones laughed heartily. Mrs. Jones, who - so not to distract Mr. Jones from an upcoming dart's tournament - had withheld information on Percy's attempted suicide, did not find this so funny.

"Come on love," Mr. Jones continued, "let's get us a brew, then we can think about what to do." Impressed with his simple rhyme, Mr. Jones extended a hand to his beloved. In a feat resembling a comic ballet, the mingled Joneses made it off the bed and, following an argument over which dressing gown to wear, proceeded to the kitchen in an awkward waltz.

Were it not for the hum-drumming and rumble of the kettle, the two Joneses would have stood in silence. Mr. Jones wondered whether his joke about a joint passport would lighten the mood. It didn't. Neither did his realisation that you couldn't spell 'cojones' without 'Jones'. The two of them then, almost in tandem, began to wonder how the morning's event would affect their sex lives. Mr. Jones remembered his mother and took some comfort in her fondness for 'necessity being the mother of invention.' Mrs. Jones pondered momentarily, before remembering: "The kids are coming today and the house is a mess!"

The two of them then began to clean the kitchen. A description of this seems a little superfluous, but it was amusing to say the least, though not as amusing as their argument about going to the bathroom. After falling over for the fourth time, Mr. Jones decided not to get up, which made cleaning rather difficult for Mrs. Jones, as did the broken glass on the floor. They were quite content once, Mr. & Mrs. Jones, though there is a gulf between contentment and happiness. I love how closely the French for paradise, 'paradis', resembles the pronunciation of parody. Perhaps this would be funnier in French?

'Les vrais paradis sont les paradis qu'on a perdus.'

It's okay, Mr. Jones found French scary too: It's a diplomat's language, so difficult to pin down but so great for punning... In fact, he found the English language trouble enough. Right now, Mr. Jones was rather tongue tied. In a curious frenzy, the two were kissing like teenagers and rolling around the floor – knocking into everything! Then the doorbell rang.

See I forgot to mention that Ms. Jones, the daughter of Mr. & Mrs. Jones, had just gotten off the bus at the Joneses' bus stop and had been heading to the Joneses' house. The other junior Jones, who found these periodic visits a little tiresome and tedious, had decided their abstraction was a more valid use of their time.

Upon hearing the doorbell, the two Joneses looked down and noticed that the veined crochet decorating their unsightly bond had swollen into a tumorous mass which bore a striking resemblance to their daughter. Their actual daughter, in the flesh, noticed that the Joneses' door was unlocked and began to twist the handle. The two Joneses watched in horror as several tiny pustules formed in the vague shape of a mouth and a large opening collapsed in the middle of them.

Ms. Jones opened the door, only to lay eyes upon a malformed reflection of herself sprouting from between her parents. Sprout is the correct word as several veins had begun working their way through Mr. & Mrs. Jones. As Mr. Jones bled out, following a hardened blue shoot piercing an artery, he regretted not having seen a doctor about his unsightly veins. For a brief period Mrs. Jones was alive, whilst her husband, still attached, began to collapse in upon himself. The face opened its toothless jaw and emitted a strange choking sound which slowly began to resemble a scream. Searching for a tongue, it found one in Mrs. Jones, but not before taking Mr. Jones' eyes. They always said she had her father's eyes. Mrs. Jones was a real trooper and suffered through the whole ordeal until her cheekbones were required. Her husband was a real wuss.

Ms. Jones, in a state of shock, had walked in,

put her mid-price box of chocolates on the side table, and collapsed into an evening chair. She did not get up until the bizarre transformation had run its full course, and even then simply prodded the fleshy ragdoll with a spatula before sitting down again. The Jones singular arose and attempted to balance itself, bearing a striking resemblance to a scene in a popular cartoon about a baby deer. Standing in front of Ms. Jones was a being that resembled her - had she been crafted with a cookie cutter and stuffed inside a skin body sock.

At first she was terrified, but Ms. Jones slowly realised they had a lot in common. They soon became firm friends and eventually lovers. Ms. Jones also realised that her double was able to summon up the features of her parents, which was great at parties!

I scarcely enjoy didactic literature, but thought it important to write about the rarely heard side effects of varicose veins. Some details may have been exaggerated, but this is simply to make sure that a visit to a back-street dentist does not put one off practicing medical professionals, as it did to Mr. Jones.

Looking for Gloria
By Gabino Iglesias

Freddy walked into the Gravity Saloon and rushed to the bar while staring at his shoes. He knew it was a dangerous joint. Avoiding eye contact was the best technique to keep violence at bay. Although he considered alcohol-enhanced conflicts a cheap form of entertainment, the money he was about to make kept him focused. Sure, sex and power are fun but, in the end, most folks would agree it's all about the moola.

When the dark wood of the bar came into view, Freddy stopped looking at his shoes and looked up. A virus had infected the long line of stools under the bar and they were all vomiting their stuffing onto the grimy floor. The spew slowly cascaded down in the altered gravity of the place, almost as if it all happened in slow motion. A few things that looked like cigarette butts seemed to be feeding on the stuffing, but it was too dark to tell and there were more pressing issues at hand. Freddy found an empty, puke-free chunk of bar, leaned on it, and ordered a beer from a man who resembled an obese weasel.

428

As his pupils adjusted to the gloom of the place, Freddy turned around and looked at the patrons. The collection of deformed beings was almost a perfect copy of the crowd that regularly gathered at the Deformed Jackalope, his neighborhood bar. The blood stains on the floor and the stench of stale piss and stool vomit invading his nostrils were the only things reminding him this was a different bar and not his usual refuge. Instead of country-punk, the sound of metal grinding on metal poured from black speakers that hung from the ceiling behind the bar. The noise fueled the ever-tightening knot of apprehension in his chest. He was going to guzzle his first brew and quickly get a second one.

A way-over-her-prime hooker walked past Freddy, dragging her razor-sharp sadness behind her like rusty ballast. The pulsating lights of the joint enhanced the deep cellulite punctures on her four hairy legs. The short red skirt somehow reminded him of home. He wondered if there was enough time for a quick trip upstairs, but then someone interrupted his thoughts by touching his right shoulder. Freddy peeled his eyes off the dilapidated hooker and looked to his right. The woman standing there was almost entirely translucent, but some of her organs were visible and a pinkish fluid made the larger veins in her body visible. She mumbled something but was interrupted by the door opening.

Just as they'd done when Freddy walked in, every eyeball in the joint turned to the entrance. A fat man stood at the door, the lights making the copious sweat on his forehead and jowls dance rhythmically to a tune only they could hear. One look at the painfully distended stomach was all Freddy needed to know the man was Mr. Owens, his client. He waved. It caught the man's attention. Without a nod, smile or wave, Mr. Owens sauntered over.

Even under the throbbing lights, Freddy could see three weeks without going to the bathroom had taken a toll on his client. His belly was abnormally round and tight like that of a woman pregnant with an elephant. The fabric of his black t-shirt was stretched to the point of becoming somewhat transparent. But his face was worse. The skin looked like a dirty, yellowish sheet thrown over discarded furniture and there were dark bags under his eyes that would've made any boxer happy. A painful scowl brought the entire mess together and gave Mr. Owens the appearance of a man grimacing at his own impending death.

"How you doin' Freddy?" asked Mr. Owens in a strained voice.

"Getting by, Mr. Owens," replied Freddy.

Mr. Owens joined Freddy and the bar and got uncomfortably close. Sweat and fear poured from his huge pores on his face.

"I'm glad you called," said the fat man. "It's been three fucking weeks and I can't put up with this situation any longer. Did you really find the man who stole my asshole?"

Freddy felt insulted. He was known as Freddy "The Finder" for a damn reason. Since Mr. Owens was in such a desperate situation, he decided to let it slide and assured him they were going to get his stolen anus back within the hour. First, however, Freddy needed to see two things.

"You brought the cash?"

Without a word, Mr. Owens pulled a stack of bills from his right pocket and dropped it on the bar. The man was obviously new to places like the Gravity Saloon. Freddy made the stack disappear in the blink of an eye. If anyone saw the money, blood would hit the floor. He looked around. To his left,

431

two suspiciously-young females with obviously loose morals had squeezed generous mounds of purplish flesh into barely-there skintight getups. They giggled at how strange the pink liquid in their glasses moved in the lower gravity of the bar. Ironically, the giggling made their breasts shake like flan in the hands of a Parkinson's patient. To his right, Mr. Owens looked at him and, beyond him, a lip-licking pervert was busy eyefucking every woman, man, and cockroach in the joint. Freddy told Mr. Owens to meet him in the bathroom in two minutes and walked away.

His bloated appearance, the intensity and stench coming from him, and the sad desperation covering his face had convinced Freddy Mr. Owens was for real, but you could never be too sure. Complicity always has a price and Freddy made Mr. Owens drop his trousers in the john and prove to him his asshole, which he called Gloria, had indeed been stolen.

A few minutes went by and Mr. Owens shuffled his way into the john, huffing and puffing like a hog about to birth a fridge. Freddy told him what he wanted to see. Mr. Owens agreed, but said he couldn't really bend in any direction because the

432

movement made him feel like was about to burst like a hotdog in a microwave.

"That's all fine with me," said Freddy. "But if that's the case, make sure you don't drop your pants because I sure as hell am not getting anywhere near your ass or balls to help you get them back up."

Mr. Owens reached into the side of his pants and pulled out a gun. Freddy panicked for a second and was about to reach for his own piece when the fat man placed it on the filthy counter. Then he turned around right where he was and dropped his oversized sweatpants. With his right hand, he reached back, grabbed his ass cheek and pulled it aside. The sight of the two pale, hairy cheeks roughly sewn together with black thread was enough to tell Freddy the man was for real.

"That's...that's enough, Mr. Owens," said Freddy while trying to keep his lunch down.

"Well...since we're already in this uncomfortable situation, would you mind taking a look in there and telling me if it looks infected to you?"

Freddy was not getting paid nearly enough money to look into another man's ass, but then he thought about the anguish the man had to be

433

suffering from and kept his mouth shut. He leaned over a bit and took a closer look.

The sutures were amateurish at best, but they looked clean and Freddy couldn't see any pus, which he knew was a good sign.

"Looks clean to me," he said.

Mr. Owens pulled his pants up, picked up the gun from the counter, and turned around. He brought the gun up, but he was holding it out, not pointing it.

"Do you need this?"

"No, Mr. Owens, I have my own gun," said Freddy.

The hatred coating Mr. Owens' query answered the burning question Freddy had been pondering since he received the man's phone call: why would a rich man contact a lowlife like him instead of the oinkers to get his stolen property back? Now Freddy knew the answer: like any other man forced to deal with shady characters and a very personal injustice, Mr. Owens didn't want justice, he wanted retribution.

***

A few minutes later they were barreling down I-36 on Freddy's rental worm. The thing squirmed and squished a lot smoother than Freddy's old ride, so he was glad he'd spent a few bucks to impress his client.

The New Manhattan-Lower Brooklyn tunnel was only a few months old, but denizens from both places used it so much it was already full of potholes and littered with trash, rotting body parts, and vehicle carcasses. If Mr. Owens was surprised to be heading back home, he opted to keep quiet about it.

While he drove, Freddy stole glances at his client. Under the bright lights of the tunnel, it was easier to study the man.

Mr. Owens was prematurely bald. His nose was full of small red veins and his ears had enough hair to stuff a pillow. Pot-seed burns speckled the stretched cotton shirt that barely contained three weeks of accumulated feces. The man squirmed around as much as the worm that was carrying them and looked uncomfortable in every position. Freddy didn't want to imagine a life without the relief that comes from taking a dump. Feeling sorry for Mr. Owens, he decided to break the comfortable silence and fill him in. It would also be a good chance to prove to his client that when someone hired Freddy

435

"The Finder," they were hiring the best finder ever.

"We're heading to a house on the Third Circle, almost right below your street. The man who stole your anus, Omar Olivo Ortiz Oropeza, is an illegal alien who spends his days on a bed there, pushing all sorts of nasty food down his gullet and..."

"Were you able to figure out why he stole my sweet Gloria?" interrupted Mr. Owens.

Unfortunately for him, Freddy knew why: he had witnessed the man using the stolen anus.

"I really don't want to go into too much detail, but you're entitled to know what's being done with your property, so I'll tell you what I know," said Freddy. "Omar is obsessed with becoming the fattest man in the Third Circle. To achieve this, he swallows gallons of gravy, dozens of bacon-wrapped fetuses, fried fatback sandwiches, butter-stuffed cookies, and lard-covered cheesecakes on a daily basis. What comes out the opposite end of his mouth is an almost radioactive fluid so acidic that Omar's own anus is constantly in pain. With the help of a doctor from the outer ring of the Seventh Circle, Omar had a second asshole placed on his body so he can alternate them. It helps him stay

436

pain-free."

Mr. Owens nodded at the information he was receiving, but kept quiet. Then he exhaled audibly and started talking, his eyes lost and unfocused.

"I was lucky enough to be born into a family that wasn't hurting for money. My father had a successful mind control chip business. He struggled a little at first, but his product was good and the reception was fantastic. As soon as the mob learned they could control animals and people at a distance, they started shoveling cash my father's way. After the media broke a story about a herd of killer cows, he decided to sell the business. I grew up in comfort and always took things for granted. Then my dad died, my mother was bitten by a hellmaggot while tending to her roses and started rotting, and my sister, probably out of heartbreak, spontaneously combusted. I inherited everything. Let me tell you, I spent most of that money pretty damn fast. I built a giant womb and moved into it. I ate nothing but exotic species and slept only with women who were willing to be mutilated during sex. That's not a cheap thing to find, Freddy. Anyway, the point is that I never knew anxiety or pain. Then three weeks ago two incredibly tall skinny grey fellows grabbed

437

me as I was getting out of my womb, zapped me with a taser, and pushed me into a white worm that smelled like sulfuric acid and menthol. Next thing I know I wake up face down in an abandoned warehouse with no asshole and in a lot of pain. You might think I have enough reason to be angry with what I've told you, but it gets worse. Gloria was not a normal anus. After my father sold his company, it moved in different, infinitely better directions. The developed chips that tap into your conscious and unconscious thoughts to create the perfect pet. Two years ago my anus became my pet, my companion, my best friend. I hope you now understand why the man who did this has to pay the ultimate price."

Mr. Owens stopped talking. Freddy knew there was nothing he could say to that story, so he stayed quiet.

A few minutes later they pulled up in front of a house built with graffitied plywood. They got off the worm and left it tied to a post that no longer had a mailbox on top of it. A loud grumble came from somewhere inside the house. They could hear it out on the sidewalk. Whatever it was, it sent shivers down Freddy's spine. The it came again and was followed by an incredibly loud wet fart. They

438

both knew then what it was: they were listening to Omar's stomach. Just as Freddy had imagined, Mr. Owens pulled out the gun from his stretched out waistband. Now that the gloom of the bathroom wasn't hiding anything, he could see it was a .357 Magnum, a no-nonsense kind of gun. Mr. Owens asked him to lead the way.

The overpowering smell of sweat, burnt oil, and farts made them cringe and their eyes water as they walked toward the hut. They pushed open the piece of plywood that acted as a door and looked inside.

In the middle of the shack stood an enormous bed. On that bed, the blob known as Omar Olivo Ortiz Oropeza was busy drinking a few pints of melted ice cream through a piece of garden hose. Mr. Owens raised the gun and approached the man.

"Who the fuck are you?" asked Omar.

"I came to get my Gloria back, you fat fuck!" screamed Mr. Owens.

"Who's Gloria? What are you...?"

The man stopped. A phlegmy purr signaled a breath. Before he could continue, Mr. Owens pulled the trigger. Omar's forehead exploded in a crimson

439

flower and his head dropped back. Mr. Owens put the gun away and pulled a straight razor from his pocket. He asked Freddy to help him turn the dead man over. The task was easier said than done and it took them five minutes of pushing to get the man off the bed and onto his humongous, flabby stomach. When the dead robber was finally turned, Freddy saw the two anuses. They were both fresh and had the same rough stitches as Mr. Owens' wound. Although they looked identical to him, Mr. Owens began crying and caressing the one on the left. In response, and even though the man it was attached to was dead, the anus started rapidly dilating and closing. It made Freddy think of a Cyclops in the rain. As he carved around the stitches, Mr. Owens kept saying "Oh, my Gloria. Sweet, sweet Gloria."

After much slicing, Gloria was freed from her gluttonous slaver and Freddy would swear he saw the anus pucker and reply to his owner's attentions with what sounded like kisses.

With the asshole in his hand and a satisfied smile on his face, Mr. Owens thanked Freddy and declined a ride home. He knew just the man to make him right again. Claiming a surgeon friend of his lived nearby and would pick him up, Mr. Owens thanked him once again and walked away, his anus held tightly against his tear-streaked face. Freddy climbed into his rental worm and immediately felt the bundle of cash trying to burn a hole through his jeans. It was time to go back and pay that sad hooker a visit that would brighten her night.

A Path for the New Bride
By Nick Cato

Then

Ryan Lambaste (that's lamb-bass-tee) was worried the meal had been a complete failure. Sure, he could've run outside, or into another room, but he refused to let his problem control his life.

#

"I can't believe we won't be seeing each other for six months," Olivia had said when they began their last dinner together. "But I'm so excited for you. I can't believe this is finally happening."

Now

He'd read stories from his favorite bands on how lonely the road could get. His band mates spent every moment they weren't on stage getting drunk and entertaining groupies.

Not Ryan.

Even if he wasn't married to Olivia, he'd be afraid to join in on the backstage hi-jinks, worried that they'd show up for him—or something worse.

Then

Olivia helped Ryan clean up the mess; food, broken dishes and chair legs lay strewn around the kitchen and adjoining living room. Traces of condiments ran up and down the walls, a few across the ceiling. The refrigerator door had been ripped off and smashed to pieces. The air carried a distinct odor, but Olivia couldn't quite place it.

442

Now

On Scattered's tour bus, their manager counted money from the afternoon's merchandise sales. They actually made more from T-shirts and CDs then they did from being on the biggest heavy metal road show in the world, but no one was complaining; there weren't too many new bands who could get on the same stage as Killsquad, Deathhead, and several other top acts.

Ryan smiled, considering the stack of cash. He was finally living his dream after ten years of gigs in mostly empty nightclubs and countless band member changes. Yet perhaps it was his age—thirty-nine—that made him long to be back home with Olivia, in an environment where he'd be better prepared for the next outburst.

Then

They'd made love for the last time on the filthy kitchen floor. Ryan's right knee slid on a half-eaten pickle, causing him to slam into the stove

443

when he tried to get up. And when he was finally able to stand, one of them sat between the tea kettle and frying pan, leaning back on a large pot of soup.

Olivia lay on the floor, her head tilted up, purple ooze dripping over her lip. The drops slowly hit the floor, each one turning into a hovering, glowing sphere that surrounded Ryan's head.

"Mr. rock star," the thing on the stove said. "I guess this is good-bye."

"Good-bye?"

"Well, for now. I don't know if we can take being away from her for six months," it said, nodding down to Olivia. Her mouth finally ceased dribbling the peculiar liquid. "We've grown quite fond of her."

"Please—come with me. You can't—"

"We've thought about it and decided we'd rather stay," the thing said, looking at the hovering spheres making their way around the kitchen.

"But I don't want to leave you here without me around."

The thing frowned. "Have it your way."

Ryan fell to the floor, the spheres forming a force-field, holding him in place.

"You sure about this?"

444

"Y-yes. P-please don't do this to her."

"Okay. I tried," the thing said, before walking between Ryan's legs, its tiny body swaying back and forth like an obese rat.

Now

Somewhere on a stretch of road in Nowheresville, Texas, Ryan Lambaste looked out the window of his tour bus, amazed at how flat everything was. He heard the grunting, groaning and laughing of some girls his band had picked up in Louisiana, wondering how they were planning to get back home.

Then

Olivia woke up, dizzy. She watched Ryan make more of a mess near the kitchen sink as he shoved the hose attachment in and out of his throat. The cold water reached her from across the room, creeping under her body, causing severe goosebumps. Her mouth tasted like a mixture of

445

dehydrated milk and Sweet Tarts.

"Come out you son-of-a-bitch ..."

Olivia walked over to him, reached for him, trying not to slide on the slick tile.

"Come on! Get out of me!" Ryan said, his voice a mixture of anger and deep-pitched aquaticness.

Now

They stormed across the plains, nearly five thousand strong. Their sight caused many to smirk, many to laugh, but this herd was driven by a seldom-seen rage. Their dirty, white hair suggested years of flatland habitation. Despite the pleasant look of the creatures, some of their coats were stained red, hinting to a side of them unknown to the growing legion of domestic owners.

Then

Olivia washed the mustard, wine, and various other stains from her hair, reinvigorated by

446

the hot water. A blurred vision of Ryan came through the glass door. His body was perched on the toilet, his voice finally back to normal.

Perhaps he had accepted their plans.

The bathroom glowed purple when he stood up to flush.

Now

"Dallas should be in sight within thirty minutes," the bus driver said, a long cigar hanging from his lip. "Parts of this tour aren't too exciting, as I guess you can see."

"Yeah, I've noticed," Ryan said, picking up his 1978 Les Paul, strumming without a pick to relieve the boredom.

The groupies had passed out along with his band mates. He hoped the idiots would be alert in a few hours when they took the stage to perform for close to 75,000 screaming fans.

In the distance, a small cloud of dust followed them.

Then

"They're kind-of cute, but I don't know if I'd want one as a pet." Olivia ran her hand through the curly hair. "Their legs are pretty silly-looking if you ask me."

"Bite your tongue," Camile Jessie said, tossing feed to the precious animals who roamed freely across her property. "They're the best pets money can buy."

Olivia walked with her neighbor through the acreage, petting the creatures as they came and went.

"So, how's Ryan doing?"

"You know … he's excited about the tour. And all."

"And all? Does that mean missy here isn't as excited about it as her hubby is?" Camile rubbed Olivia's shoulder for motherly comfort.

"Oh no, of course I am. But it's going to get a little lonely around here while he's on the road."

"Lonely? You ever get that bored, you know I can always use your help over here." Camile tossed the last handful of feed to the ground, where it was quickly licked up.

448

"Thanks, Cammy."

A burst of purple smoke puffed out from Olivia's bedroom window, causing her and Camile to gasp.

"Ryan still havin' those attacks?"

"Yes, but he's not going to budge."

"You mind if I go 'n have another talk with him?"

"You can try, but he's probably sleeping."

Camile scratched her elbow on the back of a dark-gray alpaca. "Guess I'll wait until tomorrow."

Now

Scattered's tour bus skidded, although they were driving on very arid blacktop. The driver gained control of the vehicle and drove on.

"What was that?" John DiTello asked, running up from the rear of the bus.

"Hey! Someone finally surfaced." Ryan kept a calm demeanor despite the fact their bus was being attacked.

John looked out the windows, something the sex lair in the back didn't have. "What the hell are

449

those things?"

"You wouldn't believe it if I told you."
Then, to the driver, Ryan said, "I'd suggest stepping
on it with everything you've got."

Then

"Oh come here, honey," Camile said,
hugging Olivia who had come over in tears. "Now
there's no reason to be getting all cryin' on yourself.
Just think of the money he'll be makin'."

"I know," Olivia said, blowing her nose in a
torn-to-shreds tissue. "But I miss him so much, and
it's only been five days!"

Camile couldn't take much more of seeing
her neighbor suffer.

She could hear them groaning out in the
fields—itching to do her bidding.

Now

Scattered's two tour buses finally found their
way to Miller's Field, a large area just outside of

Dallas that was set-up to accommodate the tremendous crowd. Deathhead's bus was already unloading, as was Planned Damage's and KillSquad's. Ryan stepped off the bus and could hear the gathering fans already filling the huge area in front of the stage.

This was the life. He took his gear and headed for Skull City, the name given to the backstage tent area. On his way he high-fived several musicians he'd grown up worshipping, trying very hard to play it cool, even after nearly a week on the road with them. The novelty probably wouldn't wear off for a few more tours.

Ryan joined his band mates in tuning up and going over the set list. Food was distributed by a group of girls who looked like they belonged on a punk tour, drinks came from a bunch of hippie-looking older men, and drugs were all over the place, although his band didn't partake before hitting the stage.

He also silently prayed that they wouldn't show up until after the concert.

Then

Olivia woke up on Camile's couch. Maybe she cried herself to sleep, or perhaps she'd had a little too much brandy.

The humming came through an open window and grabbed her attention.

Camile sat cross-legged in the middle of her backyard, singing in a strange tongue. The alpacas formed a single-file line, hundreds stepping up, licking her ankles, taking pulls from her left nipple, which emitted a stream of yellow smoke, and then heading off into the pasture.

Camile's eyes glowed purple.

Now

On their way to the stage, the ground began to rumble. Ryan heard some people in the crowd scream "Earthquake!" then chaos ensued.

Within seconds the festival grounds were frantic with metalheads trying to break free from the confusion and band members scrambling for the false safety of their tents and tour buses.

452

Ryan continued to the stage, figuring it'd be safer up there than on the ground. A few people up front looked on as if nothing was happening, waiting for the show. Half the crowd went crazy as Ryan came out from behind the drum riser, but in the distance, he saw a barrier fence come crashing down, followed by a trail of rising dust.

Thousands of alpacas flooded the field, stampeding concert-goers, making a bee-line for the stage. Ryan noticed many people—even some being crushed—laughing at the puffy legs and determined faces of the unusual beasts.

Every smile in the field was inverted when the blood started flying.

Then

Olivia pretended to be sleeping as Camile came back into the house. She peeked as her neighbor went to the kitchen and stuck her feet in a large pitcher of iced-tea, the liquid turning purple and bubbling like a mad scientist's concoction.

Olivia wanted to run next door and get back into her own bed, but was afraid to move, not knowing what on Earth Camile was up to.

A few alpacas came into the house, one sitting down near Olivia's feet. One began to lick her ankle, but she kept her composure.

Now

Ryan ran with everything he had back to his tour bus, the stage and audience a growing pile of rubble.

Then

Olivia managed to make it home after Camile finally went to sleep; the alpacas had joined her—seemingly all of them. She tip-toed around them, right up to her front door, then locked it behind her.

Her body stunk of the wooly animals. She washed in the scalding water, trying to remove the purple ring around her ankle that refused to come off.

As she tried to catch up on some sleep,

Camile's voice came through her window.

Now

Ryan flew across the flatlands, heading back the way they had come.

Behind him, the concert area lay in ruins, thousands of fans were massacred, millions worth of equipment destroyed, and the Scattered tour bus had been reduced to rubbish. He could still hear his band mates and road crew screaming as the creatures stomped their faces into the earth, snapping necks and crushing skulls.

Ryan braced himself, trying to breath in the heavy motion, stuck to the side of one of the larger alpacas. Dust filled his mouth as he wondered what was bonding him to the creature.

Then

The purple ring had spread throughout Olivia's body, coloring all her skin. She screamed when she looked in the mirror.

455

Curly white hair began to grow on her arms and back.

She ran out the front door, flying into the arms of Camile Jessie.

"Now just relax there, neighbor."

Olivia fainted.

Present Mesh

Ryan was delivered back home just seven days into his first world tour. The creatures dumped him in Camile's backyard and then pulled his legs apart. The purple sphere squeezed out from between his legs, divided into countless miniature versions of itself, they finding their way inside the alpacas. Then the thing came out of him last and moseyed over to Ryan's house.

Camile took a pull from her nipple as Ryan stood up.

"Olivia really missed you." She offered him a hit.

Realizing the tour was history, he indulged. "Which one?" Ryan asked, looking through the crowd.

456

Camile snapped her fingers. A tall, slim alpaca strutted through the crowd, sticking out like a sore thumb due to its purple fur. It came face-to-face with him.

Tears welled up in Ryan's eyes.

Camile began to sing a new song as the alpacas stepped to the side and made a path for the new bride.

Ryan walked her back home, wondering if this would be his last tour as a professional musician.

AUTHOR BIOGRAPHIES

Meghan Arcuri is new to writing fiction and poetry. To date, she has three short stories and one poem published. That she writes horror and bizarro is amusing to her, especially since she cried after watching *Candyman* and is still afraid of the dark. More information on her can be found at meghanarcuri.wordpress.com or facebook.com/meg.arcuri.

Andrew Wayne Adams is the author of *Janitor of Planet Anilingus*, a bizarro novella published by Eraserhead Press as part of their 2012 New Bizarro Author Series. His short stories have appeared in *Bust Down the Door and Eat All the Chickens, The Dream People, Metazen, Zygote in My Coffee, The Magazine of Bizarro Fiction*, and elsewhere. He grew up in Ohio but now lives in Portland, Oregon, where he works in a warehouse.

Vincenzo Bilof lives in Michigan and repairs

pinball machines for a living.

Max Booth III is the editor-in-chief of Perpetual Motion Machine Publishing and the assistant editor of *Dark Moon Digest.* He is the author of *They Might Be Demons, Toxicity,* and *The Mind is a Razorblade.* He currently resides in San Antonio, TX with his life partner and dachshund. Follow him on Twitter @GiveMeYourTeeth and visit him at www.TalesFromTheBooth.com.

G. Arthur Brown pens absurd and irreal fiction, usually by the light of a candle made from the fat of an executed murder. He has published one novel, *Kitten*, part of the New Bizarro Author Series from Eraserhead Press. His fiction has appeared and disappeared of its own volition. He is currently looking for an environmentally friendly way to glue his scribblings in place permanently.

Jeff Burk is the cult favorite author of *Shatnerquake, Super Giant Monster Time, Cripple Wolf,* and *Shatnerquest.* Like the literary equivalent to a cult B-Horror movie, Burk writes violent, absurd, and funny stories about punks, monsters,

460

gore, and trash culture. Everyone normally dies at the end. He is also the Editor-In-Chief for *The Magazine of Bizarro Fiction* and the Head Editor of Eraserhead Press' horror imprint, Deadite Press.

Nick Cato's fiction has appeared in many anthologies, magazines, and websites. He is the author of the mafia-zombie novel *Don of the Dead,* the novellas *The Apocalypse of Peter, The Last Porno Theater*, and the short story collection *Antibacterial Pope and other Incongruous Stories.* He is currently co-authoring a huge film book on 70s occult horror films and has two novellas and a bizarro novel in the works. Visit his blog at nickcato/blogspot.com.

Alan M. Clark—born Nashville, Tennessee in 1957—grew up in a home full of old bones, Indian relics and dusty medical books—Bachelor of Fine Arts Degree from the San Francisco Art Institute. His short fiction appears in three collections, in the anthologies, *Tales of Jack the Ripper, The Walri Project, Last Drink Bird Head, The Thackery T. Lambshead Pocket Guide to Eccentric and Discredited Diseases, Portents, Bedtime Stories to Darken Your Dreams, More Phobias, The Book of Dead Things, Dead on Demand*, and *Darkside*, and

461

in the magazines, *Midnight Hour, The Silver Web* and *The Magazine of Bizarro Fiction*.
Novels: his Bram Stoker Award-nominated novel, written with Jeremy Robert Johnson, *Siren Promised*,—2005; his two book series written with Stephen Merritt and Lorelei Shannon, *The Blood of Father Time*—2007; *D.D. Murphry, Secret Policeman*, written with Elizabeth Massie—2009; *Of Thimble and Threat: The Life of a Ripper Victim*—2011; *A Parliament of Crows*—2012; *The Door that Faced West*—scheduled for release 2014. Mr. Clark's publishing company, IFD Publishing, has released six traditional books, the most recent of which is a full color book of his artwork, *The Paint in My Blood*, and twenty-three ebooks. He and his wife, Melody, live in Oregon. www.alanmclark.com

Edmund Colell's work has appeared in LegumeMan, Christmas on Crack, Amazing Stories of the Flying Spaghetti Monster, Bizarro Central, Detritus, Bizarrocast, and elsewhere. He survives in Tucson, Arizona, holed up in an iced coffee fortress against the vicious heat and brain-boiled citizens.

David Conover is a large brain floating in a fishbowl full of bourbon and sweet vermouth. He works with words and pictures while impatiently waiting for his mindslaves—dazed third shift workers at the nearby Louisville Ford Truck Assembly Plant—to complete his invincible transforming cybernetic body. There have been some delays, since the color he ordered, Jazz Blue Pearl Coat, is not factory standard.

William Cook is the author of the novel *Blood Related*. He is a writer of psychological horror and dark fiction that crosses genres. Many of his short stories have appeared in anthologies; he is also the editor of *Fresh Fear*, a horror anthology that includes some of the biggest names in contemporary horror fiction. Website: http://williamcookwriter.com

Christopher T. Dabrowski is a Polish author: Books in Poland: *Deathbirth* (2008), *Anima vilis* (2010), *Grobbing* (2012), *Deathbirth and other* stories (2012) and *The life of Dr. Abble* (2013).

Film based on his story: "Angel" - http://www.imdb.com/title/tt3092668/ - with famous Polish actress (Anna Mucha) and music from USA rock band Silversun Pickups.

He published his stories in: Slovak (PLAYBOY),

USA, England, Czech Republic, Russia, Brasil, Spain, Argentina, Germany, Italy, Hungary and Mexico.

Danger_Slater is the world's most flammable writer! He enjoys fast cars and slow women. Or is that slow cars and fast women? Or maybe it's *low* cars and *fat* women? Whatever the case, he writes books and short stories and shit and you love ALL of them! Purchase one his books on Amazon (seriously, fucko, get on that) or follow him on Facebook, Twitter and Goodreads and get links to all things Dangerous at www.dangerslater.blogspot.com

James Dorr's newest collection is *The Tears of Isis*, released by Perpetual Motion Machine Publishing in May 2013. This joins his two prose collections from Dark Regions Press, *Strange Mistresses: Tales of Wonder and Romance* and *Darker Loves: Tales of Mystery and Regret,* and the all-poetry *Vamps (A Retrospective)* from Sam's Dot/White Cat. An active member of SFWA and HWA with nearly four hundred individual fiction and poetry appearances from *Alfred Hitchcok's Mystery Magazine* to

Xenophilia, Dorr invites readers to visit his site at http://jamesdorrwriter.wordpress.com."Mr. Happy Head" was first published in *Wicked Mystic* in Spring 1996.

P. A. Douglas wrote a bizarro novella in 2013 called, Cucumber Punk. Douglas lives in South East Texas.
www.indie-inside.com

Ethan Evans was born in Kalamazoo, Michigan and grew up in Nashville, TN graduating from Belmont University in 2013 with a degree in biochemistry & molecular biology. He is the nephew of the artist and writer Alan M. Clark. Ethan met Daniel Pendergraft in 2009. Their friendship has since resulted in the birth of a collaboration machine, both writing together and playing aleatoric music on the piano/trombone (Daniel) and the alto saxophone (Ethan).

Randy Fox grew up in Muhlenberg County, Kentucky, and moved to Nashville, Tennessee with the obviously insane idea of making a living by writing words on paper. His fiction has appeared in several anthologies and magazines including *Imagination Fully Dilated*, *It Came from the Drive-In* and *Love in Vein II*, and his writing on music, pop culture and old, weird stuff has appeared in *Vintage Rock*, *Record Collector*, *Nashville Scene*, *East Nashvillian*, *Journal of Country Music*, *Jack Kirby Collector*, *Scary Monsters* and many other publications printed on the remains of dead trees. From 1997 to 2010 he hosted The Hipbilly Jamboree on WRVU-FM in Nashville, a weekly program of rockabilly, western swing and wise-ass talk, and he's currently writing a book on how a bunch of n'er-do-well hillbillies helped create a thing called rock'n'roll.

Daniel W. Gonzales is a person. He is a person who lives in a place. That place is Washington. He doesn't want to say anymore than that because you might be one of THEM. The people watching him, the people who want to eat him and drag him into that dark dimension where the shadow things live. Oh yeah and he runs this magazine called Surreal Grotesque, www.surrealgrotesque.com. What the fuck else is there to know?
Email: SurrealGrotesque77@hotmail.com.

R. A. Harris writes bizarre, strange and surreal fiction from his home in England. His published work includes the bizarro novella *All Art is Junk* (Bizarro Pulp Press, 2013) and the mind-buggering

Apparatus of Capture (Dynatox Ministries, 2013). Find out more at www.leakylibido.wordpress.com

Emily Hunerwadel is an engineering student at Belmont University hailing from a small, small town in mid-Alabama. With this background, she likes to bring some science themes and ideas into her writing. When she graduates, she intends to completely disregard her science-y roots and delve fully into the world of writing and publishing.

Gabino Iglesias was born in the Caribbean and then moved around trying to escape his nightmares. He's been a dog whisperer, witty communications professor, and ballerina assassin. He now lives near a dumpster in Austin, Texas, where he works (well, goes hungry) as a freelance journalist and impersonates a PhD student. His nonfiction has appeared in rags like *The New York Times*, *El Nuevo Día* and *Z Magazine*. The stuff that's made up has been published in places like Flash Fiction Offensive, Bizarro Central, Paragraph Line, Divergent Magazine and a few horror and bizarro anthologies. His first book, *Gutmouth*, was published by Eraserhead Press. When not writing or fighting ninja squirrels, he devours books and regurgitates reviews for places like Verbicide, The Rumpus, Word Riot, HorrorTalk, The Magazine of Bizarro Fiction, Zouch Magazine, Chiaroscuro, Buzzy Mag, Tweeds Magazine, and a few others. He's currently working on overcoming his crippling hippopotomonstrosesquipedaliophobia and writing weird stuff. You can send insults his way at gabinoiglesias@gmail.com

MP Johnson's short stories have appeared in more than 30 underground books and magazines. His debut book, *The After-Life Story of Pork Knuckles Malone*, was recently released by Bizarro Pulp Press. His second book, *Dungeons and Drag Queens*, is due soon from Eraserhead Press. He is the creator of Freak Tension zine, a B-movie extra and an obsessive music fan currently based in Minneapolis.

Dawid Kain – born November 7, 1981, in Köln (Germany), is a Polish novelist and short story writer, author of four critically acclaimed novels: *Right, Left, Broken*, *Mug in the Sky*, *Five to Revolt* and *Square One*. He lives in Cracow.

In 1987, after hearing Poison's "Look What the Cat Dragged In" for the first time, **Sean Leonard** decided he wanted to play drums. After realizing all rock stars wore leather pants, he traded in those dreams of fortune and fame for 80's sitcoms, horror movies (which he reviews at HorrorNews.net), and punk rock. Sean's short stories can be found in Solarcide's "Flash Me! The Sinthology," Bizarro Plup Press's "Bizarro Bizarro: An Anthology," and online at Cease, Cows. www.seanofthedead.net

Jan Maszczyszyn was born in Poland in 1960. In 1989 he migrated to Australia, where he is currently living. He specializes in writting dark SciFi, Bizzaro Fiction and Horror and often tries to combine them where he can. Jan succeeded in publishing an anthology of his own stories *Testimonium* 2013 where he explored the possibilities that crossing over of genres could create. His characters often say: "Stop dreaming about the future - start to hate it! The future ?- for us ?- is to be dead!". He made his debut in "New word" magazine in 1977 with his story " Guardian ", later his stories were published in "Fantastyka", "Politechnik", "Facts"," Merkuriusz

"," Sounds ", and in fanzines: Somnambul, Fictions, Quasar, Phoenix, Spectrum, a quarterly literary" Matafora ", and they also appear in a wide range of press within the Polish community in Australia. A few stories appeared in anthologies *Meeting in the Skies*, *Get the Universe*, "Devourer of gray", "Dira necessitas" and recently "Bizzaro Bazaar" in 2013. He also publish his stories in polish portals of bizzaro fiction "Bad Letters" , "Horror Online", "Carpe Noctem","Qfant", "Shortal","Tea at Helen's place", "Ex Fabula" and " New Fantastica".
He was one of the founders of the first Polish SF& Horror club fiction "Somnambul" issuing periodical with the same title. Website: jahusz.com

Todd Nelsen's literary and film interests include horror, fantasy, and science fiction. He cites Stephen King, Robert E. Howard, Hermann Hesse, and R.B. Clague as influences. He is an avid fan of metal music and currently resides in Denver, Colorado, where he writes, reads, and is constantly fantasizing. His short fiction has been featured in numerous publications, including *Schlock*! *The Pulpateers* and *Tales of the Undead – Hell Whore Volume III*.

Daniel Pendergraft was born and raised in north Texas in a town called Allen. He moved to Nashville, TN to study jazz piano in '09, graduating in 2013. He has an optimistic view of the future despite the fact that he has yet to contribute anything of value to society, save a mystic collaboration (with Ethan Evans) which produced the first recorded testament of our Gelatin Savior, better known as *Wildberry Christ*. May his delicious, gooey tendrils of Jello embrace your currently unflavored soul, for now and ever, amen.

Tony Rauch is an architectural and urban designer, and an all around great guy filled with nothing but good things. Good things. He has been interviewed by, or had his books reviewed by, The Prague Post, Oxford University, MIT, Savanna Collage of Art and Design, and Raintaxi, among many others.Rauch has three books of short stories out –
- *I'm Right Here*, from Spout Press (funky/jazzy/arty short stories)
- *Laredo*, from Eraserhead Press (funky/jazzy/arty fairytale short stories)
- *Eyeballs Growing All Over Me... Again,* from

Eraserhead Press (fairy tale surreal fantasy action adventure sci-fi short stories and story starters for young adults and reluctant readers)
For more info and story samples, refer to his website: http://trauch.wordpress.com/

Dustin Reade lives in Port Angeles, Washington in a trailer park behind a BBQ restaurant. His book, *Grambo* was released as part of the 2013 New Bizarro Authors Series, and his short stories can be found in The Magazine of Bizarro Fiction, and online at Bizarro Central. When not writing, he perform atheist wedding ceremonies, plays keyboard, and edits the online surrealist magazine, The Mustache Factor.

James Reith is a writer, musician and computer-game designer hailing from a 'back-end-of-nowhere' village in Somerset, England. Here are 10 marginally interesting things about him:

• He lived in Germany for 9 years
• He once delivered a paper on Paul Muldoon's poetry to Paul Muldoon
• He really doesn't like talking about himself in the 3rd person

472

- He once replaced the replacement for the percussionist from 'The Happy Mondays' for a band, which was not 'The Happy Mondays', at a music festival
- He doesn't think there is anything wrong with long, cumbersome sentences
- As a child, he discussed the politics of Thomas the Tank Engine with a Czech ambassador
- As an adult, he briefly worked as a professional odour-sniffer
- Physically, he has been likened to 'a hot Charles Darwin'
- No one believes this, but he is distantly related to Florence Nightingale

As a schoolboy, a cowboy once helped pick up his textbooks (no one believes this either, but James is adamant it happened)

Michael Allen Rose is a Chicago based writer, musician and performance artist. He has several stories in publication including his debut novella *Party Wolves in My Skull* from Eraserhead Press and a limited edition chapbook from Dynatox Ministries called *Declension*. His short pieces have also appeared in Surreal Grotesque, Phantasmagorium, Kizuna: Fiction for Japan and others. His musical project Flood Damage is loud and strange, and an album is forthcoming. He thinks dumplings are suspicious. He likes cats better than people. Often times, he can be found either naked, or in nothing but a bathrobe. If you ask him about it, he'll tell you it's part of a performance piece, but you'll know better. He loves good beer, good tea and good people who aren't dicks. Find him on the worldwide information superhighway at www.michaelallenrose.com and various other sites.

Craig Saunders lives in Norfolk, England, with his wife and three children, who he pretends to listen to while making up stories in his head. He holds a degree in Japanese, and lived in Japan for five years where he held a number of jobs; editor, translator, and carpenter among them. He knows enough jujitsu, karate, aikido and kendo to be a danger only to himself. He has published more than two dozen short stories, and is the author of many novels including *Rain* (Crowded Quarantine Publications), *The Love of the Dead* (Evil Jester Press) and *A Stranger's Grave (*Grand Mal Press). He writes horror and fantasy for fun and humour when he's feeling serious, which isn't often. He blogs at www.craigrsaunders.blogspot.com, or find him on

Amazon.com or Amazon.co.uk.

Bruce Taylor, aka., "Mr. Magic Realism" writes magic realism (think "Twilight Zone". His writing has also been described as a cross between Bradbury and Kafka). Recently, he co-edited with Elton Elliott, former editor of "The Science Fiction Review", the ground breaking anthology, "Like Water for Quarks" which examines the intersection of the magic realist writing form with science fiction, with such contributors (in the original anthology, Ray Bradbury) as Ursula K. LeGuin, Brian Herbert, Kevin J. Anderson, Connie Willis, Greg Bear, William F. Nolan and many others (now available from baenebooks.com). His book, *Kafka's Uncle and Other Strange Tales* with introduction by Brian Herbert, was nominated for the &NOW Award for Innovative Writing (SUNY, NY). Another book, *Edward: Dancing On the Edge of Infinity* with introduction by Jay Lake, based on the work by Karl Capek (who gave us the word, "Robot") has received favorable reviews. Bruce is also presently completing the third book of a spiritual trilogy (introduction to be written by Brian Herbert) due out 2014.

475

Kevin Ward is a native of Nashville, Tennessee, who fell in love with illustration early in life. He started drawing at age three because there were not enough pictures of dinosaurs at the local library to satisfy him. From elementary school onward he was encouraged to pursue art.

After studying fine art in college he became fascinated by the idea of suggesting stories through images. His ongoing love of science, music, fantasy, and genre fiction provided a melding of images with subject matter so that illustration became the natural outlet for his creativity.

By 1980 he had worked his way into the science fiction subculture,. his first exhibit a near sell out providing the contacts for his first published work in Future Life Magazine. He has provided illustrations for publications in the US and in Europe including covers for books by Anne McCaffrey, Piers Anthony, Norman Spinrad, and others. His clients have included the Doubleday Publishing Group, Grolier Science Encyclopedia, Funk and Wagnalls, TSR, Inc., and NASA. Still residing in Nashville, he has recently achieved a revitalized career after a long hiatus from illustration. He is currently producing e-book covers for an ongoing urban fantasy series.

Wol-vriey is Nigerian and quite tall. He is the author of *The Bizarro Story of I*, *Chainsaw Cop Corpse*, *Vegan Zombie Apocalypse*, and *Meat Suitcase*. Wol-vriey blogs at http://oddityfarm.wordpress.com

THE COVER ARTIST

Alan M. Clark grew up in Tennessee in a house full of bones and old medical books. He has created illustrations for hundreds of books, including works of fiction of various genres, non-fiction, textbooks, young adult fiction, and children's books. A major influence for his art comes from the Surrealists, particularly Max Ernst. He is fascinated with the use of what he calls "controlled accidents" and the possibility of "finding" images within the paint. A great advocate of collaboration, he has worked with many others in both literary and visual art. Mr. Clark has illustrated the writing of such authors as Ray Bradbury, Robert Bloch, Joe R. Lansdale, Stephen King, George Orwell, Manly Wade Wellman, Greg Bear, Edward Lee, Peter Straub, and Lewis Shiner, as well as his own. He is the author of 12 books, including seven novels, a lavishly illustrated novella, four collections of fiction, and a nonfiction full-color book of his artwork. His latest novel *The Door That Faced West* is due for release in Feb. 2014 from Lazy Fascist Press. Awards for his illustration work include the World Fantasy Award and four Chesley Awards. Mr. Clark's company, IFD Publishing, has released six traditional books and twenty-three ebooks. Alan M. Clark and his wife, Melody, live in Oregon. www.alanmclark.com

478

CUCUMBER PUNK

On the fringe of an acceptable society, Pete's a
cucumber-headed punk whose thoughts of rebellion
against the social order frustrate him to no end.
Sometimes, there's a shortage of tomato sauce. But
there's no shortage of fear for the Veg-heads, as they're
hunted down to satisfy the Norms and their consumer
culture...

WWW.BIZARROPULPPRESS.COM

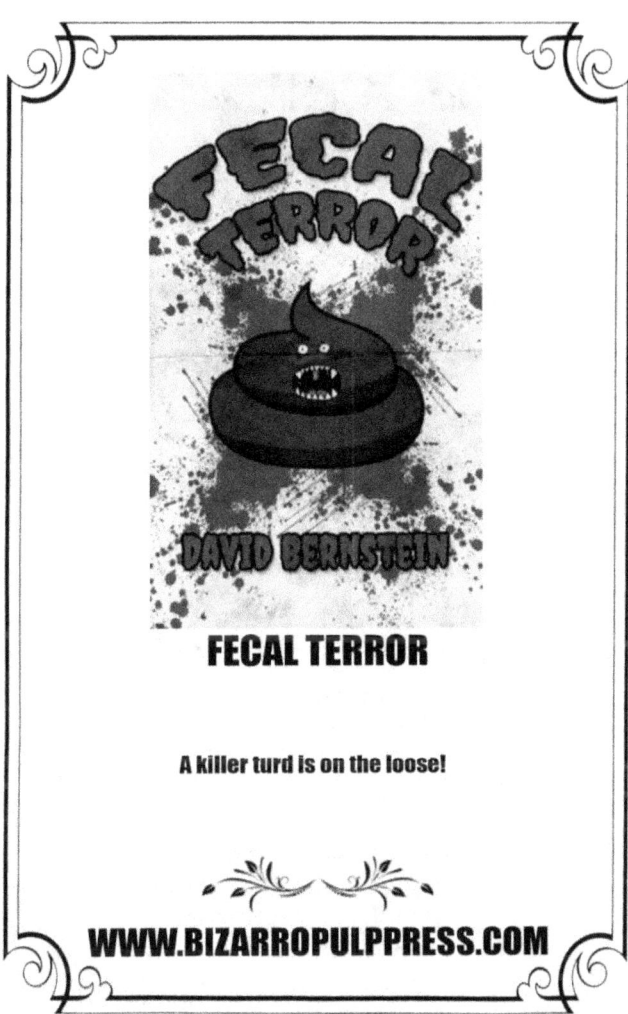

FECAL TERROR

A killer turd is on the loose!

WWW.BIZARROPULPPRESS.COM

MOOSEJAW FRONTIER

Juan wakes up in the racist town of Moosejaw after suffering a near fatal
snake bite. As he battles for the right to live he begins experiencing
vivid nightmares of a symbiotic dream-twin who seems determined to
take over complete control of Juan's existence. 'Moosejaw Frontier' is a
terrifying journey through the various plateaus of reality, fiction, and
one man's intrinsic desire to become more than just a minor character...

WWW.BIZARROPULPPRESS.COM